Ireland, the Irish, and the Rise of Biofiction

Biofiction Studies

Biofiction is literature that names its protagonist after an actual historical figure, and it has become a dominant literary form over the last thirty years, resulting in publications from global luminaries as varied as Gabriel García Márquez, J.M. Coetzee, Margaret Atwood, Joyce Carol Oates, Mario Vargas Llosa, Laurent Binet, Peter Carey, Olga Tokarczuk, and Hilary Mantel. **Biofiction Studies** explores the history, rise, evolution, and nature of biofiction. Because it raises questions about the nature of the subject, of selfhood, on the ethics, politics and psychology of representations, on the relationships between what is perceived or constructed as factual and fictional, **Biofiction Studies** will be of interest to students and scholars in numerous fields, including philosophy, ethics, literary and genre theory.

Ireland, the Irish, and the Rise of Biofiction

Michael Lackey

BLOOMSBURY ACADEMIC
NEW YORK • LONDON • OXFORD • NEW DELHI • SYDNEY

BLOOMSBURY ACADEMIC
Bloomsbury Publishing Inc
1385 Broadway, New York, NY 10018, USA
50 Bedford Square, London, WC1B 3DP, UK
29 Earlsfort Terrace, Dublin 2, Ireland

BLOOMSBURY, BLOOMSBURY ACADEMIC and the Diana logo
are trademarks of Bloomsbury Publishing Plc

First published in the United States of America 2021
This paperback edition printed 2023

Cover design by Eleanor Rose | Cover image © Getty Images

A catalog record for this book is available from the Library of Congress.

ISBN: HB: 978-1-5013-7847-8
PB: 978-1-5013-7851-5
ePDF: 978-1-5013-7849-2
eBook: 978-1-5013-7848-5

Series: Biofiction Studies

Typeset by Integra Software Services Pvt. Ltd.

To find out more about our authors and books visit www.bloomsbury.com
and sign up for our newsletters.

For my children, Anya, Katya, and Willie

Contents

Acknowledgments viii

Introduction: Ireland, the Irish, and Biofiction 1

Part One Historical Context for the Rise of Biofiction

1 Oscar Wilde and the Invention of a Life-Creating Fiction 15
2 George Moore's *The Brook Kerith* and the Scandal of the Biographical Novel 55

Part Two Irish Figures as Biofictional Symbols

3 Roger Casement and the Transnational Origins of "Irishness" 99
4 Traumatized Agency in Eliza Lynch Biographical Novels 141

Part Three Theoretical Reflections about Biofiction

5 A Poetics of the Biographical Novel: Agency, History, Fiction 181
6 Why Names Matter: Concluding Reflections about Autonomy and Biofiction 205

Appendix: Interview with Mario Vargas Llosa 223
Notes 234
Bibliography 259
Index 268

Acknowledgments

In 2012, when I first started working on biofiction, there were a handful of scholars researching the literary form, but most of us were working in isolation. By 2015, we all started to find each other and to form meaningful bonds, and since then, the study of biofiction has exploded. Julia Dabbs, Kelly Gardiner, Bénédicte Ledent, Martin Middeke, Naomi Miller, Julia Novak, Catherine Padmore, Stephanie Russo, Daria Tunca, and Valentina Vannucci have all contributed in one way or another to my thinking about biofiction, specifically as it is manifested in this book. I am grateful to all of them for their insights and support.

Special thanks go to Todd Avery, Ingo Berensmeyer, Lucia Boldrini, Laura Cernat, Kathleen Costello-Sullivan, Adrian Frazier, Alison Gibbons, Suzanne Hobson, Elizabeth King, Monica Latham, Bethany Layne, Brian McHale, James Phelan, and Virginia Rademacher, who have given me valuable feedback on chapters and/or ideas in this book. Their scholarly generosity has been a great gift to me.

Many creative writers of biofiction have been extremely gracious in sharing with me their thoughts about their work, which has helped me better understand individual works as well as biofiction more generally, and to them I will always feel immense gratitude. In particular, I would like to thank Russell Banks, Barbara Chase-Riboud, Michael Cunningham, Emma Donoghue, Bruce Duffy, David Ebershoff, Robert Harris, Colum McCann, Anchee Min, Barbara Mujica, Sabina Murray, Joyce Carol Oates, Joseph O'Connor, Lance Olsen, Jay Parini, Joanna Scott, Susan Sellers, Chika Unigwe, Mario Vargas Llosa, and Jane Yolen.

To Ludwig Pfeiffer I owe a special debt of gratitude. His scholarship has heavily influenced me, his mentorship has broadened me, and his friendship has buoyed me. Without Ludwig's guidance and support over the last twenty years, my scholarly life would be much different and certainly less intellectually rich.

In the spring/summer issue of 2018, *Éire-Ireland: An Interdisciplinary Journal of Irish Studie*s published a special issue about Irish biofiction, which I guest-edited, and I would like to thank the editors, Nicholas Wolf and Vera Kreilkamp, for their support for that project, which has clearly impacted the ideas in this book.

Many students have assisted me with this project and contributed to my understanding of biofiction, and I want to specifically thank Anika Eaves, Ariel Ebaugh, Diondra Franklin, Abigail Giordano, Madeline Gould, Bailey Kemp, Claire Larson, Nora Lund, Corinne McCumber, Kimberly Norwood, Sarah Severson, and Johannah Woodley. These are the kinds of students who make teaching so gratifying.

The University of Minnesota, and my campus (Morris) in particular, has been amazingly generous in giving me leave time and in financially supporting my research. Simply put, this project would not have been possible without the University of Minnesota's commitment to humanities research. I am lucky to work in this system.

To Haaris Naqvi and Bloomsbury I owe my greatest thanks. The massive surge in biofiction studies would not have happened without the support of Haaris, and we can safely say that Bloomsbury has become the best and most dominant press for scholars of biofiction.

Finally, I would like to thank my wife, Julie Eckerle, who always supports my work but also holds me intellectually accountable, who inspires me through her first-rate scholarship, and who keeps me sane and hopeful through her unconditional love. Gratitude!

Introduction: Ireland, the Irish, and Biofiction

Biofiction is literature that names its protagonist after an actual historical figure, and it has become a popular, and even dominant, literary form over the last thirty-five years. Gabriel García Márquez's *The General in the Labyrinth* (1989), J. M. Coetzee's *The Master of Petersburg* (1994), Penelope Fitzgerald's *The Blue Flower* (1995), Michael Cunningham's *The Hours* (1998), Daniel Kehlmann's *Measuring the World* (2005), Hilary Mantel's Thomas Cromwell novels (2009, 2012, and 2020), Laurent Binet's *HHhH* (2009), Olga Tokarczuk's *The Books of Jacob* (2014), and George Saunders's *Lincoln in the Bardo* (2017) are just a few stellar works by world-renowned novelists. It has only been in the last ten years, however, that the scholarship has finally started to catch up with the three-decade surge in biofiction. This is not to say that there were no studies about biofiction before 2010. There were.[1] But recent years have witnessed a significant escalation in the study of the literary form.

And yet, there is still much confusion regarding what biofiction does, as the following anecdote about Peter Carey's Booker Prize–winning novel *True History of the Kelly Gang* illustrates. The work opens with a vivid two-page description of the final shootout between the Australian police and the Irish bushranger Ned Kelly, concluding with the caption: "Undated, unsigned, handwritten account in the collection of the Melbourne Public Library (V.L. 10453)." This note suggests that the introduction is a transcription of a handwritten manuscript held in the Melbourne Public Library. Indeed, according to an archivist at the State Library Victoria in Melbourne, Australia, which houses the draft versions of Carey's novel, librarians received requests to see the original handwritten document after *True History* was first published. The archivist, of course, told such petitioners that Carey's book is fiction, and not history or biography, so there is no such document. But one puzzled patron asked: "Can Carey do that? I mean, can he just make up a source like that?" The archivist said, "yes, because it is fiction, Carey can do that." The implication is that had Carey written a history or a biography, it would have been unethical for him to fabricate a source. To be more specific, if a biographer or a historian invented a documentary source and then claimed that it was housed in the archivist's library, one suspects that the staff would expose the writer as a fraud and publicly denounce him or her. But instead of condemning or even criticizing Carey for referencing a nonexistent source, the archivist chuckled at the cleverness of the novelist's literary deception.[2]

The librarian understands that what is in the pages of Carey's novel is a fictional figure, a paper character not to be confused with the person in history. In other words, while the story is based on an actual person, *True History* is true in a fictional sense, which is different from being true in a biographical or historical sense, so the author of biofiction can concoct a nonexistent source. This story usefully captures some of the confusion about biofiction. The problem in interpretation among scholars started in the 1930s, when Georg Lukács suggested in *The Historical Novel* (1937) that the biographical novel is a subgenre or version of the historical novel and that biographical and therewith historical accuracy are the primary criteria for determining the quality of a particular work—I will clarify why Lukács's approach is so problematic in Chapter 1. In a 1938 essay, Lucien Febvre, a French historian and one of the founders of the Annales School of history, took a similar approach when he condemned "novelistic biographies"[3] for inevitably altering facts about an actual person's life. Taken as a given within this tradition of interpretation is that fidelity to the biographical record should be one of the defining features of biofiction, which is one reason why the American scholar and cultural critic Carl Bode draws the following conclusion in a 1955 essay with the telling title "Buxom Biographies": "the biographical novel deserves more to be pitied than censured."[4] Paul Murray Kendall solidified this scholarly tendency in his 1965 book *The Art of Biography*, in which he faults what he refers to as "the novel-as-biography" because it is a "radical left" invention that is "almost wholly imaginary."[5]

More recently, scholars have used the biographical-accuracy approach to condemn biofiction as an unethical genre. Lucia Boldrini published *Autobiographies of Others* in 2012, and in that work she does first-rate analyses of many important biographical novels, including Carey's *True History*. Boldrini praises the work for giving voice to a marginalized figure like Kelly. However, after clarifying how Carey's novel functions in relation to the law, she says that the work "posits a choice between two ethical positions, each of which involves a symmetric unethical risk: either refuse the appropriation of another's voice but leave them without any voice; or give them the possibility of having their history represented, but at the cost of substituting one's voice for theirs, appropriating it, and with that, their identity."[6] Ethically, Carey does something praiseworthy by recovering and portraying Kelly's history as an impoverished and thus politically marginalized figure. But Carey's instrumental appropriation of Kelly inadvertently displaces the identity of the real person, which is why his novel, according to Boldrini, borders, at the very least, on the unethical.

Marie-Luise Kohlke's 2013 article "Neo-Victorian Biofiction and the Special/Spectral Case of Barbara Chase-Riboud's *Hottentot Venus*" builds on Boldrini's claim that biofiction is a form of "identity theft," which leads her to conclude that neo-Victorian biofictions participate, wittingly or not, in either an unethical "imposition" on the biographical subject or, "at worst," an "imaginative grave robbery—the stealing of a voice, life, and identity."[7] The logic underwriting the position of these two writers goes something like this: the actual biographical subject has a history. The contemporary author, in writing a biography of sorts about this person, has used, rather than represented, the actual historical figure, and in the process, the writer has done an injustice to the biographical subject by misrepresenting or displacing him or her. Ina Schabert, Jonathan Dee, Julia Novak, Fredric Jameson, and Binne de Haan are just a few writers who have analyzed and assessed biofiction through the lens of biography and have, consequently, distorted or overlooked what biographical novelists actually do with their reality-based protagonists.[8]

However, as I will demonstrate throughout this book, the biographical-accuracy approach is in irreconcilable conflict with the way many biographical novelists think about their works, because it treats biofiction primarily as biography rather than fiction.[9] To illustrate why this is a problem, it is useful to look at a major development in portraiture aesthetics, which contributed to or at least paralleled the rise of biofiction, as I will explain in Chapter 2. The Arabic author Hassan Najmi best expresses the nature of this aesthetic transformation in his 2011 biographical novel about Gertrude Stein (*Gertrude*). In the work, the artist Henri Matisse claims that his painting "The Moroccan Amido" is not really about the figure who is the subject of the artwork. When the character Muhammad, who knows the actual Amido, tells Matisse that the portrait does not resemble the actual person, the French artist says, " 'I didn't do the painting to resemble him.' Rather, 'it's supposed to look like me.' " At this point, Muhammad offers an insightful interpretation of the work, which, according to the novel's Matisse, is "the main thing." Matisse then makes a clarifying distinction about art that will prove central for the novel: "you always need to bear in mind that, when we paint, we're not presenting actual reality, only artistic reality. Of course it's not actually Amido; it's a work of art." Based on this exchange, Matisse admonishes Muhammad, and readers more generally, to make an epistemological adjustment in relation to art:

> "You need to adjust your eyes a bit," Matisse told him as he bade him a gentle farewell by the door. "The human eye is not merely an organ that reflects what it sees or even what it knows (the way you know Amido, for example). It's a shaping tool."[10]

Is the purpose of the artwork about a historical person to accurately reflect the reality of the real-life figure? If so, then Matisse's "The Moroccan Amido" could only be characterized as a failure because, as Muhammad notes, the painting fails to faithfully picture the actual person. But Matisse indicates that such an assumption by the viewer is a mistake. Viewers of art need to shift their expectations about what the art object signifies and does. Such works are supposed to activate the mind of the viewer, which is why Matisse praises Muhammad's response to the painting. Given this example, a work of art about a particular person could be effective and successful, even if it strategically distorts or totally misrepresents that which it signifies.

A little later in the novel, Najmi has Pablo Picasso add another layer of complexity to the newly emerging form of portraiture aesthetics. In a conversation with Muhammad, the Spanish artist says that his goal with his Gertrude painting, a bioportrait of sorts, "was not simply to portray her, but to show her in a different guise, to use her to create a new way of looking." His description of his actual experience painting the work is instructive. As Najmi's Picasso says to Muhammad: "Are you aware that at some point I no longer needed Gertrude? I was no longer bothered—if you prefer—about having her with me every day. At that point I started looking for her other face, the ideal face perhaps. When I finally located that face, Gertrude was not even there!"[11] Picasso starts his painting of Stein by representing the famous salonnière and writer, but after he gets from her what he needs, he turns his attention away from the actual woman to his own vision, which is why Muhammad concludes that "Picasso never really painted Gertrude."[12] The shift from representation to creation is where art begins, and Picasso makes this move for the benefit of his viewers, that is, in order "to create a new way of looking" at the world. Since *Gertrude* is a verbal portrait of Stein, we can say that the picture of the American expat in the novel is not supposed to resemble Gertrude Stein; it is supposed to look like Najmi. And this is the case because Najmi's goal is not to represent the modernist author; rather, it is to transform her into a work of art in order to create a new way of looking at life and the world.

Najmi's novel is primarily set in the early twentieth century, but the developments in portraiture aesthetics that he foregrounds were at work in the mid- to late nineteenth century, and it was George Moore and Oscar Wilde who would most clearly appropriate those ideas, use them in their fiction, and contribute to what would become the current boom in the biographical novel and biofiction studies. Understanding how the newly emerging form of portraiture aesthetics parallels what happened in the world of fiction will enable us to expose some of the glaring problems with dominant approaches to contemporary biofiction and to better understand and appreciate what biographical novelists actually do and accomplish in and through their works. If readers know that the final product is not supposed to be seen as a paper version of the actual historical figure, if they know that artists use the real-life person to project into existence a new way of seeing and being, then readers could adjust their eyes in such a way that the Boldrini–Kohlke idea of displacing the original person through biofiction would be incoherent. To put this in the words of Wilde's narrator from the aptly titled biofiction "The Portrait of Mr. W.H.," Boldrini and Kohlke "confuse an ethical with an aesthetical problem."[13] Artists are different from historians and biographers because they embellish and fabricate, so saying things that are historically and/or biographically untrue is acceptable and sometimes necessary. Therefore, to dub the creative liberties that artists take with the biographical subject unethical is to misunderstand the nature of art and the function of the artist. This becomes increasingly apparent when we note how Wilde and Moore incorporated developments within the world of portraiture aesthetics into their corresponding form of literature, what we refer to today as biofiction.

Taking my critical cue from Wilde and Moore, this study foregrounds the aesthetic. Above all, this is a book about biofiction, a form of literature that invites analysis from a wide range of theoretical approaches. Insights from gay studies and queer theory would be appropriate for Wilde's "The Portrait of Mr. W.H.," Moroccan studies and postcolonial theory for Najmi's *Gertrude*, and religious studies and postmodern theory for Moore's *The Brook Kerith*, to give just a few examples. All of these approaches would yield worthwhile contributions to each respective area of study. But what I am doing in this book is more fundamental. I am a scholar of biofiction, so my critical objectives revolve around the literary form: why it came into being, how it signifies and functions, how it has evolved, and why it has become so popular and even dominant. Therefore, I make no claim to being a scholar of postcolonial theory, feminist theory, or queer theory, nor do I pretend that this book will add something of substance to any of those or other theory-specific fields of study, even though I discuss novels that would benefit from such theoretical approaches. But I do believe that an accurate understanding of the history of biofiction and the way the literary form signifies would enable scholars to make noteworthy contributions to many fields of study through their analysis of specific biofictions.

My focus on biofictional aesthetics should explain the limited number of texts I examine. Were this a book primarily about Irish biofiction, then I, if I defined Irish biofiction as works by Irish authors as well as about Irish figures, would need to do an extensive analysis of many more texts such as Kate O'Brien's *The Lady* (1946), Thomas Kilroy's *The Big Chapel* (1971), John Banville's *Kepler* (1983), Duncan Sprott's *Our Lady of the Potatoes* (1995), Margaret Atwood's *Alias Grace* (1996), Kevin Barry's *Beatlebone* (2015), Nuala O'Connor's *Miss Emily* (2015), Gavin McCrea's *Mrs Engels* (2015), Marita Conlon-McKenna's *Rebel Sisters* (2016), Annabel Abbs's *The Joyce Girl* (2016), and Jo Baker's *A Country Road, A Tree* (2016), among many others. Additionally, since I have done the only interviews with Colum McCann and Emma Donoghue that focus exclusively on their biofictions, it would only make sense that I would devote one chapter to the study of *Dancer* (2003), *TransAtlantic* (2013), and *Apeirogon* (2020) and another to *Life Mask* (2004), *The Sealed Letter* (2008), and *Frog Music* (2014). Moreover, because of my admiration and respect for Joseph O'Connor, a section about *Ghost Light* (2010) and *Shadowplay* (2019) would be warranted. A comprehensive study of Irish biofiction would include such analyses and would be a valuable contribution to Irish studies, but *Ireland, the Irish, and the Rise of Biofiction* is not such a work. To reiterate, this study is primarily about biofiction, specifically how and why the Irish as creative writers and biographical subjects played a crucial role in its origins, evolution, legitimization, and now dominance. So I have strategically selected only the authors and texts that help clarify my main claims about the history, rise, and legitimization of the literary form.

Of crucial importance for the rise of biofiction were newly emerging theories of human subjectivity, which required a corresponding form of literature. Friedrich Nietzsche was important for understanding the emergence of and need for biofiction (*Thus Spoke Zarathustra*, as I show in Chapter 2, qualifies as a biofiction, and this work had a significant impact on Moore), and in his 1888 work *The Case of Wagner*, he makes an observation that clarifies why such a literary form needed to come into being. After clarifying why Richard Wagner and his art are so dangerous and sick, something about which he had direct knowledge since he was once a disciple of the Bayreuth composer, Nietzsche makes a stunningly insightful claim about the human condition: "all of us have, unconsciously, involuntarily in our bodies values, words, formulas, moralities of *opposite* descent—we are, physiologically considered, *false*."[14] Humans are born into a system of knowledge, and they unconsciously and involuntarily internalize that system, even if it is the opposite of what they consider themselves to be. For instance, many gays and lesbians are raised in heteronormative communities, which leads some to believe that they are heterosexual, even if they have strong sexual inclinations for someone of the same sex. When a gay person psychologically internalizes the culture's heteronormative discourse "of *opposite* descent," this makes him or her physiologically false. For Nietzsche, this experience of being physiologically false is an inevitable condition of being human, because so much of what happens to us is unconscious and involuntary. Therefore, being physiologically true is impossible. The most we can hope for is to become increasingly less physiologically false over time.

The first part of this book (Historical Context for the Rise of Biofiction) explores some of the distinctive forces that necessitated an aesthetic form like biofiction, and it is my contention that works by Wilde and Moore best express the cultural service biofiction could perform. Consistently, authors of biofiction (and not just among the Irish) rejected deterministic models of history as well as their aesthetic correlative, the historical novel, and instead developed a literary form that would foreground and promote individual agency and political autonomy. The primary difficulty, authors realized, is that humans have unconsciously and involuntarily internalized the dominant discourses of opposite descent, so personal and communal freedom are more complicated, challenging, and difficult than previously thought. Biofiction could play a vital role in exposing the cultural structures that subtly and strategically shackle minds without their conscious awareness and thereby provide readers with a roadmap to a limited but real form of liberation, which could result in a healthier and more socially just way of thinking and being. So, in a historical sense, exposing deterministic, debilitating, and destructive systems of thought and proposing more agential, more health-bringing, and more socially just ways of thinking and being are why biofiction came into being and became increasingly more popular, and I do a close analysis of Wilde's "The Portrait of Mr. W.H." and Moore's *The Brook Kerith* to illustrate this point.

Biofiction's origins as a literary form centered on cultural diagnosis and human agency help explain the kinds of figures that authors select as their protagonists. Part Two (Irish Figures as Biofictional Symbols) foregrounds complicated Irish figures whom authors convert into literary symbols. For instance, Roger Casement was born in Ireland, but since the country belonged to England at the time, he was raised to believe he was British. After working in the Congo and the Amazon, after observing what colonization entails and coming to despise colonialism and colonizers, Casement slowly cast off his British identity and reconstructed himself first as a non-British and then as an anti-British "Irishman." Picturing this subjective process of identifying and rejecting a pre-given identity of "*opposite* descent," an act that we today describe as the decolonization of the mind, and forging within the smithy of one's own soul a new and original identity enable the biographical novelist to give readers a model of a person who has achieved a certain level of individual agency and political autonomy. In other words, authors of biofiction convert a figure like Casement into a literary symbol that could provide readers with an existential template for doing something similar. Such are the central ideas in the Casement biographical novels by Mario Vargas Llosa (*The Dream of the Celt*) and Sabina Murray (*Valiant Gentlemen*). This psycho-political journey to agential living, I argue, is the stuff biofiction is made of, and it is one of the primary features that distinguishes it from historical fiction, as I demonstrate throughout this book.

But not all forms of agency result in better human living. Oppressive systems and their concomitant trauma oftentimes derange human interiors and generate Caliban-like forms of psychosis, thus posing a serious challenge to those scholars and theorists who treat agency, especially in relation to traditionally disempowered groups, as a good in itself. Numerous biographical novelists have fictionalized the life of the Irishwoman Eliza Lynch to explore the potential dangers of what I term traumatized agency in my fourth chapter, which focuses on biofictions by Graham Shelby (*Demand the World*) and Enright (*The Pleasure of Eliza Lynch*). Lynch was born in Cork, and her family suffered because of the Great Famine—that, at least, is what happens in both novels. That devastating personal and political experience was more the consequence of British power than a natural disaster, and it created within Lynch a propensity for agential excess, which she was able to enact through her relationship with Francisco Solano Lopez, who was the son of the dictator of Paraguay and would soon become dictator himself. With no check on her power, Lynch began to engage in the kind of oppressive behavior that led to her own traumatic experience in an Ireland under British rule. Biographical novelists use the life of Lynch to brilliantly anatomize the way traumatic forms of political oppression can and oftentimes do lead to horrific types of agential excess.

The last part of the book (Theoretical Reflections about Biofiction) theorizes the nature of the literary form. While biographical novelists fictionalize the life of an actual historical figure to diagnose psycho-political and sociocultural ailments, they also use this figure to imagine into existence alternative ways of thinking and being. Unfortunately, developments in postmodern theory have prevented scholars from taking the specific visions of contemporary biographical novelists seriously and have thereby led them to overlook one of the most important features of biofiction. For example, Linda Hutcheon's 1988 *A Poetics of Postmodernism*, generally considered an extraordinary landmark study, has done significant damage to the study of biofiction, as I argue in Chapter 5. Recognizing the degree to which history conditions the way people see and experience the world, postmodernists argue that we do not see the past as it was in itself. Rather, we see and value what we have been historically conditioned to see and value, thus rendering our judgments limited and suspect. Hutcheon applies this idea to the treatment of history in postmodern literature. Within this postmodernist framework, the protagonist of those novels with a focus on history formulates an interpretation of the past which is subsequently undermined through a self-reflexive critique about the way products of thought are historically conditioned and constructed. She refers to this type of literature as historiographic metafiction and includes John Banville's *Doctor Copernicus* as an example. But I demonstrate that Banville's biographical novel and biographical novels more generally signify very differently than a historiographic metafiction. While Banville understands and even accepts the postmodernist distrust of overarching ahistorical metanarratives, he, like Nietzsche, still holds that humans should project into being conceptual systems about life and the world. Therefore, instead of casting a self-deconstructive glance at the newly constructed system, Banville makes the literary case for a particular way of seeing and experiencing the world, even though he knows it is nothing more than his own provisional construction. In other words, he takes ownership of his uniquely constructed model, which is why he resists the postmodern impulse to deconstruct his own literary vision. With knowledge of the way biofiction functions and signifies, readers draw very different conclusions than Hutcheon about Banville's *Doctor Copernicus*. Specifically, instead of endlessly critiquing and deconstructing conceptual systems, many Irish writers committed themselves to the affirmative project of knowledge formation and subject construction, knowing full well that such creations were human invented and temporally limited. But it is important to note that in this book, Irish biofiction is not just literature by Irish authors. It also includes works about Irish figures, even if written by non-Irish writers, as we see in the biographical novels about Casement. The Irish struggle for individual agency and political autonomy is so nuanced, complex, and inspiring, I argue, that many prominent non-Irish writers have mined it for resonant symbols that could illuminate the more universal desire for freedom in a political world designed to thwart it.

To conclude the book, I explain why naming matters so much in relation to the biographical novel. Calling a work like Mary Morrissy's *The Rising of Bella Casey* a historical novel leads to a distorted understanding of the way it functions and/or signifies. For instance, the protagonist of a historical novel is a representative symbol or figure from a specific time and place in the past, while the protagonist of a biographical novel is an exceptional model of originality and/or agency for the present and future. To approach the protagonist of a biographical novel as if it is a protagonist in a historical novel leads readers, as I show, to see in the main character something that is not there and to overlook things that are there. But naming also matters because it adds legitimacy, meaning, and power to a work, as we see most clearly in Carey's *True History of the Kelly Gang*. Readers could say that the purely imagined story is a concoction of the writer's imagination strategically designed to serve the author's ideological agenda. By naming the character after an actual historical figure, the author signals to the reader that this story is rooted in the historical and the empirical, thus increasing the impact on readers and legitimizing to a greater degree the truth and value of the story.

Biofiction is an incredibly rich aesthetic form, and it needs to be treated in a unique and distinct manner. It is not biography. It is not history. It is not a historical novel. And it is not a historiographic metafiction. It is its own thing. To clarify what it does and the nature of its power, I examine some of the origins and evolutions of biofiction over the last 150 years. Because I am primarily concerned in this book with biofiction as an aesthetic form, I unapologetically discuss many non-Irish writers and even many non-Irish-focused texts, like Najmi's *Gertrude*. And yet, there is an emphasis throughout this book on the Irish. Specifically, I trace some of the aesthetic form's main roots back to Ireland, which was in need and search of an aesthetic form that would mirror the constructed Irish interior and would help the Irish to achieve the kind of personal agency and political autonomy they so desperately sought. Ireland is of central importance to many Irish and non-Irish authors of biofiction because its history so incisively expresses the yearning for and the ever-evolving reality of what it means to be an agential being and many Irish men and women could so easily be converted into symbols or metaphors of a more universal and comprehensive form of emancipation.

Part One

Historical Context for the Rise of Biofiction

1

Oscar Wilde and the Invention of a Life-Creating Fiction

When discussing the origins, rise, and contemporary legitimization of biofiction, Oscar Wilde is a crucial figure. This is not just because he authored one of the first and most important reflections about the aesthetic form, but also because he became the subject of many biofictions, most notably Desmond Hall's *I Give You Oscar Wilde: A Biographical Novel* (1965), Peter Ackroyd's *The Last Testament of Oscar Wilde* (1983), Louis Edwards's *Oscar Wilde Discovers America* (2003), and Colm Tóibín's *The Master* (2004). Some, of course, would question and challenge my decision to include Tóibín's novel in this list, as many would say that *The Master* is a biographical novel about Henry James. But as I will demonstrate, Tóibín has a commanding grasp of literary history, and *The Master* accurately foregrounds the crucial role Wilde played in both the rise of the biographical novel and the fall of the historical novel, which is why I argue that Wilde is the primary master of *The Master*.

I

The past is the key to the future.[1]

To understand Wilde's role in the rise of biofiction, some context is needed. The French Revolution had an enormous impact on the European psyche, so much so that scholars believe it gave birth to history programs.[2] After 1789, professors started to develop and refine the Enlightenment's scientific instruments of analysis in order to identify and define what caused cataclysmic historical events. The hope was that systematizing knowledge of what happened would enable those in the present to predict and thereby avoid future catastrophes. This attempt to make history into a rigorous science partly contributed to the rise of the historical novel, an aesthetic form that visualizes the laws and causes of human-generated disasters.[3]

In his landmark study *The Historical Novel*, Lukács clearly articulates how the nineteenth-century's scientific approach to history animated aesthetics. What the historical novel gives readers is "a rational periodization of history, an attempt to comprehend the historical nature and origins of the present rationally and scientifically."[4] Within this framework, Lukács stipulates that one of the first and most important aesthetic laws is that the protagonist of the historical novel must be an invented figure, which differentiates it from the biographical novel. This is not just an idiosyncratic recommendation on Lukács's part. It is the logical consequence of his scientific approach to history and his Marxist view of the novel. The protagonist must function as a representative symbol of the people, the nation, and the age, a figure that embodies "social trends and historical forces,"[5] which is why this character must be ordinary and average. According to this paradigm, the development and evolution of the protagonist are not important. Rather, the focus should be on the objective societal, political, and economic forces that shape and determine the character's being. Lukács refers to this as the "derivation of the individuality of characters from the historical peculiarity"[6] of the specific age. To illustrate, Lukács uses the work of Sir Walter Scott as an ideal. With his focus on the sociohistorical, Scott does not spotlight the evolution of a protagonist's identity: "Instead, he always presents us with the personality complete. Complete, yet not without the most careful preparation. This preparation, however, is not a personal and psychological one, but objective, social-historical."[7] The personal and the psychological are subordinate to the "objective, social-historical" realities that shape and determine the representative protagonist's identity. To put the matter succinctly, the protagonist must be an invention so that the author can use him or her to illustrate how the objective historical and social forces from the past have dictated the form of his or her identity.

We get additional insight into the nature of the invented protagonist of the historical novel when we attend to the way this character functions. Symbolic not just of an average person, this figure represents the whole nation and age. This explains why Lukács believes that "the central figure" of the work should be a "mediocre, prosaic hero."[8] To give the character too much personality, individuality, or autonomy would undermine the protagonist's function to symbolize a larger representative reality from the past. As Lukács says of Scott: "he never creates eccentric figures, figures who fall psychologically outside the atmosphere of his age."[9] Important to note here is not just the way the literary symbol functions in the historical novel, but also how Lukács engages the historical. A perfect example is seen through Lukács's description of the impact that a shift from mercenary to mass armies had on everyday people. In the pre-Revolutionary period, wars "were waged by small professional armies."[10] This changed during the French Revolution, which required political leaders to make the case to the masses for fighting in the name of the national cause. A transformation such as this had "a direct effect upon the life of every individual."[11] In essence, what happens at the level of the political dictates the interiority of the masses, what Lukács refers to as the "inner life of a nation."[12]

This approach has specific implications for the way the novelist must represent the historical. Having mentally reached back into the past in order to identify and define the objective social and political forces that determined the interiority of the masses, the artist can then construct a representative character and/or scene that accurately pictures much more than just one individual. Lukács uses Leo Tolstoy's *War and Peace* to illustrate. Tolstoy takes "an episode from the war which is of particular importance and significance for the human development of his main characters. And Tolstoy's genius as an historical novelist lies in his ability to select and portray these episodes so that the entire mood of the Russian army and through them of the Russian people gains vivid expression."[13] After identifying and defining the important social and political forces of a particular period from the past, the author then invents a figure that represents this "objective, social-historical" reality, thus enabling the character to accurately symbolize the whole population from a specific time and place.

The biggest benefits of the historical novel are related to its predictive capacity. With an ability "to comprehend their own existence as something historically conditioned,"[14] people in the present would be in possession of "one of the most important theoretical preliminaries for the future transformation of society."[15] In other words, the historical novel, in using the scientific method to accurately represent the past, enables us to understand what made us who we are in the present. Moreover, this aesthetic form provides us with a concrete framework for understanding what led to cataclysmic events and thus makes it possible for us in the present to predict and thereby avoid similar catastrophes in the future.

As a mere twenty-five-year-old, Wilde reflected at some length and in some depth about history as a science, and he arrived at conclusions strikingly similar to Lukács. Herodotus is for Wilde one of the greatest historians because "in him we discover not merely the empirical connection of cause and effect but that constant reference to Laws which is the characteristic of the Historian proper."[16] Put differently, in Herodotus we can discern "the rise of that *historic sense* which is the rational antecedent of the science of historical criticism."[17] Here is Wilde's characterization of that approach: "the one scientific basis on which the true philosophy of History must rest, is the complete knowledge of the Laws of Human Nature in all its wants, its aspirations, its powers, and its tendencies."[18] This knowledge is valuable as it enables us to predict the future: "For the very first requisite for any scientific conception of History is the Doctrine of uniform sequence, in other words that certain events having happened certain other events corresponding to them will happen also. That the past is the key of the future."[19] In short, Wilde intelligently registers how the Enlightenment's valorization of science inflects history.

II

Our historical sense is at fault.[20]

Wilde developed these ideas in "Historical Criticism," an essay he submitted "for the Chancellor's English Essay Prize at the University of Oxford in 1879."[21] Given the positive nature of his views about the scientific approach to history, it would seem that Wilde would have formulated an aesthetic model similar to Lukács.[22] But in the late 1880s and early 1890s, when he did his most important theorizing about aesthetics ("The Decay of Lying," "The Critic as Artist," and "The Soul of Man"), Wilde came to the conclusion that the scientific approach that he applied to history was not only unsuitable for but also in irreconcilable conflict with the world of art. Therefore, instead of formulating an aesthetic model similar to Lukács, which uses the Enlightenment's scientific method to define art, he seeks to expose why subordinating art to history (increasingly defined over the course of the nineteenth century as a hard science) would damage aesthetics, the human, and even life (I will examine this idea in more depth in the next chapter). A close examination of Wilde's "A Portrait of Mr. W.H.," a borderline biofiction, usefully demonstrates how and why Wilde's work reads as if it were a direct refutation of Lukács's model in *The Historical Novel.*

This 1889 short story focuses on the dedicatee and sometime-subject of Shakespeare's sonnets, who is simply referred to as Mr. W.H. Wilde's character Cyril Graham hypothesizes that W.H. is actually Willie Hughes, a boy-actor who performed in Shakespeare's plays. Graham's theory initially convinces his friend Erskine and the narrator, but both figures eventually have their doubts, because there is no empirical evidence to verify the existence of Willie Hughes. As Erskine says to the narrator: "The one flaw in the theory is that it presupposes the existence of the person whose existence is the subject of dispute."[23] There are two interpretive apparatuses we could apply to this story in order to illuminate what biofiction is and what it is not. These approaches come from Lukács, who wrongly uses historical-novel criteria to analyze and interpret biofiction, and Wilde, who not only anticipates but actually contributes to the rise, evolution, and now dominance of biofiction.

Lukács is a complicated figure for scholars of biofiction. In *The Historical Novel*, he identifies and defines the intellectual and political forces that gave birth to the historical novel and establishes a compelling framework to clarify how the historical novel functions. To his credit, Lukács devotes a whole section of his study to the biographical novel (300–22), which means that he understands that the biographical novel is different from the historical novel, but unfortunately, instead of noting that different forces gave birth to the biographical novel and thus necessitated unique and distinctive criteria for analyzing and assessing it, he uses historical-novel criteria to interpret and evaluate the aesthetic form, and consequently, he concludes that it is an irredeemable mistake.[24]

As noted above, for Lukács, "the historical novel is interested in the prehistory of the ideas which are being fought out today."[25] Within this framework, the author must use a "scientific approach" to disclose the "economic-social, political and cultural life" of a previous time. This life is best pictured through "objective laws" as seen in "connections"[26] between the fictional individual and the sociohistorical reality. From this vantage point, what biographical novelists give readers is too particular: "the facts of a great man's life tell us at best the particular occasion on which something great was achieved, but they never give us the real context, the real chain of causation as a result of which this great accomplishment played its part in history."[27] This commitment to history is the basis for Lukács's biggest error, which is to define the biographical novel in terms of representational aesthetics. He discloses this most clearly when he articulates one of his primary critiques of biofiction: "The better the writer's work, that is, the more truthfully he portrays the particular occasion on the basis of scrupulously checked and selected material from the given life, the more noticeable and striking will its occasional and objectively accidental character appear."[28] A work is good insofar as it accurately portrays the reality of the actual person's life. But this is also the basis for the biographical novel's failure. The author of a historical novel invents a mediocre protagonist that symbolizes the objective social-historical reality of the time. When an author bases the novel on an actual historical figure, especially an extraordinary or unique life, much in the protagonist will fail to symbolize or represent the social-historical reality of the distinctive place and age. Thus, the main figure of a biographical novel will contain much that is irrelevant ("accidental"), and it will give the reader a distorted picture of the representative historical reality, because in focusing on the individual biography, it will overlook and/or distort the larger social-historical picture, which is of ultimate importance. As Lukács concludes:

> We may generalize this weakness of the biographical form of the novel by saying that the personal, the purely psychological and biographical acquire a disproportionate breadth, a false preponderance. As a result the great driving forces of history are neglected. They are presented in all too summary a fashion and relate only biographically to the person at the centre. And because of this false distribution of weights what should be the real centre of these novels—the given historical transformation—cannot make itself felt sufficiently strongly.[29]

Failing to subordinate the biographical to the "objective laws" and reality of history necessarily distorts the picture of the past.

Given Lukács's approach, "The Portrait of Mr. W.H." would be an unambiguous failure. On the surface, this is the case because the protagonist is supposedly named after a real person, the heretofore unidentified dedicatee of Shakespeare's sonnets. In the historical novel, the main character is an empty vessel that the author can and should fill with the distinctive cultural and political cargo of the subject's time and place.[30] Since Wilde's Willie Hughes is based on a real person, the author, according to Lukács, is bound by that figure's actual biography. Portions of this character's life might symbolically reflect the place and age, but, as Lukács contends, much in that biography will fail to accurately represent the historical reality. What also makes Willie totally unsuitable as a representative character is his exceptional beauty. For Lukács, the protagonist should be mediocre, an everyday kind of figure. But Wilde's Willie is so captivating that he is described as the "tenth Muse" who inspired Shakespeare to produce "Eternal numbers to outlive long date" (PWH 265).

More than a character's name or status, however, what would make "The Portrait of Mr. W.H." a failure according to Lukács is Wilde's critical treatment within the story of the empirical method's intrusion into the world of art. As history-as-science was gaining intellectual momentum during the nineteenth century, there was the possibility that it would encroach upon the world of art, thus subordinating the imaginative and the creative to the factual and the empirical. Lukács welcomed this development, and his systematization of this idea into the historical novel is the logical product. But it is my contention that Wilde's story brilliantly dramatizes the anxiety about the scientific method's encroachment upon aesthetics.[31] Moreover, it is this concern about and rejection of science's intrusion into the world of art that mandated the rise of a literary form like biofiction.

Throughout "The Portrait," Erskine and the narrator are captivated by Cyril's theory about Willie. Yet, because of the empirical method, both harbor serious doubts. Erskine is initially enamored of Cyril's theory. But shortly afterward, the age's empirical method takes possession of him, which leads him to reject the theory:

> After some time, however, I began to see that before the theory could be placed before the world in a really perfected form, it was necessary to get some independent evidence about the existence of this young actor Willie Hughes. If this could be once established, there could be no possible doubt about his identity with Mr. W.H.; but otherwise the theory would fall to the ground.
>
> (PWH 266)

The theory hinges on its correspondence to historical fact. If the facts cannot be empirically verified, then the theory is null and void, which is why Erskine asks Cyril to promise to "not publish his discovery till he had put the whole matter beyond the reach of doubt" (PWH 266). The narrator draws the same conclusion. As he says: "But the proofs, the links—where were they? Alas! I could not find them. It seemed to me that I was always on the brink of absolute verification, but that I could never really attain to it" (PWH 277). In both cases, the men despair of the theory's value because they cannot find empirical evidence to verify it, which suggests that they subscribe, at least for a while, to a theory based on the scientific method.

Given the intrusion and privileging of the empirical approach, it might seem that "The Portrait of Mr. W.H." is working within the Lukács tradition. But the last section of the story suggests otherwise. After a prolonged study of the theory, the narrator briefly comes to accept it, so he sends Erskine an impassioned defense. But shortly thereafter, the narrator is afflicted with doubts, so he visits Erskine in order to encourage his friend to reject the theory. As the narrator says: "For heaven's sake don't waste your time in a foolish attempt to discover a young Elizabethan actor who never existed, and to make a phantom puppet the centre of the great cycle of Shakespeare's Sonnets" (PWH 279). But Erskine, who by this point has adopted a new version of the theory, one more in line with what

Cyril thinks, retorts: "I see that you don't understand the theory" (PWH 279). In essence, there are two separate theories in "The Portrait," one based on the historical novel's empirical method, the other based on what would become the axioms of biofictional aesthetics.[32]

The dominant aesthetic paradigm of the time emphasized accurate representation, so using empirical evidence to establish and justify the existence of Willie Hughes is of paramount importance. Cyril realizes this, so to satisfy Erskine, he had a portrait made of Willie "with his hand resting on the dedicatory page of the *Sonnets*" (PWH 267), thus seemingly validating his theory. But Erskine discovers by chance that Cyril had the portrait made, so, he concludes, the theory fails. But the theory would fail only if it is premised on an aesthetic of accurately representing reality in the external world. Since Cyril does not subscribe to that theory, verifying the existence of Willie is not that important to him. Readers see this most clearly when Erskine confronts Cyril about the forged painting. But Cyril responds: "I did it purely for your sake. You would not be convinced in any other way. It does not affect the truth of the theory" (PWH 268). Within the context of Cyril's theory, which Erskine would eventually adopt, proof of Willie's existence is irrelevant, so even if there is no empirical evidence to verify Willie's existence, this would not invalidate the theory. This is the case because Cyril subscribes to a different aesthetic theory, one, as I will now demonstrate, that aligns with the aesthetics of the biographical novel and stands in opposition to the aesthetics of the historical novel.

That Wilde is highly attentive to the significance of distinct conceptual fields of meaning he makes clear in the opening paragraph of "The Portrait of Mr. W.H." When discussing literary forgeries, specifically those of Thomas Chatterton, the narrator notes that from one perspective they are problematic, but from another they are perfectly legitimate. As readers, we have "no right to quarrel with an artist for the conditions under which he chooses to present his work," because "all Art" is "an attempt to realise one's own personality on some imaginative plane out of reach of the trammeling accidents and limitations of real life." Authorial self-actualization rather than a faithful representation of mundane reality—that is the aesthetic goal. Thus, to critique the artist for taking liberties with the facts is "to confuse an ethical with an aesthetical problem" (PWH 259). The story's opening logic is: if you want a faithful representation of an actual life, read a biography. But if you read a fiction (something "aesthetical") of someone's life, you cannot demand or expect biographical accuracy, because that is not what fiction writers give readers.

This distinction between the aesthetical and the non-aesthetical explains Cyril's unapologetic rejection of the scientific method as the basis for art. As Erskine says of Cyril's approach: "This was Cyril Graham's theory, evolved as you see purely from the Sonnets themselves, and depending for its acceptance not so much on demonstrable proof or formal evidence, but on a kind of spiritual and artistic sense, by which alone he claimed could the true meaning of the poems be discerned" (PWH 264–5). To use science's empirical sense to analyze and assess the artwork could only have distorting consequences, because art and the imagination should not be subordinate to science and fact. Needed is an "artistic sense" in order to understand and appreciate the poems. Cyril reiterates this point to Erskine: "I remember he more than once told me that he himself required no proof of the kind, and that he thought the theory complete without it" (PWH 267). Given these remarks, it might seem that Wilde adopts an anti-science position, but this is not correct. Wilde does not oppose science. He objects to the intrusion of science into the world of art and the attempt of science to subordinate creativity and the imagination to the empirical method.

To clarify what is at stake for writers within this particular aesthetic tradition, let me briefly reference Colum McCann, who has authored three spectacular biographical novels, *Dancer*, *TransAtlantic*, and *Apeirogon*. Like Wilde, McCann has some concerns about history's intrusion into the novel. As McCann says in an interview with Robert Birnbaum: "I hate the term 'historical novel.'"[33] He provides more insight into his reasons why in his interview with Synne Rifbjerg: "I hate the idea of the term 'the historical novel,' not that I hate history and not that I hate the novel, but I hate the way those two words match each other and plunge themselves down into an aspic, a softness; it almost wears a bodice of sorts."[34] McCann's metaphors (aspic and bodice) suggest that the historical novel contains and straitjackets the human, thus inhibiting expansion, development, and growth. In essence, the historical novel is a contradiction in terms, because the historical defines, confines, and restrains, while the novel imagines, liberates, and creates. Put differently, Lukács lauds and favors the historical novel, and his theoretical model succeeds, but it does so at the expense of art. He subordinates art to history-as-science, thus compromising art's autonomy. For writers like Wilde and McCann, if history-as-science plays a dominant role in fiction, this will attenuate and perhaps negate the aesthetic. By stark contrast, when art dominates, history-as-science must have, at most, a subordinate role within the work. The problem is not with history-as-science, nor with art. It is the ill-fated combination of the two.

When Erskine says that Cyril's theory is based more on an "artistic sense" than a scientific sense, he perfectly captures the distinction between the historical novel and the biographical novel. The historical novel uses the scientific method to identify the forces that have shaped and determined the past, thus clarifying how we have come to be as we currently are. Biographical novelists reject this approach, so they shift the focus from deterministic history to biographical autonomy. Here is how Wilde's Gilbert expresses the matter in "The Critic as Artist": "The longer one studies life and literature, the more strongly one feels that behind everything that is wonderful stands the individual, and that it is not the moment that makes the man, but the man who creates the age."[35] Literature should not be about the way the moment (history) creates the human but the way the human shapes "reality." Based on this distinction, it would be wrong to think that Wilde was trying to give readers an accurate picture of the true dedicatee of Shakespeare's Sonnets in "The Portrait of Mr. W.H." Wilde's Vivian from "The Decay of Lying" articulates the best way to approach Wilde's story and biofiction more generally: "The only portraits in which one believes are portraits where there is very little of the sitter, and a very great deal of the artist."[36] Applying this maxim to "The Portrait of Mr. W.H.," what readers get in the story is very little of Shakespeare's dedicatee and a great deal of Wilde, an idea consistent with the aesthetic approaches of Matisse and Picasso in Najmi's biographical novel, as I illustrate in the introduction.

But what exactly does Wilde give readers in this story? The answer is his view of art, which is premised on the idea of life as a critical form of endless creation. For Wilde, the critical faculty is of crucial importance because it is that which suggests a "fresh departure of thought, or passion, or beauty."[37] Within this framework, for art to be art, the invention of something new must be present. In fact, invention is what makes art art. This explains why Vivian makes the following claim from "The Decay of Lying": "No great artist ever sees things as they really are. If he did, he would cease to be an artist."[38] Merely seeing things as they seemingly are would make a person a Bartleby-like scrivener (a biographer, a historian, or a realist) rather than a Prometheus-like artist. To be an artist, a person must create a new way of seeing and/or being. This is the exact opposite from Lukács. For the Hungarian Marxist, there is an objective historical reality, and it is the artist's job to picture that reality with as much precision and accuracy as possible:

> A writer who deals with history cannot chop and change with his material as he likes. Events and destinies have their natural, objective weight, their natural, objective proportion. If a writer succeeds in producing a story which correctly

> reproduces these relationships and proportions, then human and artistic truth will emerge alongside the historical.[39]

What Lukács calls "artistic truth," Wilde would dub mindless copy. This is the case because the historical novel, as Lukács defines it, lacks the essential component of art, which is the invention of something new.

The two positions generate contradictory criteria for assessing a particular work. In the Lukács tradition, if a work captures the essence of the biographical subject and therewith the specific age, then it would be considered a success. But if not, it would be considered a failure. For Wilde, a different set of criteria is needed. Artists are not historians or biographers, neutral and objective recorders of past events. To the contrary, they are inventors of a new reality. So while Lukács favors literature that gives "living human embodiment to historical-social types,"[40] Wilde draws the exact opposite conclusion: "We are no longer in art concerned with the type. It is with the exception that we have to do."[41] According to this model, a work would succeed only insofar as it brings into existence a new way ("exception") of seeing or being. Wilde makes this point when he offers what is perhaps the first theoretical reflection about biofiction. As Vivian says in "The Decay of Lying": "if a novelist is base enough to go to life for his personages he should at least pretend that they are creations, and not boast of them as copies. The justification of a character in a novel is not that other persons are what they are, but that the author is what he is."[42] The justification of a person in a history or a biography is that the paper figure is an accurate representation of what the real person was. But the justification of a historical figure in fiction is much different. Specifically, for the author of biofiction, of utmost importance is the artist and his or her creative vision, and not the historical past or the biographical subject, because, as Vivian says: "Literature always anticipates life. It does not copy it, but moulds it to its purpose."[43] Therefore, in the realm of art, the aesthetic object should be judged a success insofar as it invents something new, which will subsequently give birth to a new reality in life, so accurate representation of the biographical subject and therewith history is not the author's aesthetic objective.

In short, biofiction writers fictionalize, rather than represent, the life of the biographical subject, a fact to which numerous biographical novelists attest. For example, in 1916, George Moore published *The Brook Kerith*, a biographical novel in which Christ survives the crucifixion and eventually renounces some of his earlier teachings as fanatical and dangerous (I will discuss this novel at considerable length in the next chapter). Moore's Christ is not supposed to be seen as a fleshed-out version of the true Jesus. As Moore says in a letter to his friend W. K. Magee: "You must look upon my Jesus as an independent creation, and not as an attempt to discover what the real man was from the Gospels."[44] In 1973, Gore Vidal published *Burr*, a biographical novel about Aaron Burr. In a 1974 interview with Gerald Clarke, Vidal says: "my Burr is not the real Burr."[45] Joanna Scott has written three brilliant biographical novels, and in an essay on biofiction, she says about Egon Schiele, the protagonist of her biographical novel *Arrogance* (1990): "I was not trying to pretend that my Schiele was the real Schiele. I just wanted him to be real."[46] In 2018, Paula McLain published *Love and Ruin*, a biographical novel about Martha Gellhorn, and in her concluding note on sources, McLain says: "my Gellhorn isn't *the* Gellhorn."[47] From 1916 until today, the pattern is consistent. As these and countless other biographical novelists argue, the paper person in the biographical novel is not supposed to be seen as an accurate reflection of the actual historical figure. It would be more accurate to say that the author fictionalizes the actual figure in order to communicate his or her own vision of life. What, in part, makes a biofiction successful, then, is the degree to which the protagonist appears real to the reader and is an effective figure for expressing the author's vision.

This biofictional approach provides readers with an intellectual framework for understanding and assessing much in Wilde's story. Cyril's portrait of Willie is a success, because, as Erskine says: "Willie Hughes became to me as real a person as Shakespeare" (PWH 265). Success here is not defined on the basis of accurately representing the actual dedicatee of Shakespeare's Sonnets. It is based on Cyril's ability to make Willie seem and feel as real as Shakespeare. But making the character feel and seem like an actual being is merely a beginning. The ultimate aesthetic goal is the invention of a new way of seeing and/or being, and this is the effect that Cyril (as a kind of "author" of Willie Hughes) has on the narrator. After committing himself to the theory, the narrator is inspired by Willie in the same way Shakespeare was: "Every day I seemed to be discovering something new, and Willie Hughes became to me a kind of spiritual presence, an ever dominant personality" (PWH 274). The seemingly real presence of Willie inspires the narrator to set into motion a process of endlessly ("Every day") discovering "something new."

To get a more precise understanding of what this idea of discovering something new means, it is useful to look at *The Incomparable and Ingenious History of Mr. W.H.* Wilde realized that the core ideas in "The Portrait of Mr. W.H." had considerable power, so he decided to expand the short story into a book. Wilde did not complete the project during his lifetime, but the draft version sheds specific light on Wilde's view of the biographical figure that functions to inspire a critical form of unending creation. The works about Mr. W.H. focus less on Willie Hughes than on the inspirational effect he has on people. For instance, Willie's "physical beauty" was so intense "that it became the very cornerstone of Shakespeare's art; the very source of Shakespeare's inspiration; the very incarnation of Shakespeare's dreams."[48] But beauty in itself is not what makes a figure so valuable. It is that this "beauty had given a new creative impulse to" an "age."[49] In short, beauty gives birth to something new, and Willie is the basis for two inspirational ideas in Shakespeare.

The first relates to "the ambiguity of the sexes."[50] A "boy-actor" who convincingly dresses and performs as a female, Willie occasions new ways of thinking about sexual identity. As the narrator of *The Incomparable and Ingenious History of Mr. W.H.* says:

> Indeed, if sex be an element in artistic creation, it might rather be urged that the delightful combination of wit and romance which characterises so many of Shakespeare's heroines was at least occasioned, if it was not actually caused by the fact that the players of these parts were lads and young men, whose passionate purity, quick mobile fancy, and healthy freedom from sentimentality can hardly fail to have suggested a new and delightful type of girlhood or of womanhood.[51]

Wilde's narrator, anticipating the work of Virginia Woolf and Judith Butler, entertains the possibility that sex is not so much an ontological reality as an "artistic creation," something that can be altered and shaped by skillful artists. In Shakespeare's case, a figure like Willie enabled the Stratford Bard to imagine into being "a new and delightful type of girlhood or of womanhood." And given Wilde's aesthetic, the artist's imagined reality would give birth to a reality in life.

Second, Willie inspires an understanding and appreciation of the legitimacy, power, beauty, and value of the homoerotic relation.[52] Here is how *The Incomparable*'s narrator describes Shakespeare in relation to Willie:

> Willie Hughes! How musically it sounded! Yes; who else but he could have been the master-mistress of Shakespeare's passion, the lord of his love to whom he was bound in vassalage, the delicate minion of pleasure, the rose of the whole world, the herald of the spring decked in the proud livery of youth, the lovely boy whom it was sweet music to hear, and whose beauty was the very raiment of Shakespeare's heart, as it was the keystone of his dramatic power?[53]

This sounds like something out of the courtly love tradition. But in this instance, the lover and the beloved are two males. To indicate that Wilde wants readers to consider this relation in sexual terms, he strategically references Plato's *Symposium*,[54] a work that takes sexual intimacy between men as a natural given.[55]

As readers, we might be wondering if Cyril, Erskine, the narrator, and Wilde have given us a reliable portrait of Shakespeare and/or Mr. W.H. But to ask such a question is to miss the point of Wilde's aesthetic, which is why the theory based on empirical evidence is irrelevant. Artists do not give their viewers the status quo, a well-established cultural truth ("things as they really are"). They imagine something new into being, something original and unique that disrupts and challenges accepted norms and reified values. This approach explains how critics should engage Wilde's story. As Ernest says in "The Critic as Artist": "the primary aim of the critic is to see the object as in itself it really is not."[56] Gilbert adds to this idea: "To the critic the work of art is simply a suggestion for a new work of his own, that need not necessarily bear any obvious resemblance to the thing it criticises."[57] A great work of art does not picture what supposedly is. That is what history and biography do. The great artist uses history or biography to create a work that inspires the viewer to see the world in a new way, which will thereby enable the person to create a new way of living.

Interpreting the theory in "The Portrait of Mr. W.H." with this aesthetic approach in mind compels readers to focus not on accurate representation of the biographical subject and his or her time and place but instead to activate their own critical-artistic sense in the present and for the future.[58] Let me apply this model to "The Portrait of Mr. W.H.," in which Shakespeare is understood to have used the life of Mr. W.H. to produce a sonnet sequence that illustrates "the true relations between the art of the actor and the art of the dramatist" (PWH 265).[59] These sonnets clarify how drama can give birth to more ideal forms in the real world: "Shakespeare invites us to notice how the truth of acting, the truth of visible presentation on the stage, adds to the wonder of poetry, giving life to its loveliness, and actual reality to its ideal form" (PWH 271). Shakespeare's artistic work was a success because it inspired Cyril to generate a new way of thinking about women and homosexuality, and Cyril's critical work in turn was a success because it inspired Erskine and the narrator to see "something new" each day. What Wilde gives readers in "The Portrait of Mr. W.H.," therefore, is a clear articulation of the way art, specifically biofiction, functions to inspire people to become active creators of new ways of seeing and living. According to this paradigm, we should not be asking: Did Wilde get Willie's life and times right? That question is premised on the empiricism-based theory that scholars took as a given. Rather, we should be asking: Did Shakespeare and Cyril effectively use the life of Mr. W.H. to set into motion a life-generating orientation toward the world?

The point I have been building toward is this: Wildean aesthetics is a tacit rejection and refutation of the historical novel, specifically as Lukács would define it decades later. Therefore, to use a Lukácsian model to analyze and interpret a work like "The Portrait of Mr. W. H." could only yield the most hideous form of interpretive deformity. Moreover, the aesthetic that Wilde establishes in and through "The Portrait of Mr. W.H." is the one that has become dominant among biographical novelists. A brief look at the remarks of a few contemporary biographical novelists will illustrate. The Nigerian-Belgian author Chika Unigwe has published a biographical novel about Olaudah Equiano (*De Zwarte Messias*), and she is currently writing one about Equiano's daughter, Joanna, about whom almost nothing is known, which makes it a borderline biofiction similar to "The Portrait of Mr. W.H." In an interview, I asked Unigwe if it is possible to do a biographical novel about someone when there is almost no historical record. Her response is illuminating:

> In a historical novel, the author is invested in being true to the realities of that time, so there is little space to create characters that transcend their time in a very radical way, which you can do with biofiction. So in that way I think that Joanna is certainly more biofiction than historical fiction. There are things that Joanna does that I doubt that she would have been able to do if I were writing historical fiction. So I think in biofiction you are able to dream a lot more, a lot wider. Your dreams are more expansive, as a writer, than in historical fiction.[60]

Given the differences between the historical and biographical novel, readers come to the works for very different things. As Unigwe concludes: "Readers don't come to biographical fiction for truth. They come to biographical fiction for possibilities."[61] What readers want from the historical novel is an accurate representation of "the realities of that time," but what they want from the biographical novel is a model of a figure that transcends the deterministic forces of history and the environment, and this is something that places the protagonist of the biographical novel in irreconcilable conflict with the protagonist of the historical novel.

Spanish novelist Rosa Montero usefully clarifies what readers get from biographical novels. For Montero, the goal of the biographical novel should not so much be to depict a real life as to use the life "to try to better understand the world in its greater complexity." This, she explains, is what Robert Graves achieves in his novel *I, Claudius*: "He wasn't telling us the story of Emperor Claudius, but rather making an impressive fresco of the human condition."[62] Montero specifies exactly what fiction writers give readers in a discussion about the human "capacity for symbolic understanding."[63] Biography is of crucial importance because it provides humans with an "existential map," which is a framework about "how to live."[64] This has direct relevance for understanding the function of a particular life in the biographical novel. In Montero's case, it would be incorrect to say that her goal was simply to give readers a picture of Marie Curie in her biographical novel about the famous Polish scientist. Montero is a novelist, not a biographer. Therefore, Montero unapologetically says that she "used Marie Curie as an enormous screen on which to project [...] possibilities."[65] Like Unigwe, the biographical subject is a figure that the author uses in order to imagine into existence possible ways of thinking and being for readers in the present and the future. As David Ebershoff says in an interview about *The Danish Girl*, his biographical novel of Einar Wegener/Lili Elbe, the first person to undergo sex confirmation surgery: "Artists are visionaries; they see something that does not yet exist. They can bring into creation something that is not yet there."[66]

In 1996, Margarat Atwood authored *Alias Grace*, a biographical novel about the Irish servant Grace Marks, who was convicted in Canada of murdering her employer. In a lecture about this work, Atwood sheds considerable light on her aesthetic objectives, and it is clear that she is working in the same tradition as Wilde. Atwood told her audience that "such stories are not about this or that slice of the past," a claim that certainly disqualifies the work as a historical novel. To the contrary, "they are about human nature," they are "about truth and lies, and disguises and revelations."[67] To conclude the lecture, Atwood references a scene from a then-contemporary film to express not just what she does but what biographical novelists do more generally:

> In the recent film *Il Postino*, the great poet Pablo Neruda upbraids his friend, a lowly postman, for having filched one of Neruda's poems to use in his courtship of a local girl. "But," replies the postman, "poems do not belong to those who write them. Poems belong to those who need them." And so it is with stories about the past. The past no longer belongs only to those who once lived in it; the past belongs to those who claim it, and are willing to explore it, and to infuse it

> with meaning for those alive today. The past belongs to us, because we are the ones who need it.[68]

As a creative writer, Atwood unapologetically lays claim to history in order to give life meaning for readers in the present and the future. Implicit in Atwood's apologia is a distinction between doing and using history. For those who do history, giving readers established facts about the past is of crucial importance, so altering them is unacceptable. But biographical novelists use rather than do history, so taking liberties with the facts is not just acceptable but also sometimes necessary. Put simply, biographical novelists fictionalize lives from the past to enhance life in the present and future. This is the same model at work in Wilde's texts about Mr. W.H. While it might seem that the narrator's insights about women and homosexuals in *The Incomparable and Ingenious History of Mr. W.H.* derive from his analysis of Willie Hughes, they are actually Wilde's ideas, and he is merely using Willie Hughes to invent new ways of seeing and living in the future. As Wilde says in "The Soul of Man": "The future is what artists are."[69]

Ebershoff can further illuminate the method of Wilde and the biographical novelist more generally. In the Author's Note of *The Danish Girl*, Ebershoff states explicitly that the "reader should not look to this novel for very many biographical details of Einar Wegener's life." Ebershoff found "some important facts about Einar's actual transformation,"[70] and he then used those details in order to craft a narrative that would underscore the degree to which "there is universality to Einar's question of identity."[71] In short, Ebershoff converted Einar/Lili into a symbol. Thus, Ebershoff used rather than represented Einar/Lili, and he did this to express his own views about the link between a constructed identity and human agency. In sum, biographical novelists take something of significance from a particular figure's life, and they then fictionalize that life in order to project into being their own view of life and the world. Within this aesthetic framework, biographical novelists alter biography and history in order to convert the main character into a symbol, which is why Ebershoff says: "*The Danish Girl* is a metaphor."[72]

To return to my central claim in this section: If we use the scientific sense as the basis for the construction or assessment of an artwork, a sense that privileges past factual realities and the empirical method, then we would have to say that Wilde's work and biographical novels more generally are failures because they do not accurately represent history or biography. But if we use the "artistic sense" as the basis for the construction or assessment of an artwork, a sense that prioritizes creative invention and future possibilities, then we could say that these works succeed insofar as they lead to the creation of something new, which subsequently becomes a living reality in the present and future. Understanding that there are two separate theories at work in this story significantly impacts the way we interpret the wonderfully ambiguous conclusion. The narrator inherits the forged painting, which he shows to his "artistic friends," who speculate about the identity of the painter. The narrator, however, chooses not to disclose that the painting is a forgery: "I have never cared to tell them its true history" (PWH 281). Knowledge of the painting's "true history" would seem to render the theory about Willie Hughes null and void, because, as the narrator earlier said to Erskine about the painting, the "only evidence for the existence of Willie Hughes is that picture in front of you, and the picture is a forgery" (PWH 279). To punctuate this empiricism-formulated point, the narrator intones: "Whatever romance may have to say about the Willie Hughes theory, reason is dead against it" (PWH 279). Based on these claims, we could say that the narrator subscribes to the evidence-based theory. But by the end of the story, this clearly changes, for as the narrator says of the painting in the closing sentence: "sometimes, when I look at it, I think that there is really a great deal to be said for the Willie Hughes theory of Shakespeare's sonnets" (PWH 281). Since the narrator stipulates that the empiricism-based theory is valid only on condition that the painting verifies Willie's existence, we can conclude from the narrator's personal reflections that he considers the theory valid in an "artistic sense," which is to say that the portrait must have succeeded in generating a new way of seeing and being. To be more specific, just as Wilde's Shakespeare used Willie Hughes to create works that inspired Cyril to see "something new" in life, and Cyril used Willie Hughes to create a work that inspired Erskine to see "something new" in life, so too did the painter of Willie Hughes inspire the narrator to see "something new" in life. It is in this "artistic sense" that the painting confirms the Willie Hughes theory. But more importantly, this "artistic sense" would become the foundation for biofictional aesthetics, as we will now see in biographical novels in which Wilde plays a crucial part.

III

Instead of mastering life,
I allowed it to master me.[73]

Wilde's colorful life and theories about art are so compelling that they have generated a disproportionate number of biofictions, though not all are of equal value or significance. For instance, Hall's *I Give You Oscar Wilde* is noteworthy because it was the first biographical novel about the Irish writer. But in the tradition of biofiction, it lacks the originality, creativity, and substance we find in the works of Ackroyd, Edwards, and Tóibín.[74]

In *The Last Testament of Oscar Wilde*, Ackroyd has his protagonist write his memoir during the last four months of his life, and that memoir, with two concluding pages from Wilde's friend Maurice Gilbert, is the novel. It is the work's clever narrative strategy that makes *The Last Testament* such a success, as we see Wilde reflect on the strengths and weaknesses of his art and life. Therefore, what readers get in the novel is less about Wilde and more about aesthetics, existence, and the art of living.

Ackroyd makes it clear that "The Portrait of Mr. W.H." is one of Wilde's most significant works. As his Wilde says:

> In *The Portrait of Mr. W. H.*, that extraordinary essay in which I reveal the identity of the boy who haunts Shakespeare's sonnets, I limned a portrait of perfect masculine beauty, in which both sexes have left their touch. This book was my homage to Greek love, and never had I put my learning to more artful use. It was of no concern to me if the facts were accurate or inaccurate: I had discovered a truth which was larger than that of biography and history, a truth not merely about Shakespeare but about the nature of all creative art.
>
> (LT 121)

The "truth" of this work is "larger" than what is found in biography and/or history, which is why a correspondence to established facts is of secondary concern. The objective here is the "artful use" of Willie's life in order to create an "homage to Greek love." If we apply this approach to *The Last Testament*, we could say that Ackroyd makes "artful use" of Wilde's life in order to communicate his own vision of art and life.

For Ackroyd, Wilde's story captivates not only because he was an extraordinary writer and thinker, but also because he was such a spectacular failure. Of central importance to Wilde's aesthetic is idealism, the view that through an elevated self-consciousness a person could evade biological or environmental determinism and thereby behave as a legislator of reality. Within this framework, it is when Ackroyd's Wilde "abjured the wonderful idealism of" his "art" that he "took the first step on the path which was to lead" him "into the wilderness" (LT 102). To clarify precisely what he means, Ackroyd's Wilde strategically alludes to Plato's *Symposium*: "I had been sitting with Socrates, but now I had found Alcibiades on my other hand, and I took my meat, and drank my wine, with him"

(LT 102). The strategic reference to Socrates and Alcibiades provides a framework for understanding Ackroyd's usage of Wilde's life.

In *The Symposium*, a group of thinkers attends a party, where each person makes a speech "in praise of love."[75] Taking his inspiration from the philosopher and priestess Diotima, Socrates argues that the function of love is "procreation," which "can be either physical or spiritual,"[76] though he contends that spiritual procreation is superior to physical. But the goal is not simply procreation: "Its object is to procreate and bring forth in beauty."[77] For those committed to material procreation, their progeny are children, but for those committed to spiritual procreation, their progeny "is wisdom and virtue in general."[78] Applying this hierarchical model to love, Diotima clarifies how physical forms of love and beauty are merely the beginning of an ascent toward more noble and sublime realities, which are spiritual in nature:

> This is the right way of approaching or being initiated into the mysteries of love, to begin with examples of beauty in this world, and using them as steps to ascend continually with that absolute beauty as one's aim, from one instance of physical beauty to two and from two to all, then from physical beauty to moral beauty, and from moral beauty to the beauty of knowledge, until from knowledge of various kinds one arrives at the supreme knowledge whose sole object is that absolute beauty, and knows at last what absolute beauty is.[79]

According to this model, love of a boy like Willie Hughes should be the beginning of what would become an increasingly more spiritual form of love, one that would transcend the physical and particular and culminate in something spiritual and universal.

To clarify how this model functions in the realm of action, Plato concludes *The Symposium* with a particular encounter between Alcibiades and Socrates that functions to distinguish a base, sensual, and corruptible form of love from a spiritual one. Described as a beautiful man, Alcibiades arrives at the end of the party. Drunk and uninhibited, he berates Socrates, who is clearly attracted to such young men. Through "mere words,"[80] Alcibiades claims, Socrates seduces young men like himself, but he does not take seduction to its logical end, sexual fulfillment. This surprises Alcibiades because he believes that his beautiful appearance should induce the older man to sexual action. But in his retort Socrates exposes Alcibiades's flawed assumptions:

> You must see in me a beauty which is incomparable and far superior to your own physical good looks, and if, having made this discovery, you are trying to get a

> share of it by exchanging your beauty for mine, you obviously mean to get much the better of the bargain; you are trying to get true beauty in return for sham; in fact, what you are proposing is to exchange dross for gold.[81]

Intellectual beauty is gold, and, by comparison, physical beauty is mere dross. This is the case because the progeny of intellectual beauty is eternal, not subject to decay or death, as is Alcibiades's physical appearance.

Central to Ackroyd's novel is Wilde's realization that he chose Alcibiades's dross over Socrates's gold. This discovery enables Ackroyd's Wilde to reflect on the senses in which his life and art have failed and succeeded, and it enables Ackroyd to use Wilde's life and art to picture a more effective aesthetic. That Ackroyd's Wilde regrets much is one of the novel's refrains. Comparing himself to Balzac, who fashioned life "into shape as a sculptor will fashion stone into a beautiful form," Wilde understands that he "did not know life at all" (LT 63). Instead of keeping his eye on the real prize, which should have been the progeny of intellectual beauty, Wilde succumbed to the ephemeral praise of flatterers: "I did not disillusion those who listened to me, and there lay the most serious flaw in my character. I enjoyed praise, I admit it. I like to be liked" (LT 89). Given his focus on the momentary and the superficial, he "sought for visible rather than intellectual success," which led him at times to write "quickly and without thought" (LT 97). Therefore, instead of maturing and developing as a person and an artist, his "growth" had "been arrested," and this, Wilde claims, is the "tragedy of" his "life" (LT 101). Having lost himself in his sins ("I had lost myself in my sins; with my own hands I had blinded myself and I stumbled into the pit" [LT 119]), Ackroyd's Wilde takes full responsibility for his failings: "the vanity and hypocrisy were mine" (LT 122). Thus, the life of Ackroyd's Wilde serves as a cautionary tale: "If I am anything, I am a warning" (LT 179).

With all these scorching self-incriminations, it would be easy to conclude that Ackroyd's novel pictures Wilde as an unambiguous failure. But this is not correct. It was in his early years that Wilde formulated his aesthetic "mission," which was "to bring art into life," and it was in drama that he "discovered that the two become perfect in combination" (LT 88). Given his comprehension of and contribution to aesthetics, he compares himself to some of the world's most prominent artists and thinkers:

> Every great creation involves a rupture of equilibrium, and the finest things in art have come from that fever of the passions which I and others like me

> have experienced. It was male love which inspired Michelangelo in his perfect sonnets; it inspired Shakespeare to immortalise a young man in words of fire just as it guided the hands of Plato and of Marlowe.
>
> (LT 112–13)

In the tradition of Shakespeare, Michelangelo, Plato, and Marlowe, Wilde concludes that he "was the greatest artist of" his "time" (LT 170). With such extraordinary talent, he "could have been the voice of the coming age" (LT 179).

To understand why he could have been the voice of the coming age, it is important to see how Wilde aesthetically registered a major shift in intellectual history. Plato established a model in which Truth exists independent of human communities. Thus, it is the responsibility of thinkers and artists to discover and subsequently represent such Truth, which is co-eternal with the Divine. Within this framework, established Truths are immutable and inviolable. But this paradigm renders artists of negligible significance. Plato's *Ion* is a perfect case in point. As Socrates says, inspired poems "are not of man or human workmanship, but are divine and from the gods." As such, "the poets are nothing but interpreters of the gods." This approach to truth renders artists passive recipients of pre-existent Truth rather than active creators of "truth." Having accepted the poets as godly seers and ministers of the divine, the listeners come to believe "that it is not they [seers and ministers] who utter these precious revelations while their mind is not within them, but that it is the god himself who speaks, and through them becomes articulate to us."[82] According to this model, Truth is valid and trustworthy only insofar as the human has played no role in its construction. In essence, Plato used the God-concept to establish, ground, and legitimize a model of objective and immutable Truth in which the artist must subordinate the self to the absolute Truths that are what they are whether humans apprehend them or not.

The phenomenological turn of the late eighteenth and early nineteenth centuries shifted the focus from seemingly established ontological Truths to phenomenologically constructed epistemological "truths," and this shift significantly elevated the position of the artist. Instead of being the gods' amanuensis, a being that merely takes dictation from the Divine, the nineteenth-century artist became a figure that shapes and determines "reality"—recall William Blake's famous formulation: "I must Create a System, or be enslav'd by another Mans."[83] So rather than subordinating self to a pre-existent ontological Reality, which Ackroyd's Wilde exposes as a "conventional reality" (LT 138), the artist should unapologetically acknowledge and affirm the artistic self that creates a new conceptual "reality." This shift explains the valorization of personality in Wilde's work—only those beings with a personality can create a compelling and lasting "reality." Ackroyd's Wilde sees himself as the one who has "written so much about the powers of the personality" (LT 92). And yet, he failed as an artist because he lost sight of what should have been the focus, which is the construction of a new conceptual "reality" (an updated version of Plato's intellectual progeny) that would have created more life. Here is how Ackroyd's Wilde expresses the matter:

> To a larger extent, I realise now, my power—and the power of my personality—depended upon my position in society. As soon as that position was taken away, my personality counted for nothing whatever. In similar fashion, I once saw reality from a great height since it was from the pinnacle of my individualism: now I have fallen so low that reality rises above me, and I see its shadows and its secret crevices.
>
> (LT 14)

Foregrounding his flamboyant and mesmerizing personality garnered Wilde much attention when he was in his prime, but now that he has lost his cachet, "reality" overtakes him.

Ackroyd uses Wilde's response to his "gross indecency" trial to illuminate his protagonist's failings. As an artist, Wilde should use his piercing intelligence to expose the flawed, unjust, and debilitating assumptions on which cultural and political laws ("conventional reality") of his age are premised. Then he should imagine into being a new set of assumptions ("reality"), ones that would lead to healthier and more just ways of seeing and experiencing the world. Reflecting on the major mistakes of his life, just as the actual Wilde does in *Epistola*,[84] Ackroyd's Wilde details how he failed at his trial to do what he should have done as an artist:

> My lawsuit was unforgiveable—the one really foolish action of my life. Instead of mastering life, I allowed it to master me; instead of being the extraordinary dramatist which I was, I became an actor merely, mouthing the lines of others and those which fear and cowardice murmured to me. I let my fate rest in the hands of Society rather than shaping it myself: I appealed to the very authorities whom I professed to despise. For that I cannot be forgiven, and the memory of my failure haunts me still.
>
> (LT 135)

Society has an established system of rules, laws, and norms in place, and most people mindlessly accept them as an inviolable Reality. But as an artist, Wilde is not one of the masses. Therefore, instead of merely accepting society's edicts as incontrovertible Truths, a response in which life masters him, it is his responsibility as a master to examine society, diagnose its ailments, and prescribe something new and better for it. Simply accepting society is to abdicate his responsibility as an artist and a master of life. Had he lived up to his calling as an "extraordinary dramatist," he could have used his personality to make the case for a new way of seeing Uranian love, thus challenging the foundational idea that was used to criminalize and persecute him.

The problem here is not necessarily Wilde's focus or emphasis on personality. It is that Wilde failed to use his personality in service of something greater than himself. There is a practical example to illustrate how this aesthetic-into-life process should—ideally—function. From 1895 until 1897, Wilde was imprisoned for "gross indecency." After his release, Wilde wrote *The Ballad of Reading Gaol*, a biopoem about the life of Charles Thomas Wooldridge, who was executed in 1896. Prison life was outrageously inhumane, and part of Wilde's aesthetic goal with *The Ballad of Reading Gaol* was to inspire reform, which explains why he proudly announced that his "poem 'had been twice quoted in the House'" at a "parliamentary debate" about a prison reform bill and that through his poem he was "able to deal a heavy and fatal blow at the monstrous prison-system of English justice."[85] Important to note here is the kind of change the poet wanted. Wilde's verbal picture of Reading Gaol led the home secretary to propose increasing "the number of prison inspectors and official visitors."[86] But Wilde felt that such a proposal fails to address the real problem. Increasing staff to ensure that the regulations are upheld does not alter the regulations, which are the basis for the inhumane conditions. As Nicholas Frankel observes: "It was the regulations themselves that needed changing, he insisted, since as presently constituted they seemed to have the destruction of both the prisoner's physical and mental capacities as their object."[87] As an artist, Wilde exposes a foundational system that is destructive, and he imagines into being something else, a system that is more productive of life.

This is precisely what Wilde tries to accomplish in "The Portrait of Mr. W.H." Wilde uses Shakespeare's dedicatee to create a new reality, specifically an original way of thinking about women and homosexuality, which will lead in the future to new ways of female and homosexual being. Through the aesthetic power of their (Cyril, Erskine, the narrator, and Wilde) personality-rich presentations, these four could give birth to a new reality, so even after they are no longer alive (Cyril dies, and the narrator picks up where Cyril left off. Wilde is now dead, and I am picking up where he left off.), the "realities" they created continue to live. By foregrounding his own personality over his intellectual progeny, Ackroyd's Wilde failed himself, his art, and others, because now that he no longer has a captive audience, his work can no longer have an impact. This explains why Ackroyd has him make the following claim: "As it is, my personality has destroyed my work: that is the one unforgivable sin of my life" (TL 66). The novel's logic goes something like this: because Wilde did not use his personality to effectively make the case for a new "reality" like Uranian love, which should have been his intellectual progeny, in other words, because he used his mesmerizing personality to aggrandize only himself, now that his reputation is in tatters, nothing substantive of him remains.[88]

Reliant as this aesthetic is on *The Symposium*, it is important to clarify precisely how Wilde departs significantly from Plato. By suppressing that which is of the human or human workmanship, Plato's artist is receptive to the revelations of the gods, Truths that are valid for all people in all places at all times. Within this Platonic system, gratification comes from discovering an immutable Truth: "This beauty is first of all eternal; it neither comes into being nor passes away, neither waxes nor wanes." Unchangeable, this Truth has universal and atemporal validity, which is why it is described as having "a beauty whose nature is marvellous" and considered "the final goal."[89]

Wilde rejected this view, because the world is not—ontologically—what it is. Rather, it is—phenomenologically—what we have conceptualized and subsequently naturalized it to be.[90] Therefore, the goal should never be a final and absolute characterization of Reality. The goal should be endlessly creating new ways of seeing and experiencing life and the world. This explains why Ackroyd's Wilde makes the following claim: "But I became aware of a peculiar but now to me familiar phenomenon: as soon as I had expressed my philosophy, I ceased to adhere to it. Once I had given perfect form to my ideas and attitudes, they became wearisome to me. When people believed in me, I ceased to believe in myself" (TL 53). For Wilde, life is found in the activity of endlessly critiquing the truths we inherit, determining whether they have relevance or meaning for us, and, if not, creating new and better truths for the future. Those who fail to critique the present and then to counter-construct more relevant truths for the future are nothing more than slaves. Wilde formulates this view most clearly in "The Soul of Man": "Art is Individualism, and Individualism is a disturbing and disintegrating force. Therein lies its immense value. For what it seeks to disturb is monotony of type, slavery of custom, tyranny of habit, and the reduction of man to the level of a machine."[91] Since the essence of life is perpetual growth and endless development, the establishment and reification of Truth would result in human stagnation and ultimately cultural death. What makes the final and absolutist model of Truth so dangerous is that it leads people to let their critical, intellectual, and creative guard down. They accept the culture's provisionally constructed truths as universal and eternal, and thus become, wittingly or not, the slaves of epistemic custom and the vassals of societal habit. In other words, instead of acting in accordance with truths that are suitable for them in their time and place, they subscribe to Truths that were constructed for people from an alien culture and age.

And this idea applies to the contemporary artist, which is why Ackroyd's Wilde ceases to adhere to his own ideas and attitudes after they have been brought to perfection. What artists do is to disrupt and destabilize dominant orthodoxies, even their own, so aesthetic fulfillment is not achieved through the establishment of a new absolute Truth. It is realized through the artistic activity of constructing a new provisional truth. Put differently, the aesthetic goal is active creation, and not the establishment of an inviolable Truth. This explains why Plato's model is not only wrong but also dangerous, as his devotion to an immutable and universal Truth leads to stagnation and ultimately death.

IV

To live is the rarest thing in the world.
Most people exist, that is all.[92]

Edwards's *Oscar Wilde Discovers America* is an excellent biographical novel, certainly worthy of extensive study, but I want to conclude this chapter by looking closely at Tóibín's *The Master*, as this work best articulates the crucial intellectual developments that led so many writers to turn away from the historical novel and to the biographical novel. Central to the novel is James's life- and fiction-altering transformation, and it is Wilde who makes this metamorphosis possible. For the sake of clarity, let me start by explicitly stating the nature of the change. Early in the novel, James believes that his role as an artist is to encourage submission to society's seemingly ineluctable laws. In a sense, he has adopted a version of Alexander Pope's idea that "Whatever is, is right."[93] Within this aesthetic framework, the goal is not to examine and diagnose a culture and subsequently change it, making it thereby healthier and more life-promoting. Rather, it is to accept reality as it is and thus to counsel renunciation of one's seemingly wayward desires, an act that does nothing to change the social and the political. By the end of the novel, however, Tóibín's James rejects his renunciation aesthetic and instead affirms the individual self over societal dictates and prizes an aesthetic and culture of experiment, creativity, and the sensuous.

Tóibín opens the novel with James's renunciation aesthetic. The year is 1895, and James is anxiously awaiting the premiere of his play *Guy Domville*. The work's theme is of crucial importance for the whole novel, so Tóibín has James strategically reveal it, which is that "Guy Domville, despite his vast wealth and golden future, decided to renounce the world and devote himself to a life of contemplation and prayer in a monastery."[94] To underscore that renunciation will be a dominant motif, Tóibín uses the idea to differentiate James from Wilde. On the opening night of his play, James, to settle his fraying nerves, attends a performance of Wilde's play *An Ideal Husband*. James, certainly no fan of Wilde's work at this point in the novel, compares the play to his own, and he finds his rival's work wanting: James's "drama was about renunciation, he thought, and these people [who were watching Wilde's play] had renounced nothing. At the end, as they called the actors back for further bows, he saw from their flushed and happy faces that they did not appear to have any immediate plans to amend their ways" (M 16). James's play encourages renunciation of self, while Wilde's play rejects the idea of renunciation altogether.

To indicate that the renunciation aesthetic is not a onetime affair for James, Tóibín returns to the idea near the end of the novel, when James's niece reads *The Portrait of a Lady*. Isabel Archer has made some bold and daring choices as a young woman by venturing to Europe and marrying someone whom everyone opposes. Eventually, Archer realizes that she has made a horrible mistake by marrying her husband, but she remains with him nonetheless. James's niece is puzzled by this decision, so she asks her uncle why Archer made this choice. James says: "Making such leaps [as Archer did when she was young] requires us to be brave and determined, but doing so also may freeze any other possibilities. It is easier to renounce bravery rather than to be brave over and over" (M 325). What James does not vocalize is just as important. He believes that it was a matter of "duty and resignation" (M 324) that Archer stay with her husband. This is the same theme in James's play.

Renunciation does not just play a major role in James's fiction; it is an essential component of his life. The early Jamesian strategy in *The Master* is to show people how to cope with the life-thwarting laws and norms of society, and this is achieved by renouncing seemingly wayward desires. For instance, Tóibín's James wrote a story many years before about a personal matter, but he destroyed it. Now, in January 1895, he decides to record what happened, which was about him standing in the rain outside the Paris room of Paul Joukowsky, a man who has encouraged intimacies and for whom James clearly yearns. This scene, so reminiscent of Michael Furey's death-bringing pursuit of James Joyce's Gretta Conroy, evokes a sense of thwarted love, but in James's case, what leads to failure is his philosophy of renunciation. Instead of venturing into the unknown by approaching Paul, which would violate a cultural prohibition about love between men, James waits outside until the light in Paul's room fades, and then, consistent with his philosophy of renunciation, he slowly walks home. However, in his fictional story of the event, James "had alerted Paul to his presence and Paul had come down and they had walked up the stairs together in silence. And it was very clear now—Paul had made it clear—what would happen" (M 10). What makes this moment so poignant is James's failure to imagine his way beyond his culture's prohibitions. As the narrator says, rather than thinking about what would happen next with Paul, James "had never allowed himself to imagine beyond that point. It was the closest he had come, but he had not come close at all" (M 10). The energy expended on renouncing one's wayward impulses prevents James from imagining into being a new way of sexual intimacy between men, a way that would be in conflict with and transcend his culture's restrictions. Having failed to pursue the experience with Paul, James confined the imagination to what is culturally predetermined. The outside-the-norm life experience would have opened up the possibility for the imagination, which would have made possible the creation of something new. But that did not happen, so from a Wildean perspective, James failed as a person and an artist, because his philosophy of renunciation did not result in a new way of seeing and being first in art and then in life.

This scene with Paul parallels what happens with an army corporal who serves as James's manservant during his visit to Ireland. The character's name is Hammond, and he is as drawn to James as James is drawn to him. Significant are the changes made about Hammond from the drafts to the published version of the novel, which indicate that Tóibín struggled to get the nuanced and suggestive language of the James/Hammond (Andrews) interactions exactly right. Hammond, who is named Andrews in the draft versions, enters James's apartment when the author most yearns for a soul-comforting intimacy. Here is the version that Tóibín ultimately included:

> He put his hands behind his head in the darkness of the bedroom, the firelight having fully dimmed. He was disturbed by the idea that he longed, now more than ever before, in this strange house in this strange country, for someone to hold him, not speak or move even, but to embrace him, stay with him. He needed that now, and making himself say it brought the need closer, made it more urgent and more impossible.
>
> (M 37–8)

Compare this with the version of the first draft in which Hammond (Andrews) is mentioned:

> He put his hands over his face in the darkness of the bedroom, the firelight having fully dimmed. In that moment when Andrews had appeared until he left the room Henry knew that he longed for someone to hold him, not speak or move even, simply embrace him, stay with him, rest with him. He needed that now and saying it to himself brought the need closer, made it then more urgent and, he sighed, as impossible as it always had been.[95]

In the published version, there is no indication that the someone for whom James pines should be a male or that the idea of comfort is related to Hammond. But in the draft version, by specifically mentioning Andrews (Hammond) in the same sentence in which James yearns for intimacy, Tóibín makes his James more conscious of his own homosexual yearnings. But this is a mistake because Tóibín's James cannot imagine his way, at least at this point in the novel, to such a form of same-sex intimacy, which perhaps explains why Tóibín had to eliminate the reference to Hammond.

Let me give one more example to illustrate. In the fourth typed draft of the novel, Tóibín includes the following line in a scene in which Hammond—strangely—asks James if he wants a book he was previously reading (M 28). After Hammond makes this offer, "Henry lay in bed and wondered if Hammond had intended to offer him comfort or something more than comfort." But Tóibín crossed out this sentence, and in the margin he wrote: "Crosses the line."[96] To give James too much consciousness at this point in the novel would conflict with the limited and flawed character that Tóibín is creating. James's philosophy of renunciation has extremely negative consequences on his life and aesthetic; it causes a huge blind spot, which leads to some of the novelist's most grievous mistakes as an artist and a person. To have his James entertain the possibility of intimacy with Hammond would cross the line by making James more conscious and daring, which would be inconsistent with the character Tóibín created, so he decided not to include the sentence in the final version.

The weaknesses and failures in James's character, deriving or resulting as they do from his commitment to renunciation, negatively impact his relationships with others. To understand how and why this is the case, it is important to note the novel's focus on the cultural role the artist should play in enabling people to better see the world and in improving the quality of human life. Tóibín suggests that the early James has failed to some degree as an artist in the opening three pages. James struggles with nightmares, and the first section concludes with a haunting image of his mother appealing to her son for help. In the dream, "he had locked eyes with his mother, and her gaze was full of panic, her mouth ready to cry out. She fiercely wanted something beyond her reach, which she could not obtain, and he could not help her" (M 3). Everyday people, like James's mother, make a tacit appeal to artists, who are the unacknowledged legislators of the universe. As artists, their cultural job is to identify and expose cultural ailments and to prescribe a cure by offering a better and healthier way of seeing and/or being. What people like James's mother do not need is an artist who basically says: "Life is exactly as it should be, and my job as an artist is not to change the society but to reconcile you to reality as it is by counselling you to renounce your wayward impulses and desires."

Again, an early draft of the novel will prove illuminating. Tóibín clearly wants to establish two facts about James's character in the first part of the novel. Like James's mother, his sister, Alice, makes an implicit plea for help. Alice has had some mental and health challenges, so she goes to England with Miss Loring, who is ambiguously described as Alice's caregiver or perhaps lover. Here is the passage about Alice's request of her brother: "Miss Loring accompanied her when Alice decided to come to England to avoid being cared for by her aunt Kate, an act of defiance and independence and also, of course, a cry to Henry for help" (M 56). In the first draft of the novel, the narrator says in this same section that Henry "at various times took care of her [Alice]," but Tóibín did not include this passage in the final version.[97] Why? The problem with Henry at this point is that he is epistemologically limited and flawed, which leads him to overlook a great deal and consequently to fail many people around him. Therefore, Tóibín had to eliminate the suggestion that James took care of his sister in order to underscore his failure to see and then to properly respond to his sister's plea for help.

James's personal and aesthetic limitations and failures are best brought into sharp focus through his interactions with Constance Fenimore Woolson. A famous novelist and an astute reader of James's work, Tóibín's Woolson quietly and privately suffers in the novel until she commits suicide. Her death has a staggering effect on James, who subsequently wonders if he bears any responsibility. It is in a conversation with Woolson about Alice and women more generally that readers see the exact nature of Henry's limitations in the worlds of seeing and action. After Henry observes that "'Life itself seems to be the root of" his sister's "malady," Woolson replies: "I think it's difficult for all of us. The gap is so wide." The "us" in this case might seem to be all people, which would include Henry. But this is not correct, as becomes clear when Woolson further clarifies what she means. Henry does not quite get her meaning, so he asks if she means the gap "between her imagination and her confines." But Woolson has a more gender specific idea in mind. She says: "I mean between using our intelligence as women to the full and the social consequences of that" (M 230). The us is women, and it would certainly include someone like Woolson, who has clearly used her intelligence to the full. Indeed, shortly after making this remark, Woolson says that "the consequences" for women like her and Alice "get into the marrow of your soul" (231). Read in relation to all the other females in the novel who make a plea to Henry for help, this scene is devastating. Woolson is subtly telling Henry that a form of despair has made its way into her marrow, but instead of attending to what his close friend is implying and following up with suitable questions, James makes a dismissive remark that is meant "as a joke, or a sign of gratitude, or a way of reducing the intensity of their exchange" (M 231).

Throughout the novel, Henry is in search of appropriate material for new work. But instead of engaging in a rich conversation with Woolson about the situation of women like Henry's mother, Alice, and Woolson (the unnamed wife of Prince Oblisky and Henry's cousin Minny Temple would also fit into this category), he dismisses the scene as irrelevant. And yet, had he done what he should have done as an artist, which is to diagnose and expose what ails the culture and then to imagine into being a healthier and more life-promoting way of being, he could have used his art to alleviate the burden on all the women who are clearly turning to him for help.

While Tóibín's early James fails in some significant ways, the James of the late 1890s undergoes a major transformation, which leads him to adopt a much healthier and more life-promoting worldview and aesthetic. The most important figure to effect this metamorphosis is Wilde. Shortly after the performance and failure of his play *Guy Domville*, Wilde is put on trial for committing homosexual acts, and it is through James's obsessive attention to this very public event that he undergoes a fiction- and life-changing transformation. Initially, James had little respect for or interest in Wilde, but once he learns that Wilde had thrown sexual "caution away," the "story of Wilde filled Henry's days" (M 68). In *The Master*, this fascination with Wilde significantly impacts James's aesthetic. From *The Portrait of a Lady* (1881) to *Guy Domville* (1895), renunciation of self to what is considered a moral or societal duty is a central theme in the work of Tóibín's James, thus making James and his characters representatives of the age. But in the closing pages of *The Master*, Tóibín's James renounces renunciation and adopts an aesthetic much closer to Wilde's.

To understand the nature of James's transformation, it is important to define two separate aesthetics that Wilde identifies in *De Profundis*. One begins with an established, immutable Truth to which humans must submit. But Wilde rejects this aesthetic because it reduces the human to a mathematical equation. Such an aesthetic, which is premised "on a careful calculation of ways and means," is for people who "know where they are going." At first glance, this might seem like a good thing. But for Wilde, this aesthetic is for the "more mechanical people," those who become mindless automatons. By stark contrast, Wilde favors a more dynamic approach to art and life:

> But with the dynamic forces of life, and those in whom those dynamic forces become incarnate, it is different. People whose desire is solely for self-realisation never know where they are going. They can't know. In one sense of the word it is of course necessary, as the Greek oracle said, to know oneself: that is the first achievement of knowledge. But to recognize that the soul of a man is unknowable, is the ultimate achievement of Wisdom. The final mystery is oneself.[98]

Instead of giving readers precise answers to perplexing questions about the human, artists in the dynamic aesthetic tradition seek to expose the degree to which life is ultimately unsystematizable and mysterious. Within this framework, the aesthetic objective is to reveal rational depictions of humans as limited, reductive and potentially dangerous and to immerse readers into the dynamic mystery of endlessly creating being.

James adopts Wilde's dynamic aesthetic approach by the end of *The Master*. When asked what he plans to write next, James, clearly thinking about *The Ambassadors* (1903), says that he has in mind a story about "an American of middle age, with much intelligence and a sensuous nature which has remained hidden throughout his life" (M 334). When pressed about the message of this projected novel, Tóibín's James says: "The moral is the most pragmatic we can imagine, that life is a mystery and that only sentences are beautiful, and that we must be ready for change, especially when we go to Paris" (M 334). The James of 1881 or 1895 would have this character renounce his sensuous nature and subordinate his personal desires to a moral or societal duty. But this is the James of 1899, the one who, like Wilde, has come to question his culture's societal truths and moralities. Therefore, instead of having his protagonist submit to a clearly defined duty, James dispenses with certain knowledge of such obligations and privileges life, mystery, and perpetual change.

It is for this reason that Tóibín's James would reject a literary form like the historical novel. This is not mere speculation. Tóibín strategically includes a scene in order to indicate that his James opposes and even rejects the historical novel. Late in the novel, Henry's brother William expresses concern about Henry's work. He encourages his sibling to abandon the novel of manners about the superficial and materialistic English and to turn his attention to a "novel which would deal with our American history," specifically "about the Puritan Fathers" (M 317). Henry not only rejects William's proposal, but also uses this occasion to express his contempt for the historical novel: "'May I put an end to this conversation,' Henry said, 'by stating clearly to you that I view the historical novel as tainted by a fatal cheapness'" (M 317). To punctuate his point, Henry ends the discussion by dismissing William's proposal with a single word, "humbug" (M 317). The significance of these remarks is staggering. In one of the most celebrated biographical novels, the protagonist denounces the historical novel, which clearly suggests that *The Master* should not be considered a historical novel.

In fact, Tóibín makes this point directly in his recent interview with Bethany Layne. When asked if there is a difference between the historical novel and the biographical novel, Tóibín says that there is. He then provides an example. Tóibín notes that James's apartment in Kensington was wired for electricity in 1896. A historical novelist, Tóibín claims, would incorporate such a detail in his or her work: "If you're writing a historical novel this is a marvelous scene for you where you're actually getting a key moment in history and you're integrating it into lives and you're seeing what the next day will be like." Tóibín does not write such novels, because "it would ruin my novel. It would be the end of the novel."[99]

Readers get additional insight into the nature of the historical novel through a brief analysis of Tóibín's source text for his construction of this scene with

William. Sarah Orne Jewett sent James a copy of her historical novel *The Tory Lover*, and in 1901 James responded, but instead of using the occasion to discuss the quality of Jewett's work, he uses it to reflect on the irredeemable vices of the historical novel. For James, this is an aesthetic form that is characterized by "a fatal cheapness," the same phrase Tóibín's James uses. The historical novelist gives readers a multitude of "little facts that can be got from pictures and documents, relics and prints," but what it lacks is "the real thing," which consists of "the invention, the representation of the old consciousness, the soul, the sense, the horizon, the vision of individuals in whose minds half the things that make ours, that make the modern world." All of these are "non-existent" in the historical novel, an aesthetic form that James calls "humbug." Of crucial importance for James is the mysterious, indefinable, semi-autonomous dimension of human consciousness, which is not just different from but diametrically opposed to the "conditioned"[100] consciousness represented in the historical novel.

The suggestion that the historical novel is "tainted by a fatal cheapness" is of crucial importance. For both James and Tóibín, there is a fatalistic dimension to the historical novel, because it underscores how humans are at the mercy of ("conditioned" by) external forces—the wiring of the house will have necessary and discernible consequences on the inner life of characters. But the historical novel is also a cheap literary form because it lacks the richness of creativity—the historical "novel" merely copies what is. Like McCann, James and Tóibín hold that there is something in the nature of the historical novel that is in irreconcilable conflict with art, and that something is the derivative and deterministic dimension of history. To put the matter succinctly, the historical novel foregrounds the conditioned consciousness in order to clarify how we have come to be as we currently are, while the biographical novel foregrounds how people can evade or transcend environmental and/or biological conditioning in order to emphasize future possibilities of what we can become.

That this is the case, however, is not as important as why, and Tóibín provides a clear answer by setting Henry off from William. As Henry says: "While my brother makes sense of the world, I can only briefly attempt to make it come alive, or become stranger" (M 334). Like traditional historical novelists, William seeks to make logical and rational sense of the world, which is one reason why he would like his brother to author a historical novel. But by this point in the novel, Tóibín's Henry, like Wilde and McCann, does not think that history's truths and methods can be usefully deployed within the novel. This is not to say that Tóibín's James would oppose William's desire to make sense of the world.

It is just to say that what William desires is not quite right or suitable for what Henry does as a novelist. Tóibín's Henry is not really interested in the historical forces that have conditioned being. Rather, his aesthetic focus is on making life strange so that people can feel emboldened to move forward by creating new ways of being for the future.

In *The Master*, Tóibín strategically references another artist who is working within this dynamic aesthetic tradition. Early in the novel, Tóibín's James expresses admiration for Nathaniel Hawthorne, because he makes life dynamic, meaningful, and rich. Notice how Tóibín describes the young James's response in a way that will foreshadow the 1899 James's rejection of the historical novel: "Hawthorne had not observed life, Henry thought, as much as imagined it, found a set of symbols and images which would set life in motion" (M 163). The aesthetic objective is not to passively observe and then represent what happened; that is what the historical novelist does. The goal is to activate life, to create a way of seeing and being that would promote and advance new and rich life forms. Tóibín's James refines this view in relation to his own aesthetic when he says that his goal is to make the world "come alive, or become stranger." Historical novelists give readers logical and rational ways of understanding and representing the past, thus clarifying how we have come to be as we currently are, while biographical novelists convert a biographical subject into a literary symbol in order to create startling, strange, and new ways of seeing and being in the present and future. In short, the very thing that historical novelists give readers (a logical and rational representation of the past) is precisely what biographical novelists seek to unsettle and disrupt ("The one duty we owe to history is to rewrite it,"[101] Wilde says in "The Critic as Artist"), and they do so because life is to be found in the act of dynamically creating fresh ways of being for the future rather than mindlessly submitting to seemingly established Truths about the past. As such, what we get in *The Master* is not an accurate representation of James or even history so much as Tóibín's vision of life and the world, and he fictionalizes Wilde and James to bring that vision into sharp focus.

With this distinction between the historical and biographical novel in mind, we are in an excellent position to appreciate the title of Tóibín's novel. Early James was no master. He took his personal and aesthetic cue from his environment, and if any of his private desires conflicted with his culture's dominant ideals, he renounced his desires and authored fiction to counsel others to do the same. In a sense, the early James would have been predisposed in favor of the historical novel, because his passive philosophy of renunciation is consistent with the axioms on which historical fiction is premised. But after obsessing over Wilde's trial and internalizing some of Wilde's aesthetic ideas, Tóibín's James undergoes a transformation, which readers see most clearly through his unambiguous rejection of the historical novel. Instead of being a passive observer who merely reports on what happened, someone who is mastered by the environment, James becomes a master by setting life into motion through a literature that makes life strange and admonishes readers to seek and embrace change. As such, the 1899 James becomes a master, and it was Wilde who enabled him to do so, which is why Wilde is the primary master of *The Master*.

V

Life is Art's best, Art's only pupil.[102]

The title of my chapter is purposely ambiguous. On the one hand, biofiction is a life-creating fiction, by which I mean that Wilde creates a life of Willie Hughes in "The Portrait of Mr. W.H."; Ackroyd creates a life of Oscar Wilde in *The Last Testament of Oscar Wilde*; and Tóibín creates a life of Henry James in *The Master*. But on the other hand, what all these writers do is to use an actual life (a biographical subject) in order to produce a life-giving type of fiction: "A great artist invents a type, and life tries to copy it."[103] Life, in this instance, means active creation rather than being passively created. For someone like Wilde, most people are automatons, individuals who mindlessly accept their culture's truths as final and absolute, and thus they never actually live because they do not create something uniquely and distinctively their own. In a sense, many of the masses are the walking dead because they merely exist rather than live. Since the historical novel is premised on the idea that social and political forces shape and determine the identity of individuals and cultures, it would be considered a death-bringing aesthetic form, as James, Tóibín, Unigwe, and McCann suggest, because it presupposes that humans are nothing more than the logical product of their time and place. By stark contrast, biographical novelists, with their emphasis on agency, take life, defined here in terms of individual autonomy, as the ideal, and as such, the biographical novel is a life-bringing aesthetic form in that authors provide readers with an "existential map" for agential living in the present and for the future. This irreconcilable difference explains why the biographical novel should be considered not a version or subgenre of but a reaction against and a counter to the historical novel.

When I say that the biographical novel emphasizes autonomy as a form of life, I have three separate forms of autonomy in mind (relating to the author, the biographical subject, and the reader), and for the sake of clarity, let me examine each separately. As Wilde consistently notes, the author is free to alter facts about the biographical subject because the aesthetic goal is to stimulate and inspire critical and creative thought for the future, and not to accurately represent an actual person and therewith history. To illustrate, take Tóibín's usage of Jewett's letter. The scene occurs sometime around October 1899. If a person expects biographical accuracy, then this section of Tóibín's novel can only disappoint, because the actual letter was written on October 5, 1901. A persnickety scholar could easily say: "Tóibín's novel fails because he attributes to James ideas that the novelist would not formulate for another two years." But such a critique would indicate a failure to understand the genre conventions of a biographical novel. As an author of fiction rather than biography, Tóibín's goal is to convert James's life into a symbol in order to "set life in motion." To achieve his aesthetic objective, Tóibín feels free to take liberties with biographical facts, which is something a responsible biographer and historian would not and should not do. Author autonomy is the freedom to alter biographical and/or historical facts in service to the author's larger "truths" in the present and for the future.

The second form of autonomy relates to the biographical subject. What Tóibín charts in and through *The Master* is James's evolution, specifically how he develops from being a slave to habit and custom to becoming an autonomous master, which makes life possible. This transformation from non-agency to agency, from being mastered by life to becoming a master of life, is of central importance in the biographical novel, and so authors structure their narrative in order to chart and accentuate this characterological development, a development that sets the active and semi-autonomous protagonist of the biographical novel apart from the determined protagonist of the historical novel. Tóibín emphasizes how Wilde's life and work enable James to overcome his life-denying philosophy of renunciation, a philosophy that leads life to master him, and instead to adopt an aesthetic that uses art to set life into motion. It is James's painfully tragic journey from a passive acceptance of a seemingly ineluctable Reality to a reasonable, albeit limited, form of autonomy that makes the novel so deeply effective and gratifying.

The last form of autonomy relates to the reader, and McCann gives us the best way to think about this idea. Rudi Nureyev is the protagonist of McCann's *Dancer*, and he functions as the quintessential biographical subject, which is to say that he is the living refutation of the historical novel. A loyal Soviet, Nureyev's father has adopted Karl Marx's political philosophy, which holds that it "is not the consciousness of men that determines their being, but, on the contrary, their social being that determines their consciousness."[104] Nureyev's father tries to indoctrinate his son with that ideology. As the elder Nureyev says to the young Rudi: "Your social existence determines consciousness, son."[105] But this is precisely the philosophy that Rudi and McCann ultimately reject as flawed, limited, debilitating, and unacceptable. McCann brilliantly articulates his view of art's uncanny power to assist readers and viewers in the process of evading determinism and of constructing self through his description of the genesis of *Dancer*. At first blush, it might seem that what motivated McCann to write the novel was his passionate interest in Rudi's life. But actually, it was Nureyev's impact on McCann's friend Jimmy Smallhorne that inspired McCann. In my interview with him, McCann admits that he "wasn't really interested in Rudolf Nureyev." Rather, he "was much more interested in the story of Jimmy Smallhorne, a working class friend of mine from Dublin who was mesmerized when he saw Rudolf Nureyev on television. It was a story like Jimmy's that mattered, and that was my beginning of stepping into the biographical novel." The goal of the biographical novelist is not to accurately represent the life of the biographical subject—McCann admits that his Nureyev is "probably 90 percent imagined."[106] Rather, it is to use the life story of the historical figure to make the reader "come alive in a different body, in a different time."[107] In short, the artist's goal is to "embody us in wakefulness,"[108] and this is what Rudi seeks to do through dance and McCann through fiction.

Let me briefly illustrate how this functions in *Dancer*. As an artist, Rudi does not simply project into being a moment of beauty. He sets into motion a process of endlessly discovering and creating a new reality. Here is how one character in the novel describes Rudi's impact on her: "Rudi had stood upon that stage like an exhausted explorer who had arrived in some unimagined country and, despite the joy of the discovery, was immediately looking for another unimagined place, and I felt perhaps that place was me."[109] Rudi's art mentally transports his viewers into the unimaginable, a psychic space that transcends imagined borders and limitations. In sum, Rudi does what Wilde's Willie, Ackroyd's Wilde, and

Tóibín's 1899 James do, which is to use art in order to set life into motion. As one character notes:

> Rudi gathers a group around himself, launching into some diatribe about dance as an experiment, all its impulses going to the creation of an adventure and the end of each adventure being a new impulse towards further creation, *If a dancer, he is good*, says Rudi, *he has to straddle the time! He must drag the old forward into the new!*[110]

Rudi uses dance to introduce his audience to the dynamic power of endlessly creating life, and Wilde, Ackroyd, Tóibín, and McCann do the same through their works. Within this framework, it is Wilde's usage of Willie, Ackroyd's usage of Wilde, McCann's usage of Rudi, and Tóibín's usage of James that enable them to achieve their aesthetic goals. Biographical and/or historical truth—these are subordinate to the more important goal of liberating the reader into the embodied wakefulness of a creating and creative consciousness, a consciousness that leads to new possibilities in seeing and being.

As I intend to demonstrate in the next chapter, what Wilde did was no anomaly. Countering history-as-science's intrusion into the world of art was a dominant idea of the second half of the nineteenth century and the first quarter of the twentieth century, and it led many prominent artists to emphasize biography over history, autonomy over determinism. Within this intellectual context, the aesthetic goal was not to depict a life. Rather, it was to use a life in order to create an existential map for experiencing a health- and life-generating form of autonomy. While the artists I discuss in the next chapter are very different from Wilde, the pattern I intend to expose is roughly the same for all of them, and it goes something like this: The intrusion of history-as-a-science into the world of art, which resulted in the historical novel, generated the need for a counter-aesthetic, and the most compelling and effective form to emerge was biofiction, which—for good reason—has now become one of our age's most dominant literary forms.

2

George Moore's *The Brook Kerith* and the Scandal of the Biographical Novel

Any serious study of the history of biofiction must include something about George Moore. At first this might seem to be the case because Moore published in 1916 *The Brook Kerith*, a daring, controversial, and stellar biographical novel about Jesus. But the more substantive reason is that Moore had direct and indirect connections with a wide range of artists and thinkers who played a crucial role in the origins and evolution of the ideas that would give rise to biofiction, so he, more than anyone else, was able to register the political need and cultural value of the aesthetic form as it took shape in the late nineteenth and early twentieth centuries. Central to my argument in this chapter is that there was a growing awareness that biofiction could be one of the most effective aesthetic forms to combat the culture's death-bringing forces and to advance and promote life.[1] Furthermore, it is my contention that Moore intelligently registered the significance and value of biofiction as an aesthetic form and that *The Brook Kerith* is one of the best and most important in the genre. What makes the work so spectacular is what also makes it so scandalous, and as I intend to demonstrate, *The Brook Kerith* is far more scandalous than previously suggested and for reasons that have not yet been clearly or fully articulated.[2] But before analyzing Moore and *The Brook Kerith*, I will discuss at some length the work of Émile Zola, Edouard Manet, Friedrich Nietzsche, and Houston Stewart Chamberlain, figures who in one way or another contributed to Moore's groundbreaking biofiction.

I

> *The work of the great artist is himself …*
> *Manet's art was all Manet.*[3]

Manet's 1868 *Portrait of Emile Zola* (see Figure 2.1) anticipated contemporary biofiction.

Figure 2.1 *Portrait of Emile Zola* (1868)

This portrait marks a significant shift in the nineteenth-century art world, as scholars have noted, but it is groundbreaking for reasons, specifically in relation to biofiction, yet to be articulated.[4] In 1865, Claude Bernard published *An Introduction to the Experimental Study of Medicine*, which uses the laws of science to make the case for a deterministic approach to life and the human. This work had an enormous impact on Zola. In his 1879 essay "The Experimental Novel," Zola clarifies precisely how Bernard's scientific approach could and should function in literature. For Zola, the implacable laws of cause and effect apply not just to "physical life" but also to "the passionate and intellectual life."[5] After illuminating "the determinism of inanimate bodies," researchers, Zola argues, should move to the "determinism of living beings," for the "fixed laws that govern the human body" also dictate "the laws of thought and passion."[6] Given that determinism dominates everything, there is a need for a corresponding form of literature, what Zola refers to as the experimental novel. Founded on science's experimental method, authors of such fiction enable readers "to possess a knowledge of the mechanism of the phenomena inherent in man,"[7] knowledge that allows them "to solve scientifically the question of how men behave when they are in society."[8] The goal is not simply to define the human. It is also "to foresee and direct phenomena."[9] As Zola says: "Here is our role as intelligent beings: to penetrate to the wherefore of things, to become superior to these things, and to reduce them to a condition of subservient machinery."[10] With scientific knowledge of the human comes the ability "to master certain phenomena of an intellectual and personal order, to be able to direct them."[11] More specifically, should this model come to dominate "in history,"[12] it would enable us to avoid human-generated disasters and thus improve social and political life.

In *From Chaos to Catastrophe?* (2018), K. Ludwig Pfeiffer clarifies why a Zola-type approach is naïve and unrealistic. Central to Pfeiffer's project is the link, or rather the questionable possibility of a link between the processes and products of consciousness. People generate a conscious system of thought, and they believe that it will translate into a corresponding program of action. But as Pfeiffer convincingly argues, this rarely occurs, mainly because unconscious factors impinge upon established conceptual systems, thus disrupting the line of connection between the conscious processes and products of thought. Pfeiffer contends that contemporary neuroscience has begrudgingly had to acknowledge this condition of human being, which results in the humble recognition of the limits of conscious conceptual systems. To clarify and justify his claim, Pfeiffer focuses the second part of his book on "Consciousness and History: Biographical 'Novels' and their 'Liberal' Extensions."[13] Within this framework, the biographical novel best illustrates his thesis that the conscious processes and products of thought rarely work in unison.

Pfeiffer is responding to the same forces that resulted in Manet's painting of Zola. What prompted Pfeiffer to pursue this project was his realization that contemporary theory has assigned "a merely peripheral position to persons, individuals or, to use a more distinguished term, subjectivity." Thus, "individual chances of intervening into, interfering with and perhaps actively shaping larger processes playing by their own ('self-referential') rules have always been slim. They have diminished, or so it appears to many observers, to the extent that an awareness of the metastatic growth of the systemic control of life has come to rule more or less in undisputed form."[14] To counter this deterministic state of affairs, Pfeiffer turns to the biographical novel, which emphasizes agency over history, individual autonomy over deterministic systems. The same energies animating Pfeiffer's work led, as I will argue, to Manet's painting of Zola. But there is one crucial difference. While Pfeiffer holds that the deterministic model is limited at best and unrealistic at worst, Manet suggests that Zola's aesthetic is damaging and destructive for both artists and life. Since the objective laws of science are of ultimate importance according to Zola and his deterministic model, the artist must efface self so that viewers can accurately see the rational laws governing the human and the universe. What artists are and what their vision of life is are subordinate to the neutral and objective realities of the material world, which renders life nothing more than mechanical motion and the artist of negligible significance.

Zola published "The Experimental Novel" in 1879, but he had formulated a scientific and deterministic model as early as 1867, when he authored his first major work about Manet. As James H. Rubin says of Zola's writings about Manet: "Zola believed that positivism and science represented the progressive direction of modern French culture. His approach to Manet was tied directly to his conviction that Naturalism was modern because it was governed by empirical principles." Thus, in his verbal portrait of Manet, he uses his own aesthetic principles to frame and define the French painter and his work: "Zola put quasi-scientific words in Manet's mouth and then exclaimed, 'He is above all a Naturalist.' "[15] Robert Lethbridge puts the matter succinctly: Zola's "references to Manet as an 'analytical painter' are grounded in the same pseudo-scientific jargon characteristic of his own emerging Naturalism."[16]

Manet's *Portrait* is a wonderfully comic refutation of Zola's aesthetic. By virtue of the title and the central figure, it would seem that the subject is Zola. But to degrade Zola's status within the painting, Manet places just above and to the right of the French naturalist's head a reproduction of his famous painting *Olympia*. Instead of boldly looking directly at the viewer, as she does in the original painting, Manet alters his own painting by having his subject cast a condescending glance down at the novelist, thereby subordinating Zola to Manet.[17] Further accentuating this peripheral status is Zola's 1867 work about Manet, pictured just below the representation of *Olympia*. In that work, Zola praises Manet because he gives his audience "a truthful and literal interpretation" of Nature. In other words, what viewers get from Manet are unadulterated facts, which is why Zola uses scientific language to characterize him as an artist: "I see him as an analyst painter. All problems have been re-examined; science requires solid foundations and this has been achieved by accurate observation of facts. This approach is not confined to the world of science alone."[18] In short, Manet is an empty vessel through which Nature is rendered: "Art as practiced by him leads to ultimate truth. This artist is an interpreter of things as they are, and, for me, his works have the great merit of being accurate descriptions."[19] Given this approach to Manet, one can better understand and appreciate the French artist's representation of Zola's essay in *Portrait*. Manet's name is prominently displayed, while Zola's is so small that it is perceptible only when one stands close to the painting (see Figure 2.2).[20]

Since this is the only legible work in a painting with numerous texts and even an open book in Zola's hands, the writing with Manet's name stands out. In essence, the painting of the literary titan, rather than effacing self and thus "imitating and reproducing" Zola "as exactly as possible,"[21] is a brazen assertion of Manet, his art, and his vision. As such, Manet merely uses Zola to picture his own vision of life and the world.

Scholars have noted that Manet's painting signals a major shift in portraiture aesthetics, but I want to clarify why that transformation anticipated and even contributed to biofiction. In a landmark study, Richard Brilliant defines "portraiture as a particular phenomenon of representation," specifically insofar as it illuminates "changes in the perceived nature of the individual."[22] Based on this approach, the portraiture artist has three main objectives, which can be defined in relation to three questions the artist answers for the biographical subject: (1) "*What do I (you, he, she, we, or they) look like?*" (2) "*What am I (you, she, he, etc.) like?*" and (3) "*Who am I (you, etc.)?*"[23] The best portraits effectively answer one or all of these questions. But with Manet's shift from representing the subject to representing himself, a new question was needed, which is: how does

Figure 2.2 Close-up of *Portrait of Emile Zola*

the artist use the biographical subject to project into existence his or her own vision of life and the world? Within this framework, biographical accuracy is subordinate to the artist's vision, which explains why Manet was willing to alter his own painting *Olympia* in his portrait of Zola.

Strangely, Brilliant notes the aesthetic shift that so many scholars have seen in Manet's painting, but that did not lead him to formulate a new set of criteria for assessing this type of portraiture. This failure leads him to make a questionable claim about the Manet work of Zola. To locate his approach within a specific tradition of interpretation, Brilliant cites Richard Shiff, who says: "'The Portrait of Zola … becomes Manet's self-expression, his own vision and his own portrait.'"[24] Unfortunately, instead of seeing Manet's work as an example of a new and legitimate approach to portrait painting, Brilliant dismisses it as the product of "Manet's selfish eyes."[25] Therefore, he uses his tripartite model to claim that Manet's painting effectively characterizes what Zola is like. Specifically, the portrait pictures "Zola's critical acumen."[26] If my reading of the painting is correct, there are two reasons why Brilliant's interpretation is unconvincing. First, the portrait primarily portrays Manet, not Zola. Second, instead of depicting Zola in a positive manner, it actually exposes one of his most flagrant intellectual flaws and thereby offers an alternative way of thinking.

Manet's subtle critique of Zola is certainly fascinating, but what makes it so significant for this particular chapter is the degree to which it aligns with the work of Wilde and Moore, thus contributing to what would become a central component of biofictional aesthetics. Wilde provides a conceptual framework for understanding the rejection of Zola's scientific model and the rise of the countervailing biofictional approach. For Wilde, the artist is irrelevant within Zola's science-based paradigm. All that matters, according to Zola, are the scientific laws and facts that make the world and the human what they are. Within this framework, the artwork is great only insofar as authors negate themselves so that they can correctly identify, define, and expose what is of ultimate importance, which are the laws and facts governing the material universe. Wilde unambiguously rejects this aesthetic approach because it denigrates the artist and therewith life. In direct response to Zola, who praises Honoré de Balzac for incorporating science's experimental method into his novel *Cousin Bette* in order to give readers "scientific knowledge" of both "individual and social relations,"[27] Wilde rejects the French novelist's approach to Balzac. For Wilde, Zola's work "is entirely wrong from beginning to end," and he specifies the sense in which this is the case: it is "on the ground of art."[28] Balzac is different from Zola, Wilde contends, because Balzac "created life, he did not copy it."[29] Let me bring the differences between the two into sharp focus. For Zola, the great "artist is an interpreter of things as they are," while for Wilde, "no great artist ever sees things as they really are. If he did, he would cease to be an artist."[30] What makes an artist great, according to Zola, is the ability to subordinate self so that he or she can accurately represent the material world (Wilde refers to this as copying reality). But what makes an artist great, according to Wilde, is the ability to project self by imagining into being a new "reality" (to create life) in the present and for the future.

Moore, who claims that Manet has "deep roots in my mind,"[31] met the French artist in the late 1870s, and Manet introduced the Irish novelist to Zola.[32] We know that Moore was enthralled by Zola's scientific approach to literature, which would make it seem like he would have been more suited to write a historical or experimental, rather than a biographical, novel. In *Confessions of a Young Man*, Moore admits that he was initially intoxicated by Zola's approach after reading his work:

> The idea of a new art based upon science, in opposition to the art of the old world that was based on imagination, an art that should explain all things and embrace modern life in its entirety, in its endless ramifications, be, as it were, a new creed in a new civilisation, filled me with wonder, and I stood dumb before the vastness of the conception, and the towering height of the ambition.[33]

However, Moore would eventually turn against Zola and his scientific approach. Moore's biographer Adrian Frazier insightfully explains how Manet contributed to Moore's critique and ultimate rejection of Zola. In July of 1879, many artists in Moore's milieu believed that "the scientific method has put its imprint on all the arts." But Moore was no longer enamored of Zola's aesthetic by this point, because he had come to adopt the position of Manet. Here is Moore's characterization of Manet's view: "The work of the great artist is himself … Manet's Art was all Manet." This put Moore in irreconcilable conflict with Zola, for "Zola's art did not claim to be Zola; it was offered as the truth of society and nature."[34] According to Zola's approach, in accurately representing the reality of a figure from the past, the artist discloses the laws of society and nature, an aesthetic feat that implicitly negates the artist and his or her vision. But according to the countervailing approach of artists like Manet and Moore, a visual or verbal portrait of a historical figure is not supposed to be seen as an accurate representation of that biographical subject. To the contrary, the artist merely uses the historical figure in order to give viewers him- or herself. So instead of negating the self when picturing a biographical subject, the artist uses the life of an actual person in order to unapologetically picture his or her own self or vision of life. With this approach in mind, Moore's *The Brook Kerith*, a novel supposedly about Jesus, is really about Moore.

II

History [...] is a nightmare from which I am trying to awake.[35]

In this same aesthetic tradition is Nietzsche, whose writings had an enormous impact on Moore.[36] Indeed, a brief analysis of *Thus Spoke Zarathustra* and the context in which that work came into being will shed new and significant light on Moore's *The Brook Kerith*. Like Wilde, Nietzsche focused early in his career on history-as-science, which he best articulates in his 1874 essay "On the Uses and Disadvantages of History for Life." Here are the central questions of the work: "Is life to dominate knowledge and science, or is knowledge to dominate life? Which of these two forces is the higher and more decisive? There can be no doubt: life is the higher, the dominating force, for knowledge which annihilated life would have annihilated itself with it."[37] When scientific knowledge weds itself to history, there are devastating consequences, for as Nietzsche claims, "it is possible to value the study of history to such a degree that life becomes stunted and degenerate" (UDH 59). For the *Übermensch* philologist, the "mighty historical movement" (UDH 59) of his age has significantly injured humans and even life. Nietzsche is not saying that history *per se* has had this effect. He stipulates that history could, under the right conditions, contribute to life. He is saying that history as it has been configured in his day is the problem. For Nietzsche, when history becomes a "pure, sovereign science" (UDH 67), it subjugates human life to the dictates of knowledge, which leads to degeneration and ultimately death. Therefore, instead of history, science, or knowledge, life should be the first principle of any system. According to this paradigm, history must serve human life; it must enable and empower human life to grow and develop. As Nietzsche concludes: "Let us at least learn better how to employ history for the purpose of *life*" (UDH 66).

His age's reification and fetishization of historical knowledge as a science led Nietzsche to emphasize the need for biography. But not just any kind of biography. Nietzsche calls for a biography that would underscore the human ability to evade determinism. Given that Nietzsche privileges life over history-as-science, the goal of writers should not be to illuminate the social-historical reality that shapes and determines human life in a given time and place—that is what historical novelists do. Rather, authors should showcase the human ability to defy or evade environmental conditioning or cultural determinism: "if you want biographies, do not desire those which bear the legend 'Herr So-and-So and his age', but those upon whose title-page there would stand 'a fighter against his age' " (UDH 95). For Lukács, the protagonist of a historical novel should function as a representative symbol of "the age,"[38] what he refers to as a historical-social type.[39] This figure represents the dominant forces that contributed to the making of representative people of the time. But for Nietzsche, needed is a turn to the biographical subject, specifically a figure that transcends the culture and environment, what he refers to as a "fighter against his age."

The ideas in Nietzsche's 1874 essay mandated the formation of a corresponding aesthetic form. *Thus Spoke Zarathustra* is that work, and it fulfills the definition of biofiction. Just as we see in Manet's painting, Nietzsche's verbal portrait, which is supposedly about the Persian prophet Zarathustra (also referred to as Zoroaster), is an unapologetic representation of himself and his own worldview. Nietzsche makes this claim in *Ecce Homo* when he says something that every scholar of biofiction should consider: "I have not been asked, as I should have been asked, what the name of Zarathustra means in my mouth."[40] His answer to this question is surprising, that is, if one were working within a Zola or Lukács literary tradition. Zola and Lukács believe that the artist should give readers an objective representation of the world as it is, Zarathustra, for example, as he really was and therewith the society that made him into what he became. But Nietzsche freely admits that the Zarathustra in his book is the opposite of the actual historical person, and as such, his protagonist is actually Nietzsche. To be more specific, the real Zarathustra invented morality, but Nietzsche's character overcomes and overturns the simplistic good-and-evil model: "the self-overcoming of the moralist, into his opposite—into me—that is what the name of Zarathustra means in my mouth."[41] Instead of representing reality as it is, as Zola urges, Nietzsche fictionalizes the historical person in order to give his readers himself and his own vision of life, which places Nietzsche in the same tradition as Manet, Moore, and Wilde.

Nietzsche's response to a bewildered reader of *Thus Spoke Zarathustra* gives us additional insight into the way his biofiction should be read: "When Dr. Heinrich von Stein once complained very honestly that he didn't understand a word of my *Zarathustra*, I told him that this was perfectly in order: having understood six sentences from it—that is, to have really experienced them—would raise one to a higher level of existence than 'modern' men could attain."[42] What readers get in *Thus Spoke Zarathustra* are the will-to-power, the death of God, the eternal recurrence, and the *Übermensch*, ideas that are not to be found in the *Zend-Avesta*, and for Nietzsche, a commanding grasp of these ideas would transform the reader into a new and healthier person. As should be clear, the focus here is not on the past or a person from the past but on the present and the future and who and what readers could become after reading a work like *Zarathustra*.

My objective here is to examine *Zarathustra* in order to clarify how biofiction functions and signifies, specifically insofar as this work anticipates and informs Moore's *The Brook Kerith*. The most striking feature of both biofictions is the degree to which they identify Christ as the figure that is doing most damage to their contemporary cultures and that supplanting Christ is necessary in order to save the culture.

Nietzsche's critique of Christianity is pointed and direct throughout his career. As he says, Christianity "is the extremest thinkable form of corruption" and "mankind's greatest misfortune,"[43] which is why he concludes: "I call Christianity the *one* great curse, the *one* great intrinsic depravity, the *one* great instinct for revenge for which no expedient is sufficiently poisonous, secret, subterranean, *petty*—I call it the *one* immoral blemish of mankind."[44] This is the case because "sickness belongs to the essence of Christianity."[45] While Christianity pretends to be a noble religion premised on love, what really animates it is a ruthless will to dominate: "To dominate barbarians Christianity had need of *barbarous* concepts and values: sacrifice of the first-born, blood-drinking at communion, contempt for intellect and culture; torture in all its forms, physical and non-physical."[46] But the ultimate crime is Christianity's tendency for extreme hatred and fanatical violence: "A certain sense of cruelty towards oneself and others is Christian; hatred of those who think differently; the will to persecute."[47] In a larger political context, what concerns Nietzsche most is "the fatality that has crept out of Christianity even into politics!"[48] In other words, there are compelling reasons to be worried, as Christianity has gained a foothold within German politics.

This critique of Christianity is central to *Thus Spoke Zarathustra*. Throughout the work, the relationship between a mental orientation and human relationships is of central concern. Those who have adopted a debilitating and destructive mentality Zarathustra refers to as "despisers of life."[49] By stark contrast, Zarathustra represents "the voice of the healthy body" (Z 22), which is a body that is perpetually open "to create beyond itself" (Z 24). Consistent with Nietzsche's earlier works, Zarathustra holds that "life wants to climb and to overcome itself by climbing" (Z 78). But what prohibits life from healthy and perpetual growth is a closed will-to-power. Instead of seeing truth as a servant of life, most believe that it is possible to reduce and even cage life through the "thinkability of all being" (Z 88). At first, the problem here would seem to be the fetishization of truth. But for Nietzsche's Zarathustra, the real problem is the will, specifically what Nietzsche would refer to as a closed system of will in *On the Genealogy of Morals*, which I will discuss shortly. Zarathustra and Nietzsche praise the liberating and liberated will, the courageous and autonomous will that endlessly creates, but they believe that the will could easily be poisoned, which would lead it to damage everything it touches. What does the most harm is the God-concept ("God is a thought that makes crooked everything that is straight" [Z 66]), because it leads to the formation of a tyrannical and absolutist will-to-power that translates into a faulty and even destructive form of truth.

In *Thus Spoke Zarathustra*, it is Christ who is the primary culprit, because he deploys the fanatical and absolutist will-to-power by effectively persuading people that life is an argument that he has successfully decoded. Thus, his Truth, a seemingly God-constructed reality, is eternal, universal, inviolable, and absolute, so humans must submit to it as the one and only legitimate way of being. But for Nietzsche, since "life is no argument,"[50] as he claims in *The Gay Science*, it is not only impossible but also dangerous and destructive to reduce life to an argument through a system of immutable Truths. This does not mean that people should stop constructing truths or arguments about life; Nietzsche claims that we could not live without such truths and arguments. The issue is the function and form of truth in an age in which a stable and immutable Truth is no longer credible.

What makes Christ so seductive and dangerous is the way he effectively persuades people that his Truths have a divine origin, so they are incontrovertible. But for Zarathustra and Nietzsche, Christ's truths are epistemic constructions of his will rather than ontological facts of divine being, and what makes Christ so dangerous is that he wields a tyrannical will-to-power.[51] It is important to note that, while Zarathustra discusses the will-to-power, Nietzsche would not explicitly nuance the idea of the will until 1887. Given Nietzsche's consistent praise of the will, specifically the will-to-power, it might seem that it is a sacrosanct reality, something beyond criticism. But here is how Nietzsche describes the tyrannical and destructive will in *On the Genealogy of Morals*. The "closed system of will" is distinctive in that "it rejects, denies, affirms, and sanctions solely from the point of view of *its* interpretation," and "it submits to no power, in its absolute *superiority of rank* over every other power—it believes that no power exists on earth that does not first have to receive a meaning, a right to exist" except as a "means to *its* goal, to *one* goal."[52] Within the closed system-of-will framework, there is only one Way and one Truth.

The closed will-to-power has staggeringly negative consequences on the way people interact with one another. For instance, Christ set up a model in which he is the shepherd and his followers are sheep.[53] But this model makes Christ a tyrant and his followers slaves, since Jesus claims that he is "the Way, the Trueth, and the Life" and that there is no other way to the Heavenly Father except through him.[54] By stark contrast, Zarathustra, who has adopted an open will-to-power, claims that the idea of there being a Way is nothing more than a phantom of an overheated imagination: " 'This—it turns out—is *my* way—where is yours?'—That is how I answered those who asked me 'the way.' *The* way after all—it does not exist!" (Z 156). Instead of desiring to be an overbearing shepherd or hoping for sheepish followers, Zarathustra rejects the Christ model in favor of one based on parity and friendship: "It dawned on me: let Zarathustra speak not to the people, but instead to companions! Zarathustra should not become the shepherd and dog of a herd!" (Z 14).

The Zarathustra model shifts the locus of autonomy and power away from himself and to others. To put the matter bluntly, while Christ formulates a model that ultimately validates and empowers him, Zarathustra formulates a model that provisionalizes his own truths and power and admonishes others to seize control over their own lives. Zarathustra is unambiguous on this score. After sharing his view of life with others, he says: "I counsel you to go away from me and guard yourselves against Zarathustra! And even better: be ashamed of him! Perhaps he deceived you" (Z 59). Implicit in this approach is the humble recognition of human fallibility, and since everyone, including Christ, is all-too-human, all people should be reluctant to accept any truth as final and/or absolute. So instead of urging others to turn their lives over to him, Zarathustra admonishes them to construct their own vision of life and the world:

> You say you believe in Zarathustra? But what matters Zarathustra! You are my believers, but what matter all believers!
>
> You had not yet sought yourselves, then you found me. All believers do this; that's why all faith amounts to so little.
>
> Now I bid you lose me and find yourselves; and only when you have all denied me will I return to you. (Z 59)

To be a follower of Christ, believers must submit to Christ's Truths, because they are immutable, eternal, universal, and Divine. The New Testament Christ does not acknowledge that he may have inadvertently deceived his followers, nor does he encourage them to distrust him. But to be a companion of Zarathustra, the person must reject Zarathustra and formulate a vision of his or her own, because truths are provisional and evolving. Within a Christian system, to be a Christian, one must be a follower of Christ and his Truths. But within a Nietzschean system, to be a Nietzschean, one must reject Nietzsche and formulate his or her own "truths." In short, what Nietzsche does in this work is to use the Persian prophet in order to make the case for and model human agency.

The critique of Christ in *Thus Spoke Zarathustra* is extensive and substantive—I have only mentioned a few central ideas. But what prompted it? The answer has something to do with the rise of an extremely dangerous anti-Semitic Christian nationalism, and it was in and through his relationship with Richard Wagner that Nietzsche became aware of this political danger. In 1868, Nietzsche met Wagner,[55] and over the next few years he would become a disciple. But by 1874, Nietzsche started to become critical of his mentor and father figure,[56] mainly for three reasons: Christianity, nationalism, and anti-Semitism. In *The Case of Wagner*, Nietzsche claims that Wagner is "one of my sicknesses"[57] and that he "makes sick whatever he touches."[58] In "Nietzsche Contra Wagner," the philologist specifies what divides him from the famous composer: Wagner "had condescended step by step to everything I despise—even to anti-Semitism." To indicate that there is a link between Christianity and anti-Semitism, Nietzsche shifts immediately to his other main reason for rejecting his former master: "Richard Wagner, apparently most triumphant, but in truth a decaying and despairing decadent, suddenly sank down, helpless and broken, before the Christian cross."[59] That Wagner's anti-Semitic version of Christianity posed a major political threat Nietzsche makes clear in "*The Case of Wagner*" section of *Ecce Homo*, where he unambiguously condemns German nationalism as "this most *anti-cultural* sickness and unreason there is, nationalism, this *nevrose nationale* with which Europe is sick."[60] For Nietzsche, the combination of anti-Semitic Christian nationalism would have a deadly political impact, and he had specific reasons for drawing this conclusion.

While Nietzsche started to distance himself from Wagner by the mid-1870s, his sister, Elisabeth, remained involved with the Wagner circle, and in 1876, she met her future husband, Bernard Förster,[61] who was totally devoted to the German luminary.[62] Elisabeth was a Christian anti-Semite, and it was through Förster and the Wagner circle that her Christian anti-Semitism was strengthened, clarified, and formalized. For instance, Förster argued that there is an inextricable link between Christianity and Germanness. As he claims in his 1881 book *Das Verhältniss des modernen Judenthums zur deutschen Kunst* (The Relationship of Modern Jewry to German Art), it is a fact that Christianity and Germanness have become so completely united that were one to decline, so too would the other. Förster consistently blends Christianity and Germanness, which enables him to define Jews as anti-Aryans who stand in mortal opposition to that which is German and, therefore, Christian.[63] Within this framework, that which is non-Christian is not just indifferent to Christians and Christianity. It is in mortal opposition to that which is Christian, which, in part, explains Förster's anti-Semitism. In his 1883 book *Parsifal-Nachklänge* (Parsifal Reminiscences), Förster argues that Christianity is the product of the Aryan Geist. Given this definition of and approach to Christianity, Jesus could not have been a Jew. As Förster claims: "Based on his origins, Jesus was *no Jew*, rather he was a Galilean. Also, he was not a 'Semite,' rather he was the 'son of God,' the fulfillment of all yearnings of Aryan humanity."[64]

What probably made Nietzsche so fully conscious of the looming political danger of Christian anti-Semitism was Förster's April 13, 1881, petition to Bismarck, which was signed by nearly 270,000 people.[65] The petition begins by nationalizing Christianity and oppositionalizing Germans and Jews: "The Jewish hypertrophy conceals within itself the most serious dangers to our national way of life. This belief has spread throughout all the regions of Germany. Whenever Christian and Jew enter into social relations, we see the Jew as master and the native-born Christian population in a servile position."[66] Notice how the petition frames the conflict in religious rather than racial terms. The oppressed in Germany are the Christians, who are presumably Germans. Therefore, the petition goes on to argue, "if the inward connection between German custom and morality and the Christian outlook and tradition is to be maintained, then an alien tribe may never, ever rise to rule on German soil."[67] The implication: to correct the current problem in Germany, eliminating the "alien tribe" (Jews) is necessary.

Wagner's cult-like following, which included prominent cultural and political leaders; the nature of the circle's anti-Semitic Christian nationalism; and the loss of his sister to this group of people—this is the context that gave rise to the vicious critique of Christianity found in Nietzsche's work, specifically *Thus Spoke Zarathustra*. As such, we could say that the work is a cultural intervention, an attempt to expose the imminent political threat Christianity poses and to offer an alternative to Christ through Zarathustra. And for Nietzsche, what will bring most psychological health is a comprehensive experience of a life-promoting agency, something that Christ thwarts but Zarathustra promotes. Given Nietzsche's objections to Christianity, anti-Semitism, and nationalism, we can see *Thus Spoke Zarathustra* as an implicit rejection of Wagner and his circle, as they were the source of the anti-Semitic Christian nationalism that Nietzsche targets in and through his work.

III

Christ is the first great enemy of the Jews.[68]

My central claim is this: as a biofiction, *Thus Spoke Zarathustra*, seemingly about a real historical figure, is actually an unapologetic intervention into the present, an attempt to diagnose a then-contemporary cultural sickness and to project into existence a new and healthier way of seeing and being for the future. So instead of accurately representing a person from the past and therewith a specific time and place, the author merely uses the historical individual in order to create a new and better present and future, an aesthetic objective that places the biographical novel in irreconcilable conflict with the historical novel. That I have spent so much time discussing Nietzsche, Wagner and his supporters, and *Thus Spoke Zarathustra* should not be seen as only tangentially related to Moore and his biographical novel about Christ. As I will now demonstrate, there are profound connections that link Moore to the politically dangerous version of Christianity that took shape in and through the Wagner group, and, like Nietzsche, Moore authored a work to combat the rise of that politically toxic form of faith.

In the concluding chapter of *George Moore and German Pessimism*, Patrick Bridgwater does the best and most extensive analysis of Nietzsche's impact on Moore and his writings. Bridgwater argues that Moore's Preface to the 1904 reprint of *Confessions of a Young Man* (originally published in 1888 in serial and then in 1889 in book form) foregrounds Moore's similarities to the *Übermensch* philologist;[69] identifies the "first echo of Nietzsche in Moore's work," which "comes in *Evelyn Innes* (1898)";[70] clarifies how Moore appropriated Nietzsche's idea of "Stellar Friendship";[71] and illustrates how Moore adopted the Nietzschean view of "life as an aesthetic phenomenon."[72] Bridgwater's chapter is detailed, comprehensive, and precise, so it is surprising that he fails to mention what is perhaps the one Moore text most inspired by Nietzsche, *The Brook Kerith*.

Moore's Jesus novel was published in 1916, and it was a landmark work for many reasons. The novel pictures the life of Christ, but instead of dying and then rising from the dead, as recorded in the gospels, Jesus is taken down from the cross before he dies and nursed back to health. Moore's Jesus then lives for many more years and eventually renounces his teachings as fanatical. Here is Moore's description of his aesthetic objective in a March 28, 1916, letter to W. K. Magee:

> You see my plan was to accept the fact that the Jesus we read of hated priests and organized religion; and my plan also was to show a great change in this man after the crucifixion, a greater change than happens to most men, because the events of his life were more calculated to change his nature than any that could happen to-day … Being a man of strong intelligence he did not try to cling to beliefs that had been proved to be false. He became a new man.[73]

Moore's Jesus undergoes a major transformation after nearly dying on the cross, and this is the case because he had a "strong intelligence." As such, there is no way he could have remained faithful to his earlier teachings, which have proven to be incorrect or outdated. Striking about this passage is how similar it is to one from Nietzsche's *Thus Spoke Zarathustra*. For Zarathustra, Christ "died too early." A longer life, Zarathustra continues, would have resulted in a much different and a much better man: "Believe me, my brothers! He died too early; he himself would have recanted his teaching if he had reached my age! He was noble enough for recanting!" (Z 54–55). Nietzsche and Moore speculate about Jesus living longer and suggest that if he had lived longer he would have recanted his flawed teachings and adopted a more life-affirming worldview, because Jesus was a noble and intelligent man. The ideas are so similar that it is hard to imagine that Moore did not take his inspiration from Nietzsche.

And there is much evidence to suggest that Nietzsche's *Zarathustra* had a significant impact on Moore. In 1902, John Quinn, a patron of modernist writers and artists, wrote a letter to William Butler Yeats, who had a contentious relationship with Moore, telling the Irish poet that he spotted a copy of Nietzsche's *Thus Spoke Zarathustra* on Moore's library table. His remarks to Yeats are noteworthy:

> I mailed to you a week ago my copy of Nietzsche's *Thus Spake Zarathustra* … Another reason for my sending it was that I saw a copy of it in the French edition on Moore's library table when I called at his house … before I went down to Galway. If he is writing a novel of the subject, he may be reading Zarathustra with the plan of the novel in his mind.[74]

Moore's idea about fictionalizing Jesus surviving the crucifixion did not come to him until 1910, so the suspected novel Quinn mentions could not have been *The*

Brook Kerith. But Quinn's reference to Zarathustra indicates how important the work was to Moore as early as 1902.

But there is even more important evidence about *Zarathustra*'s impact on the Irish iconoclast from Moore's first biographer. Joseph Hone notes that Moore admired Daniel Halévy, a French historian who authored *Vie de Nietzsche* (*The Life of Nietzsche*). Moore told Hone that Halévy's book was the "way that biography should be written."[75] *The Life of Nietzsche* is notable for many reasons, but most significant for understanding Moore's work is its focus on *Zarathustra*. Of all of Nietzsche's works, this is the one to get the most attention. Halévy describes both the origin and the content of the work as a response to and a refutation of Wagner and Christ. As Halévy says: "The work was immense: it had to be a poem which would make the poems of Wagner forgotten; a gospel which should make the Gospel forgotten."[76] In a sense, Nietzsche's Zarathustra would overshadow and supplant the charlatans and demagogues, Wagner and Christ. As a "Fifth Gospel,"[77] which is how Nietzsche described the work to his publisher, *Zarathustra* would not so much add to the picture of Jesus found in Matthew, Mark, Luke, and John as overturn everything about the supposed God-man. Moore had the same objective as Nietzsche. In a March 1914 letter to Magee, Moore told his friend that he had just returned from a research trip in Palestine and was going to dedicate himself "to the composition of the Fifth Gospel."[78] Both Nietzsche and Moore refer to their works as Fifth Gospels. But it is not calling the works the "Fifth Gospel" that makes the two so similar. It is how *Thus Spoke Zarathustra* and *The Brook Kerith* function in relation to the four gospels that makes these two works so radical, rich, and fascinating. Neither author tries to get the life of Christ right or to contribute something new to the fund of knowledge about the man. To the contrary, they seek to discredit and delegitimize the gospels-Christ and to imagine into being a more informed and humane way of thinking, one that would have a more positive impact on the present and future.

It is my contention that Moore published a blistering work about Christ for the same reason Nietzsche did. Moore had connections with the Wagner circle, where an anti-Semitic Christian nationalism took shape during Wagner's lifetime and was formulated into a comprehensive philosophy that would eventually become the basis and foundation for the Nazis' version of Christianity. The key figure in relation to Moore and the Nazis is Houston Stewart Chamberlain, who praised Wagner, authored a biography about him, promoted his work, and eventually married his daughter. But Chamberlain is most famous because he is generally considered "the 'spiritual founder' of National Socialist Germany."[79] In 1899, he published *The Foundations of the Nineteenth Century*, a book that was subsequently hailed "as the 'gospel of the Nazi movement'"[80] in the Nazis' official newspaper, the *Völkischer Beobachter*. This two-volume work was immensely popular, selling more than a quarter of a million copies by 1938.[81] Given Chamberlain's comprehensive vision of religion, politics, and Germany, Alfred Rosenberg, author of *The Myth of the Twentieth Century* and editor of the *Völkischer Beobachter*, "hailed him as a pioneer and spiritual forerunner and viewed himself as Chamberlain's true successor,"[82] which is why he felt so honored when he was commissioned to write a book about Chamberlain's work. In 1923, the Nazis' propaganda minister Joseph Goebbels read the *Foundations*, and when he met Chamberlain in 1926, he indicates in his diary how important Chamberlain was to National Socialism by referring to him as a "spiritual father," dubbing him a "Trail blazer, pioneer!"[83] Chamberlain's biographer, Geoffrey G. Field, notes that Hitler read the *Foundations*.[84] But more importantly, Field indicates how crucial Chamberlain was by describing Hitler's response to the famous writer's public endorsement. After getting word of Chamberlain's support, members at the Nazi Party headquarters in Munich were euphoric, and Hitler was so giddy that he was supposedly "like a child."[85]

As was the case with Förster, Chamberlain's version of Christianity entails the negation of the Jew. As Chamberlain claims: "Whoever wishes to see the revelation of Christ must passionately tear this darkest of veil from his eyes. His advent is not the perfecting of the Jewish religion but its negation."[86] Chamberlain makes this same claim in a slightly different way later in the *Foundations*: "We certainly do the Jews no injustice when we say that the revelation of Christ is simply something incomprehensible and hateful to them. Although he apparently sprang from their midst, he embodies nevertheless the negation of their whole nature" (FNC I.338). In political terms, there is an inverse relationship between the revelation of Christ and the elimination of the Jew within a Christian polity. The Christianization of the body politic both implies and necessitates the negation of the Jew. Or, conversely, insofar as the Jew is present within a culture, the revelation of Christ and the formation of a Christian polity cannot be realized. This is the version of Christianity that the Nazis incorporated into their Party Program, which reads: "The party as such represents the standpoint of a positive Christianity, without tying itself to a particular confession. It fights the spirit of Jewish materialism within us and without us."[87] Notice how the Nazis define their version of Christianity in opposition to that which is Jewish.

What makes Chamberlain particularly important in relation to Moore's *The Brook Kerith* is his justification for a violent version of Christianity. According to Chamberlain, one of the biggest shams of the nineteenth century has been the ultra-passive and -tolerant portraits of Christ: "We have had represented to us as Christianity a strange delusive picture of boundless tolerance, of universally gentle passivity, a kind of milk-and-water religion" (FNC I:194). By stark contrast, Chamberlain wants his readers to recover the true Christ. Here is how he describes that savior: "Not peace but the sword: that is a voice to which we cannot shut our ears, if we wish to understand the revelation of Christ" (FNC I: 193). For Chamberlain, the "life of Jesus Christ is an open declaration of war" (FNC I:193), and this is a war that he directs mainly against the Jews.

There is good reason to believe that Moore was aware of Chamberlain's militant anti-Semitic Christian nationalism. Nietzsche experienced that version of Christianity in and through his sister and brother-in-law, who were heavily involved with Wagner and his circle, while Moore would have experienced it in and through Chamberlain, who adopted and disseminated the Christian anti-Semitism that was dominant among Wagnerians and that would become the basis and foundation for the Nazis' Christian, anti-Semitic political agenda. The evidence that Moore knew Chamberlain and/or his work is highly suggestive. As Frazier notes, Moore made five trips to the Wagner Festival in Bayreuth (1894, 1897, 1899, 1901, and 1910), and Frazier speculates that Moore met Chamberlain during his 1897 visit.[88] This would have happened because Moore's longtime friend Edouard Dujardin was also a close friend of Chamberlain's.[89] But even if Moore did not meet Chamberlain, it is highly likely that he would have known Chamberlain's work, because Chamberlain had such an enormous impact on Dujardin and his writings.[90] Given Moore's multiple visits to Bayreuth, he would have been familiar with the mood and atmosphere of the place and would have realized how impactful the group was. Here I want to take issue with Zuleika Rodgers, who takes note of the anti-Semitic theories of both Chamberlain and Dujardin. According to her interpretation, "Moore departs from his friend Dujardin in presenting a more sympathetic picture of first-century Jewish society. There is no attempt to align his views in support of the race theories of Chamberlain and the blatantly anti-Semitic perspective of Dujardin."[91] While it is true that Moore rejected the anti-Semitism of both Chamberlain and Dujardin, it is also true that Moore's novel incorporates Chamberlain's Christian anti-Semitism into the novel in order to subject it to extensive scrutiny and vicious critique, and he does this, I argue, in order to clarify how this anti-Semitic version of Christianity was gaining traction within Europe at the time. For the sake of clarity, let me identify the line of connection between Chamberlain's Christ and the one the Nazis would adopt.

Hitler adopted Chamberlain's militant, anti-Semitic version of Christianity, as is clear from an April 12, 1922, speech before the German Landtag. A man by the name of Count Lerchenfeld said that his faith as a Christian "prevented him from being an Anti-Semite." But Hitler countered by saying: "my feeling as a Christian points me to my Lord and Saviour as a fighter. It points me to the man who once in loneliness, surrounded only by a few followers, recognized these Jews for what they were and summoned men to the fight against them and who, God's truth! was greatest not as sufferer but as fighter." To support his view of Christ, Hitler then quotes the New Testament: "In boundless love as a Christian and as a man I read through the passage which tells us how the Lord at last rose in His might and seized the scourge to drive out of the Temple the brood of vipers and of adders."[92] For Hitler and the Nazis, the violence of Christ is necessary, because if Christians allow the Jews to take possession of the culture, then civilization will be totally destroyed. In short, Christians have no political choice but to vanquish the Jew—such is the nationalist logic underwriting the rise of the Nazis' violent Christ. It is for this reason that Hitler draws the following conclusion in *Mein Kampf*: "*by defending myself against the Jew, I am fighting for the work of the Lord*."[93]

Dietrich Eckart was a prominent Nazi who also worshipped the militant anti-Semitic Christ. Eckart died in 1923, but he had a profound and lasting impact on National Socialism, which is seen most clearly from Hitler's decision to dedicate *Mein Kampf* to him (among the heroes of National Socialism, Hitler asserts in his concluding dedication, Eckart was "one of the best, who devoted his life to the awakening of his, our people, in his writing and his thoughts and finally in his deeds").[94] In Eckart's *Bolshevism from Moses to Lenin*, which consists of an imagined conversation between Hitler and Eckart, Eckart says that "we [National Socialists] want Germanism, we want genuine Christianity,"[95] a rhetorical formulation that equates Germanism and Christianity. But if true Germanism necessarily implies genuine Christianity, then true Jewishness would necessarily imply genuine anti-Christianity, which is why Eckart's Hitler concludes that Christ and the Jew belong to "two fundamentally different worlds [which] were opposed to one another."[96] To support this view, Eckart references the New Testament as it justifies the Nazis' view that Christianity signifies a decisive rupture with Judaism and the Jew: "Christ was not so tolerant. With a whip he put a stop to the business of the 'children of the devil.' "[97] For Eckart, Christ was justified in taking this stance, because the Jews have a propensity to undermine governments, specifically Christian nations. Indeed, this is exactly what the Jews are doing today in Germany, for as Eckart's Hitler says: "And the game they're playing today, they have been at for two thousand years."[98] What Germany is experiencing with the Jews in the present is identical to what happened in the time of Christ, so, the logic goes, if Germans do not take violent action against the Jews, the Jews will crucify Christ yet again.

Founder of the anti-Semitic newspaper *Der Stürmer*, Julius Streicher was one of the primary figures to shape the way everyday Germans defined Jews, for as Streicher's biographer claims: *Der Stürmer* "had been one of the most widely circulated papers in Germany, the one paper Hitler himself claimed to read from cover to cover."[99] According to the International Military Tribunal at Nuremberg, which concluded that Streicher's newspaper inspired everyday Germans to commit atrocities against Jews, *Der Stürmer* "reached a circulation of 600,000 in 1935."[100] Ann and John Tusa differ with the Tribunal's figure, claiming instead that *Der Stürmer* reached its peak in 1937 with "a circulation of 500,000." However, they claim that the "readership was higher" than its circulation, because "display cases for the paper were set up in public places."[101] As a political leader of the Nazi Party (he was *Gauleiter* of Franconia, a region in Bavaria), Streicher wielded immense power. With regard to the concentration camps, he did not have a direct role in their making, but his newspaper certainly inspired the ideology of hate that allowed so many Germans to perform their duties in the death mills, which is why he was among the first group of Nazi leaders to be sentenced to death at the Nuremberg Trials. What separates him from the others, however, is that there is no evidence that he killed a single Jew or that he ordered anyone to kill a Jew. Referring to him as "Jew-Baiter Number One," the Nuremberg Tribunal concluded that "he infected the German mind with the virus of anti-Semitism, and incited the German people to active persecution."[102] In essence, Streicher was one of the highest-ranking Nazis to be executed, and he was hanged for providing the ideology and justification for everyday Germans to take violent action toward Jews.

That ideology was an anti-Semitic Christian nationalism, and images from *Der Stürmer* best visualize its distinctive nature. I could provide scores of examples to illustrate, but let me supply only one representative image.[103] The 1929 Easter issue, which is titled Resurrection ("Auferstehung"), pictures marching German soldiers saluting the Crucified Christ, who is perched on the top of a hill (see

Figure 2.3).[104] Retreating in fear is a Jew, who looks on the scene with horror. The suggestion is that Christ is being resurrected in Germany by the Nazis, a political situation that logically and necessarily terrifies the Jew, who intuitively realizes that Christ's political Resurrection entails his physical negation. Given

mord in Hanau

Auferstehung

nert. Diese Stellen, sowie die mit den Händen geknickten iglein der nächsten Sträucher zeigen deutlich, daß sich arme Knabe verzweifelt gewehrt hat. Schließlich gelang och der Bestie, das Schlachtmesser in die Lungenhalsschlag- einzustoßen. Die Tatsache, daß nur wenige Blut-

spritzer an dem Mordplatze vorhanden sind, läßt auch den Unwissenden erkennen, daß der Zweck des Mordes die Gewinnung von Menschenblut war.

Von dieser Stelle aus hat dann der Mörder sein Opfer noch 15—16 Meter weiter in den Wald hinein geschleppt.

Figure 2.3 Image entitled *Resurrection* (*Auferstehung*) in a 1929 issue of *Der Stürmer* (March 1929, no. 13).

the nature of this image, the political rise (Resurrection) of Nazi Germany is incomprehensible without Christ. Moreover, based on the anti-Semitic content of the image, which vividly pictures the version of Christianity contained in Point 24 of the Nazis' Party Program, there is an inverse relationship between the Christianization of Germany and the negation of the Jew. Germany will become more truly Christian only insofar as it eliminates all Jews and everything Jewish. Or, conversely, eliminating Jews is a prerequisite for the Christianization of Germany.

In his novel *Michael*, Goebbels pictures this Christian political agenda most clearly. The eponymous character is a disillusioned German who wants to restore Germany's greatness. Significant is his conception of Christ, who gives modern Germans the needed framework for instituting their Christian Reich. Goebbels sets Christ against the Jews, which allows Goebbels's Michael to suggest that negating Jews is a prerequisite for establishing the Nazis' Christian Reich. Within this framework, Christians and Jews are in irreconcilable conflict: "Christ is the genius of love, as such the most diametrical opposite of Judaism, which is the incarnation of hate."[105] This conflict epitomizes the way history has functioned for two millennia: "The Jew is the lie personified. When he crucified Christ, he crucified everlasting truth for the first time in history. This was repeated dozens of times during the next twenty centuries and is being repeated again today."[106] The logic of this model is pernicious and deadly. For Michael, a "nation without religion is like a man without breath," and since the "German quest for God is not to be separated from Christ,"[107] this means that Germans have no alternative but to take decisive action against the Jews, for "Christ is the first great enemy of the Jews."[108] To be clear, what Michael suggests is a need for the ruthless Christ of Chamberlain, Eckart, and Hitler to serve as a model for political action in the present:

> Christ is hard and relentless.
> He drives the Jewish money-changers out of the temple.
> A declaration of war against money.[109]

Prominent Nazis from major sectors of the Party were in agreement about Christ, who supports violence and even war against Judaism and Jews in the name of faith.

Moore published *The Brook Kerith* in 1916, so he would not have been aware of the way the Nazis adopted and made use of the violent Christ found in

Chamberlain's book. But this fact actually helps clarify what biographical novelists do. My major claim in this chapter is that biographical novelists are cultural diagnosticians who use the life of an actual historical figure in order to expose what ails a particular society. In the case of Wagner, Förster, and Chamberlain, their anti-Semitic Christ is the primary sickness, and, left unchecked, it will metastasize into something horrific, like the Christ of Hitler and the Nazis. It is this metastasizing view that led Nietzsche to exclaim: "The very next century will bring the fight for the dominion of the earth—the *compulsion* to large-scale politics."[110] My task at this point is to illustrate how the Wagner-Förster-Chamberlain-Nazi context can power and enrich our understanding of Moore's biofictions about Jesus.

IV

Life is at an end where the 'kingdom of God' begins.[111]

In 1910, Moore published "The Apostle," a work he refers to as a "Scenario" that consists of "the working notes that a writer has made to help him to write a play."[112] The 1910 Scenario reads like a short story, but with knowledge of Moore's oeuvre, one realizes that it is an early version of his 1911 play *The Apostle*, his 1916 novel *The Brook Kerith*, his 1923 revised version of *The Apostle*, and his 1930 play *The Passing of the Essenes*.[113] Moore would develop, complicate, and nuance the core ideas found in the 1910 Scenario, but the provocative premise—that Jesus survived the crucifixion and, twenty years later, informs the apostle Paul that his teaching of Christ risen is untrue—remains the same in all works.

To illuminate biofiction, specifically as Moore first imagined it, I start with an analysis of the Scenario, because Moore's alterations from the 1910 work to the 1911 play and then to the novel shed considerable light on his understanding and the unique power of the aesthetic form. Given the provocative nature of the work's key idea, it would be easy to focus mostly on Jesus. But the title of the Scenario and the first play is "The Apostle," which suggests that the real story and main character is Paul. Understanding that shifts the scandal from the blasphemy of Jesus surviving the crucifixion and not rising from the dead to Paul's concluding act, which is to murder Jesus so that Christianity could survive and flourish.

After Jesus' near crucifixion, he retreats in the Scenario to an Essene monastery, where he lives a simple life. Unencumbered by and even indifferent to theological speculation, Moore's Jesus finds meaning "by looking at the glory of the sky" and "the sunshine behind the mountains."[114] But he appears to experience a certain kind of repressed anxiety about coercive forms of theology, which explains his reluctance to engage in religious debate. For instance, when the Prior asks a lay brother and his spiritual brothers what they did during the day, the lay brother "tells of a preacher whom he has seen exhorting an unwilling multitude." After making this remark, "fear seems to come over the face of" the lay brother, which leads the Prior to ask: "Would'st thou say it is not well for men to preach?" The lay brother responds: "I would say nothing, giving no orders to other men, for the divine order is implanted in the heart, and every man knoweth what is best for him to do."[115] Why is the lay brother fearful of preaching? Part of the answer relates to the degree to which preachers will go in order to convert the "unwilling multitude."

At this point in the Scenario, the reader does not know that this "lay brother" is Jesus. But when that becomes apparent, readers get a better understanding as to why Jesus fears preachers who impose on the "unwilling multitude." During his stay, Paul tries to convert the Essenes to Christ's teaching, but as he tells the brethren about Christ, it becomes clear that their living Jesus is supposedly the Christ who ascended into heaven. At a crucial point in the telling of Paul's story, Jesus asks the apostle if he ever tried to confirm his facts: "So much thou knowest of the man's story, and no more. Didst thou care to inquire out?" Paul avoids answering the question, so Jesus asks if Paul ever talked to his brother or disciples to get reliable information: "And thou didst dispute with them, Paul, without ever caring to learn the words of Him whose name thou invokes in vain." But, again, Paul avoids answering the question by calling Jesus a "blasphemer"[116] and then quickly departs in order to locate witnesses who could corroborate his story about Christ risen.

Paul returns, and with him is Mary Magdalen, who immediately recognizes Jesus. But even with corroborating evidence that he is indeed the true Jesus, Paul remains committed to his fanatical religious agenda, which is why Jesus tells Paul that his faith, supposedly in Jesus, is really a faith in himself: "It is faith in thyself, Paul, that prevents thee from believing in me." Paul finally acknowledges that Jesus is who he says he is, but instead of relinquishing the faith, "Paul appeals to Jesus, telling him of the suffering it will cause many if a monk should come out of the Essene monastery and declare that it was he who had died on the cross and that the Resurrection was a fable preached by Paul." Jesus' reply is of crucial importance not just for understanding Moore's Scenario but also all of Moore's subsequent biofictions about Paul and/or Jesus: "But into this fable," Jesus replies, "other fables will be interwoven, and better that thy friends should suffer than that the whole world should suffer ever afterwards." There is something in the nature of Paul's version of Christianity that could have deadly consequences for the "whole world." To give readers a specific example to illustrate, Moore has Paul kill Jesus and then justify this murder in the name of the faith. As Paul reasons after the killing: "If this man hath spoken a lie he has merited death, and by his death Christianity is saved."[117] We are now in a position to answer the question: how far will a preacher go in order to impose *his faith* on an unwilling multitude? For the apostle, saving Christianity is of ultimate importance, and there is no limit to what he will do in order to accomplish his goal, even if it means murdering the person on whom the faith is based.

The 1911 "play" version of *The Apostle* is confusing for many reasons. On the title page it is referred to as "A Drama in Three Acts," but the play frequently reads like his Scenario or a short story. There are long sections of description in which characters speak and the plot is advanced, but there are no clearly designated speaking parts for actors. This confusion is made worse by the content of the book (as opposed to the play). As with the Scenario, Paul is portrayed in the play as a self-deluded fanatic who is willing to kill Jesus in the name of faith. But the work begins with "A Prefatory Letter" to Moore's friend and translator Max Meyerfeld, which describes how the idea of the work came to Moore and his first time reading the Bible. In stark contrast to the play, Paul is portrayed in this letter as a "very wonderful figure,"[118] "who accomplished a work so extraordinary as the interpretation and foundation of Christianity."[119] Based on the effusive content about Paul in the opening letter, the reader would have no idea that he would be portrayed as a dangerous fanatic in the play. In fact, the letter contradicts at times the portrayal of Paul in the play.

It is my contention that the "Prefatory Letter" was written after Moore completed the play, and that it signals a shift in Moore's thought that would lead to the writing of *The Brook Kerith*, a work that is very different from *The Apostle* (1911) in its treatment of Jesus. For readers of *The Brook Kerith*, stunning must be the fact that Jesus and his Gospel are treated as human and divine ideals in *The Apostle* (1911). When Mary Magdalen reunites with Jesus, she tells him not to look at her, because time has ravaged her appearance. But Jesus retorts: "And in love of me thy beauty liveth, and it shall live for ever on earth, wherever my Gospel is preached, and in heaven among the saints from everlasting to everlasting."[120] For the Jesus of *The Apostle* (1911), his Gospel is noble and sublime, so much so that angels and saints will celebrate it in the heavens. Within this framework, what vitiated Christianity is Paul, who created a religion that is really a reflection of his own narcissistic ego rather than the beauty of Jesus' Gospel.

How different is this portrayal of Jesus and his Gospel from what we find in *The Brook Kerith*. When the older Jesus reflects on his former life, he looks with horror on what he became and what his teachings inspired. In a moment of searing self-recrimination, Jesus says: "I fear to think of the things I said at that time."[121] He is specific:

> My teaching grew more and more violent. It is not peace, I said, that I bring to you, but a sword, and I come as a brand wherewith to set the world in flame. I said, too, that I came to divide the house; to set father against mother, brother against brother, sister against sister.
>
> (BK 447)

In "The Apostle" and *The Apostle* (1911), Paul's construction of Christianity is the reason why "the whole world should suffer ever afterwards," but in *The Brook Kerith*, it is Jesus' fanatical teaching that poses a serious threat to the world, as I will illustrate in the following pages.

Something changed in Moore's thinking that led him to shift the burden of responsibility from Paul, who is solely guilty of perverting Christianity in the Scenario and the 1911 play, to Jesus, who is culpable in large measure in the novel. Moore's reading of the Gospel of Luke contains one potential explanation for the transformation in Moore. In the 1911 "Prefatory Letter," Moore had a tepid response to the work. He "was disappointed almost from the first," and he acknowledged that a "great weariness certainly overtook" him "about the middle of" Luke's "narrative."[122] What is missing from the Gospel is life: "In Luke's narrative Christ seems a lifeless, waxen figure, daintily curled, with tinted cheeks, uttering pretty commonplaces."[123] The focus here is on the writing. At this point in his biofictions about Jesus, Moore is more interested in the writer's ability to make a paper character seem real and alive. Notice how Moore talks about the Gospel of Mark: "How far the story told by Mark is true in fact we shall never know, but it is certain that it is true on paper."[124] Mark succeeds where Luke fails, and what defines success for Moore is the rhetorical skill of making the paper character of Christ real and meaningful to the reader.

But in a July 27, 1914, letter to Magee, when Moore was deep into the writing of *The Brook Kerith*, the Irish author shifted his focus from Luke's failures as a writer to the content of Jesus' teaching, and he was horrified. "Are you aware," Moore asks Magee, "that Jesus was one of the most terrifying fanatics that ever lived in the world?" After making this claim, he specifies the Gospel: "Pretty bad occasionally in John but in Luke he shocked me."[125] When focusing in 1911 on the writing, Moore considers Luke a failure, because the Gospel writer did not bring the character to life. But when focusing in 1914 on the content and consequences of Christ's teaching, Moore considers Luke dangerous because he unleashed a fanatic on the world. This shift in focus had a significant impact on Moore's characterization of Jesus. Paul is the only criminal in "The Apostle" and *The Apostle* (1911), but in *The Brook Kerith* the pre-crucifixion Christ is the primary culprit because he codified a religious ideology that would lead to and justify large-scale atrocities. Within this framework Paul is a secondary villain because he is merely a carrier of Jesus' poisonous doctrine and proselytizes many with it. Absent from the Scenario and the 1911 play are the incriminating passages about Jesus' fanatical teachings.

As is the case in Nietzsche's *Thus Spoke Zarathustra*, mental and emotional orientations are of crucial importance. The pre-crucifixion Jesus adopted a way of thinking that led to and even necessitated at times epistemic and physical forms of coercion and violence. The post-crucifixion Jesus refers to this way of thinking as a "great harshness of mind," which leads Jesus to turn from his "natural self" (BK 446). What Moore does so well in the novel is to picture Jesus' internalization of his fanatical worldview and to illustrate how it functions. My focus here sets my approach apart from a scholar like Suzanne Hobson, who claims that Moore's novel "begins in an environment of theological skepticism and anticlericalism."[126] My argument is that for Moore it was less skepticism about God and Christianity and more concern about the then-present political dangers of the militant Christ that gave rise to *The Brook Kerith*. In other words, Moore was less interested in the "truth" of Christianity than the dangers it posed to the social and political order.

Post-crucifixion Jesus says that his decline into madness and fanaticism began when he "read the Book of Daniel" (BK 352). Much of the novel is told from the perspective of Joseph of Arimathea, and he, too, is startled by Jesus' passionate engagement with and response to this Old Testament narrative. Specifically, what concerns him is Jesus' propensity to think of himself as the Messiah. In the Book of Daniel, Nebuchadnezzar orders three men to be thrown into a furnace. But when the Babylonian King looks inside, he notices a fourth form, which "is like the son of God" (BK 153). This is what Moore's Jesus tells his disciples. While the disciples fail to understand Jesus' purpose in narrating this story, Joseph realizes that Jesus tells it in order to indicate that he is "like the son of God" (BK 154). And the message implicit in this idea is clear: Jesus, like Daniel, is invulnerable: "Jesus has told the marvellous stories of Daniel's escapes from death so that his disciples might have no fear that the priests of Jerusalem would have power to destroy him: whomsoever God sends into the world to do his work, Jesus would have us understand are under God's protection for ever and ever" (BK 154–5). As the Messiah, Jesus is a more-than-human force. But the idea of being the Messiah was not the demonic end of Jesus' self-aggrandizement. Judas tells Joseph that he feared Jesus "will be driven by the demon into the last blasphemy," which Judas specifies: "He will declare himself God" (BK 226). To his credit, the post-crucifixion Jesus comes to realize that his fanatical claim to being first the Messiah and then God was a "sin" (BK 450). As he says to the president of the Essene cenoby: "I had once believed myself to be a precursor of the Messiah like many that came before me, but unlike any other I began to believe myself to be the incarnate word" (BK 450).

Within a Nietzschean tradition, imagining oneself to be God leads—necessarily—to a destructive relationship with others. Humans are fallible, limited, and biased beings, and consequently, they come to reliable knowledge, if at all, through trial and error. A God is different, because divine knowledge is intuitive, comprehensive, and infallible. Thus, to oppose God would be to oppose Truth. Once Jesus declares himself the Messiah and then God, he becomes a tyrannical master who must be unquestionably obeyed. Having internalized this view, Jesus demands absolute submission from his sheep: "those who would be saved from the fire must follow me. I am the word, the truth, and the life. Follow me, follow me, or else be for ever accursed and destroyed and burnt up like weeds that the gardener throws into heaps and fires on an autumn evening" (BK 224). Jesus' logic is that, since he, as God, has the Truth, people must submit to him and his Truth. And if they don't, they must be eliminated.

What makes this model particularly dangerous is that Jesus' followers will adopt their Master's fanatical view, so they will enact violence on those who challenge or oppose Christ and his Truths. Post-crucifixion Jesus realizes this, which is why he says: "It was not enough for me to love God, I must needs ask others to worship him, at first with words of love, and when love failed I threatened, I raved; and the sin I fell into others will fall into, for it is natural to man to wish to make his brother like himself" (BK 368). Since others will adopt his destructive and deadly way of thinking, Jesus refers to his earlier teachings as an "evil seed" that he has "sown" (BK 448).

According to this paradigm, the Apostle Paul is extremely dangerous, as he commits his life to and has considerable success spreading Christ's Gospel of hatred and death. In a conversation, the president of the cenoby tells Jesus that the world lives on lies. Therefore, Jesus should ignore Paul because "one lie more will make no difference" (BK 454). But Jesus cannot easily accept the president's advice: "A counsel that tempts me," Jesus retorts, "for I would begin no persecution against Paul, but the lie has spread and will run all over the world even as a single mustard seed, and the seed is of my sowing; all returns to me" (BK 454). Notice how Jesus calls attention to his own culpability. This is very different from the Jesus of "The Apostle" or *The Apostle*, works in which Jesus is innocent of disseminating a death-bringing theology. But in *The Brook Kerith*, Jesus is the parent and original of the pernicious doctrine of hatred, violence, and death, while Paul is merely guilty of persuading others to adopt Jesus' barbaric Gospel.

One of my central claims is that biofiction, seemingly about a figure from the past, is consciously and strategically about the authorial present. Therefore, instead of asking whether Moore has given readers a new but more insightful and/or accurate picture of the historical Jesus, we should be asking: Why did Moore write a novel about Christ in the early twentieth century? And what was he trying to accomplish for his present through his usage of Christ? I argue that Moore, who had direct and/or indirect contact with Chamberlain via his association with the Wagnerites at Bayreuth, was aware of the militant anti-Semitic Christian nationalism that was taking shape in Germany after the publication of *The Foundations of the Nineteenth Century*. Like Virginia Woolf, Moore sees literature as an attempt "to criticise the social system, & to show it at work, at its most intense."[127] But unlike Woolf, who uses fictional figures to achieve her aesthetic goal, Moore realizes that literature can be more effective if it is anchored in the historical and the empirical.

In *The Brook Kerith*, what gets most attention is the violent rupture between Christianity and Judaism that pre-crucifixion Christ instituted, and this only stands to reason as this rupture would become the Nazis' dominant idea. But what needs to be clarified is the theology that justifies such violence. One of the prevalent interpretations of Christianity holds that there is a continuity between Judaism and Christianity, that Christ, having been born and raised in a Jewish community, sprang from a Jewish environment, and, therefore, his teaching blends Judaism and his own thought. Those who adopt this approach emphasize that Christ did not come to abolish the Law (Judaism) but as its fulfillment. Another view, however, holds that Christ's birth signifies the death and even negation of Judaism. This is the idea found in Chamberlain, Hitler, Eckart, Goebbels, the Nazi Party Program, and so many other Nazi writings. It is my contention that Moore, as a frequent visitor to Bayreuth and a close friend of Dujardin, must have been aware of this version of Christianity, and this explains Moore's construction of Paul's character.

As in "The Apostle" and *The Apostle* (1911), so in *The Brook Kerith*, just before Paul arrives at the Essene monastery, he preaches to a "multitude" (BK 386), but whereas the people are referred to as an "unwilling multitude" in the first two works, they are identified as Jews in the novel. Paul says to his hosts that "Timothy and myself were assailed by the Jews," and he specifies that they "barely escaped drowning in the Jordan" (BK 391). This reference to the Jews who would destroy a Christian like Paul dominates the text. After establishing an opposition between Christians and Jews, Paul tells the Essenes that God will ultimately abandon the Jews: "only by faith in him the world may be saved, and the Jews will not listen. A hard, bitter, cruel race they are, that God will turn from in the end" (BK 392). It might seem that Paul only opposes a certain group of Jews because he specifies those of Jerusalem—he does not want to "fall into the hands of my enemies the Jews, of Jerusalem" (BK 403). But as he continues his story, he indicates that a wide-range of Jews are his enemies. The Jews of Damascus "rose up against me and would have killed me" (BK 406). The "Jews" from a town neighboring Lystra denounced Paul and Barnabas and then "dragged Barnabas and myself outside the town, stoned us and left us for dead" (BK 409). What happened near Lystra is repeated: "But I am behoven to tell that wherever we went the persecution that began in Lystra followed us. As soon as the Jews hear of our conversions they assembled either to assault us or to lay complaints before the magistrates, as they did at Philippi, the chief city of Macedonia" (BK 413).

Since Jews consistently oppose and even persecute him and Christians more generally, Paul eventually stops making qualifications. As he says: "I have preached faithfully, followed wherever I went by persecution from Jews determined to undo my work" (BK 410). In his narrative to the Essenes, he says that he was "eager [...] to tell of the persecutions of the Jews" (BK 415) and "the interventions of the Jews" (BK 417). Here I am citing only a small fraction of the examples laced throughout his narrative, but the point should be clear: Paul establishes a deeply antagonistic relationship between Christians and Jews, and according to his version, Jews have the goal of destroying Christians and Christianity.

But what, in part, leads the Jews to persecute the Christians is Christ's message, which is that he represents the death of Judaism. As Paul says of Christ: "By his life and death he abolished the Law, whereby we might live in faith in Christ, for the Law stands between us and Christ" (BK 421). The only way to get to Christ is to reject Judaism. This is the case because there is no continuity between the two religions, only an irreconcilable and violent rupture. To indicate that this is not a clearly settled position, Moore pictures Paul in conflict with James about the very topic. After a three-year absence from Jerusalem, Paul returns, but to his horror he discovers that James made Jesus palatable by misrepresenting his message: "for James had made his brother acceptable in Jerusalem by lopping from him all that was Jesus, making him according to his own image; with these Christians he no longer stood up as an opponent of the Law, but as one who believed in it, who had said: I come not to abolish the Law but to confirm it" (BK 407). Paul, of course, rejects this idea, for as he later says: "James, the brother of the Lord, answered that Jesus had not come to abrogate the Law but to confirm it, which was not true" (BK 419).

It is worth noting that Moore underwent a transformation about this idea while working on the various versions of his Jesus story. In the Scenario, Paul tells the Prior that "he [Paul] is a Jew," and "that he holds by the law."[128] In *The Apostle* (1911), when the Prior suggests that Paul must be a Jew, Paul says: "None more a Jew than I."[129] But in *The Apostle* (1923), Paul says to his followers: "We are Jews no longer, but Christians,"[130] and as such, instead of seeing the Law as an incomplete but essential part of Christianity (Paul "thinks that the law was not complete in the Bible, but it is completed now—"[131]), as the Paul of the Scenario believes, the 1923 Paul considers the Law a curse from which Christ has liberated humanity. As Paul says to the Essenes: "The Lord Jesus has raised the curse of the law from you."[132] Clearly, Moore was working through the logic of the Christian anti-Semitism that was taking shape in Germany during the first couple decades of the twentieth century and would become a dominant ideology among the Nazis.

What makes Paul's appropriation of Christ's anti-Semitic teaching so troubling and even haunting is how it would function when Christians have political power. In Paul's day, Christians were a small minority, so they were politically impotent. Therefore, when Moore's Christ says that those who refuse to follow him should be "destroyed and burnt up like weeds," there was no secular possibility of doing that. But in the early twentieth century, when Christianity dominated in Germany, Christians had political power, and there were thus fatal consequences for the "enemies" of the faith.[133]

By having his Jesus live many years after his crucifixion, Moore is able to picture his protagonist reflecting on his former teachings and to register why they were so dangerous and destructive. Post-crucifixion Jesus does not become an atheist; he becomes a pantheist: "God is not here, nor there, but everywhere: in the flower, and in the star, and in the earth underfoot" (BK 366). Where pre-crucifixion Christ went wrong was to "gather the universal will into an image and call it God" (BK 366). This act, Jesus now understands, is the "starting-point of all our misery," because "he who yields himself to [this restricted and consolidated image of] God goes forth to persuade others to love God, and very soon his love of God impels him to violent words and cruel deeds" (BK 366). It is for this reason that post-crucifixion Jesus wonders if his former view of God "were not indeed the last uncleanliness of the mind" (BK 366).

For post-crucifixion Jesus, rejecting the view that he is the incarnate word would effectively disable, at least from the Christian side of things, the mechanism that leads to religiously inspired violence. In a conversation with the president of the monastery, Jesus says that he should go to Jerusalem to inform the Jews that he survived the crucifixion and did not rise from the dead. Were he to do this, the Jews would "welcome" him, because they would realize that he is "no longer the enemy; Paul is the enemy of Judaism and I am become the testimony" (BK 454). To save the social order, renouncing the idea of God as the exclusive possession of anyone is a political must.

V

I live in an imaginative country which is defined by the concrete.[134]

What I am trying to clarify in this chapter are the distinct ways that biographical novels signify, and to do that, I will briefly show how Moore's biographical novel contrasts with the work of prominent modernists. William Faulkner published no biofiction, but his ways of thinking about literary symbolism can be used to illuminate a distinctive feature of the biographical novel. In 1932 Faulkner published *Light in August*, a novel that insightfully documents the Christian nationalist thinking that leads to the brutal murder of the protagonist, Joe Christmas.[135] The person who commits the horrific deed is Percy Grimm, and in

1957, Faulkner described his character as "a Nazi Storm Trooper." But, ironically, Faulkner admits that he had not "heard of Hitler's Storm Troopers" when he first published the novel.[136] How is it possible for a character to symbolize something of which Faulkner had no knowledge? The answer has something to do with Faulkner's concept of a limited universal. Faulkner made his Storm Trooper comment in a classroom at the University of Virginia, where he was a Writer-in-Residence from 1957 until 1958. During his stay, Faulkner took questions from students, and one asked him if Grimm is "the type of person that is [...] prevalent in the South today, perhaps in the White Citizens Councils." In response, Faulkner simultaneously limits and expands the student's idea: "I wouldn't say that there are more of him in the South, but I would say that there are probably more of him in the White Citizens Council than anywhere else in the South, but I think you find him everywhere, in all countries, in all people."[137] Not all people in the South have adopted Grimm's white Christian nationalism, thus limiting the universal application of the Grimm character, but in the South, his white Christian nationalism can be found more in the White Citizens Councils than anywhere else. Furthermore, this racist Christian nationalist type is not solely the product of the South, which is why Faulkner's Grimm is more expansive than the student question suggested, for the Grimm type exists "everywhere, in all countries, in all people." In other words, there are Grimms in the North, in the West, in the East, and in Nazi Germany. As a cultural diagnostician, it is Faulkner's job as a writer to identify, define, and then picture with as much precision and accuracy as possible the ideologies that produce Grimms. Thus, Faulkner's Grimm can be seen as a portrait of a Nazi Storm Trooper, even if he had no knowledge of the Nazis.

But in light of Nietzsche's compelling critique of Truth, twentieth-century writers became increasingly skeptical about such overarching symbols, which function as universal truths. Woolf's evolution is useful within this context. In 1927, Woolf published *To the Lighthouse*, a work that examines the patriarchal thinking embedded within Western philosophy, and she uses the character of Mr. Ramsay to symbolize that mental orientation.[138] But by 1929, with the publication of *A Room of One's Own*, there was a shift in Woolf's thinking, which poses some challenges to the kind of symbolism at work in her earlier novels. This 1929 work is obsessed with the idea of truth: "a nugget of pure truth," "the true nature of fiction," "one cannot hope to tell the truth,"[139] "the essential oil of truth,"[140] "the pursuit of truth,"[141] "the grains of truth,"[142] and "truth had run through my fingers."[143] These are just a few of the references to the concept of truth in Woolf's work. But what Woolf was setting up through her discussion of truth was a critical analysis of her fictional Professor von X and his "monumental work entitled *The Mental, Moral, and Physical Inferiority of the Female Sex*."[144] Symbolic of the typical patriarchal scholar, this professor has been engaged in a massive project to define "the true nature of woman,"[145] but as Woolf's narrator engages his work, she realizes that there are two levels of truth: the surface truth, which consists of claims about the true nature of woman, and the "submerged truth,"[146] which are the motivations that lead someone like the professor to say what he does about the true nature of woman. After reading what the professor "wrote about women," the narrator thinks "not of what he was saying," the surface truth, "but of himself," which is the "submerged truth." And she concludes that the professor does not give readers an accurate picture of women, but rather uses women as an instrument (an idea anticipating Adrienne Rich's "Diving into the Wreck") to exalt and aggrandize men: "Women have served all these centuries as looking-glasses possessing the magic and delicious power of reflecting the figure of man at twice its natural size."[147] Woolf's insightful characterization of the two-tiered knowing subject in the process of constructing truth raises serious questions about the reliability of surface truth claims. If a submerged ideological agenda plays a crucial role in the formation of a surface truth, then the surface truth can be both inaccurate and even oppressive.

It was this two-tiered model of truth that, in part, led to the rise of postmodernism, which Jean-François Lyotard defines "as incredulity toward metanarratives."[148] Overarching ahistorical Truths, like the nature of women, were subject to intense scrutiny, thus leading to a questioning of such claims. This development, I contend, also led to a radical questioning of the traditional literary symbol, such as a figure like Grimm who is supposed to represent a type found "everywhere, in all countries, in all people." There is something problematic and untrustworthy in the nature of the metanarrative truth claim, as Woolf so deftly demonstrates in *A Room of One's Own*, and since traditional literary symbols function in the same way, there was a need, I contend, for a new type of literary symbol, one that would still serve the purpose of cultural critique but also be more reliable and trustworthy. Biofiction was the logical answer.

Contemporary writers of biofiction have registered this intellectual shift. In a recent interview Susan Sellers, who has authored a biographical novel about Woolf, notes that the "proliferation of biographical fiction has its roots in postmodernism, with its twin suspicions of truth and fiction."[149] What many biographical novelists realize is that authors could use fiction's overarching ahistorical symbols to prove whatever they want. Laurent Binet, who has authored biographical novels about Reinhard Heydrich and Roland Barthes, puts the matter clearly: "it is too easy to demonstrate something by resorting to fiction. If we can invent any situation, any event, and place any character in any fictitious situation, then we can demonstrate anything we want about this character."[150] Since the protagonist of a biographical novel is based on an actual historical figure, this grounds the narrative more firmly in the concrete and puts some limits on the authors' freedom to construct whatever they want. As David Lodge, author of biographical novels about Henry James and H. G. Wells, says about including real documents in a fictional narrative:

> If you say at the beginning that all the letters are real letters, then there is a documentary element in the novel, which persuades the reader to trust the story. If your priority was not to create this illusion of fact, of factually reporting this life, then you wouldn't do it and you would be free to use your imagination and make your characters do whatever you feel you want them to do.[151]

An immersion in the factual and the empirical is a central component of Tóibín's aesthetic. As he says in an interview: "I live in an imaginative country which is defined by the concrete." According to Tóibín, "facts" are something that authors of biofiction "have to deal with," but the facts are "nourishing as well as restricting." To clarify what he means, he uses a maritime metaphor. With biofiction, the author gets "an anchor from certain facts, and that anchor is not merely factual but emotional, and it brings a great deal with it, it carries you. And because it carries you, you can get a great deal of energy from it."[152] The biofictional symbol is different from the traditional literary symbol in that it is more anchored in fact.

In the early half of the twentieth century prominent Christians devised subtle, sophisticated, and sometimes vicious strategies to enforce submission to Christian Truth.[153] In the world of literature, there were two separate approaches to exposing and criticizing the Christian social system at its most intense. Those in the Faulkner tradition created a fictional world that illuminated the dangers and potential horrors that could and did emanate from a highly charged Christian system. Modernists in this tradition include E. M. Forster, who invents the character of Mr. Ducie in the novel *Maurice* (1913–4) in order to symbolize how Christian teaching mandates a coercive form of heteronormativity that psychologically tyrannizes and ultimately destroys many in England;[154] Woolf, who invents the character of Miss Kilman in *Mrs. Dalloway* (1925) in order to symbolize how a Christian psychology can justify brutal forms of imposing on others, an imposition that can lead to death, which is why the Christian Kilman's name is so symbolically significant (as a Christian, she is the killer of men);[155] and Nella Larsen, who invents the character Helga Crane in the novel *Quicksand* (1928) in order to symbolize how "ten million black folk"[156] have been metaphorically gang-raped into a form of Christian belief that justifies their poverty, inferiority, degradation, and subjugation.[157]

These three novels as well as Faulkner's *Light in August* are extraordinary works, now considered canonical modernist texts. And yet, from a biofictional perspective, they cannot expose and criticize the Christian social system as effectively as they could and should because there is something arbitrary in the nature of the works' literary symbolism. Grimm, Ducie, Kilman, and Crane are invented characters that authors could easily manipulate in order to express whatever their creators wanted. To more effectively criticize the Christian social system, a form of fiction that is more anchored in fact would be required. Biofiction, specifically *The Brook Kerith*, was a newly emerging literary alternative, as the author's imaginative vision is anchored in and defined by the concrete, thus eliminating, at least to some degree, the charge of having invented from whole cloth a fictional world that conveniently serves the author's political and ideological agenda.

Let me clarify how the anchored imagination functions in *The Brook Kerith*, which should be treated as fiction rather than biography. If readers see *The Brook Kerith* as a form of biography, they will assess it on the basis of its accurate representation of Jesus. According to this approach, Moore's novel would be a failure because he misrepresents the facts of Christ's life. But as I have already demonstrated, Moore does not consider his Jesus to be "the real man" found in "the Gospels." His Jesus is "an independent creation." More specifically, he is a figure that Moore converted into a literary symbol. In a December 18, 1915, letter to Magee, Moore makes this point directly. In the novel, Jesus "continued to live after the Cross, and must therefore advance, if he is to stand for intellectual advancement."[158] His Jesus is not supposed to stand for the actual person. He is supposed to symbolize intellectual progress, which means advancing beyond the Christ found in the New Testament. So we could say that Moore's pre-crucifixion Christ is in large measure a faithful representation of the man from the Gospels, while the post-crucifixion Jesus is a figure that Moore invents in order to project into existence his own vision of life and the world.

There are two separate ways of thinking about Moore's Jesus as the symbolic incarnation of advancement. According to the first, Christ gave us specific Truths, which were supposed to be valid for all people in all places at all times. Within this framework, Moore gives readers in and through his Jesus new Truths, ones that supplant Christ's Truths from the New Testament. But this approach, I contend, is misguided and untenable because Moore, clearly working within a Nietzschean tradition, considers the idea of a singular, immutable, God-created Truth intellectually incoherent and politically destructive. For Moore, and this is the second approach, intellectual advancement means a thoroughgoing rejection of the model that makes possible and generates one way and one Truth and one life. As such, Moore is in the same tradition as Nietzsche, Wilde, and Tóibín, which privileges life over Truth. As Moore says in a July 30, 1914, letter to Magee: "my story will be the repentance of Jesus for his blasphemies against life."[159] In essence, we should not be at the mercy of a pernicious system of thought that was established 2,000 years ago. Our destiny as autonomous beings is to create new ways of thinking and being that are more suited for our contemporary world. That act of behaving as an autonomous being is the very definition of life, according to Moore, and consequently, killing the New Testament Christ is a political must for the construction of a healthier and more socially just polity.

Given all this, the real scandal of *The Brook Kerith* is not Moore's de-divinization of Christ or his decision to have Jesus survive the crucifixion. It is his suggestion that the New Testament Christ formulated a model of God and Truth that can and will in certain situations lead to political catastrophe. Thus, the only way to safeguard the contemporary social and political order is to reject the New Testament Christ and his model of Truth. To be more specific, if Moore's contemporaries do not replace the New Testament Christ with a more informed and humane Jesus, one that embodies Moore's idea of intellectual advancement, then mass political destruction and death will be inevitable. But what this new Jesus is has been the source of some confusion because scholars have failed to understand the conventions of biofiction. As Harold Orel claims, when it comes to the representation of post-crucifixion Jesus, the novel is supposed to be read as "a version of what may have been the case, it is a plausible simulacrum of history."[160] In a sense, Orel sees *The Brook Kerith* as a speculative biography, which provides readers with a plausible version of the past. This view, however, makes no sense. By his own admission, Moore acknowledges "that there is no real man in the Gospels, but a collection of odds and ends regarding one man, compiled from different sources and very often in conflict."[161] If Moore cannot access the real Jesus, it would be even more incoherent to think that he would try to give readers a reliable speculative extension of the man and his time.

Therefore, instead of seeing the post-crucifixion Jesus as a legitimate version of the "real man," it would make more sense to locate Moore's work within the tradition of Manet ("Manet's art was all Manet"), Wilde ("The only portraits in which one believes are portraits where there is very little of the sitter, and a very great deal of the artist"), and Nietzsche ("the self-overcoming of the moralist, into his opposite—into me—that is what the name of Zarathustra means in my mouth"). In other words, Moore's post-crucifixion Jesus, who stands for intellectual advancement, is unapologetically Moore. As such, there is no effort or even pretense on Moore's part to get post-crucifixion Jesus right. To the contrary, there is an effort to fictionalize Jesus to project into being Moore's vision, which he does by constructing an intellectually enlightened and tolerant character for the purpose of countering and combatting the rabid form of militant Christian nationalism that was taking shape in Moore's day.

Worth noting is that it is not just the content of *The Brook Kerith* but also the form of the work as a biographical novel that communicates Moore's new view of Jesus. In the Christian tradition, Christ established a model in which Truth is valid for all people in all places at all times, and as the God-man, he incarnated that Truth. The biographical novel implicitly rejects this model of Truth. Instead of ceding agency by turning to the past for a Truth that dictates who and what we are in the present, as is the case in the historical novel, the biographical novel fictionalizes a figure from the past in order to model the process of human agency so that readers can activate an agential way of being in the present and future. Moore gives us such a model in the person of Jesus. But it is important to note which Jesus. For Moore, the Christ from the New Testament is an unstable fanatic, a figure certainly not to be trusted, revered, or followed. The New Testament Christ is the one who has come to dominate from Wagner through the Nazis, and he is the basis for the social sickness that Moore seeks to expose. The alternative Jesus, the one worthy of the reader's admiration and respect is the one Moore created, the figure who renounces his former violent teachings and symbolizes intellectual progress. Therefore, it is in the fiction (the new Jesus rather than the New Testament Christ) that the artist gives new life and reality to the society, for as Wilde says: "A great artist invents a type, and life tries to copy it." Moore created a more tolerant, intelligent, non-violent, non-fanatical, and humane Jesus than is found in the New Testament, and, given the logic of biofiction, it was his hope that his culture would take its cue from the Moore Jesus rather than the New Testament Christ. Stated more strongly: if the culture does not reject the New Testament Christ and replace him with Moore's Jesus, a massive political catastrophe is inevitable. That is the real scandal of *The Brook Kerith.*

Moore's *The Brook Kerith* provides a template for what biographical novelists do more generally. Moore starts by accurately representing the reality of the biographical subject, specifically identifying a psycho-political sickness inherent within an individual's way of thinking and being. Christ's delusional view of Truth and his narcissistic belief in exclusive access to the Divine are his fatal flaws. After accurately representing the biographical subject's destructive and deadly mentality, the author then turns to fiction in order to project into existence an alternative way of thinking, which is intended to provide readers with a much healthier and more life-producing way of being. Moore's post-crucifixion Jesus, who renounces Truth and divinizes all life, is Moore's life-enriching alternative. In essence, the ordering of the terms biographical fiction perfectly expresses what authors do. They take their inspiration from the biography of an actual historical figure, but once they get from that personage what they need, they then fictionalize the life in order to communicate their own vision of the world. As I suggested at the end of Chapter 1, authorial autonomy, biographical autonomy, and readerly autonomy are the ultimate goals, which are achieved through the author's construction of something new.

And yet, even though the aesthetic accent in the biographical novel should fall on the creation of something new, like post-crucifixion Jesus, *The Brook Kerith* ends with a scene of haunting despair, thus suggesting Moore's growing concern about the deteriorating religious-political situation in his day. Paul, realizing that Jesus will not expose his narrative about Christ rising from the dead as a sham, does not kill Jesus in *The Brook Kerith*, as he does in the Scenario and the play, and this is what makes the conclusion of the novel so ominous. In the closing pages, Paul begins his journey to evangelize the whole world "from morning to evening" by preaching "on all matters concerning Jesus, his birth, his death, and his resurrection" (BK 486).[162] Paul is a zealous, tireless evangelist, and when his anti-Semitic version of faith will finally catch fire in a Christian nationalist context, the logic of the novel implies, his followers will feel and believe that they have no choice but to do what Christ demands. As Hitler would say just nine years after the publication of *The Brook Kerith*: "*by defending myself against the Jew, I am fighting for the work of the Lord.*"

Part Two

Irish Figures as Biofictional Symbols

3

Roger Casement and the Transnational Origins of "Irishness"

In Inventing Ireland, Declan Kiberd examines the political and economic conditions that generated specific "works of art" during the late nineteenth and early twentieth centuries, but he foregrounds those literary "masterpieces" that possess an uncanny power to "float free of their enabling conditions."[1] Since Kiberd's focus is on the literature that contributed to the making of the modern nation, there is very little discussion of Roger Casement, the late nineteenth, early twentieth-century Irishman who did humanitarian work in the Congo and the Amazon; was involved with the 1916 Easter Rising; and was hanged by the English for treason. Yet, a wide range of contemporary scholars and writers have been drawn to Casement for exactly the same reason Kiberd is drawn to writers like Wilde, George Bernard Shaw, Lady Gregory, Yeats, and many others, which is because they believe that the Irish humanitarian played a crucial role in the invention of Ireland. But there is an additional reason why Casement has become such a major figure of interest over the last twenty-five years. The English wanted to execute Casement for his involvement in the Easter Rising, but given his widely publicized humanitarian work, he was well respected and immensely popular. Moreover, there was a huge campaign from famous people to spare his life. The English, however, wanted him dead, and during their investigations into his supposedly treasonous behavior, they discovered his "Black Diaries," which document some of his homosexual behavior. The English used these diaries to destroy Casement's reputation and to turn the public against him. But now that cultural sensibilities about homosexuality have flipped, Casement has become an icon in gay studies.

Brian Inglis's 1973 biography is certainly an important work in the list of studies celebrating Casement, but it did not lead to the surge in scholarship about the controversial figure. Roger Sawyer's *Casement: The Flawed Hero* (1984) and

B. L. Reid's *The Lives of Roger Casement* (1987) had a more substantive impact, but it was the publication of W. G. Sebald's *The Rings of Saturn* (1995) and Adam Hochschild's *King Leopold's Ghost* (1998) that contributed significantly to what would become a whole industry of scholarship about the life of this extraordinary and complicated man. This certainly makes sense. The combined critique of colonialism and the belief in the gift of homosexual vision enabled Hochschild and Sebald to indicate that Casement was a crucial figure in history not just because of his noble campaign against ruthless forms of economic exploitation and political oppression; his life is noteworthy because he developed ways of thinking and systems of thought that enabled people to overcome epistemological blind spots, the very blind spots that lead good-hearted people like Casement to unwittingly contribute to political oppression despite their desire to the contrary.

The titles of some of the twenty-first-century books about Casement testify to the nature and value of his contribution: Reinhard R. Doerries's *Prelude to the Easter Rising: Sir Roger Casement in Imperial Germany* (2000), Jeffrey Dudgeon's *Roger Casement: The Black Diaries with a Study of his Background, Sexuality and Irish Political Life* (2002), Séamas Ó Síocháin's *Roger Casement: Imperialist, Rebel, Revolutionary* (2008), and Jordan Goodman's *The Devil and Mr. Casement: One Man's Battle for Human Rights in South America's Heart of Darkness* (2010) are just a few works that underscore Casement's commitment to social justice and his liberationist impact. But what scholars do with a figure like Casement is very different from what a fiction writer does. As noted in Chapter 1, Atwood underscores how biographical novelists fictionalize, rather than represent, lives from the past in order to help us live better lives in the present and future, and writers do that, as Montero claims, by using the lives of others to create an "existential map" for their readers. Within this framework, what makes Casement so extraordinary is not that he provides us with clearly formulated propositional truths about who we are and what we can become but that he models the struggle, both heroic and tragic, to negotiate and even generate a semi-autonomous and socially just approach and identity in an age beset with confusion and anchored in injustice. In contrast to scholars, therefore, the objective is not to inform readers about the past. It is to use the past in order to empower readers in the present to live as more autonomous beings and to construct a better and healthier polity for the future, and Casement is one of the most effective figures for novelists to achieve this goal.

I

Draw round, beloved and bitter men,
Draw round and raise a shout;
The ghost of Roger Casement
Is beating on the door.[2]

A good Nietzschean, Yeats understood the idea of transvaluing all values (*die Umwertung aller Werte*). Before the twentieth century, imperialism and colonialism were primarily seen as noble political and economic enterprises, designed for "the development of civilisation in the centre of Equatorial Africa,"[3] as King Leopold II claims, or "To seek another's profit,/And work another's gain,"[4] as Rudyard Kipling declares. But by the beginning of the twentieth century, there was a mounting critique of colonialism and imperialism, so what was once celebrated as a manifestation of western altruism would, through a Nietzschean transvaluation of values, eventually be exposed as a massive global atrocity. Given his commitment to the Irish nationalist cause, Yeats brilliantly juxtaposes the figures of John Bull and Casement to signify this cultural and political inversion.

As a symbol, Bull represents the average Englishman, with his good-hearted, down-to-earth honesty, his general sense of fairness, and his willingness to defend God and country. In his 1938 poem "The Ghost of Roger Casement," Yeats formulates not so much a spatial whited-sepulcher view of Bull, which would highlight the disparity between surface beauty and inner corruption, as a temporal transvaluation-of-values approach in relation to the English symbol, which emphasizes how virtues in one age become vices in the next. "John Bull has stood for parliament,"[5] Yeats's narrator claims, and this is the case because he knows how to advocate on behalf of his country and its people by indicating "That all must hang their trust/Upon the British Empire,/Upon the Church of Christ."[6] Evidence of his greatness is that "John Bull has gone to India"[7] to prove "That none of another breed/Has had a like inheritance"[8] to the English.

But Yeats's narrator does his own research, and what he finds contradicts the British version of the story:

I poke about a village church
And found his [John Bull's] family tomb
And copied out what I could read

In that religious gloom;
Found many a famous man there;
But fame and virtue rot.[9]

There are two separate ways of thinking about fame and virtue rotting. According to the first, something like virtue is eternal in nature. Virtue rotting, therefore, would mean that something extrinsic to virtue caused corruption, thus turning a specific virtue into its opposite. Within this framework, "the virtues of colonialism and the Empire,"[10] as a character refers to them in Vargas Llosa's *The Dream of the Celt*, are valid for all times, but flaws in British policy and management led to the corruption of something intrinsically noble and pristine. In other, more capable hands, colonialism and Empire would have retained their purity and thus continued to be the virtues they essentially are. According to this paradigm, Bull would symbolize an eternal ideal. He might have momentarily corroded from within because of vice or ineptitude, but in himself he remains intact as the incarnation of British goodness and justice.

The second approach dispenses with the idea of virtues as eternal and suggests that what was once considered a virtue can now, in a new light, be seen as a vice. In this system, there is something intrinsic to seeming virtues like colonialism and Empire that make them actual vices, and with time, when people have formulated and adopted a totally different or more informed system of knowledge, they will be able to clarify precisely why seeming virtues at one time are actual vices in another. Woolf's brilliant analysis of the Angel in the House in her "Professions for Women" speech/essay intelligently enacts this approach—the virtues of the ideal nineteenth-century woman are considered vices in the feminist twentieth century. If we apply this transvaluation-of-all-values approach to Yeats's poem, then the John Bull symbol would have an expiration date. Thus, what was considered a sumptuous political delicacy in the nineteenth century can now be seen as putrid offal in the new age. To be more specific, Bull has become a toxic symbol, while Casement, who was once demonized as pure poison because of his homosexual orientation, has become the symbol of justice for the new generation. Yet, Yeats celebrates Casement not because of but in spite of his homosexuality, thus indicating that Yeats's own transvaluation journey was incomplete.

We see Yeats's conflicted view through his two very different poems about Casement. The meaning of "The Ghost of Roger Casement" is derived from a *via negativa* approach. After giving readers information about Bull, the narrator concludes each stanza with the following couplet: "*The ghost of Roger*

Casement/Is beating on the door." The suggestion is that Casement is in the process of supplanting Bull as a new type of political symbol, one that better reflects a more humane and just social order. Since the focus of the poem has been on the British Empire's colonial project, we can safely assume that Casement symbolizes the opposite, which is an anti-colonial or postcolonial future.

While Yeats unambiguously celebrates his Irish compatriot in "The Ghost of Roger Casement," he is more guarded and defensive in his 1937 poem "Roger Casement." The epigraph to the work indicates that Yeats wrote it "*After reading 'The Forged Casement Diaries' by Dr. Maloney*."[11] Without mentioning the crime of "gross indecency," Yeats notes how the British turned "a trick by forgery"[12] in order to blacken Casement's "name."[13] Rather than transvaluing the value of heteronormative sexuality, a semiotic act that would have been consistent with his transvaluation of British colonialism, the poem takes it as a given that Casement is innocent of the sexual crime of homosexuality, thus making him a "gallant gentleman."[14] The implication, of course, is that, if the Black Diaries are not a forgery, then Casement would have been a homosexual, in which case he would have been a criminal whose reputation had been rightly "blackened." What makes the Casement poems so fascinating is Yeats's simultaneous insight and blindness regarding his countryman's liberationist politics. Using a Nietzschean model of transvaluing all values, Yeats condemns Britain's colonial agenda and celebrates Casement's postcolonial approach, but because of an epistemological blind spot, Yeats could not apply the transvaluation model to Casement's sexuality, which leads him to celebrate Casement, but only on condition that the Black Diaries are a forgery and that, therefore, he remains heterosexual.

By 1995, with the publication of *The Rings of Saturn*, Sebald was able to extend the transvaluation-of-all-values approach from the realm of politics to sexuality. But more than that, Sebald prioritized sexuality by suggesting that Casement's homosexuality was an epistemological aid that contributed significantly to his liberationist politics. Sebald begins and ends Chapter 5 with a discussion of Casement, but most of the chapter concentrates on Joseph Conrad's biography, focusing specifically on his trip to the Belgian Congo during the early years of its formation. This, obviously, was the origin of *Heart of Darkness*. In the Congo Conrad met Casement, whom he considered a man of integrity. The chapter concludes with a brief summary of Casement's reflections about "the nature and origins" of political "power and the imperialist mentality that resulted from it,"[15] thus leading Casement to draw links between the English and the Belgians and the Congolese and the Irish. Significant for my purposes is the lesson learned from the narrator's presentation of the material: "We may draw from this the conclusion that it was precisely Casement's homosexuality that sensitized him to the continuing oppression, exploitation, enslavement and destruction, across the borders of social class and race, of those who were furthest from the centres of power."[16] Sebald's narrator certainly does not earn this conclusion, nor is there much evidence in Casement's writing to justify his assertion, but that he drew it indicates the degree to which the transvaluation of all values had progressed from 1937 to 1995, or from Yeats to Sebald.

What Yeats and Sebald do is to elevate Casement into a cultural icon of postcolonial justice. As readers, we are not given compelling reasons to accept this view. We are merely invited to trust Yeats and Sebald. Writers like Vargas Llosa (*The Dream of the Celt*) and Sabina Murray (*Valiant Gentlemen*) are different because, as biographical novelists, they clarify precisely what made Casement so extraordinary; they illustrate how he was able to expose his culture's values "of *opposite* descent," to use Nietzsche's terminology, as destructive and deadly and how he was able to imagine into existence a new, more autonomous, and more socially just way of seeing and being. Put differently, these authors use Casement to picture what made him epistemologically capable of exposing and transvaluing the dominant ways of seeing and being from his time and to imagine into existence more humane and socially just alternatives. As such, Casement's life serves as an existential map for those who would live in a more autonomous and socially just manner.

II

Characters don't have the view of God.
None of us does.[17]

In 2016, Alan Lewis published *Dying for Ireland: The Last Days of Roger Casement*. While this is a biographical novel, it fails as such for many reasons, but its shortcomings are useful for understanding what makes first-rate biographical novels so powerful, effective, and impactful. The biographical novel came into being in part to counter the weaknesses and limitations of the historical novel, as I have demonstrated in Chapters 1 and 2. Bruce Duffy has authored two spectacular biographical novels, one about Ludwig Wittgenstein (*The World as I Found It*) and one about Arthur Rimbaud (*Disaster Was My God*), and in an interview about these works he explains why the historical novel is such a problem. History is the foreground of the historical novel, while the protagonist is of secondary importance. But this is backwards, argues Duffy, because the "hero of the novel should be the foreground, and the history should be the background."[18] From this perspective, authors of historical fiction necessarily impose inauthentic and bulky frameworks on their characters. Faulting Lukács, in particular, Duffy explains why the historical-novel approach misrepresents and falsifies human experience: Lukács "demands this imposed, matrix-like system, this historical overlay over the characters—a vast and an inflexible theater in which, I guess, he gets to sit as the judge."[19] In the real world, Duffy argues, "characters don't have the view of God," because "most of us live in the fog of the day to day. We're not aware of giant sweeps of history around us in which we are the cogs."[20] Thus, it is Duffy's objective "to put" his "characters into the fog of the day to day—into what is really going on right around them, the odd and even silly things."[21]

For someone like Duffy, what would make Lewis's novel so misleading and unsatisfying is the *ex post facto* historical perspective. Living in the moment entails much uncertainty, confusion, and disorientation, and even if characters believe they are behaving as autonomous agents, they could be merely doing the bidding of cultural and political power brokers or acting in accordance with a well-established conceptual system, despite their intentions to the contrary. Embeddedness in the present makes original thought or autonomous action extremely difficult at best and nearly non-existent at worst. For intellectually honest and clear thinking characters to have too much certain knowledge about the nature of new, original, or unsettled experience would, thus, falsify the way people experience themselves in historically non-determined situations.

Given all this, Lewis's characterization of Casement fails to accurately represent the tortured interior of his character's experience of himself. Take, for instance, the way Lewis's Casement reflects on his own homosexuality. Told from the perspective of Casement, who is sitting in prison awaiting execution, the narrative reflects on the events that led to Casement's revolutionary action and ultimate capture. But there are also brief discussions of Casement's private life, specifically his homosexuality. Here are the thoughts of Lewis's Casement:

> Every large city—especially a large port city such as Manhattan—has places where men who are new in town may meet like-minded souls, or at least enjoy conversation and a glass of wine in a congenial atmosphere. The safely married

> segment of society is always shocked to find that such places exist, although how could they expect otherwise? Exist they do, but only to the extent they can pay off the constabulary and officialdom to suffer their existence. Before long, a raised price is not met or the lure of voters to be aroused overshadows that of bribes to be collected, and the weight of public morality comes down upon such establishments and drives them underground, like a gleeful child playing whack-a-mole at the fun fair.[22]

This sounds more like the reflections of a contemporary sociology professor describing a societal state of affairs than a conflicted 1916 homosexual in a staunchly heteronormative polity. Duffy refers to this as the standing-in-judgment epistemological stance we typically find in the historical novel.

In short, Lewis fails to understand the epistemological significance and narrative importance of turning from history to biography, from an epistemological position of intellectual clarity and certainty to a subjective position of disorienting complexity and conceptual uncertainty. But locating characters in the fog of the day to day is not an end in itself. The goal is to picture the subject in the process of negotiating and constructing a unique, original, and semi-autonomous way of seeing that would enable the protagonist to bring into existence something new and more productive of life. Murray makes this point directly in an interview about her biographical novel *Valiant Gentlemen*. When discussing this work, Murray speculates that "the biographical novel's embracing of personal psychologies offers an alternative to the historical novel's performance of understood notions."[23] The embedded and uncertain personal psychology stands in stark contrast to history's "understood notions." As is the case with Wilde, Nietzsche, and Moore, Murray is intensely concerned about the condition of being epistemologically and socially overdetermined, but instead of identifying history or science as the primary culprit, she first targets technology:

> Why this interest in biographical novels now? Perhaps as we deal with the onslaught of technology, we forget that life is determined by people. There is not a moment in time where one doesn't interact with some dehumanizing element of technology. In the midst of all this, we wonder what it is to be a person.[24]

For Murray, personhood is defined by that ability to evade being determined, which is why she decided to write specifically about Casement:

> I wanted to look at colonialism, the Belgian Congo, the First World War, and to question what it is to be alive in the present of those situations. Decisions are made by people. I said to myself: "This is what's important here, human

> psychology. Important here are interactions." And I was lucky to find someone like Casement, who was dealing with massive historical movements: the opening up of Africa, the First World War, the Barings Bank Crisis, emerging gay identities.[25]

Casement was not so much immersed in a transvaluation-of-all-values moment as he was one of the primary catalysts for a transvaluation-of-the-seeming-virtues of colonialism and Empire. What makes Casement so extraordinary is his ability to construct new realities in a time of so much upheaval and confusion, and some of the realities he constructed have now come to dominate, which, in part, explains the emergence of a whole industry of scholarship and literature about him.

III

> *Underneath all and unsuspected almost by myself I had remained an Irishman.*
>
> (Roger Casement)

When doing research for *The Dream of the Celt*, Vargas Llosa visited the archives at the National Library of Ireland in Dublin, which houses Casement's letters to Alice Stopford Green, the author of important books about Irish history, legends, and myths. These works had an enormous impact on Casement, as Vargas Llosa makes clear in the novel: she "contributed more than anything else to giving Roger the 'Celtic pride' he boasted of so vigorously" (DC 49). But it was in the letters to Green that we get spectacular insight into the emotional and psychic transformations that make Casement such a noteworthy and remarkable figure. Not surprisingly, Vargas Llosa makes extensive use of these letters in the construction of his protagonist.

Before turning to those letters, let me briefly discuss one of the standard practices of biographical novelists, which is to take something significant from the life of someone and then to build a fiction around that event, trait, or character. In *The Dream of the Celt*, what interests Vargas Llosa most is the transformation of individual identity, an idea he introduces in the novel's epigraph: "Each one of us is, successively, not one but many. And these successive personalities that emerge one from the other tend to present the strangest, most astonishing contrasts among themselves." This quotation comes from José

Enrique Rodó's *Motives of Proteus*, and Vargas Llosa clarifies in the epilogue how Casement embodies Rodó's ideas. After explaining how a "revolution in customs" in Ireland led to a partial rehabilitation of Casement's reputation, Vargas Llosa discloses what he thinks of his protagonist. He is "one of the great anticolonial fighters and defenders of human rights and indigenous cultures of his time, and a sacrificed combatant for the emancipation of Ireland." Casement's contemporary compatriots have recently come to this conclusion, Vargas Llosa notes, but to do so they had to accept "that a hero and martyr is not an abstract prototype or a model of perfection but a human being made of contradictions and contrasts, weakness and greatness, since a man, as José Enrique Rodó wrote, 'is many men,' which means that angels and demons combine inextricably in his personality" (DC 354).

It was in the letters to Green that Vargas Llosa got some of his best inspiration for developing Rodó's ideas about the strange evolutions and transformations of Casement's successive personalities. Of crucial importance is the link between perception and being as well as being and perception—the ordering of the terms is significant. In an April 24, 1904, letter, Casement claims that had he been English, he would not have been emotionally, psychologically, or epistemologically capable of seeing or empathizing with the exploited and suffering Africans: "I am quite sure that if I had not been an Irishman and an ardent believer in the nationality and rights of Ireland I should have passed thro' those scenes of Congo suffering humanity with a cold, or at any rate so reserved a heart, that I should never have committed myself as I did"[26] to writing the report about the atrocities. Being English would have prohibited him from feeling compassion for the Congolese, thus preventing him from seeing the suffering right in front of him. What made Casement able to see the human agony and then to have compassion for the Congolese was his being an "Irishman."

But being an Irishman or an Englishman is not an easily definable reality for someone like Casement. In an April 20, 1907 letter, Casement explains how he nearly became an Englishman:

> It is a mistake for an Irishman to mix himself up with the English. He is bound to do one of two things—either go to the wall, if he remains Irish, or become an Englishman himself. You see I very nearly did become one once! At the Boer war time. I had been away from Ireland for years—out of touch with everything native to my heart and mind—trying hard to do my duty and every fresh act of duty made me appreciably nearer the ideal of the Englishman. I had accepted Imperialism—British rule was to be extended at all costs, because it was the best

> for everyone under the sun, and those who opposed that extension ought rightly to be 'smashed'. I was on the high road to being a regular Imperialist Jingo—altho' at heart, underneath all and unsuspected almost by myself I had remained an Irishman. Well, the war gave me qualms at the end—the concentration camps bigger ones—and finally when up in those lovely Congo forests where I found Leopold I found also Myself—the incorrigible Irishman![27]

Notice how Casement defines Britishness. It is based on a dutiful acceptance of imperialism, Britain's right to dominate others. The more Casement internalizes and enacts that political agenda, the more British he becomes. But implicit in this view is a behavioral mandate in relation to resistors and opponents, who should be "smashed."

This passage is important because it illuminates the political, intellectual, and emotional logic that leads colonizers to feel no compassion for the colonized and no remorse for having violated them. If Britain has a legitimate right to extend its rule over others, then the righteousness of the cause would effectively render the feelings and sufferings of those who resist and oppose Britain's noble political agenda of negligible significance. The emotional logic is linked to one's national identity. The more intensely British a person is, which is defined on the basis of a person's commitment to imperialism, the less compassion can one experience for resistors and opponents of British rule. Contrariwise, the less intensely British a person is, the more compassion can (but not necessarily will) one experience for victims of British colonialism. Therefore, as Casement shuffles off the mortal coils of Britishness and becomes increasingly more Irish, the more capable is he of seeing Congolese suffering as suffering and feeling compassion for those who suffer.

The letters to Green are important because they enable Vargas Llosa to understand and chart the subtle and complex transformations in Casement's identity, which lead to a very different relationship to the colonized and a polar opposite response to their sufferings. For instance, to construct Casement's letter to his cousin Gee (Gertrude Bannister), Vargas Llosa takes many of his ideas directly from the 1907 letter to Green:

> This is why, dear Gee, it may seem like another symptom of madness to you, but this journey into the depths of the Congo has been useful in helping me discover my own country and understand her situation, her destiny, her reality. In these jungles I've found not only the true face of Leopold II. I've also found my true self: the incorrigible Irishman.
>
> (DC 80)

The references to finding Leopold in the Congo, discovering his true self, and being an "incorrigible Irishman" indicate that Vargas Llosa used the Green letter as his source text for his construction of Casement's letter to Gee.

Both the Green letter and the Vargas Llosa construction of the Gee letter are crucial for understanding Casement's stunning metamorphosis. In the novel, Casement has an intense conversation with Green, and here is how Vargas Llosa's narrator characterizes his protagonist's thoughts: "there in the Congo, living with injustice and violence, he had discovered the great lie of colonialism and begun to feel 'Irish,' that is, like the citizen of a country occupied and exploited by the Empire that had bled and weakened Ireland" (DC 88). The logic of this passage is stunning. As an Englishman in Ireland, Casement felt that he was part of a dominant nation that is righteously empowering an inferior people to become one with a superior race. That is how Casement felt before renouncing his Englishness and becoming "Irish." As an Irishman, he sees his experience very differently. Instead of being a part of a righteous and just political cause, one that sanctions the smashing of resistors and offenders, he identifies with the "Irish," which converts the colonizing action into its opposite, something unjust and criminal.

Significant here is Vargas Llosa's decision to put the word Irish in quotation marks, thus underscoring the provisional nature of national identity, specifically Irishness. Uncritically internalizing the colonizer's definition, which his father did, led Casement to think himself British, which, in turn, resulted in him being British. But after having emancipated himself from his father and the British, Casement casts a critical and regretful glance at his previous self:

> He was ashamed of so many things he had said and believed, repeating his father's teachings. And he vowed to make amends. Now that he had discovered Ireland, thanks to the Congo, he wanted to be a real Irishman, know his country, take possession of her tradition, history, and culture.
>
> (DC 88)

The shift in perspective inspires Casement to become something else—to become "Irish." And as he does this, it alters his whole understanding and experience of colonialism. Rather than looking at the Congolese with a cold and indifferent heart, he views their suffering with compassion, which is why he resolves to help them.

But there is a perplexing question when we look at the Green letters as the primary source text for Vargas Llosa's construction of Casement's character.

Note how Casement suggests in his letter to Green that his Irishness enabled him to see Congolese suffering:

> There is so much to be done in the Congo matter that we shall need all our strength and the effort of every friend of the weak and the oppressed to help these poor persecuted beings in Central Africa. It is a tyranny beyond conception—save only, perhaps, to an Irish mind alive to the horrors once daily enacted in this land. I think it must have been my insight into human suffering and into the ways of the spoiler and the ruffian who takes 'civilization' for his watchword when his object is the appropriation of the land and labour of others for his personal profit and which the tale of English occupation in Ireland so continually illustrates that gave me the deep interest I felt in the lot of the Congo natives.[28]

Based on this letter to Green, what made Casement capable of seeing and registering the "tyranny beyond conception" in the Congo was the fact that he witnessed and experienced all of this through the lens of his "Irish mind," but based on Vargas Llosa's *The Dream of the Celt*, what made Casement capable of seeing and registering Irish suffering was the fact that he witnessed and experienced the atrocities in the Congo ("thanks to the Congo"). Did Vargas Llosa fail to read the Casement letters to Green closely and carefully? How can we explain that he got this particular fact so wrong? Or, is there an alternative way to think about Vargas Llosa's usage of both the letters to Green as well as Casement's biography?

We get some answers to these questions in the source text for the novel's epigraph. Taking Proteus as an ideal, Rodó holds to the principle that "to renew oneself is to live."[29] "Time is the supreme innovator,"[30] and in his attempt to clarify what this means, Rodó imagines how "a traveller who returns to his fatherland after a long absence" would see the people "whom he left in" his "youth."[31] This, of course, describes exactly what happened to Casement in both real life and Vargas Llosa's novel, and not surprisingly, Rodó's very next sentence is the one that Vargas Llosa uses as the epigraph to *The Dream of the Celt*. Relevant to my argument is Rodó's characterization of the way human interiors experience and register transformations in and through time:

> Each thought of your mind, each rhythm of your feelings, each determination of your free-will, and, even more, each instant of the seeming truce of indifference or of sleep which interrupts the process of your conscious activity (but not the process of that other activity which develops within your self without the participation of your will, without even your own knowledge), all these are but

> one impulse more towards a modification whose accumulated steps produce these visible changes from age to age, from decade to decade.[32]

There are both conscious and subconscious processes that impact and inflect a person's personality. Therefore, defining the "*actual causes*" of the motives or the transformations within us is extremely difficulty, which is why Rodó concludes that the "*actual causes* are the key to many enigmas of our destiny."[33] Certain knowledge of human motives and interior transformations is highly elusive, and Casement acknowledges this by saying that he thinks rather than knows that it was his experiences in Ireland that led to his clarity in vision about and compassion for the Congolese. Given this approach, it is possible that someone like Casement would consciously and rationally say that his experiences as an "Irishman" led him to feel compassion for the Congolese, while the actual cause of his behavior could be that his experiences in the Congo led him to feel for the Irish. Semiotic slippage in relation to the exchanges and negotiations between the conscious and the subconscious make it difficult to establish clearly defined causal relations with regard to human interiors.

In other words, when it comes to human motives, certainty is nearly impossible. What knowledge we do possess is provisional at best, signaled by quotation marks ("Irish"). Yet, Vargas Llosa holds up Casement as a model, albeit flawed, because he has cultivated some effective strategies for overcoming epistemological limitations, thus making it possible for him to counter-construct himself as a more unique, a more authentic, and a more socially just individual. But Casement was not always a spectacular individual, and it is through his transformation that readers get an "existential map" of autonomous behavior, to use Montero's phrasing. Specifically, Vargas Llosa uses Casement's character to chart and illuminate the evolution from being a passive, culturally determined figure to becoming an active, culture-determining individual. Vargas Llosa highlights how Casement was in danger of becoming what Rodó refers to as a dissipated spirit: "How many spirits are dissipated in sterile living or reduced to the theatricality of a role that they illusively thought was part of their nature!"[34] Human character is dynamic by nature, so change is inevitable. But there are those who allow external forces to determine their transformations, while there are others who take some control over the developments in their personality. Education, intellect, and an active will—these are the things that could empower a person to have some control over their internal transformations and to direct them in a productive and life-promoting way, according to Rodó.

Throughout the novel Vargas Llosa pictures many characters who fail to take any control over their own personality. They merely play a role that has been scripted for them, and over time they have come to "illusively" think that the role "was part of their nature." Within the context of *The Dream of the Celt*, this principle applies most to many of the colonizers who have mindlessly accepted the colonizing narrative, which holds that colonizers are in possession of a redemptive ideology that will enable them to save African savages. As was the case with Casement, the more intensely the colonizers internalize this ideology, the more would they incarnate the official identity of their nation. To put this in Rodó's language, acting in accord with the colonizing nation's official script would make one a genuine member of the colonizing power, an act that would lead the person to illusively think of the scripted role as his or her nature.

This describes how Casement viewed himself and behaved in his early years in the Congo. But as Vargas Llosa has Casement reflect on his transformation, his character takes note of the numerous dissipated spirits who surround him, thus giving readers insight into the mental and epistemological orientations that power the colonizing project. Casement first went to Africa because he believed in the three pillars that "justified colonialism: Christianity, civilization, and commerce" (DC 29). But when he finally gets to serve under one of his inspiring idols, Henry Morton Stanley, he makes crucial discoveries about knowledge and epistemology. With regard to knowledge, Casement believed the surface rhetoric about the "redemptive principles" (DC 25) of colonialism, seductively disseminated by King Leopold II, which holds that the socio-political goal in the Congo is to exterminate "the social degradations of slavery and cannibalism" and to free "the tribes from the paganism and servitude that kept them in a feral state" (DC 25). But after witnessing how the horrid realities in the Congo contradict what he thought he was going there to accomplish, Casement shifts his focus from knowledge (the information that he has been given) to epistemology (the mental orientations that enable a person to know or prevent one from knowing). Notice how Casement characterizes his earlier self in epistemological terms: "*I wasn't aware because I didn't want to be aware*, he thought" (DC 25). In this instance, desire inflects the capacity to know. Specifically, a human desire can lead a person to overlook a reality right before one's eyes.

But after making this initial observation, Casement expands his foray into epistemology by noting that "worse than being a willing blind man was finding explanations for what any impartial observer would have called a swindle" (DC 25). On the basis of a willing desire, some people see what they want to see or do not see what they do not want to see. Different and even worse from this is that epistemological orientation that functions once a redemptive ideology has been established and internalized. The second approach is worse for two reasons. First, for those in thrall to the redemptive-principles epistemology, breaking free from it is extremely difficult. Contrasting the willing-blindness and the redemptive-principles epistemologies will prove instructive at this point. Casement wants to believe in the nobility of colonialism, or he does not want to believe that colonizers would commit atrocities, so he fails to see colonial atrocities. But when he finally witnesses firsthand the flagrantly criminal behavior of colonizers, he can no longer deny the reality. This is how the willing-desire epistemology is undone.

The redemptive-principles epistemology is different because it can rationalize and justify the most extreme atrocities. Casement clarifies how this model works in the same paragraph about finding explanations to justify the colonial swindle. Stanley had African chiefs who could not read or understand the language sign contracts which would basically divest their tribes of rights and force them into slavery. Here is how the young Casement responded to this situation: "*They don't know what they're doing, but we know it's for their good and that justifies the deceit*, the young Roger Casement thought" (DC 26). Casement clearly knows that what they are doing is wrong, but the redemptive-principles idea epistemologically transforms the present wrong into an ultimate right, thus justifying the violation.

But how far can one push this redemptive-principles ideology? In *Heart of Darkness*, Joseph Conrad suggests that it can sometimes justify genocide. It is worth noting that Conrad makes an important appearance in *The Dream of the Celt*. Indeed, Vargas Llosa's Conrad was so influenced by Casement that he says the following:

> "You should have appeared as co-author of that book, Casement," he declared, patting him on the shoulder. "I never would have written it without your help. You removed the scales from my eyes. About Africa, about the Congo Free State. And about the human beast."
>
> (DC 52)

One of the narrators of *Heart of Darkness* is Marlow, and he distinguishes the Roman conquest of the earth from then-contemporary colonization on the basis of a redeeming idea. Both events are brutal, but one can be justified while the other cannot because a redemptive principle converts the horrific action into something necessary, noble, and sublime:

> The conquest of the earth, which mostly means the taking it away from those who have a different complexion or slightly flatter noses than ourselves, is not a

> pretty thing when you look into it too much. What redeems it is the idea only. An idea at the back of it; not a sentimental pretence but an idea; and an unselfish belief in the idea—something you can set up, and bow down before, and offer a sacrifice to…[35]

Significant in this passage is the concluding ellipsis. In the name of the redeeming idea (referred to as "redeeming principles" in *The Dream of the Celt*), colonizers can do anything, because the governing principle is so magnificent that it can redeem all atrocities, no matter how extreme. The escalating series of terms after the reference to the "unselfish belief in the idea" testifies to the extent to which colonizers can go in the name of the "noble cause."[36] They can set up something for it, they can bow down to this idea as they would to a god, and they can even offer a sacrifice to the idea. But what makes the passage so chilling is the unspecified reality implicit in the ellipsis. Given the increasing intensity of the litany of terms, the ellipsis has to be something even more than a sacrifice, and since Kurtz will make a plea for genocide ("Exterminate all the brutes!")[37] at the end of his manifesto celebrating the ennobling glories of colonialism, and since Marlow affirms Kurtz and his mission as "a moral victory" ("It was an affirmation, a moral victory paid for by innumerable defeats, by abominable terrors, by abominable satisfactions. But it was a victory! That is why I have remained loyal to Kurtz to the last"),[38] it is not unreasonable to suggest that the redeeming-idea principle can justify the extermination of indigenous populations.[39] And it is worth noting that Vargas Llosa told me in an interview the he is "a great admirer of Joseph Conrad," who "has had a great influence on my writing."[40]

This strategic allusion to Conrad is epistemologically significant because the nobility of the redeeming idea can transmute a seemingly barbaric atrocity into something unworthy of notice, thus blinding colonizers to the sufferings of the natives they have come to serve and save. Casement acknowledges this epistemological reality when he reflects on the number of colonizers who could feel compassion for the colonized:

> How many of the colonizers—businessmen, soldiers, functionaries, adventurers—had a minimum of respect for the native and considered them brothers or, at least, human beings? Five percent? One in a hundred? The truth, the truth was that in the years he had spent here he could count on one hand the number of Europeans who did not treat the blacks like soulless beasts whom they could deceive, exploit, whip, even kill, without the slightest remorse.
>
> (DC 44)

Multiple factors, including a yearning for wealth and a view of the native as a "soulless beast," dictate how a colonizer comes to know and register what he sees, but it is the intensity of the redeeming idea that determines the extent to which colonizers can commit atrocities with emotional, psychological, and political impunity. The more semiotic and cultural legitimization the redeeming idea has and the more intensely it is internalized, the more capable are colonizers of perpetrating atrocities without seeing or experiencing them as crimes against humanity. For Vargas Llosa, the redeeming-idea epistemology is extremely dangerous because it can totally blind perpetrators to some of the most horrific acts of barbarism.

As a symbol, what makes Casement so rich for writers is his dual nature. He started his career as a young British colonizer, but after a long and tortuous evolution, he became an Irish anti-colonial fighter, who discovered that he was a colonized subject even when he was a colonizer. Vargas Llosa places Casement's "Irish" epiphany in 1903, just after he completed his journey through the Congo in order to document Belgian atrocities. Reflecting nostalgically on the Ireland of his youth gives Casement some momentary relief from the trauma he experienced for having witnessed unspeakable crimes against the natives. But it is through these reflections that Casement draws a logical connection between Ireland and the Congo:

> Wasn't Ireland a colony too, like the Congo? Though for so many years he had insisted on not accepting a truth that his father and so many Ulster Irishmen like him rejected with blind indignation. Why would what was bad for the Congo be good for Ireland? Hadn't the English invaded Ireland? Hadn't they incorporated it into the Empire by force, not consulting those who had been invaded and occupied, just as the Belgians did with the Congolese? Over time the violence had eased, but Ireland was still a colony whose sovereignty disappeared because of a stronger neighbor. It was a reality that many Irish refused to see.
>
> (DC 80–1)

Only by seeing the structural similarities between Ireland and the Congo can Casement finally understand and appreciate the nature of England's crimes against Ireland and the reality of Irish subjugation under the English. In short, going to Africa in order to learn about the Congo enabled Casement to discover Ireland for the first time. Such is the epistemological value of transnational thinking.

What empowers Casement to finally see what he, his family, and the Irish more generally could not is his ability to make important epistemological distinctions. For instance, when Casement visits the African village of Walla to get information about atrocities committed there, the inhabitants complain about the Belgians' unrealistic work quotas. It is simply not possible to do and produce all that the Belgians expect. This response leads Casement to wonder: "Here too, in Walla, he was surprised that none of those poor creatures complained about the main thing: With what right had the foreigners come to invade, exploit, and mistreat them? They took into consideration only the immediate problem: the quotas" (DC 71). The Congolese realize that the Belgians are behaving in an unjust manner, but they cannot think beyond the immediate injustice to the foundational and originary crime, which is the invasion of their land, the subjugation of their people, and the divestment of their autonomy and rights.

When Casement confronts colonizers, he discovers that they, too, suffer from the same epistemological limitations. After telling a captain about the atrocities in Walla, the military man gives Casement an Adolf-Eichmann-like response. He is merely fulfilling orders. Only those in a position of policy-making leadership can alter or establish an official system dictating human behavior: "Changing this system is not the task of the military but of judges and politicians. Of the Supreme Government" (DC 73). Such an approach, premised on what Hannah Arendt refers to as a banality-of-evil mentality, turns humans into mindless automatons, robot-like figures that can only do what they are programmed to do. Doing something like programming is beyond their ken, ability, and authority.

All of these experiences occur in the first section of the novel, which is titled The Congo. Section two is called Amazonia, while the last section is dubbed Ireland. This is significant because the novel strategically charts the evolution of Casement's character in order to clarify how he eventually came to see Ireland as structurally similar to the Congo and the Amazon, thereby clarifying a major shift in Casement's thinking and approach to Ireland. At the end of the Congo section, when Casement finally realizes that Ireland is like the Congo insofar as it is a colonial possession deprived of autonomy and sovereignty, he starts formulating strategies for Irish emancipation, which would include boycotting "British products," refusing "to pay taxes," replacing "British sports such as cricket and soccer with national sports, and literature and the theater as well" (DC 110). Such an approach would have a desired effect, for as Casement concludes: "In this way, peacefully, Ireland would break free of colonial subjugation" (DC 110).

But Casement's experiences in the Amazon force him to change his view. Instead of taking a gradual, methodical, nonviolent approach to Irish independence, Casement realizes, based on what he witnesses in the Amazon, that the Irish situation is urgent and dire, so there is a call-to-arms tone in his thinking. Vargas Llosa has Casement arrive at his new view while he is making his way through the Amazon jungle:

> We Irish are like the Huitotos, the Boras, the Andoques, and the Muinanes of Putumayo. Colonized, exploited, and condemned to be that way forever if we continue trusting in British laws, institutions, and governments to attain our freedom. They will never give it to us. Why should the Empire that colonized us do that unless it felt an irresistible pressure that obliged it to do so? That pressure can come only from weapons.
>
> (DC 186)

The Amazon transformed Casement from a nonviolent anti-colonialist into an aggressive fighter against colonialism who supports a violent overthrow of colonial power.

What enabled this conversion was an understanding and awareness of the stages of colonial domination and subjugation. When Casement initially went to the Congo in 1884, he was part of the first stage of colonial domination, in which colonizers establish contact with indigenous populations and build roads for easy and ready transportation of colonizers, soldiers, weapons, and goods. To make this possible, colonizers force natives to do the grunt work, and when they resist or oppose, violence and death are used to enforce communal submission. Having been a part of Stanley's 1884 team of explorers and Leopold's installation of official colonial rule in 1885, Casement witnessed the horrible realities of the first stage of colonial domination.

The second stage is different because the colonial outposts have already been established, so newly arrived colonizers step into roles that have been clearly defined. Casement goes to the Amazon in 1910 to investigate atrocities in the rubber industry, which was established in 1893. Those seventeen years of colonial domination had a substantial impact on the psychology of the colonizers. Here is how Vargas Llosa's Casement describes the second stage to himself as he is preparing his official report: "Impunity and absolute power had developed in these individuals sadistic tendencies that could be manifested freely here against natives deprived of all rights" (DC 183). Taking their cue from previous colonizers, the new recruits step into a world of naturalized sadism. Therefore, it should come as no surprise that "three-fourths of the indigenous population" had already been "annihilated" (DC 193), and the remaining subjects were living in such a state of emotional and psychological defeat that they had lost their humanity. Observing the surviving natives in this second stage leads Casement to reflect on the degree to which the Irish are like the colonized people in the Amazon: "*We should not permit colonization to castrate the spirit of the Irish as it has castrated the spirit of the Amazonian Indians. We must act now, once and for all, before it is too late and we turn into automatons*" (DC 192). No longer capable of autonomous thinking or action, the indigenous populations have become unwitting and *de facto* slaves. Putting aside for the moment the glaring difference in the amount of time the regions were living under colonial subjugation (seventeen years in the Amazon, while centuries in Ireland), Casement's realization that what the Amazonians are experiencing could be the fate of the Irish explains why he believes that Irish emancipation is an urgent necessity. Delaying or postponing action could have catastrophic effects on the Irish interior life and therewith the possibility of an Irish nation.

Given all the specific details Vargas Llosa provides readers about Casement's experiences in the Congo and the Amazon, it could be easy to treat *The Dream of the Celt* as a form of biography. But it is important to keep in mind the distinctive kind of truth biographical novelists give readers. Biographers are committed to giving readers an actual life with as much precision and accuracy as possible, so embellishing the truth, fabricating stories, or altering established facts would not be permissible. As a fiction writer, Vargas Llosa is less interested in biographical facts than he is in using the life of his protagonist in order to symbolically represent a trans-historical and transnational truth about what it means to be human. He was very clear about this in his interview with me. According to the Peruvian writer, "a good novel is always full of lies, inventions, fantasies, all distortions of real facts." The novelist does this for three reasons: (1) to "make people much more conscious" of "brutal inequalities," (2) to give readers "a vivid experience of what happened, of what is happening, or what will happen," and (3) to empower people to challenge and even "destroy the status quo." One of the more distinctly human "truths" that Varga Llosa explores in *The Dream of the Celt* is the way most people come to "illusively" believe that the role scripted for them is "part of their nature." For instance, the young Casement was trained and conditioned to believe that, because Ireland is a legitimate possession of the British Empire, Casement is, therefore, British. But it is during his stint in the Congo that Casement rejects Britain's legal right to Ireland, and it is during his time in the Amazon that he starts to cast off his British identity and to construct himself as an "Irishman." A former overseer of a station refers to Casement as an Englishman, but Casement immediately corrects him: "I'm not English, I'm Irish" (DC 232). A former judge does the same, and Casement has an almost identical response: "I'm not an Englishman, I'm Irish" (DC 248). The English would have the Irish believe that the Irish are British, albeit inferior to the pure and true blooded Englishman, which is why the Sheriff who oversees Casement's pre-execution imprisonment condemns the Irishman "for being a traitor to your country" (DC 15). But Casement rejects the Sheriff's view, because, as he says, "my country is Ireland" (DC 15). As a loyal Brit, the Sheriff replies: "Ireland is British" (DC 16). One view holds that Ireland is a legitimate possession of Britain, thus making the Irish British. But the other view holds that, because Ireland has been unjustly colonized, the Irish are separate and distinct from the British. Casement was born and raised to believe in colonialism and, therefore, to be British, but eventually he rejects British colonialism and therewith his British identity. After which, he exclusively claims his Irish identity.

While Casement effectively rejects his British identity and begins to adopt an Irish one, he is less effective when it comes to his sexual identity. This failure is, in part, what makes Casement such a poignant and human figure. Caught in the fog of the day to day, to use Duffy's phrasing, Casement is remarkable because he was able to see and expose so many super-subtle forms of political oppression, but he also failed in some significant ways, and Vargas Llosa intelligently pictures Casement's limitations. Given his "Puritan upbringing," Casement adopted "the rigidly traditional and conservative customs of his paternal and maternal families," so he considered "same sex" attraction "an abominable aberration, rightly condemned by law and religion as a crime and a sin without justification or extenuating circumstances" (DT 219–20). But in Africa, where Puritan law did not dominate and where there was an appreciation for the body and the sensuous, the incorrigible Irishman experimented with an alternative sexuality. Yet, when Casement acts on his homosexual desire, he feels shame immediately afterward and promises "himself, for the sake of his honor, the memory of his mother, his religion, that it would not be repeated" (DT 221). The lesson: casting off a prefabricated identity is much easier than constructing a new one, and this is the central struggle and challenge at the core of the biographical novel.

Given the biographical novel's focus on the construction of something new for the unknowable and indefinable future, radical uncertainty is inevitable. Should Ireland work with England to establish home rule, which would result in Ireland maintaining a tight connection with England? Or, should

Ireland fight for national independence, which would entail a decisive break with England? And how should Ireland achieve its goal of Irish autonomy? Should its people serve the British Empire in the First World War with the hope that England would eventually reward the Irish by granting them home rule? Or, should Ireland align itself with England's enemy, Germany, in order to weaken England so that Ireland could win independence when England is at its weakest and most vulnerable? Casement chooses to align himself with Germany and to instigate a violent rebellion, but he is never certain that what he is doing is right. Many Irish soldiers who fought on the British side during the First World War were taken as prisoners by the Germans, and Casement sought to make them into a small army to fight against the British for Irish independence. But most of the imprisoned soldiers rejected Casement and his plan with extreme prejudice. Also, some of Casement's closest friends abhorred the idea of the Irish cooperating with the Germans, which leads casement to ask a Catholic priest: "Do you think that what I'm doing is the right thing or am I mistaken" (DC 324). Casement's rejection of England and British colonialism is unambiguous. But what a post-British Irish identity could and should be and how one can construct such an identity and country are not at all clear to him.

And in stark contrast to Sebald, who suggests that Casement's homosexual perspective was both an epistemological aid and a blessing, Vargas Llosa shows how queerness is, at times, a liability that significantly thwarts Casement's ability to see clearly, thus disrupting the construction of a new Irish identity and nation. On two separate occasions Vargas Llosa's Casement experiences "profound sadness" (DC 222) because he realizes that he will never experience the loving intimacy he witnesses in a "stable [heterosexual] relationship" (DC 222) and that "he would die without having tasted that warm intimacy, a wife with whom to discuss the day's events and plan the future" (DC 236). But then Casement meets Eivind Adler Christensen, a young and beautiful man. The response of Vargas Llosa's Casement is telling:

> With him [Eivind] a tide of youth, of hope, and—the word made him blush—of love had entered his life. It hadn't happened to him before. He'd had sporadic street adventures with people whose names, if they were their names and not mere nicknames, he forgot almost immediately.
>
> (DC 320)

Casement finally experiences same-sex romance, but there is a catch. Eivind is a spy, and the British use him to track Casement's movements, to monitor the anti-British activity of him and his associates, and eventually to squash the German effort to arm Irish rebels. What makes Casement so susceptible and vulnerable was his desperation for the prohibited and criminal love between men. Casement's Irish comrades in the United States, his military co-conspirator, and the Germans caution the Irish revolutionary that Eivind is a spy, but instead of heeding their warnings, Casement dismisses them as biased and unsubstantiated accusations. The problem, to reiterate what Casement says early in the novel, is this: "*I wasn't aware because I didn't want to be aware*" (DC 25). The consequences of Casement's epistemological failings are deadly. The German shipment of arms to Ireland for the Easter Rising must be sunk in order to avoid detection, thus depriving the rebels of the necessary weapons to successfully wage their rebellion, and Casement is captured and eventually executed.

By pointing out Casement's failure to construct a new way of seeing and being, it would seem that I have made the case against the biographical novel. But Vargas Llosa's extensive references to the nature and power of a person as a catalyzing symbol for future transformations suggests otherwise. In the Amazonia section, Casement sees a young boy swimming naked in a river, which leads him to think of his friend Herbert Ward, with whom he worked in the Congo and who became a sculptor. Casement believes that Ward "could make a beautiful sculpture of this adolescent," one that would be "the symbol of Amazonian man stripped of his land, his body, and his beauty by the rubber barons" (DC 196). This work of art would not just depict the boy's beauty. It would use the boy to represent a much larger political and economic reality in relation to the indigenous population. In this instance, the symbol would function exactly as it should according to Lukács, which is to say that it would accurately represent a historical reality in a specific time and place.

But as the novel progresses, Casement comes to think about the symbol in a much different way. In a conversation about the relationship between history and symbols, Stopford Green says that "history is made of symbols" (DC 276). Within this framework, even though the Easter Rising seemingly failed because the leaders were killed and the Irish were still under British rule, the lost lives have been converted into a mobilizing symbol. In short, the British executions of the leaders "have baptized this symbol with blood, giving it a halo of heroism and martyrdom" (DC 276). Late in the novel, in a conversation with a Catholic priest, Casement expresses his view that the death of the Easter-Rising leaders "can create a symbol that will move all the energies of the Irish" (DC 344). The meaning of this symbol is not in what it represents, related primarily to the cognitive act of understanding. Rather, the meaning is in what the life-converted-into-a-symbol will generate, which, in this case, will be a distinct Irish identity and then an Irish nation.

In effect, the leaders of the Easter Rising (Joseph Plunkett, Patrick Pearse, and James Connolly), whom Vargas Llosa mentions throughout the novel, symbolically set into motion what would become a successful but incomplete rebellion. Missing from the story of the battle for dignity, freedom, and rights was the homosexual. In Africa, Casement discovered that what the Belgians did and continue to do to the Congolese is what the English have done and are doing to the Irish. When Ward challenges the logic and reality of drawing such a comparison, Casement retorts: "The methods of colonization in Europe are more refined, Herbert, but no less cruel" (305). The English may not be chopping off Irish hands, the quintessential symbol of depriving a people of agency, but there are other, more sophisticated and subtle forms of divesting a people of autonomy, and for Casement, the British have perfected the art of enslaving people without their conscious awareness. Casement exposed the overt strategies of colonization used against the Congolese and the Amazonians as well as the subtle strategies used against the Irish, but he failed to understand, register, and appreciate that what has been done to the Irish is also being done to homosexuals like himself. Thus, the homosexual would continue to be denied the rights and freedoms for which Irish rebels fought. Until Casement is officially included as one of the freedom fighters of the Easter Rising, until he is acknowledged and accepted within this liberationist pantheon as a homosexual, and until Ireland secures full-fledged liberty for gays, the Easter Rising will not have realized what it set out to do. In short, the Easter-Rising symbology, which must include Casement, is an ongoing event, and Casement, as a homosexual, has now become the best and most suitable symbol for the invention of a new, free, and just "Ireland."

Seeing and understanding Casement as a symbol that will move all the energies of the "Irish" toward a comprehensive concept and experience of freedom poses a serious challenge to the way we define freedom. One of the key ideas of *The Dream of the Celt* is the power of transnational thinking and perceiving. By going to the Congo and the Amazon, Casement was finally able to see what the British were doing to the Irish and thus able to expose the subtle forms of enslavement that the Irish experienced. Living in the day to day, however, Casement failed to see how similar structures were used to oppress homosexuals. But Vargas Llosa can see what Casement could not, which is why the Peruvian novelist converted Casement into the most suitable symbol of political freedom. Within the Vargas Llosa framework, the aesthetic goal is not to illustrate how Irish rebels redefined the Irish as autonomous beings that should enjoy the same political rights as the English. More fundamentally, the novel shows how the very idea of defining the human is part of the problem for realizing a socially just approach to political freedom. This is the case for two separate reasons. Were the English to define the Irish, even if it were as a free and equal being, the incorrigible Irish would ask: Why do the English rather than the Irish have the official political right to define the Irish? But there is an even more fundamental question at the core of the novel: Is there something problematic and even objectionable to the act and project of defining in an absolute or totalizing manner a person or a people? Notice how Vargas Llosa, when discussing the Irishman's sexuality, celebrates in the epilogue the fact that it is impossible to define Casement: "It's not a bad thing that a climate of uncertainty hovers over Roger Casement as proof that it is impossible to know definitively a human being, a totality that always slips through the theoretical and rational nets that try to capture it" (DC 355). In the world of the historical novel, authors use the "theoretical and rational nets" to define and thereby entrap ("nets") the human, but in the world of the biographical novel, authors emphasize the degree to which the human evades the entrapping nets of theory and reason, thus making the act of defining the human in an absolute way epistemologically problematic at best and politically dangerous at worst.

Thematically, this idea has major significance in relation to Casement, who succeeds in remarkable ways in the Congo and the Amazon, but fails in equally remarkable ways in Germany and with regard to his homosexuality. If Vargas Llosa, by his own admission, considers Casement a heroic, anti-colonial fighter, why would he conclude the novel by underscoring so many ways in which his protagonist failed? The answer has something to do with the unique nature of the biographical novel. While biographical novelists reject the overarching systems that historical novelists use in order to define the forces that shape and determine a representative protagonist, it does not logically follow that biographical novelists totally reject truth systems. Recognizing that he is inscribed within cultural and political systems, Casement articulates a crucial idea about the human condition: "people lived inside a system in which it was practically impossible to distinguish falsehood from truth, reality from a swindle" (DC 238). Some people, like Casement, can evade determinism and imagine into being a new reality, but this ability is provisional and limited at best. In other words, even one of the most extraordinary human beings fails miserably at times. But in his successes and failures, Casement gives readers what Montero refers to as an "existential map" for becoming an autonomous being. Through the art of transnational thinking and perceiving, one can expose the limitations within one's own system of thought and can see normalized realities through a totally new lens. This makes the construction of a new, alternative reality possible. But whatever new "reality" we create will be limited, subject to a subsequent deconstruction and reconstruction, because of the inevitable epistemological blind spots and limitations that come with being human.

And that really is the core of the biographical novel. This art form is not trying to give readers reliable biographical or historical truth. It pictures biographical figures struggling to identify, understand, and expose the debilitating and destructive truth systems of their time as they seek to install a new, more socially just truth system. What the reader gets, therefore, is not the new truth or system, but a human life that has activated a way of being that evades determinism to some degree and constructs something original and new. Therein lies one of the primary appeals of the biographical novel.

IV

In his mind his resistance of injustice was wholly tied up in his Irishness.[41]

To clarify and highlight the nature and extent of human agency, Murray juxtaposes Ward, the Englishman, and Casement, the Irishman, in her novel *Valiant Gentlemen*. The two men go to the Congo, and soon they begin to hate both the Belgians and the English for perpetrating a brutal system of economic and political enslavement throughout Africa. But over time, the two develop very different views of their national identity, and these divergent perspectives ultimately doom their friendship. More than anything else, what divides the two is the cultivation and refinement of a critical capacity that makes human agency possible. Ward fails to develop the ability to think in critical ways about what he experiences, which raises some questions about Vargas Llosa's positive view of transnational thinking. Ward, like Casement, lives in multiple countries, but instead of leading him to see more deeply and clearly and thus to develop the ability to create something new, he becomes increasingly more uncritical, jingoistic, and vapid.

Since early in the novel Ward says that he hates England and the English hate him ("'I hate England,' Ward responds, 'and England hates me'"),[42] it would seem that Murray would make him into a complicated, self-reflective character. But in a key moment Ward aligns himself with Stanley for the famous Emin Pasha Relief Expedition, and from this point forward, Ward becomes increasingly more of a mindless servant of English ideology. Before Ward decides to become a part of the Expedition, Casement shares with his friend his view of Stanley, a "charlatan" who has become "the best expression of an intrepid Englishman" (VG 24). Casement was initially seduced by Stanley, but after working with him he comes to despise the man and all he represents. So when Ward, knowing Casement's views and what Casement experienced with the man, decides to follow and assist Stanley, this signals a momentous turn on Ward's part away from a potential life of critical reflection to a life of mindless nationalism. Murray spotlights this dimension of Ward's character throughout the novel. Described as "more of an adolescent than a man" (VG 29), the post–Stanley Ward "thinks that Englishness is a religion and as such is maintained by unquestioning faith" (VG 167). The irony, of course, is that "Herbert, who thinks he's utterly English, has no real idea of what being English entails" (VG 169).

The problem with Ward is not so much his nationalism as it is his epistemological limitations, which make him susceptible to becoming an empty-headed nationalist. Ward is governed more by emotion than intellect. This is seen most clearly by his treatment of an African woman who serves as his concubine while in the Congo. In a self-rationalizing moment, Ward wonders if he will be able to slip out of this role of having a concubine after he leaves Africa. To indicate the kind of man Ward is at this point, the narrator describes Ward as "a slippery creature, a man who assembles his moral code around his desires" (VG 50). It is not the firm convictions of an intelligently formulated system of thought that determine his behavior. Rather, he acts on the impulses of his immediate desires, and then retroactively constructs a "moral code" to justify his actions. Thus, he will be able to leave Africa "with whatever appetites he wishes to sate," and because there are so few people who can monitor or record what he has done, no one is "to know" (VG 50).

In addition to being governed more by emotion than thought, Ward lacks basic knowledge, which leads him to make many uninformed and misinformed claims. This is especially notable when he discusses Ireland. For instance, while on a lecture tour in Ireland, Ward has a conversation about the country with an older resident in Belfast, but the Englishman struggles to understand what is being said because of his limited knowledge: "the more Ward tries to follow the chain of conversation, the more he realizes that he doesn't understand the history of Ireland, nor even the present. He doesn't know anything about Parnell beyond Kitty O'Shea" (VG 178–9). Yet, despite his ignorance, especially about Ireland, Ward feels confident in his assessment of the Irish. Here are Ward's dismissive thoughts about Casement's pro-Irish politics: "Ward, who manages matchless sympathy for the natives of the Congo, has nothing but derision for the Irish, or rather Irishness, which he sees as some degraded form of Englishness" (VG 286). Through extensive reflection and considerable knowledge about the political and economic situation of Ireland in relation to England, Vargas Llosa's Casement realizes how Ireland is similar to the Congo. Murray's Ward, with almost no knowledge of Ireland, dismisses such a comparison as ludicrous, as he simultaneously discloses his own anti-Irish prejudices in the process.

With minimal intellectual curiosity and an impulsive nature, Ward is a figure that lacks the ability for autonomy. Murray perfectly captures this dimension of Ward's character when he first meets his wife Sarita. They are sailing on a ship, and when they meet, Sarita asks Ward what he does. This question confuses Ward, until his friend Edward Glave tells Sarita that "Ward is a great artist" (VG 80). Happy with this answer, Ward adopts a new identity: "Just like that, Ward had been reinvented" (VG 81). The syntax of character here is instructive. Ward does not reinvent himself; he is too passive and confused to generate an identity of and on his own. Sarita prompts him to declare an identity, and Glave provides him with one, which is why he has been reinvented rather than having reinvented himself.

The irony, of course, is that the identity he has been given is in irreconcilable conflict with his character. An artist fashions and creates, but Ward, lacking the ability for autonomy, is fashioned and created by his immediate environment. Murray's narrator highlights Ward's failings by linking him with Glave, who also believes himself to be an artist: "Glave's drawing is the equivalent of Ward's writing, capable of communication but not justified by some larger aesthetic truth" (VG 89). Simple communication is all these two "artists" can do. The ability to originate a compelling, comprehensive, and coherent vision of life and the world is beyond their capacity.

One of Ward's most significant epistemological limitations is his inability to formulate a coherent, overarching system of thought, something that is central in large and complicated artworks like a novel. While many quality novels consist of a wide array of characters and scenes, what makes such works both gratifying and challenging is the overarching system of thought that unifies all of the seemingly disconnected parts. Late in *Valiant Gentlemen*, as his life and marriage are falling apart, Ward notices his wife reading a book, which leads him to reflect on his own "gathering of little stories." To expose one of Ward's most flagrant epistemological weaknesses, Murray references the kind of intellectual labor that is necessary for reading a novel: "He was never much of one for reading novels and suspects that this has compromised his ability to create a narrative arc out of so much disparate, anecdotal material" (VG 450). Needed is a complex understanding and appreciation of the interaction between disparate individual anecdotes and a comprehensive vision, but this is an intellectual ability that Ward has failed to cultivate.

Casement is very different from Ward, which is why he has become a dominant and suitable subject of the biographical novel. In Kiberd's *Inventing Ireland*, a writer like James Joyce is of crucial importance because he examines how the artist replaces the priest in order to forge in the smithy of his/her soul the uncreated conscience of his/her race. In short, prominent writers played a crucial role for Kiberd in the invention of what would eventually become an independent and autonomous Ireland. Contemporary biographical novelists gravitate toward someone like Casement not only because they see something in his life rather than his writings that contributed significantly to the invention of an independent and autonomous Ireland but also because his life can continue to be used to contribute to the making of an independent and autonomous person and nation in the present.

In his interview about *The Danish Girl*, which I discussed in chapter one, Ebershoff gives us useful ways to think about how protagonists in the biographical novel function and why authors are drawn to figures like Casement. His Einar was born into an identity that felt false to him. Through critical reflection and heroic effort, he rejected his masculine identity and transitioned into a female one, and that identity was confirmed through surgery. The transformation from male to female led to a radical shift in Lili's life. Before the surgery, Einar was an artist, but since Lili considers art a man's profession, she rejects the artist identity after her sex confirmation surgery. But Ebershoff disagrees. Instead of saying that Lili rejects the role of being the artist, which is what the actual Lili says in her posthumously published memoir *Man into Woman* as well as in *The Danish Girl*, Ebershoff suggests that Lili becomes an artist of her self and the human more generally. Within this framework, Lili is not trying to create a great painting, as he did when she was a man. She is fashioning into being a new type of human:

> I believe that she [Lili] was a great artist, even after she transitioned, and her greatest creation was herself. Artists are visionaries; they see something that does not yet exist. They can bring into creation something that is not yet there. And in many ways this is what Lili is doing: she is envisioning her future self, she is seeing a version of herself that is not yet there, and she is creating it. And this is perhaps greater and more significant than any painting she could have done or did do when she lived as Einar.[43]

Through Lili, Ebershoff gives readers an "existential map" of the artistic process of imagining a new self into being. What makes Lili so significant, therefore, is not the artworks she did when she was Einar. It is the artwork she makes of her own life. The same applies to Casement. Vargas Llosa and Murray do not make Casement the protagonist of their biographical novels because he produced great artworks. They make him the protagonist because his life was a great work of art, one that can provide us with an "existential map" for agential living in the present.

To emphasize Casement's ability to create himself, Murray contrasts the Englishman and the Irishman early in the novel. Ward draws, while Casement writes poetry, and here is how Casement characterizes the difference between the two men: "He thinks of Ward's drawings, all Africans, and his poems, all Irish history. Is this what makes them different, that Ward constructs himself out of his own personal history, while Casement's personality demands a further reach?" (VG 16). Since Ward and Casement are in the Congo at this time, transnational experience is clearly not sufficient for enabling a person to invent something new and original. As Casement suggests, Ward is nothing more than the logical product of "his own personal history," which basically consists of his determining environment. Casement is different because he has a much broader reach than Ward.

One of the key traits that makes Casement unlike Ward is his tendency and ability to challenge society's established roles. While Ward non-intentionally adopts his culture's prefabricated roles ("Ward smiles, but he's aware that he's stepped into this new life—lecturer, Boston—by accident" [VG 108]), Casement endlessly questions society's seemingly legitimized roles. As Glave says to Casement: "You have acquired a reputation for lacking respect for authority." In response, Casement takes Glave's idea one step further by questioning the definition of authority: "That might be true," says Casement, "although it all depends on your definition of 'authority' " (VG 53). As in *The Dream of the Celt*, Casement is a man who probes and interrogates not so much the surface but the foundation of thought, which leads him to ask who defines reality, who has the power to do so, and why the established version should be accepted, questions that Ward never entertains.

What also divides the two men is intellectual curiosity. Both initially have limited knowledge about Ireland, but only Casement corrects this flaw. After Murray's Casement meets Alice Stopford Green, he begins to study the history of Ireland in earnest: "She has renewed Casement's interest in the Irish language and in the heathen origins of the true Ireland, before Cromwell, before Patrick" (VG 269). Such historical knowledge Ward clearly lacks. For instance, when discussing the messiness of the Boer War, Ward admonishes Casement to side with the victors: "Stand with the winners. Who would you rather be, Napoleon or the Duke of Wellington," "who was English" (VG 245). But Casement corrects Ward by noting that Wellington "was Irish" (VG 246). The jingoist retorts: "But his troops were English" (VG 246). Again, Casement corrects his friend: "The significant troops in that engagement were Irish too" (VG 246). Left with no rejoinder, Ward concludes the conversation by making a plea for alcohol: "Well, I'm English," says Ward. "And I'm ordering another round" (VG 246).

Intellectual curiosity, transnational experience and thinking, a study of history, and a complex understanding of the relationship between the individual anecdote and a comprehensive vision—these are the necessary prerequisites for formulating a probing, insightful, and comprehensive assessment of the political situation of the modern world, and these are the very qualities that enable Casement to expose the criminality of English colonialism. To contribute to a rebellion in his country, Casement agrees to work with the German military. In a conversation with a German journalist, Casement begins to articulate a coherent critique of England's treatment of Ireland. As an Irishman under English rule, Casement has come to "understand the subtle, dehumanizing way a conqueror justified his actions." Specifically, Casement "had sat through dinners listening to Englishmen joke about their 'Irishness' as a romantic, poetic, irrational thing—what made men sing when drunk" (VG 350). Irishness is in quotation marks in order to underscore that this is the English fantasy of "Irishness," a fact that the novel supports in and through Ward's distorted view of the Irish.

Casement's realization of the way the English have constructed the Irish leads him to make a significant discovery. The English have used the Irish as a template for justifying its political domination and oppression of many other countries. After noting how the English characterize the Irish as irrational, Casement draws the following conclusion: "this 'irrational' and therefore savage Irish ethos was used to shore up the sense of English civility and reason, which is what allowed the English to unleash their criminal abuse across the globe and persuade themselves that all their victims were somehow raised up in the process" (VG 350). Taking narrative control of the colonial other, narrativizing that other as "irrational," and using that "irrational" definition to counter-construct themselves as reasonable and civilized are the most effective strategies the English use to mobilize their subjects to conquer other nations and to blind the colonial perpetrators from the fact that they are committing crimes against others. In essence, Casement has been developing since his early days in the Congo the necessary system of knowledge and epistemological skills to see how and why the oppressed accept their condition of oppression and how the colonial perpetrators can effectively wield criminal and oppressive power.

But simply rejecting the English is not sufficient. As an artist of life, what Casement must also do is to seize control of personal and national autonomy, and this is what he intends to accomplish with his Easter-Rising co-conspirators. Having developed the epistemological ability to see, the Irish rebels are now ready to invent Ireland. But what will enable Casement and his fellow rebels to achieve their politico-aesthetic goal? Murray's Casement formulates an answer when Joseph Plunkett is with him in Germany. After briefly thinking about Plunkett's ability to write an inspiring document, Casement turns his attention to the powerful address of Patrick Pearse at the burial of O'Donovan Rossa, an Irish Fenian leader and member of the Irish Republican Brotherhood. Here is how Murray's Casement describes that experience:

> There, by the old Fenian's graveside, the identity of Ireland had suddenly made sense. You could see it emerge from the primordial gel and stand, fully formed, in your mind. One would have to be insensible not to join this God-ordained war against oppression.
>
> (VG 455)

But more important than this simple description is the conclusion Casement draws about the nature of inventing Ireland on the basis of this experience: "Apparently, what Ireland needed was some pretty words on a bit of paper and a body for gravity, and suddenly she was an intelligible nation" (VG 455). On the surface, this passage seems to be referring to Pearse and Rossa—Pearse's address contains the "pretty words" about Rossa's corpse, which is the "body for gravity." The logic of the passage goes something like this: to inspire people to seek and activate individual and national autonomy, needed is a hero who has given his/her life to the nation and the cause and an inspiring, sense-making document.

Casement's ability to link the O'Donovan anecdote to an overarching narrative arc testifies to the development of his intellectual capacity. But the abstract conclusion that Casement draws about Rossa can also apply to him as well. Casement commits his life to the cause of an autonomous Ireland, and both *The Dream of the Celt* and *Valiant Gentlemen*, which conclude with Casement's death (the "body for gravity"), contain "pretty words" celebrating Casement's commitment to the invention of a free and autonomous self and nation. The implication is that Casement, through his death, is a figure that inspires us today to bring about a free and autonomous Ireland. But if this reading is correct, how can it make sense, given that Ireland was already an independent country in 2010, when *The Dream of the Celt* was first published, or in 2016, when *Valiant Gentlemen* was first published? The answer has something to do with the much more complicated understanding of human and national autonomy and agency that is found in the biographical novel. The historical novel came to fruition at a time when writers and thinkers were emphasizing the degree to which the material conditions of being shaped and determined the human psyche and identity. In response, the biographical novel came into being in order to underscore the power and ability of the human to shape and determine the self and the environment. Yet, biographical novelists are not so naïve as to think that the environment does not impact the human or that humans can experience total agency or full autonomy. What biographical novelists foreground, therefore, is that complicated struggle to achieve some degree of agency in the midst of overwhelming determinative forces.

There is a reason for this. With the phenomenological turn, the transvaluation of all values became a dominant experience. So in the nineteenth century, slavery flipped from being good to bad, and by the late nineteenth and the early twentieth centuries, homosexuality and colonialism were in the process of undergoing a major transformation—Oscar Wilde's 1889 short story "The Portrait of Mr. W.H." subtly documents this metamorphosis in relation to homosexuality, while Pauline Hopkins's 1900 short story "Talma Gordon" intelligently pictures this transformation in relation to colonialism. Thus, values, instead of being immutable ideals that have been plucked out of some heaven of Ideas, are provisional conceptual "realities," depending in large measure on the position of the knowing subject and the communal structures of legitimization. This is one of the key ideas at the core of *The Dream of the Celt*, *Valiant Gentlemen*, and the biographical novel more generally. The shift from the seemingly objective realities of the external world to the surreal "realities" of the subjective world necessitated a new aesthetic, one that focused more on evolving and contingent orientations than on reliable ontological Truths. In an essay aptly titled "A Novel Truth about Casement's 'Irish' Identity," Murray sheds considerable light on her aesthetic method and approach as a biographical novelist.

Murray notes that, rather than trying to give readers an accurate representation of Casement, her objective is to "chronicle what he saw."[44] But this decision to inhabit an interior is particularly challenging when it comes to a figure like Casement, because he has different identities depending on his spatial location. As the narrator says: "In Africa, he is one of the English, but not in England. Places do that—throw you into some sort of relief against themselves. In Ireland he is both Northern Irish and Protestant" (VG 191). Time also has a significant impact. When Casement was a young man, there was no contradiction for him between being British and Irish, but as he became increasingly critical of British colonialism and embraced his Irish heritage, being simultaneously British and Irish became a contradiction in terms.

The issue of identity becomes particularly confusing when we introduce the ideas of the hero and the criminal. Murray acknowledges that she "decided to view Casement as a hero."[45] But as someone who grew up in Australia and who, therefore, admires the seeming criminal Ned Kelly, Murray sees a link between the hero and the criminal: "In Australia our heroes were bushrangers, and we knew in our blood that the criminals who had been sent to our distant shores [...] were largely victims of injustice."[46] In the case of Casement, the hero-criminal takes on totally different meanings in different contexts. For his work exposing the colonial atrocities of Belgium in the Congo, the British treated Casement as a hero by knighting him. However, when Casement sought to expose Britain's similar forms of colonial atrocities in Ireland and to liberate Ireland from British colonialism, the British hanged him as a criminal. But as an Irishman, his criminal work on behalf of the Irish made Casement a hero. Yet, as a practicing homosexual, Casement was considered a criminal, which is why so many people denounced him after his trial for treason. But now that there has been a transvaluation of the value of homosexuality, Casement's criminal sexuality is in part what makes him a hero today. For Murray, locating and defining a specific human identity, especially of someone like Casement, is nearly impossible, which is why he is the ideal protagonist of a biographical novel: "fiction was the perfect place to describe the unclear nature of being and the myriad conflicting thoughts and actions that make up our identities."[47] What readers get in *Valiant Gentlemen*, then, is not a clearly defined picture of Casement. Rather, Murray uses Casement to clarify why it is impossible to reduce someone like him to a clearly defined being.

What, in part, causes this radical uncertainty is the transvaluation of all values. Casement initially considered himself a Brit, but after exposing the horrors of colonization and totally rejecting it, he began to shuffle off the mortal coils of his British identity and to construct himself as an Irishman. But what exactly is an Irishman? As this is a being yet to be invented, Casement was not at all certain, which is why the idea of "Casement's Irishness"[48] puzzled Murray when writing the novel. Murray says that she was trying to clarify the nature of Casement's Irish identity as she was writing, but by the time she finished *Valiant Gentlemen*, she had to conclude: "Casement was racing to his tragic conclusion, and his identity was still morphing. I kept hopeful watch, but then Casement was in the dock, and then he was guilty, and before I had a chance to determine the stuff of his Irish nature—that slippery Irishness that I felt inadequate to describe—Casement had already been hanged."[49] The same type of uncertainty applies to homosexuality. Is homosexuality a criminal sexual orientation, something for which a good Christian needs to seek forgiveness? Is it a natural, God-given desire, which should be treasured as a reflection of divine love? Is it a biological disposition that has nothing to do with the spiritual or the divine? Casement died, but he had no clarity about what he considered his shameful sexual orientation. In other words, he had not yet begun the process of interrogating the representation or even the demonization of homosexuality in the way he had done with regard to his Irish identity, much less did he begin the process of actively inventing a homosexual identity of his own, as he had begun to do with his Irish identity. Casement was still morphing, as Murray says. This perpetual condition of morphing, related as it is to the transvaluation of all values, precludes the possibility of a final or fully defined self.

V

Fiction was the perfect place to describe the unclear nature of being.[50]

Murray's struggle to define Casement's identity is very telling about the nature of the biographical novel. Both Vargas Llosa and Murray conclude "that a climate of uncertainty hovers over Roger Casement," and they see this as "proof that it is impossible to know definitively a human being." The indefinability of the human is precisely why the biographical novel came into being. Through implacable logic, empirical evidence, rigorous science, and Enlightenment reason, nineteenth-century intellectuals, particularly historians and historical novelists, thought that they could define the human, thus providing intellectual communities with the necessary means for controlling and directing human progress. But those intellectuals who considered this approach to be a dehumanizing form of social engineering turned their attention away from the external forces that seemingly shape the human in a deterministic way into a specific form to the surreal world of the human interior, the psychic site of a potential human agency. This aesthetic move led biographical novelists to draw a very different conclusion about the human from the historical novelists, but it was also a move that was made in order to safeguard the human from what they considered the dehumanizing form of social engineering on which the historical novel is premised.

Within this framework, the Irish are of particular importance. In fact, one could say that there are very clear and compelling reasons why the Irish played a crucial role in the genesis, rise, evolution, and contemporary legitimization of biofiction. Colonialism is the ultimate form of social engineering. Through a systematic, comprehensive, and strategic plan, colonial powers seek to structure colonized people into willing subordinates and servants of foreign powers. In a sense, there is a naïve and optimistic hope that colonial subjects will willingly accept into perpetuity the role assigned to them. Over time, the colonized would accept their inferior and subordinate roles as a natural and essential condition of their social and political being. Such was England's plan for the Irish. But a wide range of Irish rebels not only challenged and resisted the scripted role England assigned to the Irish, but they also began to script their own personal and national role. Wolfe Tone, Daniel O'Connell, Charles Stewart Parnell, O'Donovan Rossa, and Joseph Plunkett are just a few prominent figures who rejected the English script for the Irish and made the case for the Irish to script their own personal and national lives.

But the tactics and terms of contemporary enslavement have had to become super-subtle and more sophisticated in the seemingly post-slavery age, and Ireland, having been England's laboratory for experimenting with and refining strategies and techniques for colonial domination, has produced some of the most probing critics of the new slavery, some of the most aggressive and effective fighters against colonialism, and some of the most creative inventors of a postcolonial way of thinking and being. In other words, Ireland's situation as a colonized country explains in part why the Irish have played such a crucial role in originating and refining the biographical novel, which exposes the way external forces seek to control and determine the individual and to educate readers into a life-promoting form of self-creation.

Colum McCann found a brilliant way to address the evolving ways of thinking about slavery in his biographical novel *TransAtlantic*. This text features a number of actual historical figures, but for my purposes, I will focus on Frederick Douglass. The first Douglass section is set in the years 1845 and 1846 during the early years of the famine and when Douglass is lecturing throughout Ireland and England. Douglass has been a slave for a significant portion of his life, so he speaks with confidence and authority about the nature, structures, and conditions of slavery. Therefore, although he is shocked by the staggering level of suffering all throughout Dublin, he struggles to make what the reader might see as an obvious connection between the situation of enslaved American blacks and suffering Irish whites. Instead, he works hard to find a language to distinguish his situation from the Irish, saying, "There was poverty everywhere, yes, but still he would take the poverty of a free man."[51]

Yet the Irish do not see or experience themselves as free, and this tension regarding the definitions of freedom and slavery is of crucial importance throughout *TransAtlantic*, ultimately leading Douglass to think in alternative ways about slavery and to broaden his understanding of the "peculiar institution." We see this most clearly through Douglass's experiences with the "Great Liberator," Daniel O'Connell. Douglass is moved by a public speech in which O'Connell says that "England has reduced our nation to bondage!" (T 62). A couple days later, Douglass gives his own speech, and in his extemporaneous address, he begins to process and register the significance of the Irish situation. While the Irish are sympathetic to and supportive of Douglass's abolition campaign, they want him to acknowledge the situation of Ireland in relation to England. Here is what Douglass hears from his audience:

> What about England? Would he not denounce England? Wasn't England the slave master anyway? Was there not wage slavery? Were there not the chains of financial oppression?
>
> (T 64)

Shortly after hearing these remarks, Douglass responds by saying: "What is to be thought of a nation boasting of its liberty, he said, yet having its people in shackles?" (T 65). This comment suggests that Douglass is starting to think in a more nuanced and comprehensive way about the nature of slavery.

But just as Douglass starts to refine his critique of England, his publisher pulls him aside and tells him that he "cannot bite the hand that feeds" (T 70). The English are Douglass's biggest financial supporters, so if he were to call them enslavers, this could put his primary funding source in jeopardy. This has an unfortunate effect. Instead of continuing to develop and formulate more complicated, nuanced, and comprehensive ways of thinking about slavery and freedom, Douglass reverts back to a simple binary. His mantra becomes the "Irish were poor, but not enslaved" (T 85). To correct the problem, therefore, enough money is all that is needed. But this view is harshly debunked. While traveling the Irish countryside, Douglass and his publisher witness incomprehensible forms of starvation, suffering and death. At one point, a woman carrying a dead child approaches the two men asking for help. The publisher offers the woman a coin, which she lets fall to the ground. Totally devastated by the experience, "Douglass reached for the muddy coin and placed it in the woman's hand" (T 74). But the woman just let the coin slip "through her fingers" (T 74). Money and poverty—these are superficial ways of addressing the nature of the problem. What is really at stake is Irish autonomy, the freedom to govern their nation and their own lives. Douglass later learns that there is enough food to feed everyone in Ireland. The problem, therefore, is not enough food, or even the money to buy it. It is a political system in which a chosen few control life-sustaining resources and have the power to deny the unchosen masses access to those resources.

In essence, McCann uses Douglass to brilliantly expose the freedom/slavery binary as not just profoundly limited but also dangerously misleading, because it creates a glaring epistemological blind spot. Douglass's logic goes something like this: Since the Irish are not legally enslaved, they must be free. Thus, any source of injustice that the Irish experience cannot be characterized in terms of slavery. But by the year 1889, McCann's Douglass thinks differently. In an address to the National Women's Suffrage Association, Douglass makes a call for female liberation, claiming that it "is a woman's right to equal liberty with man" (T 189). Freedom is no longer defined exclusively in terms of a legal system; women were not enslaved in the technical and legal sense of the word. Therefore, it is clear that the 1889 Douglass is now thinking of slavery in a more subtle, nuanced, and systemic way, which would mean that the 1889 Douglass would be in a better epistemological position to see the 1846 situation of the Irish as a form of slavery. It is only by the end of the novel that McCann provides readers with a suitable terminology for communicating the nature of the characters' situation. The year is 2011, and a character named Hannah has an unopened letter from 1919, which supposedly has some connection to Douglass. Hannah shows the letter to a Kenyan postcolonial scholar named David Manyaki, who focuses on "the literature of the colonial" (T 274) and "inner colonization" (T 275) and provides Hannah with some history about Douglass's time in Ireland. Namely, he explains how the woman to whom the letter is addressed supposedly helped Douglass buy his freedom, an event that would have occurred between his 1846 visit to Ireland and his 1889 speech to the Suffrage Association. Significant is the way Manyaki describes Douglass's post-slave condition. He says that Douglass "went back to America unslaved" (T 284) rather than saying he went back "free." The Douglass who believes in the slavery/freedom binary may have thought that he would return to the United States as a free man. But anyone with even a rudimentary knowledge of racial history in the United States knows that using the word freedom to describe the life of a black man in the mid-nineteenth century is a vile mockery of the word. This fact explains why the 1889 Douglass would have been more sensitive to the condition of women as a form of enslavement, as well as why Manyaki uses the term he does.

That *TransAtlantic* culminates with the insight of a Kenyan postcolonial scholar is not just an effective way to conclude the novel. It is the logical outcome of the aesthetic form of biofiction. Biographical novelists foreground the deceptions and transformations of an evolving consciousness. Manyaki's usage of the word unslaving will prove instructive here. For the early Douglass, it is a self-evident truth that slavery and freedom are polar opposites. Therefore, using this binary to illuminate political reality is both legitimate and important. But for a postcolonial scholar like Manyaki, who is thinking about multiple layers of enslavement and unslavement, the simple binary blinds people to more subtle forms of political oppression. Needed, therefore, is not just a new way of seeing but also a more nuanced language about the political. The word unslaving performs this intellectual service. In a positive sense, the word unslaving suggests that one is no longer a slave. That is a good thing. But to say that someone is unslaved is also to tacitly acknowledge that a person is not really free. This is something that the seemingly liberated Douglass would have discovered when returning to the United States. Furthermore, there is a distinction to be made when noting the subject position from which unslaving proceeds. When a person is unslaved, this means that, while the person is not officially a slave, that person is also not quite free. But from the vantage point of those in power, the word unslaved has a totally different valence. It is no longer possible to officially enslave people. Therefore, the goal is to unslave people, to find ways to control and use people to further the ends of those in power without letting the unslaved know that they lack autonomy. In this sense, while the word unslaved seems to have a positive connotation, it actually functions to conceal a pernicious form of enslavement. This accurately describes the situation of many characters in McCann's novel.

Casement is the perfect protagonist of contemporary biographical novels because he was one of the first to chart the way the new slavery ("unslaving") functions. In other words, Casement anticipated the brilliant insights of thinkers like W. E. B. Du Bois, Richard Wright, Zora Neale Hurston, Frantz Fanon, Gayatri Spivak, Edward Said, and Homi Bhabha, just to mention a notable few, who seek to expose overt and subtle forms of social and political enslavement and desire to enhance the autonomy of those who are considered and treated as culturally designated inferiors. Yet, Casement's blindness regarding homosexuality is as important for the symbolic function of his character as his success in exposing the nature of the new slavery. Even heroes have glaring blind spots and contradictions, and both Vargas Llosa and Murray refuse to ignore Casement's weaknesses and limitations. They do this not so much because they are committed to giving readers all the biographical details of Casement's life, but because they want to give readers a powerful and complicated view of the human condition.

To clarify my point let me return to Rosa Montero, whom I discussed in the first chapter. Montero praises Camilo Sánchez's *The Widow of the Van Goghs* because of the way "the author uses the life of Van Gogh, the character, to tell a greater story about the nature of existence."[52] For both Vargas Llosa and Murray, one of the key ideas about the nature of existence is that it is impossible and even destructive to define the human in a final or absolute way, because our knowledge systems about what it means to be human are ever evolving and always in flux. Given this view, the ideal protagonist of a biographical novel is a being that exists in a perpetual condition of coming to be. Therefore, within a specific context, there is no such being and there can never be such a being as a fully and clearly defined Irishman or Irishwoman. Casement incarnates this idea, and he does so as an "Irishman" whose identity remains illusive and elusive.

If this approach to the novels and the biographical novel more generally is sound, then why do both Vargas Llosa and Murray consider Casement a hero? The answer cannot be because he contributed to the making of what would become the fully defined and liberated Irishman or the transvalued homosexual. The issue is much more foundational. Casement, whose identity cannot be located and/or defined, is a model for us in the present because he activated a process of endlessly constructing, deconstructing, and subsequently reconstructing an identity. Through his transnational experiences and thinking and his brutally honest appraisal of himself and his culture, he never became satisfied or complacent. He lived in a perpetual state of striving to become something different, something more, and something new. That he failed with regard to his homosexuality should not be held against him. Failure is an inevitable part of a human's story when he or she ventures into the as yet unconstructed future unknown. Casement and the Irish could not have known or anticipated the transvaluation of homosexuality that would occur over the succeeding one hundred years, just as we in the present cannot know or anticipate the transvaluations that will occur over the coming decades. What is considered a measure of heroic success is the ability to expose the injustices of the way a person or a culture is currently constructed and to set into motion the process of counter-generating a new culture or being. How effective a person is in setting that process into motion is how one can determine the nature of an individual's success. That such brilliant authors as Vargas Llosa and Murray have made Casement the protagonist of their biographical novels testifies to Casement's achievement, as he provides us today with an "existential map" of how to live in the present.

4

Traumatized Agency in Eliza Lynch Biographical Novels

As we see in the biofictions about Wilde, James, and Casement, agency plays a crucial role, which only stands to reason, as the biographical novel came into being in order to safeguard human agency from the determinism of history-as-science and its concomitant aesthetic form, the historical novel. The implication is that agency is in itself a higher and desirable good. But what if the autonomous agent creates something new and original that is also deadly and destructive? This is one of the major struggles for biographical novelists who take Eliza Lynch as their subject. Given that women were treated as inferior and even subhuman beings, it is tempting to idolize strong females who, against all odds, managed to act as autonomous agents in cultures designed to preclude such a possibility. Within this framework, what makes a woman extraordinary is her non-determined, autonomous action, regardless of whether the action is positive or negative.

Lynch is a case in point. Born in Ireland in 1833, she and her family emigrated to Paris, where at the age of sixteen she married a much older French doctor and moved with him to Algeria.[1] After her three-year marriage failed, she returned to Paris, became a courtesan, and met Francisco Solano López, the son of the then dictator of the wealthy country Paraguay. Having impregnated the famously beautiful Lynch, López gave her enormous sums of money and brought her back to Paraguay as his paramour. After living there for seven years and mothering numerous children, Lynch's status increased dramatically because López's father died, so the son became the President and dictator of the land-locked country. Temperamentally, López was much more aggressive than his father. Consequently, a little more than two years after taking power he started a war with Brazil, Argentina, and Uruguay, and it was rumored that Lynch urged López to instigate preemptive military action.[2] From López Lynch received extraordinary wealth in the form of cash, assets, and land, but she was also a shrewd businesswoman who earned much on her own, thus making her for a period of time one of the wealthiest women of the nineteenth century. By the end of the Paraguayan War (1864–70), the country lost "between 60 and 69 percent of the total population."[3] The fighting concluded when López and his oldest son with Lynch died on the same day, and Lynch buried them while Brazilian military men watched.

Lynch's story is so spectacular and sensational that it has resulted in four biographical novels, William E. Barrett's *Woman on Horseback: The Biography of Francisco Lopez and Eliza Lynch* (1938), Graham Shelby's *Demand the World* (1990), Anne Enright's *The Pleasure of Eliza Lynch* (2002), and Lily Tuck's *The News from Paraguay* (2004).[4] But what makes her particularly important is the way authors use her life to illuminate the role trauma plays in excessive and destructive forms of agency. There have been many excellent studies about trauma, specifically by Judith Lewis Herman, Cathy Caruth, Dominick LaCapra, and Suzette A. Henke, and there have been some equally insightful works about trauma in Ireland and Irish literature, including Graham Dawson's *Making Peace with the Past? Memory, Trauma and the Irish Troubles*, Robert F. Garratt's *Trauma and History in the Irish Novel: The Return of the Dead*, and Kathleen Costello-Sullivan's *Trauma and Recovery in the Twenty-First-Century Irish Novel*, but my work in this chapter is distinctive. Costello-Sullivan usefully summarizes a dominant idea in many works of literature that foreground trauma: "At their most recuperative, novels that engage trauma can (re)present a process that is in itself healing for trauma victims. As trauma studies have repeatedly shown, trauma survivors recuperate best when enabled to *narrativize* their suffering—to represent their own histories in ways that give them a sense of control and authorship over their own lives."[5] As Costello-Sullivan indicates, the focus is on recuperation, which is linked with personal and narrative agency. While I certainly agree with Costello-Sullivan and the many trauma theorists who have emphasized the role of narrative in the process of agency recuperation, I emphasize in this chapter the potential dangers of recovering agency by those who have been traumatized but also have considerable political power. To be more specific, I look closely at the way a traumatized figure who becomes politically powerful can and frequently does exercise a monstrous form of agency.

We marvel at those rare individuals who achieve agency because they have an uncanny ability to transcend the limitations and conditioning of their culture. Studies about such people highlight what makes them capable of originating a new idea and behaving as an autonomous agent. Since the biographical novel came into being in order to safeguard and foreground human agency, it only makes sense that Lynch would be the protagonist of so many biographical novels. But what kind of trauma occurs to people who have been abused and violated and have discovered that they were emotionally and psychologically enchained and oppressed? What effect and impact does this epiphany have on the subject's subsequent agential behavior? In this chapter, I will clarify how the trauma that comes from understanding one has been conditioned to internalize one's oppression can and sometimes does lead to excessive, destructive, and monstrous forms of agency. But more importantly, I will clarify how this epiphany about one's oppressed situation is a crucial experience in so many biographical novels, thus enabling me to make some larger claims about the unique ways in which authors of biofiction dramatize and deploy trauma in their works.

I

All the fault lay with La Irlandesa.[6]

I will not do an extensive analysis of Barrett's *Woman on Horseback*, but this should not be interpreted as a dismissive comment about the novel. One of the first works to rehabilitate the reputation of López and Lynch, *Woman on Horseback* is well informed and meticulously documented. Barrett includes an impressive appendix which footnotes all the works he consulted in order to construct specific scenes. But the work rarely mentions Lynch's time in Ireland or her Irish identity, and since this is a book about Ireland and the Irish, the novel is minimally relevant to my overarching argument.

A brief contrastive analysis of the opening of *Woman on Horseback* and *Demand the World* will clarify why I will not do an extensive study of Barrett's novel. The first line of Barrett's novel reads: "Terror walked the narrow streets of Asuncion on the night of the whisper."[7] Paraguay's capital is in a state of shock because its dictator, Rodriguez Francia, has died. Given the total and ruthless nature of the leader's rule, the people are terrified and unable to believe in his death: "No man could hear that [he has died] and believe it without the consciousness of blasphemy in his soul and the fear of death in his bones."[8] Consistent with my main claim in this chapter, that trauma plays a crucial role in relation to agency, *Woman on Horseback* begins by foregrounding a dislocation in the communal consciousness, and this has something to do with the culture's naturalized conditions of oppression. But the scene is set in Paraguay, so while *Woman on Horseback* features an Irish woman, the novel's trauma belongs exclusively to the South American country.

Demand the World is different because it begins in Ireland. The Prologue of the novel (DW 9–17) is a retrospective set in 1886 Paris, on the day of Lynch's funeral. But Part One (DW 19–88) begins in Cork in 1847, when Shelby's Elisa is only twelve years old (DW 17)—the actual Eliza would have been fourteen in late 1847.[9] The Great Famine has ravaged the country, and Elisa and her family have suffered from severe hunger and deadly violence. But there are two events that most destabilize the young Elisa's sense of herself. Elisa's father, Cavan, is the Senior Clerk of Shipping Affairs at the Port of Cork. One of his responsibilities is to check the contents of the warehouses before they are shipped, and one day he discovers a building filled with massive quantities of high-quality Irish food soon to be exported. Since many Irish are starving at the time, Cavan asks the English owner (Lord Natesby) to give the food to the famished masses. But Natesby rejects Cavan and his proposal. To save as many Irish as possible, Cavan defies Natesby by distributing the food to the people, which leads to his arrest and ultimate demise—he will be killed in a prison brawl. Not Ireland's lack of food because of the potato famine, but the English control of Ireland's essential resources was the source of Cavan's death and Elisa's subsequent trauma. Notice how Shelby connects the situation of Cavan with the plight of the Irish through the response of Elisa and her mother, Adelaide, to his death: "They wept together, their tears of love and sorrow made astringent by the wider sufferings of Ireland, by the greed and brutality, by the senseless manner of Cavan's death" (DW 109).

England's political and economic stranglehold on Ireland also accounts for the death of Elisa's friend Biddy O'Brien. Biddy and her family live in Kilbreen. Because they are not paying rent, Natesby plans to evict them. Elisa and Adelaide go to help the O'Brien family, but when they arrive, the mother is already dead and the father dies. When the Lord's men begin to remove the families from their makeshift homes, Biddy is accidentally killed, thus traumatizing Elisa. In both cases, the English subjugation and violation of the Irish are the causes of Elisa's psyche-shattering trauma.

But it is important to note that both of these experiences are fabrications. The father of the actual Eliza was named John, not Cavan, and he was a Doctor of Medicine, not a senior shipping clerk. Also, the nakedly contrived story of the O'Brien family is nothing more than the seething product of Shelby's imagination. And yet, the cleverly (if not totally successfully) rendered scenes picture trauma-inducing experiences that could effectively inform subsequent ways of thinking and behavior in the life of Shelby's Elisa as well as the actual Eliza. My two major points: (1) In contrast to *Woman on Horseback*, *Demand the World* foregrounds the role Ireland and the Irish play in the formation of Elisa's traumatized character. And, (2) what is of ultimate importance in Shelby's novel is not biographical or historical fact but the psycho-epistemological structure and a traumatic experience that will impact and, to some extent, explain the protagonist's subsequent thinking and behavior.

When I use the phrase "trauma-inducing experience," I have two separate, but interrelated, ideas in mind: suffering and powerlessness. Trauma involves a psyche-shattering experience. But there is a significant difference between a natural- and human-caused experience of suffering. Getting struck by lightning and then suffering catastrophic consequences could permanently damage a person both physically and mentally. But there is not likely to be additional trauma as a consequence of subsequent discoveries about a malign actor orchestrating the event. The act of nature is a random affair, so retaliating against nature as a way of rehabilitating self makes no sense. It would seem that the Great Famine would be an act of nature—the blight destroyed the leaves and roots of the potato plant, rendering it inedible. But as Shelby rightly dramatizes in the fabricated scenes about Cavan, there was enough food to feed the Irish. Therefore, the trauma-inducing problem was not primarily an act of nature that led to a lack of food; it was more a human-generated crisis because there were sufficient supplies to feed the people. As such, the post-traumatic experience is exacerbated by the feeling of having been violated by a malign actor who deprived the traumatized subject of agency and inflicted avoidable suffering.

Trauma, as Henke compellingly argues, "threatens the integrity of the body and compromises the sense of mastery that aggregates around western notions of harmonious selfhood."[10] According to this model, restoring a sense of mastery is the challenge for the traumatized individual. But the layered trauma that the protagonist of the biographical novel experiences is far more insidious than the kind that prominent theorists like Henke, Caruth, and Herman outline. Elisa's early traumatic experiences occur when she was in Ireland. Her "childhood [was] scarred by poverty, and with memories of violence and eviction." These memories are "forever—in her mind" (DW 196). So when Shelby's post-marriage Elisa lives for a short period of time in France with the Dauvins, a happy and prosperous couple and their children, she cannot help but compare her life in

Ireland to that of the Dauvins. Notice how Elisa's mind turns to Biddy when she observes the daughter: "She would sometimes look at the Dauvins' daughter, and remember Biddy O'Brien, crushed beneath the hooves of the team that had drawn Lord Natesby's ram" (DW 196). In like manner, when Elisa looks at the Dauvin patriarch, she cannot help but think of her own father: "She compared the children's father with her own, the one [Dauvin] moving smoothly to govern or break the bank, the other [Cavan]—equally gifted perhaps—who'd sacrificed his freedom, and his life, so the contents of Warehouse Six could keep others from dying" (DW 196). In both instances, the traumatic experience (the deaths of Biddy and Cavan) dictates how Elisa sees and experiences the world.

But here I want to question and challenge what constitutes and causes the traumatic experience. Is it primarily the immediate event, like Biddy's death beneath a wagon or Cavan's arrest and subsequent murder in prison? Or, is it the more systemic violation that made the immediate event possible, like the English control of life-sustaining resources and the selective and unjust distribution of those resources? Answering these questions is important because rehabilitating the traumatized subject will entail different forms of therapeutic activity depending on what is considered the primary cause of the traumatic experience. Henke notes that "subjective reconstruction"[11] means a restoration of agency to the traumatized subject, which is of crucial importance for harmonious selfhood. But if through an immediate traumatic experience a person discovers that there is a much larger and more systemic force that compromises the person's ability to achieve agential self-mastery, then the strategies for subjective reconstruction would become much more difficult and require much different therapeutic action.

In Elisa's case, assuming that she could return to a condition before she suffered the immediate traumatic experiences of Biddy's and Cavan's deaths, she would still lack self-mastery because she now knows how the English control Irish lives, and it is that knowledge that unsettles and destabilizes the seemingly harmonious former self. Understanding these different layers of being "unslaved," to use McCann's terminology, poses a challenge to Henke's characterization of subjective reconstruction. Many traumatized women, Henke argues, author life writing as a form of therapeutic self-reconstruction. Here is how she describes the experience: "The subject of enunciation theoretically restores a sense of agency to the hitherto fragmented self, now recast as the protagonist of his or her life drama. Through the artistic replication of a coherent subject-position, the life-writing project generates a healing narrative that temporarily restores the fragmented self to an empowered position of psychological agency."[12] Given the logic of this model, Elisa, through a memoir or life writing, could experience a form of psychological healing that would restore "a sense of agency." But as I have been suggesting, Elisa discovers that her agency has been compromised in both an immediate and systemic sense, so restoring pre-trauma selfhood would be nearly impossible because now she knows that she lacked agency before the psyche-shattering event. That lack of agency is what in large measure will constitute her traumatic experience and will explain why she will take specific types of violent action against any forces that threaten her sense of agential self-mastery.

In the context of biofiction, subjective rehabilitation, I argue, necessitates a much different response than Henke suggests. Her model, which so many literary theorists adopt and deploy, is cerebral in nature. Through "life-writing" the traumatized individual can reinvent "the shattered self as a coherent subject capable of meaningful resistance to received ideologies and of effective agency in the world,"[13] an act that leads to a form of recuperation. But in biofiction, establishing "effective agency" is less cerebral and more practical. The experience of Cavan will illustrate. People are obviously starving during the Great Famine, so many resort to violence in order to procure scarce, life-sustaining resources: "With the failure of the potato crop, and no foreign enemy to blame, the Irish waylaid the Irish, villagers closing ranks against their neighbours" (DW 30). Given this ominous situation, colleagues of Cavan give him a gun to protect himself and his family. Cavan accepts the gift but he does not load the firearm, as he is uncomfortable with a deadly weapon. One night he is accosted by three men, and to protect himself he pulls out his unloaded gun. After using it to scare away the threatening marauders, Cavan reflects on the nature of the experience:

> Grateful for the gift of the pistol, he was nonetheless pleased it hadn't been loaded, else maybe he'd have fired it in panic. And, by doing so, killed a man he knew. For the one with the cooking knife was the son of a nearby farmer, a lad he'd often stopped to chat with, a once-cheerful youngster who'd offered Elisa a kitten.
>
> (DW 38)

As a potential victim of a violent crime (a traumatic experience), Cavan could easily direct his rage at the perpetrators in front of him. But instead of feeling anger, Cavan fears that he could have rashly killed someone he knew, someone who was "a once-cheerful youngster" and has done a kindness to his daughter. What led to the transformation of this happy youth into a violent criminal?

Shortly after this experience, Cavan finds an answer to this question when he discovers how Natesby plans to export much needed food to continental Europe for the sake of profit. This leads Cavan to let the Irish take the food from the warehouse free of charge. Cavan realizes that this act will lead to his imprisonment "for the duration of" his "natural life" (DW 84), but instead of regretting what he has done, he gloats. A marked man, Cavan boards his wife and Elisa on a ship for France, and it is on this vessel that Natesby has authorities arrest Cavan. What outrages Natesby most is Cavan's response: "Where's the remorse? He's just happy to stand and watch the vessels sail by!" (DW 86). Two things account for Cavan's gratified response: First, he has taken action against the force that is responsible for mass Irish trauma and thereby restored some agency to the people: "But at least there'll be families with food enough to eat, staving off the worst of this blighted winter. Far short of what they deserve, but better than nothing" (DW 87). Second, he has found a way to liberate his family from English control and tyranny in Ireland by sending his wife and Elisa to France: "And, most important of all, Adelaide and Elisa are on the boat. With an address to go to in Paris. A new life awaiting them" (DW 87).

In this case, what rehabilitates the shattered ego of the traumatized subject is direct action against the perpetrator of social injustice, and this act restores something resembling "effective agency" to Cavan, the Lynch family, and many Irish. In a sense, Cavan becomes the novel's model of a figure that has developed a healthy and effective response to the traumatic experience. But there are certainly limitations in that response. Cavan believes that Adelaide and Elisa will escape soul-crushing destitution when they establish themselves in Paris, but what they find there is another form of degrading poverty—they suffer from a lack of food and the twelve-year-old Elisa is forced to work in order to earn money to feed the family. Cavan has taken action against an English overlord, thus enabling him to reconstitute his traumatized self and to assert some agential self-mastery for himself and the Irish more generally, but instead of liberating his wife and daughter by sending them to France, as he thought would happen, he has merely transported them from one trauma-inducing political arena of agency-less being to another.

With Cavan as her model, it might seem that Elisa would develop a healthy, life-promoting way of rehabilitating her traumatized self. But such is not the case. Shelby's Elisa experiments with different ways of establishing a sense of self-mastery and effective agency by becoming the maid of a courtesan and marrying a much older French doctor, but I want to focus on her relationship with Solano, which leads her to greedily accumulate a staggering amount of Paraguayan wealth. As a victim of English colonialism, Elisa has been permanently damaged ("forever—in her mind") by her experiences in Ireland, which significantly impacts what she imagines as living a meaningful and fulfilling life. Before the deaths of Biddy and Cavan, Elisa has a modest dream about her future that foreshadows her emigration to Paraguay: "An avid reader, she sometimes imagined herself in a distant country, though her dreams were not of wealth or jeweled gowns. All she wished was that the hunger pangs would cease, and her house in that far-off land be always warm" (DW 22). This pre-trauma dream is certainly reasonable. But what will become Elisa's later-life reality is much more extreme.

It would be easy to fault Solano for Elisa's excesses, but Shelby places considerable blame on the traumatized Irish woman. When Solano first comes to Europe, he spends obscene amounts of money. During a visit to Italy, Solano asks Elisa to purchase thousands of pieces of highest-quality cutlery, and it is in this moment that Elisa's "dream" undergoes a metamorphosis. Notice how the transformation of her dream is connected with Ireland:

> All thoughts of Ireland now banished, Elisa indulged in a selective yet squandering dream. A glance to left or right, and she had the power to ensure a salesman's promotion, establish a shop's reputation, leave this one to the everyday customer, and triple the profits next door. It occurred to her that she was playing a man's game now.
>
> (DW 233)

Power, wealth, agency—these all become linked in Elisa's mind, and they enable her to banish, at least for the moment, memories of her traumatic experiences in Ireland. Thus, the new dream that Elisa establishes seems to restore health and wholeness to her previously shattered psyche. But as Shelby's narrator strategically suggests, Elisa's newly imagined reality is actually a "selective" and "squandering dream."

The main problem with Elisa is this: In Ireland she witnessed the horrors of the Lord Natesby approach to life, but instead of challenging that model of economic and political rule by imagining something totally new and different, she will adopt his system when she is in a similar position of power, agency, and wealth. Throughout the novel, Shelby underscores how Elisa becomes a version of Natesby. Here are just a few examples to illustrate. After Elisa's baby daughter dies, she asks Solano for a new residence. Solano agrees to do "so without complaint, and more than sixty child-labourers were sent by wagon to the outlying district of La Recoleta, there to build a country house for Madame Lynch" (DW 264). Elisa witnessed and experienced the horrible abuses of children in Cork, specifically her friend Biddy, but rather than denouncing and forbidding such criminal behavior, "Madame Lynch," like "Lord Natesby," now benefits from it.

To form an alliance with Brazil, Solano proposes to Emperor Dom Pedro of Brazil that he marry his daughter. The leader rejects the offer, but because Elisa feels threatened by the proposal, she uses the event to manipulate her lover into giving her "six *quintas*; one hundred and nineteen thousand acres of land; the titles to three river boats, and the sum of 812,000 pesos in gold—all of it in the name of Elisa Alicia Lynch, hers to hold in perpetuity, or dispose of as she wished" (DW 287). This is all Paraguayan wealth, and yet, "Elisa Alicia Lynch" has managed to persuade Solano to give it to her for her sole self, thereby divesting the Paraguayan people of their land and wealth as "Lord Natesby" did to the Irish.

Early in the novel, Natesby takes a coach to his Carrick Manor in Ireland, and he and his family are treated like royalty while the native population lives in squalor and serves the foreign master. During the Paraguayan War, Elisa and her children travel with Solano's battalion. Predictably, Elisa replicates the situation of Natesby in Ireland: "Interspersed with the family coaches were fifteen hundred weary, ill-fed horsemen, their tattered uniforms now stiff with sweat and mud and dust" (DW 353). In the midst of this "Elisa rode in the first of two landaus, which were positioned in the middle of the column" (DW 353). The strategic parallels between Natesby and Elisa are too conspicuous to ignore.

The issue is not just wealth. It is also political power, which enables Elisa to experience agency over herself and to determine the lives of others. When on a steamer bound for Paraguay, Elisa notes that Solano has a dream of being "the Emperor of a Unified South America," which would mean that she would be "Empress." What would make this so extraordinary are her humble origins: "Quite an achievement for a colleen from County Cork" (DW 243). But becoming the "Queen of Paraguay" (DW 313) or the Empress of South America is not simply a title for show. Elisa has every intention of seizing political control. This is seen most clearly when Solano becomes the supreme leader of Paraguay. Just before President Carlos Lopez dies, Solano gives Elisa a theater, villa, and riverboat. Elisa responds by saying that he is being extravagant: "You allow me whatever I want, *querido*, but I've no wish to dig too deep in your country's purse" (DW 269). Based on this example, it would seem that Elisa is sensitive to the financial needs and economic well-being of Paraguay and has no interest in plundering the nation's coffers for personal gain. But immediately upon the death of the President, readers get a much different picture of Elisa. When Solano hears that his father is moribund, Elisa says to him: "Go and see him. And don't forget what we talked about before. You will need both keys" (DW 270). One of the keys provides access to the vaults containing the country's wealth. After Solano gets the keys, Elisa tells him: "We can see what's in the Paraguayan purse" (DW 272).

What makes this scene so troubling is the degree to which Elisa uses the occasion of the president's death to control Solano and therewith the country. Until this point Elisa has been deferential and subordinate. But the moment the President dies she takes total charge and Solano subordinates himself and defers to her. For instance, after taking the keys, Solano notices his father's bodyguards closing in on him. Fearful that the guards intend to kill him, the cringing and terrified son tells them that his father died a natural death. Just before Solano has a total breakdown, Elisa enters the scene and says in an authoritative voice: "You see him? You see your new leader? Now raise your rifles and salute *El Presidente*!" (DW 272). Not only does Elisa save Solano's life, but she also secures his position as president, and she was able to do this because of her authoritative presence: "With this single, positive intrusion, the woman turned Don Carlos Antonio's troops into Francisco Solano's obedient defenders" (DW 272).

In the rest of the chapter, Madame Lynch becomes a modern incarnation of Lady Macbeth: "Solano Lopez wept on Elisa's shoulder, then was gently shrugged aside" (DW 272).[14] Solano is crying because he cannot believe that his father is dead, but Elisa has no patience with such trivial sentimentality: "Remembering her own father and others, Elisa said: 'All men die. It's what happens. Now stand away and listen' " (DW 273). At this point in her life, the trauma of her father's death, instead of making her more empathetic, leads her to callously dismiss her lover's emotional response. This is not to say that no lesson was learned from Cavan's demise. There was, and it is that Elisa and Solano must take dictatorial control over the nation. Otherwise, what Lord Natesby did to Cavan, others could do to Elisa, Solano, and their children. Taking absolute political control is the only way to maintain a sense of agential self-mastery. Therefore, Elisa directs Solano to do the following: (1) take charge of the military, (2) silence a dissenting Justice, (3) send his brother abroad on a trade mission, and (4) declare before the national assembly that Madame Elisa Alicia Lynch will officially serve as Solano's counsellor. In short, the Irishwoman Elisa has banished Paraguayan critics and dissenters and taken economic, legal, and military control of the nation. Given all that she does, Solano can only marvel at her political acumen: " 'You seem to know more than most,' Lopez murmured. 'You seem better primed than any of us, *mi mujer*' " (DW 273). She is better prepared than others, and there is a reason why. She has witnessed and experienced the way the English used power politics to subjugate and oppress the Irish. Therefore, instead of making herself vulnerable yet again by allowing herself to be placed in the position of the Irish, she decides to behave as the English did.

When Elisa's position of power in Paraguay is finally secure, she can then set into motion her larger political objective, which is to follow the British example of establishing an Empire. Still subordinate to Elisa, Solano asks her what he should do when he discovers that the Brazilians are using Paraguayan waterways to transport military weapons to a remote region of northern Brazil. Graham deploys an effective narrative strategy to expose Elisa's totalitarian will to political power. Solano asks her to read the letter containing the information about the Brazilian shipment. Her private response reveals what she secretly wants: "Reading the letter once, and then twice, Elisa glanced across the well-furnished parlour and asked herself if this might not be the chance to set Paraguay firmly where it belonged—as the centerpiece of the South American crown" (DW 325). Elisa realizes that she could use this event to invade a neighboring country and thereby to start the process of making Paraguay the England in a South American version of Great Britain. Within this imperial framework, Brazil would become a version of Ireland.

But Elisa does not express her secret imperial ambitions to Solano. Rather, she cleverly describes the Brazilian act as a threat to Paraguayan sovereignty, thus justifying preemptive military action: "It's an act of provocation," she said. "Nothing less. A deceitful shipping of weapons under our noses. Let the *Marques de Olinda* slip by, and Brazil will send others, sneering as they use our own river to fortify their province" (DW 325). Such is Elisa's public justification for instigating military action against Brazil, but as readers we know the private ambitions that inform her imperialist agenda.

What makes Shelby's Elisa so fascinating will be her next transformation, one in which she finally recognizes how her therapeutic efforts to reconstruct her traumatized psyche, to establish agential self-mastery, and to restore harmonious selfhood have gone too far. To signal that a transformation is under way, Shelby has Elisa recall her life in Ireland. As enemy troops launch a surprise attack, Elisa and her children are prepared because they slept fully clothed. Why did she do this? The answer is her experiences in Ireland: "She would never know *why* she had taken such a precaution, though its roots ran deep; perhaps they reached back to the time when Cavan and Adelaide had feared eviction from their small stone house above Cork" (DW 355). In this case, Elisa has been able to turn the trauma of what happened to her in Ireland into something of life-saving use for her in South America.

The more Elisa begins to cast a critical glance at her behavior in Paraguay, the more does she mentally return to Ireland as a source for inspiration and a model for healthy and life-promoting action in the present. During the dark days of the Paraguayan War, when it was becoming painfully apparent that the outcome was going to be total defeat, Elisa entertains the possibility of returning to Europe: "Why not abandon him [Solano] now, whilst he slept, and return across the Atlantic, with the coffers filled in Edinburgh, friends still alive in Paris, and Elisa perhaps remembered as the daughter of Cavan Lynch, the hero of Cork?" (DW 346). Cavan may have been crushed by the British, but his self-sacrificing behavior was heroic, certainly very different from the greedy, narcissistic, imperialist, and dictatorial action of Elisa and Solano.

When Elisa finally has her most soul-searching epiphany, she begins to register the catastrophic ramifications of what she has done:

> Oh, Solano … How much of *your* fault was mine? Did I really lead you on toward destruction? Did my presence beside you make the difference? Would my absence have left you at peace? Ah, *querido*, what a Hell we made of your Paradise, dreaming of crowns and coronets … And didn't really need them, did we, since we'd gold enough in the vaults to shape our own…
>
> (DW 400)

After a traumatic experience, individuals desperately seek to regain some sense of agential mastery over their own lives. But given the nature of their life-shattering experiences, their disordered interior lives can sometimes lead them to agential excess, and Shelby's Elisa is a perfect case in point. Agency means not simply financial independence and familial autonomy; it entails monstrously insane wealth and absolute political authority over others. In the passage above, Elisa seems to understand that she has gone too far, and as a consequence, she acknowledges that she has been partly responsible for horrific forms of death and destruction. But note that she does not totally repent. Had Solano and Elisa contented themselves with the Paraguayan wealth in the vaults, which was more than most countries have in their treasury, they would have possessed enough to "shape" their own lives as they wish. That this wealth belongs to the Paraguayan people and nation seems not to occur or even matter to the seemingly healthy and reformed Elisa. So while there seems to be some improvement in Elisa's traumatized condition, she is still a dangerous and untrustworthy figure, and it is her yearning and need for personal and familial agency ("to shape our own ... ") that makes her so.

After the war, when Elisa is forced to return to Europe, she must find a source for income. It is through this experience that Shelby's protagonist discovers an alternative way of securing a life-inducing form of autonomy. In her pre-Solano days, Elisa, as a courtesan, had a brief relationship with a munitions manufacturer (Monsieur Cravat), who did sexually criminal things to her. Given this man's extreme wealth, the post-Paraguay Elisa proposes the idea of a respectable, well-managed casino. The rich businessman would bankroll the operation, and Elisa would run the casino and receive a 30 percent stake in the business. Cravat agrees, but he sees the venture as a way of swindling as much money out of his customers as possible, which is why he says to Elisa: "Let the children wager their *bonbons* –" (DW 402). Elisa takes umbrage to his comment because she now rejects the idea of exploiting people, especially children, for personal gain: "Let our guests enjoy the evening at their own level," Elisa corrected. "We are *not*, Monsieur, setting out to steal from children" (DW 402). How different is this Elisa from the one who allowed sixty "children" to build a villa for her in Paraguay.

The business is a huge success, which leads Elisa to realize that she should have done something like this earlier: "*La Manoir* made a reasonable profit, then a healthy one, then one that far exceeded her expectations. Should have done this before" (DW 404). To experience economic agency, Elisa did not have to plunder the coffers of Paraguay and exploit child labor. She could have run a well-managed and honest business in France. Clearly, this Elisa is very different from the one who aspired to be the Queen of Paraguay, the Empress of South America, and the wealthiest woman in the world.

Had the casino had lasting success, Elisa could have ended her days having recovered from and come to terms with the trauma of her Irish childhood. But she went into business with an unscrupulous man, so when she takes a leave of absence in order to retrieve her children from Paraguay, Cravat turns the thriving establishment into a seedy brothel designed to generate as much profit as possible. When Elisa tries to claim her 30 percent stake in the business, she is summarily dismissed. From this point forward, Elisa will live a humble lifestyle.

Demand the World is not a great biographical novel. The writing is stilted at times, some of the scenes are overly contrived, and character motivation and development are not always clear and/or convincing. And yet, Shelby takes some daring risks, and these make the novel an important contribution to the genre of biofiction. One notable feature is Shelby's willingness to take considerable liberties with established facts. Take, for instance, Elisa's children. In real life, Eliza had seven children, three who died in Paraguay and one who died in England during her lifetime. In *Demand the World*, only two children die during Elisa's lifetime. More importantly, after the war, the real Eliza brings four of her children with her to Europe, whereas in Shelby's novel, Brazilian authorities refuse to allow the five surviving children to leave the country with Elisa, and she never sees them again. How can we explain this egregious violation of the historical record? And is there any ethical justification for making such changes? Answering these two questions is important for explaining what authors of biofiction do.

Traumatized children are potentially very dangerous. But what makes things worse is that they are numerous and ubiquitous. Like so many others, Elisa was a suffering and traumatized child in Ireland and France. When she goes to Paraguay as a wealthy woman, she selfishly thinks only of herself, so she ignores the fact that she will exploit children in the same way that she and many others were exploited. As the war is nearing its end, which will conclude with the deaths of Solano and Elisa's oldest son, the Irish woman's mind returns to her childhood friend Biddy. Elisa is in a tent with her children and maid, and the "girl" is shivering with fear and cold, so Elisa covers her with a cape: "Damp and threadbare, it at least drew the maid together with her mistress. *And reminded Elisa of that terrible Irish winter when Adelaide covered her daughter with a cloak as they stumbled through the snow from the hamlet of Kilbreen*" (DW 365). Kilbreen is where Biddy lived and died. What happened to Biddy in Ireland is now happening to Elisa's maid in Paraguay. But this time Elisa is not a victim helping a fellow impoverished sufferer. She is a woman who, in pursuit of incomprehensible wealth and unbridled power, has significantly contributed to the traumatic situation in which the maid finds herself.

Given the logic of the novel, traumatized children, in their effort to achieve agential self-mastery, can easily become authoritarian monsters, and this is something that rightly concerns Brazilian military and political leaders, which is why they refuse to let Elisa take her children. Since we as readers have seen how a traumatized child like Elisa responded to her suffering, we can infer that Elisa's children can become as dangerous as she. Having the five children survive underscores the looming threat of traumatized children who could enact dangerous forms of agency.

So is the novel an accurate representation of the lives of Solano and Elisa? In terms of biographical and historical facts, the answer is no. But in terms of a psychocultural and political structure, the answer is yes. I am not saying that Shelby has given us an ontological truth about humans that stands outside of time and space. I am saying that he extracted from the life story of Elisa what he considers a "truth" that could effectively illuminate a ubiquitous structure at work in both the past and present, and he has invented scenes and smudged facts in order to clarify how that structure functions. I take the word smudge from Joyce Carol Oates. In an interview about her Marilyn Monroe biographical novel *Blonde*, Oates talks about the kind of "truth" she gives readers in and through her protagonist:

> It's more a universal truth. When I write about Norma Jeane Baker I'm writing about a lot of people, even men. I'm writing about the biographical subject and smudging it a little to suggest that if you look in that mirror of Marilyn Monroe you will see something like yourself. Rather than her being this unique historical figure all by herself, I sense that there is a bond between us.[15]

Biographical novelists use the lives of actual historical figures in order to give readers more universal "truths" about the human, cultural, and political condition. In and through Elisa, Shelby vividly pictures the life of someone who, having suffered trauma, seeks to reconstitute herself as an empowered autonomous agent, but given the damage that comes with having been traumatized, Elisa's understanding of and approach to individual and political agency is excessive at best and extremely dangerous at worst. And as Oates suggests, Elisa is not supposed to be seen as an isolated figure in history. There is a bond between her and us, and that bond can effectively shed light on certain human and political structures that currently make us who we are. But that bond can also enable us to see and therefore choose healthier and more life-promoting ways of human and political being.

Were Shelby a biographer or historian, his flagrant alterations of fact would clearly be unethical because they would mislead readers who expect fidelity to established facts. But Shelby is a novelist, a writer of fiction, so the "truths" he seeks to give readers are very different from the biographer or historian. In *Demand the World*, he gives readers transcultural and transtemporal "truths" about the horrific consequences of trauma on children, and he uses the life story of Eliza Lynch to give those "truths" concrete shape and form. Within this framework, making changes to the biographical and historical record can be legitimate and effective, but only so long as they accurately represent the transcultural and transtemporal reality that the author seeks to depict—what Oates refers to as "a more universal truth." Put differently, readers should not assess the value of a biographical novel on the basis of its fidelity to biographical or historical fact. They should assess it on the basis of the quality of the story and the credibility and usefulness of its transcultural and transtemporal "truths."

II

> *Because dreadful things [...] are never the end. They are just the way through.*[16]

Of the biographical novels about the infamous Irishwoman, Enright's *The Pleasure of Eliza Lynch* is the most complicated and demanding but also one of the most insightful and gratifying. Enright's aesthetic control, twisted imagination, and destabilizing narrative enable her to transmute Lynch's story into a disturbing commentary on the nature of the insidious will to absolute political power. Patricia Coughlan claims that Enright's novel is in thematic conversation with Joseph Conrad's *Nostromo*, but structurally Enright uses *Heart of Darkness*'s maritime trope of travelling deeper into a continent in order to chart the protagonist's inward psychological journey. The novel opens with a section in which Eliza and López meet (PEL 1–15). The next section is set on a ship making its way upriver from Buenos Aires to Paraguay during the month of December 1854 (PEL 17–46). The next section jumps forward in time to 1857, when Eliza is established in Asunción as López's favored paramour (PEL 47–84). The next section returns to the river in December 1854 (85–108), which is followed by a section set in 1865 during the beginning of the Paraguayan War (109–153). This pattern is repeated two more times, with Eliza expressing her thoughts in a diary-like fashion followed by the physician William Stewart formulating his view of Eliza and their experiences in Paraguay, and the closer the boat gets to Asunción, the more does the reader come to understand the nature of the trauma that drives Eliza's character.

Different from *Heart of Darkness*, in which Marlow's inward journey culminates with "The horror! The horror!"[17] Eliza's begins with the "horrors." In the first section, Eliza thinks about the men with whom she has had coitus. Readers only get scant information about them, but one seems to be particularly important. Bennett is an older man, a doctor who is also a friend of Eliza's father. He was Eliza's first sex partner, which would make it seem like Eliza would have been the vulnerable one in the relationship. But this is not correct. After orgasm, Bennett "smiled at her, as though her insides were quite useful and nice, then suddenly he cracked open in front of her and horrors, horrors, came spilling out" (PEL 9). The Kurtzian horror has been multiplied into the plural, it comes at the beginning rather than the end of the story, and it is the outcome of a sexual encounter with Eliza. Is one of the primary horrors that Bennett destroyed Eliza by coercing her into sex and taking her virginity? This is unlikely because immediately after the "horrors" passage Eliza notes that "she was sure she had killed him" (PEL 9). This leads Eliza to reflect on all the men she was killing: "She was killing them in Paris, Algiers, Kent, and Bennett everywhere. She was killing Bennett in Mallow, where he never had been" (PEL 9). Based on this passage, Eliza is clearly not a passive and fragile creature who lacks agency. She is actually in command, even though she is only fourteen when she first begins her sexual relationship with Bennett. Striking about this passage is the prominence of Bennett and Eliza's continual murder of him, and specifically in the town of Mallow, where Bennett had never been.

For a reason not yet specified, Mallow is of crucial importance to Eliza. As the novel progresses, readers are strategically given important details to understand why the town holds so much meaning. In the first section with Eliza going upriver, readers learn that Eliza's father is "a doctor who specialized in rheumatic disorders at the spa town of Mallow in the Co. Cork. My mother suffered herself from bad health, and took the waters there, and we lived nearby for some years" (PEL 45). The family, however, had to emigrate because of the Great Famine. As Eliza says: "I was born in Ireland and lived there, near the spa town of Mallow, until the age of ten, when the hunger then raging in the countryside obliged us to leave from the harbor at Queenstown" (PEL 46). The matter-of-fact tone in this passage suggests that this experience is but a distant memory, so far in the past as to have no emotional or psychological impact on the 1854 Eliza.

But as Eliza journeys further into the heart of the continent, her memories of Mallow become more unsettling. For instance, in a conversation with Dr. Stewart, Eliza explains how her situation in Paraguay is not totally dissimilar to what she experienced in Ireland:

> You might as well be in Ireland. You might as well be in Mallow—where I grew up you know—a bitter town, it made my mother weep—but we all come from

> bitter towns, do we not, Doctor? Every unfortunate on the surface of this earth comes from some or other bitter little town.
>
> (PEL 150)

Clearly, something bad happened to Eliza in Mallow, and it cannot just be the Great Famine because what happened in Mallow happens everywhere. Put differently, all unfortunates come from a bitter little town like Mallow, thus suggesting that the Irish hamlet symbolizes a global reality. Universalizing the town in the same way Sylvia Plath does in "Daddy" ("But the name of the town is common") clarifies Eliza's earlier claim about killing Bennett in Mallow. Bennett might not have been physically in Mallow, but because he embodies the oppressive structures found in the bitter little town, he has been there in spirit.

It is when Eliza finally arrives in Asunción that readers get a clearer picture of what traumatized her in Ireland. Eliza believes that she could escape what happened to her in her youth. She is not trapped in a cycle since she can construct a new life, one significantly different from what she experienced in Ireland. But on her arrival in Asunción, she reluctantly and grudgingly acknowledges that life is a vicious circle from which there is no escape. After noticing the crowd awaiting the ship's arrival, Eliza muses: "They are altogether like the crowd I saw from the first boat I was ever on, the Plymouth packet from Queenstown. And so my life runs in circles, and not in a line, after all" (PEL 207). It all goes back to Ireland, to something that happened to her there and led the family to make its departure from the "harbor at Queenstown."

But what exactly induced the trauma? As in *Demand the World*, the situation of the father is vital. In Shelby's novel, Cavan is in prison for supplying the starving Irish with "stolen" food, where he will die from a stabbing. In *The Pleasure of Eliza Lynch*, the father is still possibly alive in January 1855, which is why Eliza wonders "where my father is, now" (PEL 207). This thought about her father triggers a memory about her Irish childhood. Eliza remembers how people were trying to kill her father when she was ten years old. At first, she thought the people coming after her father were bailiffs with the intention of evicting the family from its home after the crops failed for a second time. But the people were actually "indigent and ghastly-eyed" Irish in search of food: "There was one woman who reached out a purple knuckle to graze my cheek saying, in a soft kind of way, that she would eat me" (PEL 207). The situation escalates after Eliza and her family see "the first, or perhaps second corpse in the ditch" of the countryside, thus leading Eliza's father to take action: "my father gained sudden strength to pack us up and out of there, off to the ship in the middle of the night, pursued, as I thought, by these skeletons" (PEL 207). The family makes the escape, but the horror of the experience lingers within Eliza's psyche. As she notes about those who possibly drowned in their effort to escape their nightmarish lives in Ireland: "It was possible some of them drowned—I was terrified that they might, and there is something sickening, I still find, in the sound of a splash" (PEL 207–8). Eliza explicitly states that she does "not cry, as a rule," because she is "not the crying kind" (PEL 208). But when she arrives in Asunción, flooded with memories of her traumatized childhood in Ireland, she cannot contain herself: "It seems I am weeping. The tears slip out of my eyes, quite fast and silent, as though they have nothing to do with me" (PEL 208). The traumatic experience in Ireland is revealed near the end of the novel, but if we use the subjective rehabilitation model of trauma theory, then what happened in Ireland would explain so much of Eliza's behavior throughout the novel.

For Eliza, the goal is to reconstitute herself as a being with agency, a capacity she realizes she did not possess because British bailiffs had the power to control her day-to-day living. Meeting López was fortuitous because both have big personalities, but also because they suffer from the same kind of agency-compromising trauma. Spanish colonists, who highly prize pure Spanish blood, are the bane of López' existence, which is why he flaunts his mixed blood heritage: "The Spanish colonists were his particular enemy. There would be no such thing as 'pure' blood, he said. From now on, all blood was pure, all blood was Paraguay" (PEL 161). López says this in the presence of Whytehead and Stewart, two Brits from Scotland. Since the British are like the Spanish as colonizers, López fears that he may have offended his guests, so he tells them: "Don't worry. It is the Spanish who are the canker here, not you" (PEL 162). Insofar as assurances go, this cannot be very comforting, since López is basically saying that they are cankers elsewhere. But what makes matters worse is Eliza's follow-up claim: "Oopsa! And in case he should think me one of them, I say, 'Not like poor Ireland,' with a smirk that seems to offend everyone, even my dear friend" (PEL 162). For most Brits, the Irish are British. Therefore, Eliza's separation from and even disavowal of British identity can only be a source of much consternation to Whytehead and Stewart. But it is the situation of being a traumatized subject of a colonial power that unifies Eliza and López.

For those who have suffered soul-degrading trauma, agential overreaction is a real possibility, and given the passionate, impulsive, and intense dispositions of both López and Eliza, such excess can be extremely dangerous, perhaps catastrophic. López reveals much about the nature of his menacing interior when he confesses to Eliza that he has murdered a man. López and his brothers tied a man to their horses and dragged him through the streets of Asunción until "the white of his bones [was] sticking out of his raggedy back" (PEL 100). Eliza asks him why he did this, and López says that the man's "woman turned me down for him" (PEL 101). But after admitting this, López acknowledges that there is an even deeper reason for the act: "It was a thing we had to do. The girl was nothing. Carmencita Cordal. She thought her father owned the town, which he did not" (PEL 101). So important is this story, which is based on the murder of Carlos Decoud, that Barrett includes a lengthy section about it in his novel.[18] Here is how Siân Rees describes the Decoud situation in *The Shadows of Elisa Lynch*. There were rumors in early 1859 of a conspiracy against Don Carlos López, and Carlos Decoud was one of the people charged. The men arrested "disliked the López family for its low origins."[19] But there was also a personal reason for the deadly action taken against Decoud:

> It was said that the fiancée of one of the men arrested, Carlos Decoud, had been the object of his [Solano's] attentions and that he urged his father to find some pretext for Decoud's arrest in revenge for having been slighted. There may have been some lingering disagreement between General López and Carlos Decoud, for the Decouds were of old and European blood and the tight little inner ring of families to which they belonged despised the *mestizo* blood of the presidential family.[20]

The issue here is power. The Spanish dominated and controlled countries throughout South America, thus divesting the indigenous populations of autonomy over their own lives in the same way that the British treated the Irish. To right this political wrong and to send an unambiguous message to the colonizers, the mestizo López takes deadly action against a pure-blooded Spanish colonizer.

But this is not the worst part of the story of subject rehabilitation. When Eliza asks López how he feels about murdering the man, the future dictator gives what could only be considered the most horrifying response imaginable. López says that killing the man "changed the whole world" (PEL 101). The ensuing dialogue between the two clarifies what he means:

> "What way did the world change?" I say. "Was the sky more blue?"
> "Yes."
> "More full of birds?"

"Definitely."

"Was the grass greener?"

"And so on. And so forth." (PEL 102)

The brutal murder of an enemy has the salutary effect of improving López' life and making him a happier man. Such a response from a future political leader with unbridled power can only send shivers up the spine of those who would be under his control.

To indicate that López' response is not an anomaly, Eliza's subsequent thoughts confirm that she has had a similar reaction. The conversation with López regarding murder makes Eliza think about Mallow, where she, too, had a propensity for killing:

> My sister in Mallow would bring me to things she was too squeamish to kill; childish things; a frog or a daddy-long-legs, and I would dispatch them, and it would make her cry. And then later, of course, some blurted telltale, and the horrified face of my Mama, the two of them clinging to each other as they watch me walk towards Hell-fire. (PEL 102)

This cavalier and dismissive tone stands in stark contrast to the response of her mother and sister, who are horrified by Eliza's tendency for wanton cruelty. What would make this situation monstrously demonic would be an unholy alliance between Eliza and López, which would be founded on the demented pleasure of destroying and killing others. Later in the narrative, still on the ship bound for Paraguay, Eliza says she believes that López is welcoming her into his sadistic political world: "He is inviting me to join him in his life—his impossible life, where the sky is more blue, and the grass more green, where you can have things just by taking them" (PEL 168). The strategic allusions to the bluer sky and the greener grass recall the positive effects of murder on López' life. Enright is basically suggesting that López and Eliza form an all-powerful union premised on the perverse joy of dominating others to the point of death.

The reference to the "impossible life" adds another disturbing layer to Eliza's character. Shortly after Eliza reflects on her propensity to kill, she makes a claim about the magic and glory of money: "And I knew, at that moment, what money was for. It was so you could have things that were impossible" (PEL 103). For this Eliza, money is not simply a means to financial security. It is a way to achieve the unfathomable, the unimaginable, and the impossible. Given López' access to the Paraguayan vaults of wealth, Eliza believes that she and her lover will now have the power and right to make the impossible possible. As Stewart says of the 1865 Eliza: "Eliza Lynch was Paraguay. She had produced, for the honour of the country, three living sons. She was also, since López had deeded his lands to her, one of the richest women alive" (PEL 113).

The money, the political power, and even the killing—these are all just means to a much more important end, which is the agency that comes with "subjective reconstruction" in response to a traumatic event. Considerable light is shed on the extent of Eliza's agency when she is aboard the Paraguay-bound ship. Bored and restless, Eliza commands López to give money to play cards for her entertainment:

> we must play for money, because what is an evening without the promise of ruin? I turn to my dear friend and I say, "You must give Mr Whytehead more money, my dear, so that he can overcome his scruples and play. (I think I am a little drunk.) Or give the maid money, at least, so we can have a proper game."
>
> (PEL 169)

This occurs in December 1854, still very early in the Lynch-López relationship. But it suggests that Eliza already has considerable power over López and that their dangerously playful power dynamic is already well established. With access to mounds of money, Eliza can use the wealth in order to watch others rise financially or descend into "ruin." Since Eliza and López have all the power, "ruin" is not possible for them. For their entertainment López gives Eliza's maid, Francine, a small fortune so that they can all play cards for extremely high stakes. Stewart sees this as a golden opportunity to swindle the young woman out of her new-found wealth, but Eliza delights in the experience because it affords her an opportunity to assess what works and does not work in securing agency: "So at least I have some pleasure. To see the girl hazard more than she could earn in a year" (PEL 170). Watching Francine leads Eliza to conclude that she knows money, the value of which is found not so much in its possession but the power it gives a person. To illustrate, Eliza makes the following observation:

> I know money, I know the value of, for example, three hundred pounds—how a maid could live a lifetime on such a sum, how my father could live a month, how my mother might have raised her children on it for more than a year. I burned a note, once, that belonged to Mr Bennett. A fifty. I said to him, as I did it, "This afternoon, I think I'll love you for free." (PEL 170)

Money enables a person to procure life-sustaining resources, as with Eliza's mother. But Eliza burns a fifty-pound note because it, paradoxically, gives her more power, so the value of money is not necessarily in having it, but how one can use it to increase power over another, as Eliza does in her interaction with Bennett.

This scene hauntingly foreshadows the behavior of Lynch and López when they will have unlimited political power. In possession of an insane amount of wealth, López and Eliza can give money to whomever they want merely for their own amusement. Though the stakes for the two in power are not high, they can easily result in "ruin" for those who lack resources and agency. In a sense, this is going to become the power dynamic when López becomes president. Enright's Eliza will command him to do as she bids, even if it will result in the "ruin" of those without power, and she will do this for her own personal pleasure—*The Pleasure of Eliza Lynch*.

What makes this possible is an aura around oneself, which is something that Stewart best theorizes when he juxtaposes and contrasts Eliza and his wife, Venancia. Physically, Venancia is getting larger because "she was eating her way through her father's estate," but, phenomenologically, she is getting smaller, especially in relation to Eliza. As the narrator says: "Every time Stewart saw Eliza, she had grown. He was not surprised by this; Venancia had, for example, shrunk in his head, until she had become a sort of daughter to him—a body he might take up in his arms, fresh and light and loose as water" (PEL 133). Phenomenological "reality" ("in his head") is more important than physical "reality," so even though Venancia gets physically bigger, her aura becomes smaller, thus resulting in a littler being in a phenomenological sense. Having formed a mutually empowering bond, Eliza and López create a mesmerizing aura around themselves, which has a daunting and immediate impact on those in their presence. For instance, after Eliza and Stewart have a private conversation, there is a pregnant pause of silence, and in this moment Stewart experiences anxiety as López joins the two: "For a second, Stewart was afraid, but López was not jealous in the least. Such was Stewart's smallness, in the scheme of things. And indeed, Eliza stood and walked towards him as a Great Woman might walk towards a Great Man" (PEL 152). By this point in the novel, which is 1865, the communally perceived stature of Eliza and López is so gargantuan that Stewart can only passively take note of his phenomenological "smallness" in relation to their grandiose being and "scheme of things."

In the novel it is this phenomenological aura that makes an escalating form of agency possible. With López' assistance and through her own uncanny abilities, Eliza commands the admiration and respect of many powerful people in Asunción, thus leading many to see her as the ultimate creator of self. Here is how Stewart describes Eliza only two years after her arrival in Paraguay: "she has made herself, and it is to the woman who created this, as well as to the woman who *is* this, that they offer their deep and ironical homage, as though, in her beauty, she has transcended herself" (PEL 62). Stewart is contemptuous and dismissive of Eliza because he believes there is nothing intrinsic to the woman that justifies such respectful treatment. And yet, Stewart realizes that Eliza has considerable power precisely because of the way she is perceived as a self-creating being.

López also possesses this same agency aura, which, in a circular fashion, enables him to experience unbridled agency. Here is how Stewart describes López in 1857, five years before he will become supreme leader of Paraguay: "When López spoke, these days, things happened; when he moved, the world drew out of his way. There was no distance now between seeing, knowing, doing. Francisco Solano López had become simple and Stewart found that he was talking to an animal of sorts, as dangerous and easy" (PEL 75). With Eliza's assistance López can now make thought, will, and deed one and the same thing, and given his impulsive and sadistic nature, Stewart rightly sees him as "dangerous."

But it is Eliza who gives us the best visual for understanding the uncanny power and total danger of traumatized agency, the kind of agency that would make possible the catastrophic devastation of the Paraguayan War. Eliza's relationship with Bennett best illuminates the kind of sick and twisted dynamic that animates many relationships, both personal and political. At first Eliza's relationship with Bennett is about a seemingly innocent sexual curiosity, the fourteen-year-old leaving her school and running "down the street" with her "bonnet swinging in" her "hand" (PEL 97). But this innocent scene soon gives way to the unsettling fact that her first sex partner is a bald man with graying hair all over his body. Given this description, it might seem that the man has total power, but Enright cleverly flips expectations by making Eliza an adolescent dominatrix. Here is how Eliza describes her erotic encounter with the older man: "Bennett's touch was sweet as death to me. And oh! Death is sweet when you are fourteen" (PEL 97). Death here is not some romanticized martyrdom; it is a form of sadistic dominance. Eliza makes this clear when she reintroduces the idea about her perverse desire to kill: "What interests me is that high, lonely moment when you know that you might kill a man and he would only beg to be killed again" (PEL 99). I have already addressed Eliza's fascination with the desire to kill, but what makes this passage so much more ominous is her ability and willingness to abuse and even destroy a person and then to have the power to compel the victim to ask for more. After having sex with Bennett for a month, she has the older man "weeping on the floor" (PEL 99). What, in part, motivates Eliza is her yearning for money, for after she describes her murderous desire, she confesses that she took from Bennett "in twenty-one days, the sum of one thousand and seventeen pounds" (PEL 99). This clearly foreshadows what Enright's Eliza will do in Paraguay. Eliza and López will motivate huge segments of the Paraguayan population to sacrifice their lives and even ask to sacrifice their lives, and they will do this so that Eliza and López can enrich themselves, thereby giving the two the means for exerting an unbridled form of agency.

Their insatiable desire for wealth, power, and thus agency makes these two some of the most dangerous types of people to have political control. In interviews, Enright indicates that she is less interested in the specific facts of Lynch's life than she is in the "more universal" type of "truth" that Eliza represents, to use Oates' terminology. Enright told Clair Bracken and Susan Cahill that "a lot of the stories" in her collection *The Portable Virgin* "are about freedom," but also "about women breaking out of systems."[21] For women who succeed in doing this, it would seem they would be heroes. But when Enright discusses Eliza's character, she is anything but admirable or heroic. Here are just a few comments about her character: "Eliza is a greedy girl";[22] "Eliza doesn't exactly learn anything. In fact you could say she loses her ability to learn";[23] and "she is extremely simple."[24]

We could say that Eliza is a strong and resourceful female because she breaks out of an enslaving system and is no longer at the mercy of the British, who had the power to divest the Lynch family of their home and life-sustaining resources. As an enterprising woman, Eliza became the consort of the supreme leader of Paraguay, and as such she has considerable power and agency over her own life as well as the lives of many others, so in the South American context she has become more like a British imperial Lord than an Irish colonial subject. But Eliza is a greedy and unthinking figure who lacks the strength of character, the critical-thinking capacity, or ethical ability to question or challenge the political value or cultural legitimacy of the dominant colonial paradigm. This failing explains Enright's claim that "Eliza isn't one of those women characters that I want to liberate."[25] Flush with a sense of her power and agency, Eliza revels in her ability to transcend the limiting conditions of her upbringing and environment, but hers is a false and deceptive form of individual freedom and political autonomy, because she remains fully in thrall to the colonial politics that make overt and subtle forms of slavery, oppression, and exploitation an everyday reality.

That Enright thinks of Eliza in relation to colonialism is clear when she mentions previous studies of Lynch. In an interview with Shirley Kelly, Enright said that she read "several biographies" about the Irishwoman, and what amazed her "was how exceptionally biased they all were." To be more specific, she found the sources to be "very much in the colonial tradition, sneering at this wild Irish woman, who was seen to be sexually dangerous in a cute sort of way." As she was reading this material, she realized that "these people didn't know Eliza Lynch." By stark contrast, Enright claims that she knows "the sort of person" people say such things about, which is why she felt she "had an advantage over all of these biographers."[26] The colonial perspective generates a particular way of seeing and interpreting Eliza's behavior and being, one that is condescending and dismissive. Enright rejects this colonial approach to Eliza, but she finds it useful because it enabled her to get some actual insight into Eliza's psyche, which enabled her to counter-construct a very different type of Eliza.

The counter-constructed Eliza, I submit, is problematic for many contemporary Enright scholars, who tend to overlook the most disturbing parts of Eliza's character. The logic of the dominant approach goes something like this: Enright is a woman, so her novel must in some way use her protagonist to counter patriarchal narratives by emphasizing Eliza's agency and therewith female agency more generally. As Patricia Coughlan says, the novel "definitely explores feminine agency."[27] But the scholar whose work best represents the standard approach is Ana-Karina Schneider, who notes that the novel "constitutes a critical commentary" about the "marginalization and vilification of women in historiography." Given this critical approach, it might seem that Enright would idealize a character like Eliza. But Schneider resists this interpretive move: "Enright is unsentimental about Eliza Lynch's role in history as she portrays her surrounded by every conceivable source of pleasure while the country descends into chaos: unlike much current feminism, her project is not to lament Eliza's victimization by historians and biographers but to enquire into the processes of female agency."[28] What Enright scholars fail to consider is noteworthy: that Eliza does have considerable agency, but because of the trauma that she suffered, her agential behavior is dangerous at best and catastrophic at worst. While Coughlan and Schneider resist the impulse to glorify Eliza, they are unwilling to examine the degree to which she represents a monstrous albeit limited version of agency.

To be more specific, the reality is not just that the country descends into chaos while Eliza is in Paraguay; it is that Eliza, with so much power over López, played a role in the country's descent. At least this is the case in the novel versions of her story.

For Enright, Eliza is a dangerous, out-of-control figure whose story is derived from but could also illuminate the corrupt psychologies and politics at work in Joseph Stalin, Imelda Marcos, and the Celtic Tiger. In an interview, Enright acknowledges that her "Eliza was about the boom," and when she did the research for the project, she did not just consult sources about López and the Paraguayan War. She also "did a general sweep of dictators,"[29] including "Imelda Marcos's biography" as well as "Svetlana Stalin's biography of her father."[30] In fact, she wanted to use a line about Stalin as an epigraph to her novel, but her publisher said no. Therefore, *The Pleasure of Eliza Lynch* is not really a novel about an Irishwoman who made her way to Paraguay and experienced considerable agency in the nineteenth century. It is a work that fictionalizes the story of a prominent Irishwoman to visualize a trauma-induced interior as it results in a disastrous form of agential excess within a political context.

III

I like the restlessness before it is arrested by words.

There is no reliable evidence documenting when and why the Lynch family left Ireland. So why would Shelby and Enright make the Great Famine such a central part of their protagonist's story? And what is the significance of their aesthetic decision to foreground the Great Famine as a traumatic event in their novels? In an aesthetic sense, the Great Famine is the kind of event that explains why so many authors turned to the biographical novel.

Central to the historical novel is an accurate representation of the past, and for Lukács, this objective requires authors to turn to realism. In his 1938 essay "Realism in the Balance," Lukács argues that "literature is a particular form by means of which objective reality is reflected."[31] Within this framework, the primary task of literature is to picture "how thoughts and feelings grow out of the life of society and how experiences and emotions are part of the total complex of reality."[32] Lukács formulated this idea with considerable precision in *The Historical Novel*, where he claims: "what matters in the novel is fidelity in the reproduction of the material foundations of the life of a given period, its manners and the feelings and thoughts deriving from these."[33] Done correctly, which means with the aid of the most up-to-date instruments of science, logic, and reason, the novel would enable authors and readers "to pierce the surface to discover the underlying essence, i.e., the real factors that relate their experiences to the hidden social forces that produce them."[34]

Lukács' comprehensive, clearly formulated, and well developed justification for literary realism, the historical novel, and the necessary link between the two is what separates him from Enright and biographical novelists more generally. I have already discussed in the previous chapter Duffy's criticisms of Lukács and the historical novel, but it would be useful to indicate that other writers shared his view. Lance Olsen has authored numerous biofictions, including a spectacular one about Nietzsche (*Nietzsche's Kisses*), and in an interview about biofiction, he challenges "some of Lukács' assumptions." Olsen is specific: Lukács is "working with a set that makes me uncomfortable—the quaint notion, for instance, there is some kind of transcendental truth; the one that we can easily define what history is; the one that we can easily define what the novel is."[35] There is something epistemologically naïve about Lukács' work, and since the author of biofiction centers the narrative in a subjective individual consciousness rather an objective historical reality, the assumptions undergirding the Hungarian Marxist's approach strike writers as untenable. Joanna Scott has authored many exceptional biofictions, and in an interview she arrives at a similar conclusion. Scott notes that Lukács objects to the subjective turn in literature, what she refers to as "the modernist immersion in individual subjectivity." But for her, she "was nurtured by that immersion and it is absolutely what I love."[36] Not surprisingly, her focus on human interiors in part explains her reservations about the historical novel: "I've learned that I'm not alone in sharing some deep skepticism in terms of what we used to call the historical novel."[37] Jay Parini has authored important and influential biographical novels about Leo Tolstoy, Walter Benjamin, and Herman Melville, and he, too, has some sharp criticisms of Lukács. For Parini, Lukács makes an overly simplistic distinction between fact and fiction, between literary narrative and actual reality. But this is a mistake: "Having been a great reader of standard biographies, I realized at a certain point that it was simply all narrative, and that narrative is necessarily a form of fiction." Therefore, Parini concludes: "I came to realize that Lukács had it wrong; that, in fact, there's no appreciable difference between history and fiction in terms of narrative technique. It's all narration. Lukács' argument, for me, didn't hold much water."[38] For the rest of the interview, Parini clarifies how and why biographical fiction is different from historical fiction.

Enright does not explicitly distinguish the biographical novel from the historical novel, but a close analysis of her theoretical reflections about fiction indicate that she is working within the same tradition as Duffy, Olsen, Scott, and Parini. In her interview with Hedwig Schwall, Enright says that she is "very impatient with the real."[39] That she has literary realism in mind when she makes this claim is clear because she specifies how divergent forms of literary realism took shape differently within distinct national contexts: "Ideas of 'realism' are very culturally determined. Realism in France is Zola, realism in Ireland is naturalism, so it's very culturally specified what 'the real' is."[40] What led Enright to draw this conclusion is her subtle and nuanced understanding of the way language shapes, restricts, and determines human experience of the phenomena that language purports to describe. As Enright says in her interview with Bracken and Cahill:

> I'm very impatient with the claim to be real, okay, because I just don't think it's possible. There are many ways of writing about life itself. Language is already an act of translation from the real. So I think that once you've made that leap anything goes. And I think of people who claim to be real as people in denial of that first act of translation into words. Words are not reality, broadly speaking. The description of an act is not the act.[41]

Naïve realists believe that language neatly and naturally corresponds to the reality it signifies. But Enright, clearly working within a Nietzsche, Derrida, Foucault, Butler, and Rorty tradition, realizes that language and reality are two separate and distinct phenomena and that the relationship between the two is neither natural nor obvious. Who controls the "real?" How is the "real" figured differently from one spatial and temporal context to the next? And how do those who control language dictate something many consider "real," like history? Instead of taking the "real" as a trustworthy given, Enright exposes the problematic nature of the "real," which is why her work is in irreconcilable conflict with the tradition of historical fiction but aligns so well with the tradition of biographical fiction.

That Enright is an Irish writer in part explains her profound skepticism about the real. Since the British controlled language and history, they could determine "reality." The Irish are lazy savages. The Great Famine was a natural disaster, and not a massive political crime. Homosexuality is a perversion against God and nature. Such platitudes were taken as moral and epistemological givens rather than as linguistic constructions imposed upon people and the world for political power. Symbolically, the Great Famine was an ideal event for exposing how the "real" is constructed through language. In *Demand the World*, Shelby's Cavan initially attributes to the potato blight the transformation of many everyday Irish into criminals. But when he accidentally discovers the hidden Irish food intended for export and considerable profit by an English Lord, he concludes that the disaster is more human- than nature-generated. The British have been able to conceal crucial information and realities and thereby control the official story about something like the Great Famine, but through his accidental discovery, Cavan exposes the authoritative narrative as a strategic misrepresentation of the facts that serves the British economic and political agenda to the deadly detriment of the Irish.

Given the discovery of the way the British contributed to and even created the Great Famine, there are two diametrically opposed responses. One is to counter-construct an alternative real narrative. The British controlled the interpretation of the Great Famine by strategically concealing information and events. When the Irish discovered what the British tried to conceal, they were able to author an alternative history, a seemingly true one about the Great Famine. Enright would reject this approach. Instead, she seeks to expose the "real" as an incoherent idea, or rather, as a culturally manufactured conceptual system. After discovering that the British narrative about the Great Famine is biased, we should realize that all official narratives are ideologically inflected, so the idea of the "real" is not only misleading but also dangerous. Therefore, instead of trying to give readers an alternative "real" history, a historical novel with alternative historical content that is considered objective reality, biographical novelists like Enright destabilize all seemingly official or "real" narratives, exposing them as untrustworthy constructions of biased actors. This is the logical consequence of the shift from the historical novel to the biographical novel, from objective history to a subjective consciousness.

Enright's claims about the incoherence of the "real" is primarily useful because it helps clarify why so many biographical novelists reject the historical novel. Olga Tokarczuk has published a biographical novel about Jacob Frank, an eighteenth-century Jewish religious leader. In an interview about the novel, Tokarczuk confesses that she is "not really a fan of historical novels." This is the case because they prioritize "historic events," and the popular ones reinforce "conservative schemata."[42] In what sense does the historical novel reinforce conservative schemata? There is an established narrative about an event. The historical novel seemingly gives readers an accurate representation of what Lukács refers to as the "natural, objective" weights and proportions of historical "events and destinies."[43] Within this framework, readers are supposed to see the past as it was in itself and thus come to understand how it contributed to the making of who they are in the present. This model is conservative in nature because it asks readers to accept the authoritative version of history presented to them. Put differently, readers are asked to passively conserve rather than progressively challenge seemingly established definitions and interpretations of the real. But for biographical novelists, this is a mistake. The goal should not be to lull readers into accepting the seemingly "natural, objective" representations of "reality" as authoritative and incontrovertible. It should be to activate a form of critical agency within readers in relation to the "real," thus setting into motion an endless process of deconstructing and then reconstructing the seemingly "real."

The recognition that all truths are biased constructions that serve the ideological agenda of those who control the intellectual means of production is now a truism in postmodern circles. Yet, while many contemporary biographical novelists admit that they are postmodernists, many also express frustrations with certain forms and approaches to postmodernism. The traditional postmodernist approach, endlessly deconstructing arbitrary borders of meaning, frivolously engaging in a semantic game of perpetual play, must give way to a more serious intellectual enterprise, which is the knowing construction of a cultural framework in the name of political advancement and social justice. In his interview with Willemien Froneman, Stephanus Muller, who has authored a biographical novel about the composer Arnold van Wyk, explains how postcolonial theory altered his relationship to postmodernism:

> I am transformed by the postcolonial condition into this existential form of self-reflection. And literature and the sensibility of postmodern fiction responds to this transformation, which, as you say, pushes beyond mere play, mere intellectualism, mere narcissism. Ever since my "discovery" of various strands of postcolonial discourse in the nineties, I was struck by the political direction it added to the postmodern sensibility.[44]

This has led Muller to think about the need for literature that "takes seriously the act of writing as a political act."[45] The Spanish biographical novelist Javier Cercas simultaneously embraces and rejects postmodernism. He makes this point in his interview with Virginia Rademacher when he discusses the limitations of David Foster Wallace's fiction: Wallace "realized postmodernism saw literature as just a game. And for me, post-postmodernism would be literature as a game, but as an absolutely serious game, a game where everything is at stake."[46]

Enright makes a similar point about postmodernism in her interview with Bracken and Cahill. They asked the Irish writer to discuss a seeming contradiction in her work, that she wants to break women "out of systems," but that she also considers herself a "post-feminist writer."[47] To understand Enright's post-feminism, it is first important to take into account her postmodernism, which she claims is not like the one many others have internalized. As she stipulates: "The difference in my postmodern impulse is that I actually mean it. There's a sincerity to my discourse that isn't in most postmodern writing."[48] She goes on to say: "I realized that whatever postmodern impulse I have, it is an attempt to be more honest and not less. It's not an attempt to be clever, it's an attempt to be honest. So I was the only sincere postmodernist I know!"[49] In a strange twist given the postmodern claim that all knowledge is ideologically inflected, Enright implies that her postmodernism is non-ideological in nature, which explains why she considers herself post-feminist. In a personal sense, Enright confesses that she is "a feminist."[50] But because "fiction suffers from ideology,"[51] she does not allow her feminism to consciously determine the shape and form of her writing: "I am not a deliberately feminist writer."[52] Her aesthetic objective is much more fundamental and foundational: "Ideology is a very tertiary way of discussing the world. And the writer wants to look at things in a primary way, to make them new again. So you want to go under that existing discourse, linguistically, as well as every other way."[53] The "primary way" of seeing things is how they exist before they are codified and reified into an authoritative discourse. As Enright says in her interview with Schwall: "I realize that I am actually moving toward being all interested in irresolute states; the emotions that happen before things become clear, so all these unsettled, unresolved things. I like the restlessness before it is arrested by words. I am interested in all the disturbance that goes before that, in that, sort of, agitation, of not knowing, or nearly knowing."[54] Language has an arresting effect. Humans create a language to establish a conceptual system about that which is signified, and over time and with communal consensus and validation, that reified discourse is considered reality and forecloses alternative discursive systems and therewith alternative subjective experiences and responses. By transporting readers to that mental state before a conceptual system has been established and communally reified, Enright opens up the possibility of making something "new again."

Putting this framework in concrete terms will prove useful. The British colonial model defines one group of people (the English) as ontologically superior, and as such, they are best equipped to rule and govern what Rudyard Kipling refers to as the "lesser breeds without the law," like the Irish. Having been raised as a colonized subject within this political system, Eliza and her family suffered devastating consequences. When she meets López, she undergoes a Hegelian transformation from being a colonized subject with very little agency to a colonizing master with considerable agency. As such, it would seem that she has come to see the world anew. But this is incorrect. The colonial model is ideological in nature, so it is a tertiary rather than a primary way of seeing. Eliza did not see or make the world new in a primary sense. She did it in a tertiary way. As Enright says, Eliza cannot break out of a system because she has lost the ability to learn. In sum, Eliza has been totally shaped and determined through language into a predetermined model of being (the colonial model) because she has lost the ability to question, challenge, or break out of the culture's reified system. Making something new in a primary way is beyond her.

Given the logic of Enright's primary/tertiary distinction, the historical novel is based on an epistemology (an innocent realism) that would render people susceptible to oppression, though most people would never discover the nature of their subjugation, thus making them unwittingly complicit in their own suffering and trauma. Most people accept an official narrative: the potato blight was a natural disaster that occasioned trauma for many Irish. But for those who can see beneath the surface of the official narrative, the Great Famine was in large measure a human-generated catastrophe. However, if a person is unaware of the way the English controlled life-sustaining resources, placed profit above human lives, and crafted the official narrative about the debacle, then there would be no comprehension of the systemic forms of abuse and violation. But for those who learned the pernicious lesson of the Great Famine, they will respond accordingly by directing their anger and rage at the true perpetrators (the British colonizers). Enright's Eliza, steeped in the tertiary, responds to her trauma by transforming herself from a colonial subject into a colonizing master, a metamorphosis that enables her to kill (even if only in spirit) all those who had the power to make her life miserable when she was in Mallow. But because she does not know how to see in a primary way, she fails to realize that she merely replicates the model that produced "every unfortunate on the surface of the earth."

Writers like Enright are different because what interests them is the primary way of seeing, so instead of identifying a specific political reality (like British colonialism) as the main culprit, they identify something more fundamental as the source of all our woe. That something is the passive submission to the seemingly real, the foundational precept on which the classical historical novel is premised. Thus, the biographical novelist's goal is to jolt the reader into distrusting the "natural, objective" weights and proportions of events found in official narratives about history, including those in the historical novel. Given that the historical narrative is tertiary and that the biographical subject should be primary, the biographical novelist strategically and necessarily undercuts the seemingly established historical record. But the biographical novelist does not do this in order to induce a perpetual suspension of judgment, as is the case with historiographic metafiction, which I will discuss at length in the next chapter. Rather, the goal is to enable people to look at the world in a primary way, "before it is arrested by words," so that they can subsequently make things "new again." Therefore, casting a critical, deconstructive eye on history does not mean an end to the construction of a new way of seeing or systematizing history. Creating new ways of seeing and being are crucial for the artist, and activating the agency drive within the reader is the primary goal of the biographical novelist. Consequently, readers should not complacently accept any narrative as final and absolute. In sum, the aesthetic goal is not to subordinate life and self to a seemingly established system of knowledge; it is to use knowledge and history to activate agency and thereby to set life into motion.

We are now in a position to explain precisely why the Irish have made an important contribution to the rise and legitimization of the biographical novel. Having witnessed and experienced the trauma of that catastrophe known as the Great Famine, which is more human than nature generated, many Irish have come to distrust seemingly authoritative versions of history, which is why so many turned to an aesthetic form that demands that readers question and challenge established (seemingly real) versions of the past and instead invites them to become active critics and creators of knowledge and life. A development in Emma Donoghue's career is telling. In my interview with her, she notes that she authored a historical novel, and it functions exactly as Lukács says it should: "My very first historical novel, *Slammerkin*, is probably a bit deterministic in that while I show this girl enjoying certain limited freedoms, by the time she's sixteen, she's executed. So she's been slapped down."[55] Instead of foregrounding the protagonist's ability to counter or transcend the deterministic forces of her culture, she invented a character "mostly to show those social forces at work."[56] The shift in focus from deterministic history to individual agency, that is, from the historical novel to the biographical novel, leads to a much different type of work, as we see in Donoghue's *Life Mask* and *The Sealed Letter*. For instance, Donoghue has recently published *Frog Music* (2014), a wonderful biographical novel about Jenny Bonnet, a cross-dressing, nineteenth-century woman from San Francisco who flagrantly defied unjust laws and paid for her defiance with her life. When I suggested it is worth thinking about Jenny's character in relation to contemporary discourses about transgender identity, Donoghue responded in a way that is reminiscent of Enright's idea about a primary way of seeing. Donoghue insists that she does not "label" Jenny. Rather, she says that she is "exploring her."[57] Notice how Donoghue's subsequent remarks parallel Enright's thoughts about a primary way of seeing before an idea is arrested in language: "I quite often like to look at when things first got started, so I am very interested in something like transgender as a movement, when people were fresh and naïve in their reactions to it."[58] This is the same thing Donoghue did with her character Anne Damer in *Life Mask*: "In *Life Mask*, I really enjoyed looking at ideas of feminism and democracy in their very early, nuanced form."[59] The aesthetic goal is not to provide an authoritative statement about transgender, democracy, or feminism. It is to picture people in the process of engaging an as-yet clearly defined reality, before that reality has been reified into a seemingly final and authoritative discourse.

But why would biographical novelists do this? To answer this question, Donoghue shifts her focus to the reader and makes a larger claim about quality biofiction more generally: "So biographical fiction, it is often packaged as if it is very cozy and desirable and an escape into another era, but actually I think it should make us uncomfortable. It should provoke us."[60] The biographical novel does not give readers a comforting narrative about the past. It fictionalizes a historical figure in order to jar and provoke readers in the present. Russell Banks has authored a spectacular biographical novel titled *Cloudsplitter*, which is about the son of John Brown, Owen. In an interview, Banks explains how his protagonist is supposed to function. The novelist invents "a character out of historical and autobiographical material" that "is different from the character invented by the biographer or historian."[61] Instead of giving readers an accurate picture of the biographical subject, the "novelist is trying to present, in a sense I suppose, a higher truth, a truth of what it is to be a human being."[62] The construction of this truth about what it means to be a human is what permits the writer to alter historical facts. As Banks says: the author "uses the data of this character's life and embellishes it sufficiently and reorganizes it and restructures it in such a way that it can both be data and a portrait of human beings who are very different from John Brown. It could be a portrait of the reader."[63] Banks tells the story of his "best fan letter" to clarify and justify his point. After the publication of *Cloudsplitter*, he received a letter from "a woman who had served twenty-four years of a life sentence in Bedford Hills prison for women for crimes she committed as a member of the Weather Underground in the sixties and seventies."[64] What gratified Banks so much was her belief "that Owen Brown's life and story were her life and her story."[65] By his own admission, Banks was not trying to give his readers an accurate picture of his biographical subject or the historical past. He was fictionalizing both to give readers a way to think about and understand themselves and their world, and the letter from the former member of the Weather Underground indicates that he succeeded.

This is what Enright does in *The Pleasure of Eliza Lynch*. She takes considerable liberties with the lives of her protagonists. But if we know that she was thinking about Imelda Marcos, Joseph Stalin, and the Celtic Tiger as she was fictionalizing the biographical data and embellishing the historical facts of the lives of Lynch and Lopez, then we can explain why she did this. She fictionalizes the Lynch-Lopez story, as it best captures and reveals a particular way of human being. To be more specific, Lynch and Lopez were freedom fighters—they were casting off old models of political rule and constructing a new one, one that would provide more autonomy and agency for previously marginalized and oppressed people. It would be easy to glorify those who reject enslaving political models and seize agency for themselves and their people, especially at a time when agency and autonomy are under threat. But the story of Lynch and Lopez is a cautionary tale about the huge threats and potential dangers of political agency and autonomy, especially as enacted by those who have suffered trauma at the hands of unjust and oppressive political leaders.

Thus, the biographical novels about Eliza Lynch tell us less about the complex Irish woman from Cork than they do about the dangers of traumatized agency in multiple places and ages, especially in relation to those with political power. As mere reactionaries, such traumatized leaders live in the tertiary rather than the primary, so their form of political agency, seemingly the basis for something original and new, merely replicates the traditional models that they seek to overturn, which makes their agency far less agential than they might have thought. This failure to learn and think is precisely what makes these traumatized leaders so profoundly dangerous. For authors of Eliza Lynch biofiction, there is good reason to conclude that life is an endless cycle of death-bringing idiocy, full of sound and fury and signifying catastrophe.

Part Three

Theoretical Reflections about Biofiction

5

A Poetics of the Biographical Novel: Agency, History, Fiction

The title of this chapter is a strategic allusion to Linda Hutcheon's magisterial study *A Poetics of Postmodernism: History, Theory, Fiction*. That I take issue with Hutcheon should not be interpreted as a negative response to her remarkable and enduring contribution to intellectual and literary history. I agree with much of what she says, and I deeply admire and respect her rigor and precision. But there are some questionable claims in her book, specifically insofar as they relate to the study of biofiction, and in the following pages I intend to clarify why certain biographical novels that Hutcheon mentions (John Banville's *Doctor Copernicus* and *Kepler*, Christa Wolf's *No Place on Earth*, and Chris Scott's *Antichthon*) should not be considered what she terms historiographic metafictions, though I will focus exclusively on Banville's *Doctor Copernicus* to make my case. Indeed, I will argue that Hutcheon's model distorts what most biographical novels actually do.

The ordering of my subtitled triad of terms is crucial. Throughout this book I have been arguing that the biographical novel came into being in order to counter the rise of history-as-science and its concomitant aesthetic form, the historical novel. So instead of foregrounding history, the biographical novel emphasizes human agency, which is why it is the leading term in my triad. Thus, history is subordinate to human agency. This does not mean that history is unimportant. Biographical novelists respect and value history, but they are different from historical novelists because they use rather than do history. These writers mine the past for stories that effectively illuminate who we are but also intelligently imagine what we can become. So history is crucial in biofiction, but in a way that is very different than it is in historical fiction. In this chapter I offer some ways of thinking about the poetics of the biographical novel by setting the form off from Hutcheon's historiographic metafiction.

I

All great problems demand great love.[1]

For Hutcheon, historiographic metafiction is the logical aesthetic product of postmodernism, an intellectual movement that questions, challenges, and ultimately deconstructs "the totalizing master narratives of our culture, those systems by which we usually unify and order (and smooth over) any contradiction in order to make them fit."[2] After taking down seemingly established and trustworthy Truths about the past, postmodernists do not install a new set of overarching, ahistorical maxims. As Hutcheon says: postmodernism "never offers answers that are anything but provisional and contextually determined (and limited)."[3] The postmodern method is to install a new system but then to subvert it, because the postmodernist realizes that stable, incontestable, immutable Truths are incoherent fictions that falsify the realities they seemingly signify.

History played a crucial role in the rise of postmodernism. Postmodernists realize that history conditions the way people understand and experience the world, so when people look at the past, they will not see it as it was in itself. They will see and value what they have been historically conditioned to see and value, thus rendering their judgments limited and suspect. This is why Hutcheon says the following: "The postmodern, then, effects two simultaneous moves. It reinstalls historical contexts as significant and even determining, but in so doing, it problematizes the entire notion of historical knowledge."[4] Having used history to destabilize and to unsettle the epistemological stance of the knowing subject, the postmodernist must then look at the past with destabilized and unsettled eyes.

The postmodern model had a direct impact on aesthetics, specifically the historical novel, which is why Hutcheon briefly discusses Lukács's work. Hutcheon defines "historical fiction as that which is modelled on historiography to the extent that it is motivated and made operative by a notion of history as a shaping force (in the narrative and in human destiny)."[5] She credits Lukács, in particular, for illustrating how "the historical novel could enact historical process by presenting a microcosm which generalizes and concentrates."[6] Within this framework, the main character "should be a type, a synthesis of the general and particular, of 'all the humanly and socially essential determinants.'"[7] Given this definition, Hutcheon claims that Banville's *Doctor Copernicus* would not qualify as a historical novel. Instead of representing a type, Banville's protagonist takes "on different, particularized, and ultimately ex-centric status,"[8] which makes the work more historiographic metafiction than historical fiction, and since "historiographic metafiction espouses a postmodern ideology of plurality and recognition of difference," the Lukácsian idea of " 'type' has little function" within the work, "except as something to be ironically undercut."[9]

To clarify and justify her approach, Hutcheon uses two separate approaches to interpret *Doctor Copernicus*. She first illustrates how the work functions as a traditional historical novel. After noting how historical novels identify the causal forces that will shape and determine future subjectivities, she applies the principle to Banville's work. This causal model explains why sixteenth-century characters in Banville's novel "are made to talk like Wittgenstein."[10] If I understand the logic of her interpretation, it would be that Copernicus's revision of the Ptolemaic model and his installation of a heliocentric one logically led to Wittgenstein's language philosophy, so the work, treated in this instance as a historical novel, clarifies how we have come to be as we currently are, which is people who are deeply skeptical about Reality because we understand how a wide range of language games functions to construct "reality" in radically divergent ways. However, Hutcheon believes that there is something in *Doctor Copernicus* that makes it different from or other than a historical novel, and that something is "its intense self-consciousness about the way in which all this is done."[11] This self-reflective act of knowing makes the work "historiographic metafiction—and not historical fiction."[12] Within the Lukácsian framework, Copernicus is supposed to symbolically represent a type, a cultural universal of sorts. But because he is so particular and specific and because he is subsequently undercut, he "is not a type of anything."[13] Rather, the novel enacts a process whereby the protagonist projects a conceptual model into being which is subsequently undermined through a self-reflexive critique about the way products of thought are historically conditioned and constructed, thereby rendering specific historical truths untrustworthy and provisional.

What leads Hutcheon to misinterpret *Doctor Copernicus* in particular and biographical novels more generally is her faulty approach to the naming of characters. For Hutcheon, naming a character after an actual historical figure has a specific effect, which is "to validate or authenticate the fictional world by their presence, as if to hide the joins between fiction and history in a formal and ontological sleight of hand."[14] But authors of biofiction reject this view, because they say that their work is fiction, and not biography, so readers should know that what they get in the novel is a fictional version of the actual figure rather than an accurate representation of the person and the past. In other words, there is no pretense to giving readers an accurate or authentic version of the historical past, no attempt to conceal the fictional nature of the narrative by hiding the joins between fiction and history. For instance, when asked in an interview about the liberties a novelist takes with biography and history, Russell Banks says that that is an incorrect way to think about what writers of biofiction do. Banks claims that he is "using history to tell a story."[15] Based on this aesthetic paradigm, actual history is subordinate to the author's narrative, so readers should not approach the work as an attempt to provide an accurate version of history or a supplement or a correction of the historical record: "My real purpose is to generate and tell a story. It is not to correct history or write an addendum to the historical or biographical record. It is simply to appropriate the material that history has dropped at my door."[16] History is history and fiction is fiction, and to treat the two as if they are one and the same is a failure to understand the separate and distinct truth contracts that writers from each genre tacitly establish with their readers.

Banks is very clear when he specifies how authors enter into distinct contracts with readers. For Banks, if a work is called "a novel on the cover of the title page," then readers should know that what they are getting is fiction. The word novel "implies [...] a contract with the reader."[17] But, Banks continues, "if it's called a memoir, it has a different contract."[18] Given the distinct contracts, were a memoir writer to consciously and strategically alter a fact, then the reader would feel violated—recall the response (most notably Oprah Winfrey's) to James Frey's false claims in his memoir *A Million Little Pieces*. Now, of course, people could easily counter: when writing, authors select certain facts and conveniently ignore others, so all memoirs are really fictions, whether they admit it or not. This idea that everything is a fiction is certainly a truism in postmodern circles. But there is a difference between the inadvertent and inevitable fictionalization that comprises all writing and the strategic fictionalization found in a novel. For example, the main character of Banks's *Cloudsplitter* is Owen Brown, the son of John Brown. In real life he died in 1889, but in Banks's novel, he is still alive in 1903, when he tells his story. Were *Cloudsplitter* biography or history, readers would be outraged by this conscious and strategic alteration of fact. But since the work is fiction, readers should realize that the author has taken this liberty for a distinctly literary purpose. As Banks says, he had his character live into the twentieth century "so that his story, John Brown's story, would lose some of the antique quality it might have had otherwise and would point toward the twentieth century, to our own time."[19]

There are two divergent approaches to the role of history in literature here. For the historical novelist, the past has shaped and determined who we are in the present, so the historical novelist, by doing history, establishes a causal framework for understanding the determinative lines of connection between the past and the present. But since Banks admits that he is not doing history ("by authorial fiat, I violated history"[20]), it would be a mistake to characterize *Cloudsplitter* as a historical novel. What Banks actually does is to appropriate a story from the past and smudge it in order to make it relevant to people in the present. Banks notes that the work is "now being read as a portrait of the terrorist that can be applied to our present time."[21] Within this framework, the past does not determine who we have become. A more accurate way of characterizing the aesthetic state of affairs would be to say that stories from the past can be fictionalized such that they could illuminate ways of thinking and being in the present and the future—William Styron describes this as the author using the story from the past to create a "metaphorical diagram" that could enable us to see certain structures at work within multiple cultures and in multiple ages.[22]

To clarify precisely how biographical novels differ from historical novels, I will do a close analysis of *Doctor Copernicus*. More than a decade before the biofiction boom of the 1990s, Banville published *Doctor Copernicus* (1976), a stunningly insightful work about the life of the scientist who set into motion a paradigm-shifting model of the universe. In keeping with the practices of biographical novelists, Banville unapologetically admits in his Acknowledgements that there are "willed" "factual errors"[23] in his narrative, and the first page of the novel flaunts some of them. Banville imagines his way into the mind of the young Copernicus, just at that point when the child is acquiring language, and through free indirect discourse, the narrator has the youth offer anachronistic reflections about language that anticipate the works of Nietzsche, Wittgenstein, Jacques Derrida, Michel Foucault, and Paul de Man. The introductory emphasis on language is more than just a strategic allusion to the opening of Joyce's *The Portrait of an Artist as a Young Man*. It cues the reader to attend to one of the main ideas throughout the novel: that an uncritical approach to and acceptance of language can enslave a person both mentally and bodily.

Looking out a window, the young Copernicus sees a swaying, dancing, waving object, which his mother transmutes into a verbal sign: "*Look, Nicholas, look! See the big tree!*"[24] There is a word that neatly and naturally corresponds to the reality it signifies. But this is not how the future scientist initially understands the relationship between language and the world. As the narrator notes: "Everything had a name, but although every name was nothing without the thing named, the thing cared nothing for its name, had no need of a name, and was itself only."[25] In stark contrast to the *liber mundi* tradition, which holds that the physical universe is like a readable book, the external world is not waiting to be correctly named. In fact, it is supremely indifferent to the way humans use language to describe it. It is semiotic arrogance that leads humans to subordinate the material world to human discourse and to believe that their language accurately represents the Reality of the world as it is in itself. The young Copernicus, intuitively recognizing that there is an unbridgeable gap between language and that which it signifies and that language necessarily falsifies the reality that it purports to signify, does not accept the correspondence theory of truth. But this changes. With time the arrogant community of language users will naturalize him into their belief that discourse gives him epistemological access to the Truth about external phenomena. Therefore, instead of seeing material objects as fundamentally mysterious and insusceptible to the reductive formulations of language, he will adopt the dominant mental orientation toward the external world: "He soon forgot about these enigmatic matters [about language], and learned to talk as others talked, full of conviction, unquestioningly."[26]

The world into which the inquisitive intellectual is thrown does not value probing inquiry, healthy skepticism, and nuanced comprehension. To the contrary, it privileges epistemological submission to established orthodoxies. The ten-year-old Copernicus learns this lesson after his father's death, when he becomes the ward of his uncle, who is a Canon "with his eye on the bishopric."[27] The learned man informs the child that he will be sent "to the University of Cracow, where you will study canon law."[28] His uncle makes his expectations clear: "I do not ask you to understand, only to obey,"[29] a claim that he repeats just moments later. As a student, Copernicus will not be encouraged to critically analyze the truth or value of the way a specific discursive system functions in relation to that which it signifies. He will be sometimes subtly, sometimes overtly coerced into submitting to the authoritative discourse of the time, whether or not that system is suitable, accurate, or true.

But Copernicus is different from most, because he possesses an extraordinary capacity for comprehension, which frequently irritates his "masters."[30] One master, Canon Wodka, takes note of Copernicus, and he helps the precocious student recapture his early understanding of language. After briefly raising questions about the relationship between Ptolemy's theory of the heavens and the reality that it signifies, Wodka says: "when we are dealing with these matters, truth becomes an ambiguous concept."[31] Based on this approach, Wodka admonishes the curious youth to entertain the following possibility: "Consider this, child, listen: all theories are but names, *but the world itself is a thing*."[32] This approach to language and knowledge will make possible Copernicus's major contribution to the world of ideas.

In a conversation with one of his professors, Copernicus indicates that he has taken a major step in the direction of disobeying one of the ancient masters. Here is what he says to Professor Brudzewski:

> It seems to me, *magister*, that we must revise our notions of the nature of things. For thirteen hundred years astronomers have been content to follow Ptolemy without question, *like credulous women*, as Regiomontanus says, but in all that time they have not been able to discern or deduce the principal thing, namely the shape of the universe and the unchanging symmetry of its parts.[33]

The problem, however, is that his culture is so overwhelming and powerful that he is frequently seduced into accepting a version of the system that he critiqued and rejected. For instance, after Copernicus extensively meditates on his objectives as a scientist, the narrator notes how he suffers a serious intellectual setback: "No sooner had he realised the absolute necessity for a creative leap than his instincts without his knowing had thrown up their defences against such a scandalous notion, thrusting him back into the closed system of worn-out orthodoxies."[34] Copernicus yearns to break free from the "worn-out orthodoxies" of the past, but, without his knowledge or consent, he is frequently drawn back into the age-old system of thought. Intellectual freedom is far more complex and challenging than he could have ever imagined or anticipated.

Specifically, while Copernicus is starting to question and challenge a seemingly established model of the universe, he remains in thrall to a Platonist worldview, which holds that there is an ultimate Reality behind the deceptive world of appearances. Therefore, instead of attending to the material world in front of him, Copernicus attempts to access and validate the world of Eternal Forms. Note how he characterizes his project to himself: "The closed system of the science must be broken, in order that it might transcend itself and its own sterile concerns, and thus become an instrument for verifying the real rather than merely postulating the possible."[35] Science is only a springboard for something much bigger and more important, and as such, it has minimal significance in its own right.

What makes this epistemological orientation so unfortunate and even dangerous is how it leads a person to devalue and even overlook physical reality, including people. Banville's Copernicus realizes this on his deathbed, when he has an imagined visitation from his dead brother. Andreas was a scoundrel who died of syphilis, but instead of nurturing and supporting him, Copernicus turned his back on his family member. The imagined Andreas, who is really just a mental concoction of Copernicus's subconscious, tells the scientist how his Neoplatonist ideology and approach led him to overlook and/or dismiss the everyday: "you tried to discard the commonplace truths for the transcendent ideals, and so failed."[36] Within this framework, rather than seeing his brother, Copernicus merely used him as the outcast other against which he could set himself. As the imagined Andreas says to him: "I was the one absolutely necessary thing, for I was there always to remind you of what you must transcend. I was the bent bow from which you propelled yourself beyond the filthy world."[37] Copernicus used Andreas to catapult himself into the transcendent world of Platonic Forms. But what he did not understand is that such a realm of being is nothing more than a phantom of an overheated imagination: "There had to be a little regard, yes, the regard which the arrow bears for the bow, but never the other, the thing itself, the vivid thing, which is not to be found in any book, nor in the firmament, nor in the absolute forms."[38] In search of an ultimate Reality beyond language, Copernicus failed to see the actual reality in front of him, which is the material world, including the people around him. Therefore, rather than embracing and loving them, he "turned away, appalled and … embarrassed."[39] In sum, Copernicus secured intellectual agency by rejecting the Ptolemaic model of the universe and counter-constructing a heliocentric paradigm, but he remained captive to the dictates of his age by embracing its dominant Neoplatonist epistemology, and the consequences were deadly. Instead of meeting his human needs and those of the people around him, he failed to see worldly beings because of his pursuit of a fantastical ideal, a Platonic fiction that was seen as an ultimately Reality. And what he lost in the process "is the great miracle" of life, the one thing "that matters," which is "love."[40]

Hutcheon is certainly right to suggest that the characters in the novel talk like Wittgenstein, as I will demonstrate shortly. But the question I want to pose is this: How do genre conventions generate radically opposing interpretations of Banville's usage of Wittgenstein in the novel? If we read *Doctor Copernicus* as a historical novel, then it would picture the way a major intellectual development contributed to the making of who we are in the present. But Hutcheon rejects this approach. Instead, she reads *Doctor Copernicus* as a historiographic metafiction, because it visualizes Copernicus installing a new conceptual system, but then the novel, through an act of hyper-critical self-reflection, casts doubt on that newly installed system, thus subverting what it initially established. What these two aesthetic approaches share in common, however, is that they are "modelled on historiography to the extent that" they are "motivated and made operative by a notion of history as a shaping force (in the narrative and in human destiny)."[41] Given this fact, authors of historical fiction and historiographic metafiction reinstall "historical contexts," thereby clarifying how they are "significant and determining," though historiographical metafiction will go one step further by subsequently problematizing "the entire notion of historical knowledge."[42]

Authors of biofiction certainly understand the causal and even determinative nature of the historical past, and they accept that interpretation of the material world to some degree. But their aesthetic focus is on human agency rather than historical determinism, so deconstructing the newly installed system is not that important. This does not mean that history is irrelevant. It just means that biographical novelists fictionalize ("smudge," to use Oates's term) significant and relevant stories from the past in order to bring into existence a new way of seeing and/or being in the present and for the future. According to this model, instead of seeing anachronistic references as confirming the degree to which the present is the logical product of the determinative events from the past, they can be interpreted as the author's new way of ordering life and the world. This does not mean that Banville believes that the actual Copernicus had the epiphanies about language, truth, and love that he does in *Doctor Copernicus*; history is subordinate to agency in biofiction, so the author takes liberties with facts in order to foreground agential possibilities. It just means that Banville was able to use Copernicus's life story to communicate his distinctive views about language, truth, and love, and how those new ideas could become a reality in the present and future.

Banville's engagement with Wittgenstein's work is instructive. The Irish author concludes his 1973 novel *Birchwood* with the famous sentence from Wittgenstein's *Tractatus Logico-Philosophicus*: "whereof I cannot speak, thereof I must be silent."[43] Based on this explicit usage of Wittgenstein, it might seem that the Austrian philosopher is a major and reliable source of authority in Banville's fiction.[44] But the way Wittgenstein's work is deployed in *Doctor Copernicus* suggests otherwise. Wittgenstein makes a distinction between that which is transcendental and that which is empirical. Given that humans are historically embedded beings, they cannot stand outside their own limiting humanity. Therefore, they cannot epistemologically access or say anything with certainty about the transcendental, which for Wittgenstein includes ethics and aesthetics. What, in part, led Wittgenstein to draw this conclusion was his analysis of a Newtonian model of the world. Using a "fine square network," Newton was able to bring "the description of the universe to a unified form."[45] But Wittgenstein notes that this description "is arbitrary, because" he "could have applied with equal success a net with a triangular or hexagonal mesh."[46] From this semiotic fact Wittgenstein concludes that "Newtonian mechanics asserts nothing about the world."[47] All that this example tells us is that the world "can be described in that particular way in which as a matter of fact it is described."[48] What the world is in itself cannot be expressed in language, because "the sense of the world must lie outside the world,"[49] and since humans are embedded in the world, the sense of the world is beyond their ken. Within this framework, propositional truths about the world cannot do the semiotic work of signifying the world as it is in itself. Therefore, instead of naively believing in language, Wittgenstein turns against words and devises a showing theory for engaging the world: "What *can* be shown *cannot* be said."[50] Where language fails, showing succeeds: "That anything falls under a formal concept as an object belonging to it, cannot be expressed by a proposition. But it is shown in the symbol for the object itself."[51]

In the imagined conversation, Andreas tells his brother to stop seeking the truth, because "we *are* the truth."[52] Unsatisfied with this claim, Copernicus asks how we may speak this truth. But Andreas gives his brother a Wittgensteinian answer: "It may not be spoken, brother, but perhaps it may be … shown."[53] Copernicus needs to have much more modest semiotic expectations; he needs to reject the hyperbolic pretensions of language to access and signify a transcendent Reality and to content himself with a world that visually shows but does not semiotically reveal itself. Based on Andreas's direct appropriation of Wittgenstein's showing theory from the *Tractatus*, it might seem that Banville has wholly adopted the work of the Austrian philosopher and used it to give readers a picture of (to show) sixteenth-century developments in science.

But there are two separate reasons why this is not correct. First, Wittgenstein and Banville have different reasons for despairing about the failures of language in relation to the transcendent. For Wittgenstein, given the limiting situation resulting from human embeddedness in the material and historical world, knowledge of the transcendent or the metaphysical is simply beyond the mind.

Therefore, Wittgenstein counsels his readers "to say nothing except what can be said, *i.e.* the propositions of natural science, *i.e.* something that has nothing to do with philosophy: and then always, when someone else wished to say something metaphysical, to demonstrate to him that he had given no meaning to certain signs in his propositions."[54] To say anything above or beyond what the natural sciences would allow is nothing more than a charming and incoherent musing, and a good philosopher should demonstrate this to any would-be metaphysician. The despairing conclusion of the *Tractatus* is the logical outcome of the limits of language and knowledge, specifically in relation to the transcendent and the metaphysical.

Andreas accepts this Wittgensteinian axiom, but it is not what leads him to despair. Andreas thinks of language as it functions to determine social and human relations. After faulting Copernicus for his "quest for truth" and his obsession with "transcendent knowledge," Andreas tells his brother directly where he went wrong: "You thought to transcend the world."[55] Different from Wittgenstein, Andreas does not seem overly fixated on the limiting consequences of language for knowledge. His concern is with the way the yearning for the transcendent negatively impacts how people interact with the world and others. It is at this point that Andreas tells Copernicus how he used Andreas and others to try to catapult himself into the imagined transcendent. Copernicus may have advanced our understanding of the universe through his heliocentric model, but it is people like him, having internalized a two-tiered model of knowledge and fixated on some metaphysical yonder to the exclusion of the physical here and now, who have degraded the material world, including most people in it. Therefore, Andreas despairs, not because of the limits of language and knowledge, but because the two-tiered model of knowledge and truth logically leads to systemic violations of the real world and actual people.

The more important distinction between Wittgenstein and Banville relates to a negative versus an affirming approach to language and the world. In a coldly logical way, Wittgenstein tells his readers what they can legitimately say and not say, whereas Banville, starting with love, indicates how people can promote and advance better and more humane interactions with people and the world. Instead of turning away from the material world in disgust, treating it as a pale imitation of a transcendent Reality, or using it to catapult himself into the metaphysical, as Banville's Copernicus did, Andreas recommends that his brother privilege the emotional reality of love over the rational Reality of the intellect and then proceed to construct relations with the world accordingly. Within this framework, "absolute forms" are not the things that really matter. As Andreas says to Copernicus:

> You know what I mean, brother. It is that thing, passionate and yet calm, fierce and coming from far away, fabulous and yet ordinary, that thing which is all that matters, which is the great miracle. You glimpsed it briefly in our father, in sister Barbara, in Fracastoro, in Anna Schillings, in all the others, and even, yes, in me, glimpsed it, and turned away, appalled and … embarrassed. Call it acceptance, call it love if you wish.[56]

This passage is crucial because it illustrates that Banville is more Nietzschean than Wittgensteinian.

The kind of critique of truth, language, metaphysics, and the transcendent found in Wittgenstein's *Tractatus* can also be seen in Nietzsche's writings. But from the facts of human embeddedness and the limits of language and knowledge Nietzsche drew a very different conclusion. In *On the Genealogy of Morals*, Nietzsche expresses why a Wittgensteinian approach is misguided. Like Banville, Nietzsche realizes that Copernicus set into motion a way of thinking that would lead to our current critical views about language and truth: "Since Copernicus, man seems to have got himself on an inclined plane—now he is slipping faster and faster away from the center into—what? into nothingness? into a '*penetrating* sense of his nothingness'?"[57] The Copernican Revolution leads to a form of nihilism, a negation of human dignity and the diminution of human thought, what Nietzsche refers to as "the self-belittlement of man, his *will* to self-belittlement."[58]

This development has specific implications for historiography. After taking note of the steadily declining certainties in post-Copernican epistemologies, Nietzsche wonders how the radical questioning of overarching knowledge systems specifically impacts the study of history: "does modern historiography perhaps display an attitude more assured of life and ideals? Its noblest claim nowadays is that it is a mirror; it rejects all teleology; it no longer wishes to 'prove' anything; it disdains to play the judge and considers this a sign of good taste—it affirms as little as it denies; it ascertains, it 'describes.' "[59] Refusing to take a semiotic stance, resisting the impulse to formulate a coherent or authoritative interpretation of the past, and choosing merely to describe may seem like humble responses to the intellectual community's growing awareness of the limits of ahistorical approaches. But Nietzsche would dub those unacceptable responses: "All this is to a high degree ascetic; but at the same time it is to an even higher degree *nihilistic*, let us not deceive ourselves about that!"[60] Just to be clear: Nietzsche condemns nihilism as an anti-human worldview that leads to a senseless form of human belittlement and even self negation. In response to the growing incredulity toward metanarratives, Nietzsche, who privileges affirmation over negation, believes that thinkers should passionately and intelligently create new interpretations of the world. These new ways of seeing and being would not be considered final or absolute. Nietzsche realizes that they are provisional constructions that will serve the intellectual community for only a period of time. Within this framework, creators of new ways of thinking and being should be willing to engage in an endless contest of ideas. They must vigorously make the case for their new paradigm, but they should also be open to criticism of it, because the post-Copernican lesson is that no truth system is safe from a deconstructive critique.

My main claim is this: there were two separate aesthetic responses to the Copernican challenge to an established model of reality, and those distinct responses led to corresponding aesthetic forms. The Wittgensteinian response led to a model of perpetually challenging all conceptual systems that appealed to the transcendent and the metaphysical for validation. As soon as someone makes a metaphysical claim, it is the philosopher's duty "to demonstrate" that he or she has "given no meaning to certain signs." So the intellectual model is to install and subvert, because no reliable overarching system can be established. This Wittgensteinian model mandated the rise of a specific aesthetic form, and historiographic metafiction is that form.

The Nietzschean response led to a model of passionately and unapologetically constructing new ways of seeing and being, and while Nietzsche would invite others to question and challenge all innovative approaches to constructing the world, he would not commit himself to the Wittgenstein/Hutcheon project of perpetually deconstructing newly installed models. Through much labor and even more rigor, competent artists and thinkers should confidently construct authoritative (but not authoritarian) interpretations of the world. Given this approach, Nietzsche would reject the historiographic-metafiction project because he would consider it nihilistic in nature. Nietzsche was committed to affirming rather than negating, even if he knew that what he affirmed was provisional and subject to a future deconstruction. This Nietzschean approach mandated the rise of a specific aesthetic form, and biofiction is that form. Significantly, this literary form, focused as it is on agency, does the exact opposite of historiographic metafiction. Instead of installing and then subverting, it subverts and then installs.

There are two dimensions to subverting and installing. The first relates to the protagonist. In the novel, Copernicus subverts Ptolemy's geocentric model and replaces it with his heliocentric system. Based on this claim, it might seem that *Doctor Copernicus* should be characterized as a historiographic metafiction, because Banville's Copernicus will use a Wittgensteinian approach to criticize and even subvert his own model of the universe. As he says to one of his disciples:

> You imagine that my book is a kind of mirror in which the real world is reflected; but you are mistaken, you must realise that. In order to build such a mirror, I should need to be able to perceive the world whole, in its entirety and in its essence. But our lives are lived in such a tiny, confined space, and in such disorder, that this perception is not possible.[61]

Human embeddedness precludes the possibility of a whole-world or outside-the-world perspective, and since the sense of the world must lie outside the limited human world, Copernicus realizes that his perspective is probably flawed.

This discovery leads Copernicus to despair of the possibility of science. Trapped within the limited and limiting human perspective, there is no way to validate his specific model or any model of the universe. After describing how he and the ancients have lifted their heads to the skies in order to describe the universe, he says that without a more-than-human perspective, "all these theories are equal in value."[62] Thus, his "book is not science—it is a dream." Given this epistemic fact, he concludes: "I am not even sure if science is possible."[63] Since all knowledge systems are the biased products of a limiting and distorting consciousness, the idea of science's neutral and objective truths is nothing more than a phantom ideal.

Were Copernicus's disillusioned reflections about his book and scientific knowledge more generally the end of the novel, then it would be reasonable to classify *Doctor Copernicus* as a historiographic metafiction. But the novel concludes with Andreas using Nietzschean ideas to counter Copernicus's Wittgensteinian version of language, truth, and knowledge. That Banville admires and respects the German philologist is clear from his numerous and all positive references to him in essays and interviews. The 1990 essay "Survivors of Joyce" begins with a Nietzsche quotation, and in order to clarify what continually brings readers back to Joyce's *Ulysses*, he cites a nearly two-page quotation from *Human, All Too Human: A Book for Free Spirits*.[64] In the

1997 essay "Thou Shalt Not Kill," Banville cites from an April 7, 1986 entry from his own notebook for his novel *The Book of Evidence* (1989), and there are two quotations from Nietzsche, one from "*Beyond Good and Evil*," the other from "*Fröliche* (sic) *Wissenschaft*."[65] On the next page, Banville confesses that "Nietzsche is there in the pages [of *The Book of Evidence*], certainly, sometimes quoted directly, without acknowledgement."[66] In a 2015 interview with Aurora Piñeiro, Banville references Nietzsche three separate times in order to identify ideas that are of central importance in his own work. Two of those ideas are useful for understanding Andreas's concluding critique of his brother.

Like Plato, Banville's Copernicus believes that the material world is ephemeral, deceptive, and illusory. Behind, above, or outside the physical universe is an ultimate Reality that is not subject to secular ambiguity, human contingency, and random change. Copernicus's deepest desire and final goal is to get beyond the superficial world of appearance and to epistemologically access and accurately represent the Ideal world of Eternal Forms: "He was after the thing itself now, the unadorned, the stony thing."[67] But Andreas, like Nietzsche, rejects this two-tiered model of knowledge. Plato's surface world of material appearances is all there is, so the idea of transcending the world and the human and thereby coming to know things-in-themselves is a cute concoction of certain philosophers, but it is not a realistic model for human knowing. Banville makes this point in the interview: "As Nietzsche says, 'on the surface, that is where the real depth lies.' "[68] This is a point he makes in more depth and with more clarity in his 1993 essay "The Personae of Summer": "Nietzsche was the first to recognise that the true depth of a thing is in its surface. Art is shallow, and therein lies its deeps. The face is all, and, in front of the face, the mask."[69] Compared to Neoplatonism, art is shallow because it deals only with ephemeral surfaces, while Neoplatonism deals with ultimate Realities. But since the ever-changing material world is all that exists, the Neoplatonic project, which was once thought deep, does not even rise to the level of the shallow.

What led Nietzsche to draw this conclusion was his careful engagement with language. When talking about the nature of symmetry, Banville says to Piñeiro: "Nietzsche even denies self-identity, the identity of the thing-in-itself. He says this is merely a construction of words."[70] In a Platonic world, language is an imperfect vehicle that can mentally transport humans to an absolute Reality beyond language, a Reality that is what it is whether humans perceive it or not. Having been mentally transported to that Reality would enable people to engage and define the thing-in-itself, thus allowing humans to get beyond language and to Reality. But for Banville, "there is no 'thing-in-itself.'"[71] Or, to put this in Nietzsche's words, "there is no 'thing-in-itself.' "[72] For Nietzsche, "all concepts in which an entire process is semiotically concentrated elude definition; only that which has no history is definable."[73] Because we are all embedded in time, everything has a history. Therefore, nothing is definable. Language is all. Put differently, since humans will fashion words to mean different things in different times and places, there can be no stable, definable identity. This is why Banville draws the following conclusion: "The word 'different' should be elided from the language, because it is redundant. Everything is different."[74]

But it is important to note that Banville does not reject Copernicus's Neoplatonism simply because it is an epistemological fantasy of a bygone era. He, like Nietzsche, opposes it because it leads people to despise the world and to use people as a mere means for transcending the physical universe. In short, he renounces Neoplatonism because it is destructive and deadly. Therefore, Banville follows the injunction of Nietzsche's Zarathustra: "*remain faithful to the earth* and do not believe those who speak to you of extraterrestrial hopes."[75] From a Neoplatonic or Wittgensteinian perspective, Copernicus's construction of a heliocentric model falls far short of signifying Reality, the thing-in-itself, so what he has accomplished is limited at best and flawed at worst. But from a Nietzschean perspective, the invention of a new way of seeing can be a loving affirmation of the world, even if it is provisional and eventually deconstructed. Banville is clearly working within a Nietzschean tradition. From the Irish author's perspective, what makes Copernicus such a troubling figure is the mental orientation with which he engages people and the world, and this is the consequence of having embraced and internalized Neoplatonism. Since all things in the material universe are debased versions of ideal spiritual Realities, they are only unworthy means to a much more glorious end. Abolishing the spiritual world, centering attention on the material world, and affirming and even loving the physical universe would lead to a much healthier and more productive relationship with life, people, and the world—this is the reversal that Nietzsche hopes to effectuate, and it is this reversal that is of crucial importance in *Doctor Copernicus*.

Just as Copernicus subverts Ptolemy's geocentric model and installs a heliocentric one, Banville subverts Copernicus's Neoplatonic model and installs a Nietzschean one. But while Banville's Copernicus uses Wittgensteinian ideas to subvert his newly installed heliocentric system, thus making the work function like a historiographic metafiction, neither Andreas nor Banville calls the world-loving and -affirming model into question, thus making the work function like a biofiction, and definitely not a historiographic metafiction. To be more specific, and here I want to establish a couple key ideas regarding biofiction, Banville's primary commitment is to his own aesthetic vision of life, so historical fact and accuracy are subordinate to his objectives as a creative artist. It is for this reason that *Doctor Copernicus* would qualify neither as a historical novel nor a historiographic metafiction. The novel is full of inaccuracies, anachronisms, and fabrications. To think that Banville gives his readers history or is doing history (that he is reinstalling historical contexts, as Hutcheon would say) in his novel is simply absurd. What he actually does is to fictionalize the life of Copernicus, which is to say that he identifies some key facts about the man; strategically, consciously, and willfully alters some of those facts; and then uses those modified ideas to create a protagonist that embodies Banville's ways of thinking about life and the world. In short, Copernicus is merely a vehicle through which Banville gives us himself.

Where scholars go wrong in their interpretations of *Doctor Copernicus* is in their failure to take into account the two separate systems that are deconstructed in the novel. There has been much written about *Doctor Copernicus*, but I want to focus on the work of only two first-rate scholars: Ingo Berensmeyer and Elke D'hoker. Berensmeyer acknowledges that there are difficulties in classifying *Doctor Copernicus*. And yet, he tends to read the work as "a dense—and well-researched—mental biography"[76] or as a work that contains "a historically accurate account of the life and times of Copernicus."[77] While Berensmeyer notes that there are anachronistic references in the text, specifically to "Nietzsche and Wittgenstein,"[78] he sees these allusions in thematic terms:

> *Doctor Copernicus* thematises the lost unity and the sense of alienation characteristic of the modern human condition, which has often been attributed to the "humiliation" of man through the Copernican displacement of the earth away from the centre into the vacuum. Through frequent anachronisms, direct quotations and allusions to modern writers woven into the text, Banville makes his Copernicus a "prototype of modern man."[79]

Within this framework, there is a logical and necessary response to Copernicus's discovery, and the most articulate and emblematic response can be found in the writings of Nietzsche and Wittgenstein, whose works are compatible and mutually reinforcing.

Like Berensmeyer, D'hoker notes the text's allusions to Wittgenstein and Nietzsche. In the *Tractatus*, the Austrian philosopher exposes the limits of knowledge, but he leaves open a positive door of possibility in the mystical. As Wittgenstein says: "There is indeed the inexpressible. This *shows* itself; it is the mystical."[80] D'hoker applies this approach to Banville's works. With "Wittgenstein's ordinary language philosophy" in mind, what we see in the protagonist is a "gradual rejection of a skeptical scientific project in favor of romantic notions of the 'mystical' and the 'ordinary.' "[81] What links Wittgenstein and Nietzsche is their critique of Copernicus's epistemological overreach. Here is how D'hoker would characterize Nietzsche's view: "Nietzsche would probably castigate Copernicus's quest as an instance of scientific hubris: through vanity, Nietzsche would argue, Copernicus fatally defies his position within physical nature and puts himself on a par with the lord of creation."[82] It is when Banville's Copernicus finally realizes his inability to transcend the human or to access the metaphysical that he comes to understand the Nietzschean-Wittgensteinian vacuity of being. To quote D'hoker: "The sense of an emptiness at the heart of Copernicus's theories echoes Nietzsche's and Wittgenstein's rejection of metaphysics as empty, as not worth the trouble."[83] Berensmeyer and D'hoker bring Nietzsche and Wittgenstein together in order to identify a way of thinking that is of crucial importance for understanding Banville, his Copernicus, and his novel.

But this conflation is misleading. Take, for instance, the idea of the mystical. This is obviously a positive concept and experience in Wittgenstein's work. But here is what Nietzsche says: "Mystical explanations are considered deep. The truth is that they are not even superficial."[84] For Nietzsche, the mystical does not even rise to the level of being taken seriously as a legitimate reality. In other words, it is beneath the superficial. Since the mystical is such a crucial idea in the *Tractatus*, one toward which the whole work builds, the incompatible responses to it are of significant importance.

Let me provide two separate reasons why it is misleading to conflate Nietzsche and Wittgenstein when interpreting *Doctor Copernicus*. By his own admission, Banville knows very little of Wittgenstein's work, and what he does know seems to be only the *Tractatus*, as that is the work he directly references in *Birchwood* and *Doctor Copernicus*. From a Nietzschean perspective, the *Tractatus* would be evidence that Wittgenstein has internalized the most toxic assumption formulated in the Western intellectual world: the distinction between the apparent (the sensuous and the empirical) world and the real (the metaphysical and the intelligible) world. In *Twilight of the Idols*, Nietzsche dismisses this two-tiered model as now defunct: "We have abolished the real world: what world is left? the apparent world perhaps? ... But no! *with the real world we have also abolished the apparent world!*"[85] In his interview with Piñeiro, Banville unambiguously sides with Nietzsche by claiming that the two-tiered model is bogus. After claiming that the thing-in-itself does not exist, Banville confesses that the idea is nonetheless "a beautiful philosophical notion," a "sort of [...] philosophical Holy Grail." The problem is that, like the Holy Grail, it "will never be reached." He continues:

> The beautiful idea that we could actually strike through appearance to the reality of the thing, which is what Heidegger spent his life trying to do, what is it to be ... The notion of getting out the truth or getting out the thing-in-itself is a beautiful dream, of course it is an impossible one, but it is a beautiful dream.[86]

Nietzsche and Banville agree that "reality" is a seductive idea but a nonexistent one.

However, Nietzsche's motivation for rejecting the existence of an ideal reality above and beyond the world of mere appearance is based on more than just a critique of epistemology. The appearance/reality model leads to nihilistic despair, because epistemological failure is inevitable. Since there is no such thing as the real world, the quest for the highest form of knowledge will always result in the humiliation, debasement, and degradation of not just specific humans but of the human altogether. Here is what Nietzsche says about those who affirm the existence of a Platonic spiritual or metaphysical world: "insofar as they affirm this 'other world'—look, must they not by the same token negate its counterpart, this world, *our* world?"[87] This negation of material reality has a devastating impact on the way we see and experience the human, because after Copernicus, there was growing skepticism about the existence of other-worldly realities, so humans, no longer certain about their ability to access the metaphysical and the transcendent, have begun to see themselves as nihilistic blips waiting for extinction. As Nietzsche says in *On the Genealogy of Morals*: "Here precisely is what has become a fatality for Europe—together with the fear of man we have also lost our love of him, our reverence for him, our hopes for him, even the will to him. The sight of man now makes us weary—what is nihilism today if it is not that?—We are weary *of man*."[88] Not an affirmation of what humans can do and be, but a negation of its abilities and being is the defining feature of what it means to be human in a world that posits ultimate reality as the apex of human achievement and success and then realizes that such a reality does not exist.

More troubling, however, is the bestial form of human relations that the real-world philosophy entails. To define one's self in relation to the ideal real world, one needs to construct a culturally despised other against which one can set one's self. Within this framework, those who have ascended the epistemological ladder have access to the most noble and sublime ideas of the good accessible to the human. Nietzsche, of course, considers these ideas of the good to be provisional human constructions that their creators portray as indisputable ontological realities. To make these realities seem like inviolable, more-than-human Truths, communal consent is mandatory, and this is where the degraded other becomes useful and valuable. Instead of seeing the person with contradictory views as an ontological equal or a valuable interlocutor, the person with access to the good dubs the opponent an evil enemy: "he has conceived 'the evil enemy,' '*the Evil One*,' and this in fact is his basic concept, from which he then evolves, as an afterthought and pendant, a 'good one'—himself!"[89] By identifying and defining the other as evil, the good person can then counter-construct self as the good one, thus establishing a clearly defined taxonomy of good and evil. According to this paradigm, the Evil One is a foundational precept for building the concept of the good. This is why Andreas tells his brother that he "was the one absolutely necessary thing, for I was there always to remind you of what you must transcend." Copernicus created Andreas as the demonized other in order to propel himself "beyond the filthy world," in order to catapult himself into the imagined transcendent as the good-in-itself.

If we interpret Banville's novel solely on the basis of Copernicus's concluding encounters at the end of the novel, then the work would be bleak at best. But if we take seriously Andreas's claim to his brother that Copernicus could "have succeeded, in the only way it is possible to succeed,"[90] then the novel could be interpreted more optimistically. That Copernicus could have succeeded is not as important as why, and it is through an understanding of Nietzsche's work that we can formulate a clear explanation. Had Copernicus, like Nietzsche, rejected the two-tiered model of knowledge, he would not have felt that his contribution to the world of ideas was an abysmal failure. Copernicus believes that his heliocentric model never rises to the level of an Ideal Form. Consequently, his intellectual contribution is ultimately a failure. But if he would have internalized both intellectually and emotionally the Nietzschean view that abolishes the real-apparent world distinction, then he would not have felt that his model failed for doing what it never could have done.

The more important issue is the one pertaining to love. Instead of hating the world, instead of seeing material phenomena as a debased version of a higher spiritual ideal, Nietzsche admonishes his readers to love and affirm physical reality, which is the only reality. This reversal in thinking, which is not as straightforward as it might seem, has staggering consequences. For Nietzsche, "all great problems demand *great love*." With a traditional model of love in mind, something like Diotima's and Socrates's from Plato's *Symposium*, love is defined as such insofar as it becomes increasingly less material and human and more spiritual and divine, leading to the contradictory idea of altruism. Such love is not tainted by human desire. But Nietzsche denounces this anti-human approach as incoherent and unnatural: " 'Selflessness' has no value either in heaven or on earth." In a Nietzschean universe, which affirms the human and all things human, love entails a full investment of the self, which is not tainted by virtue of being human. Thus, "only strong, round, secure spirits who have a firm grip on themselves are capable" of great love. Notice how Nietzsche contrasts those who invest themselves in what they are doing and those who have an "impersonal" approach: "It makes the most telling difference whether a thinker has a personal relationship to his problems and find in them his destiny, his distress, and his greatest happiness, or an 'impersonal' one, meaning that he can do no better than to touch them and grasp them with the antennae of cold, curious thought."[91] Not a renunciation of all things human, but a full investment and introjection of the human self is a defining feature of Nietzschean love.

This view totally overturns many traditional models of and approaches to love. In Nietzsche's world, love is not a warm-fuzzy, feel-good experience. It involves impassioned intellectual conflict that leads to a this-worldly form of transcendence. The ones who believe in an other-worldly philosophy use the evil enemy as a means for catapulting themselves into the imagined realm of the transcendent and/or metaphysical. But those who have rejected the idea of the transcendent and the metaphysical, and therewith an immutable binary like good and evil, see human relations in a very different way. Nietzsche describes this nobler form of love in *On the Genealogy of Morals*: "How much reverence has a noble man for his enemies!—and such reverence is a bridge to love.— For he desires his enemy for himself, as his mark of distinction; he can endure no other enemy than one in whom there is nothing to despise and *very much* to honor!"[92] Honoring, valuing, and even loving one's enemy can lead to transcendence, which is why Zarathustra claims that "in one's friend one should have one's best enemy."[93] People are trapped within their own solipsistic selves, and it is easy to associate exclusively with people who will confirm everything they think, feel, and believe. Such relationships lead to stagnation and eventually death. Enemies-as-friends and friends-as-enemies challenge people to think outside of or beyond their solipsistic selves, thus enabling them to overcome their currently constructed selves and making possible the subsequent construction of a new and different self. In *The Gay Science*, Nietzsche clarifies how this antagonistic form of love makes his secular version of human transcendence possible:

> Here and there on earth we may encounter a kind of continuation of love in which this possessive craving of two people for each other gives way to a new desire and lust for possession—a *shared* higher thirst for an ideal above them. But who knows such love? Who has experienced it? Its right name is *friendship*.[94]

Through the respectfully antagonistic and honorably conducted battles of invested human love can friends-as-enemies and enemies-as-friends nudge each other beyond themselves into constructing something noble and life-promoting beyond the two.

Given this focus on transcendence, it would seem that Banville's Copernicus and Nietzsche share a similar view. But Banville indicates why the two are very different. In his interview with Piñeiro, Banville makes an important distinction between this-worldly and other-worldly transcendence. Banville holds that one of the major catastrophes in history "has been the way in which we have broken with the animal world."[95] Through an act of supreme hubris, we have come to "think that somehow, at some point in the evolutionary stage, we ceased to be animals and became gods, but we are not gods: we are capable of god-like actions, but we are not gods."[96] To challenge the author, Piñeiro responds by noting that Banville uses the word transcendence, thus suggesting that he is complicit in the more-than-animal tradition that he critiques. But Banville replies:

> I use the word transcendence, but in a very special sense. To me transcendence is to be transcendent into the world, not out of it. Transcendence is where the world suddenly bears into existence. This is what art does, this is what art is for, it is not for telling us how to live, it is not for making us better people, just to make reality become reality.[97]

The artist creates a reality in and through the artwork, and if it is successful, then that "reality" becomes "reality" outside the text. To be more concrete, Copernicus, and here I am treating him as an artist rather than a scientist, created a new model for seeing, understanding, and experiencing the world, and it succeeded because so many people internalized it as a legitimate picture of the universe. Put simply, the artist constructs a new way of seeing and being, and through communal awareness, that model changes the world: "That extreme of self-awareness, that is what art seems to do to the world."[98] Within this framework of secular transcendence, Copernicus could have succeeded in his personal relationships had he treated others like Nietzschean friends-as-enemies or enemies-as-friends, that is, as people with whom he engaged in an honorably antagonistic relationship that translated into a shared secular ideal that stands above the two. Affirming the other, even in dissent as an enemy, has mutually beneficial consequences, and stands in stark contrast to the other-worldly transcendent approach of demonizing, negating, and annihilating the other, who then becomes the means by which one defines self as good-in-itself. Had Copernicus adopted Nietzsche's affirmative, agonistic view of love, he would have realized his desire for transcendence but in the only way possible, which is a form of secular transcendence that starts with a loving affirmation rather than a demonizing negation.

We are now in a position to explain precisely why *Doctor Copernicus* is a biofiction and not a historiographic metafiction, why it is more Nietzschean than Wittgensteinian. Were *Doctor Copernicus* a historiographic metafiction, Banville would either deconstruct or call into question Andreas's concluding model. But the work is biofiction, so deconstruction is not the goal. As Banville says of his art: "I believe, with Hermann Broch, that art is, or should be, a mode of objective knowledge of the world, not an expression of the subjective world."[99] Saying that art is a mode of objective knowledge might give readers the impression that Banville believes in ultimate reality, the kind of knowledge associated with an Ideal Form or the thing-in-itself. But like Nietzsche, Banville is clear that no such knowledge exists. What Banville means here is knowledge that is more than just the solipsistic product of an individual's "subjective world." This is knowledge that has been validated through communal understanding and assent. Through logic, evidence, and reason, the model of reality can be presented to and seen and accepted by many, thus making it more than just an idiosyncratic vision of one isolated consciousness. In *Doctor Copernicus*, what readers get is a life that succeeds (in constructing a new model of the universe) but also fails (by remaining in thrall to the destructive and deadly Neoplationism of his age). But through an insightful presentation and critique of Copernicus's life, Banville offers in and through Andreas an alternative "mode of objective knowledge of the world," one in which Nietzschean love and artistic creation work hand in hand to make a more life-promoting form of human agency possible.

6

Why Names Matter: Concluding Reflections about Autonomy and Biofiction

The confusing and complicated journey to individual agency and political autonomy in part explains why the Irish have led the way in the origins, evolution, rise, and now dominance of biofiction. Having sometimes subtly and sometimes overtly been deprived of the freedom to control, manage, and determine their own lives, the Irish are particularly sensitive to political and economic systems designed to enslave or "unslave" them, to use McCann's phrasing. This focus on agency is what distinguishes the biographical novel from the historical novel, and it is my contention that locating a work within a specific genre has enormous interpretive ramifications. To illustrate, I want to briefly examine Marisol Morales-Ladrón's approach to Mary Morrissy's insightful novel *The Rising of Bella Casey*, which features the life of Sean O'Casey's sister. Morales-Ladrón sees Morrissy's novel as part of a "resurgence of the genre of historical fiction in Irish literature," and this is important because "it has placed women back in a national narrative and has enhanced its awareness of the silences, gaps and interstices of history through which marginal or subaltern subjects were conspicuously ignored."[1] Within this aesthetic framework, Morrissy's "main motive" is "to restore the missing years"[2] of Bella, and Morrissy does this in order "to contribute to the debate on the roles of women as the unheard voices of the community and to their restoration into the annals of Irish national history."[3] Morales-Ladrón uses a postmodern approach to justify her specific interpretation. Postmodernists note that textual reality shapes the way people see and experience the world. By this logic, "what is forgotten remains untold; and what is untold, never happened."[4] By filling in the gaps in Bella's story, Morrissy pictures an alternative history not just of Bella Casey but of women from the time more generally. For this reason, Morales-Ladrón concludes that *The Rising of Bella Casey* "is as much a historical novel as a fictional biography, considering that in the discussion of biographies, fictional biographies, and memoirs there is a vague line that separates the 'real' from the 'invented.' "[5] Since the border between the invented and the real is arbitrary and unstable, Morrissy's fictional narrative about Bella's life can be justified, thus making the work a legitimate form of history or biography.

But in what sense does it qualify as history or biography? And how specifically does it signify? According to Lukács, a protagonist in a historical novel effectively embodies a specific reality from the external world, and that figure comes to represent a significant cross section of the people from that time and place. Using this Lukácsian approach, Morales-Ladrón describes *The Rising of Bella Casey* as "a historical novel told from the perspective of the Other and an autobiographical account that rewrites the past filling in the fissures left by it." Consequently, the novel "contributes to sustaining the true discourses of history." What specifically makes the work so successful is that it "stands as a true portrayal of women from the late nineteenth to the early twentieth century, when they were regarded as mere spectators of the drama of history."[6]

There are many problems with Morales-Ladrón's approach, but I want to isolate just a couple. Like Morales-Ladrón, I would say that Bella, who is a disempowered figure for most of the novel, eventually emerges "as an empowered female with agency."[7] But how Bella functions as a representative symbol of late nineteenth- and early twentieth-century women is unclear. In her role as a schoolteacher, Bella is raped by Reverend Leeper, a totally fictional character and scene. Leeper impregnates Bella and gives her syphilis. To save her reputation from the scandal of being an unwed mother, Bella seduces Nick Beaver and dupes him into believing that he is the father of her child. Nick is an abusive husband, and eventually he descends into madness because of syphilis, so he is institutionalized. It is while he is in the asylum that Bella re-encounters Leeper, who is also suffering from a syphilis-induced form of insanity, which leads her to despair, because Bella now realizes that she probably gave her husband his insanity- and death-bringing sickness.

How does this unique and idiosyncratic story translate into a representative example of female history from the late nineteenth and early twentieth centuries? Were most women being raped and then seducing innocent men into marrying them? Were many women giving their husbands syphilis? How specifically does Bella's story signify a worthwhile contribution to history? And why should readers trust that Bella's story best captures the essence of the life of women from the late nineteenth and early twentieth centuries? Morales-Ladrón does not answer any of these questions, and I suspect that her interpretive model would self-destruct were she forced to do so. But what I want to suggest here is that there are two irreconcilable approaches to the novel and that one makes more sense than the other. The historical-novel approach contends that the author of the fictional narrative gives readers a plausible or even legitimate picture of the past—this is, as Morales-Ladrón contends, Morrissy's "main motive." But, as biographical novelists like Atwood, Montero, Banks, and Oates say, the goal of the biographical novelist is to fictionalize something from the life of a person from the past, reorganize and restructure that person's story, and smudge it a little in order to make it meaningful and useful for readers in the present and the future. From this perspective, it makes no sense to see the biographical subject as a representative figure from the past. Rather, it would make more sense to see the main character as a unique and exemplary model of someone who has seized and secured some level of agency in a world designed to make autonomous behavior almost impossible. Therefore, Bella is a captivating character not because she is a representative symbol but because she is atypical and extraordinary.

Throughout the novel Morrissy foregrounds the degree to which characters are enslaved without their conscious awareness. Realizing that she is pregnant, Bella resolves not simply "to charm" Nick into marriage but "to ensnare him,"[8] and in a chapter titled "Manoeuvres," suggesting Corporal Beaver's military exercises, Bella "had, it seemed, manoeuvred Nick Beaver into seeing a future with her"[9]—this would qualify as the kind of traumatized agency we see in the behavior of Eliza Lynch. Having been violated, Lynch and Bella engage in an irresponsible and even destructive form of agency in relation to others in order to rehabilitate themselves as autonomous beings. Bella's union will be neither fortunate nor happy, and it will set her family up for a modern type of enslavement, which is how O'Casey describes his sister's legacy to her children: "A life of miniature slavery."[10] Within this framework, history plays a crucial role. The year is 1897, and Bella is a Protestant loyal to the English crown. There is going to be a public celebration of Queen Victoria's sixtieth year on the throne, so Bella proposes attending the "Queen's Jubilee" because it is "history in the making." But her brother has a different view: "History, he thinks, history is our undoing."[11] The overpowering public ritual will reinforce the view of England's legitimate rule over Ireland and the Irish, thus contributing to the de-Irishization and Britishization of Ireland and making the goal of Irish emancipation (and a distinctive Irish history) increasingly more unrealistic. Given O'Casey's critical remark about history, it should come as no surprise that he has contempt for the ideal historical novelist. As O'Casey says to his sister: "Walter Scott," he'd snort, "he's old hat."[12] History is not the protagonist of *The Rising of Bella Casey* or the biographical novel, as it is in the historical novel. Agency is, and within biofiction, history is oftentimes an oppressive force that must be overcome, which is why it is deeply problematic to refer to or treat Morrissy's work as a historical novel.

What Morrissy does so brilliantly is to chart Bella's decline into miniature slavery and her eventual rising, which, for important symbolic reasons, coincides with the Easter Rising. Morrissy characterizes agency for Bella as being the "Mistress of Her Circumstances." This is the title of the novel's second chapter, and it pictures the young Bella's intellectual gifts and her time in College. The implication is that knowledge is one of the primary ways to become a mistress of one's own circumstances. But after being raped, Bella marries the hapless Nick, resulting in a rapidly declining financial situation that precludes access to spirit-elevating resources like education and art. Nick and Bella have syphilis, and within the context of the novel, this sickness functions as a metaphor describing the unhealthy mental lives of many Irish. Morrissy has O'Casey reflect on a transformation in Bella to signify the destructive consequences of poverty. O'Casey suggests that Bella go back into teaching in order to finance her children's education. But Bella dismisses this idea as unrealistic. Indeed, she just took her son out of school and set him up as an apprentice in a print shop. This act brings to O'Casey's mind the time when his own mother withdrew him from school and sent him to work at the age of fourteen. Bella berated her mother for doing this, but now she does exactly the same thing, which leads O'Casey to note the differences between the two separate Bellas: "she had been Miss Casey in spirit then: bright, indignant, full of mettle."[13] This stands in stark contrast to what she has become. O'Casey describes what happened to her: "First, the hardening of the heart, then the dimming of the intellect."[14]

The degeneration of the mind has destructive consequences on the ability of people to interact with others in a healthy and productive way. This is something the narrator clearly expresses when Bella visits the asylum where Nick stays. She notes that the inmates are oblivious: "They took no notice of her; madness, as she knew, bred incurious solipsism."[15] To indicate that this type of behavior occurs in everyday society, Morrissy dramatizes Bella's response to a child who looks like "a walking skeleton." The girl asks Bella for a cup of sugar, but she tells the child to leave. When O'Casey asks what ails the little one, his sister says consumption, which leads O'Casey to fault "the inequitable system." But Bella puts all the blame squarely on the shoulders of the "neglectful mother." O'Casey then asks Bella: "Where is your mercy?" And Bella replies: "I cannot afford mercy towards those who despise me."[16] Because the girl comes from a Catholic family, the people who despise her and whom she despises, Bella makes no effort to understand their living situation—she retreats into her "incurious solipsism" and stands in cruel and heartless judgment over them. The irony, of course, is that Bella's circumstances probably mirror what the Catholic family experiences, because they are all "living in the ruins of Empire."[17] The "incurious solipsism" in the asylum is prevalent throughout society more generally, thus making the madhouse a suitable metaphor of certain segments of the Irish population.

To correct this situation, needed is some personal and political autonomy, the freedom to manage, control, and determine one's own life and destiny, which would give life a sense of magic and meaning. This is what happens during the Easter Rising, when Bella finds a stranded piano in the desolate streets of rebellion-torn Dublin. After "the [ambiguous] Rising happened"[18] and Bella brings the piano into her house, "strains of Beethoven's *Moonlight Sonata* emanating from the Beavers' front room"[19] are heard. The music has an inspiring effect: "It seemed to open the door on her girlish self, so serious and high-minded and bent on improvement."[20] She now believes that she can infuse life with meaning: "with a piano in residence, could not the schoolroom come to her? She saw herself again as a teacher, schooling the children of the gentry in scales and in notation and with it regaining some semblance of her former self."[21] Were she to do that, "that would put a stop to all those prophets of doom, her own flesh and blood included, who took her for some broken-down creature, who failed to see the flame of elevation that burned fiercely within."[22]

With her piano and a belief in her ability to improve and elevate herself, she takes a job as a charwoman, which for a pre–Rising Bella would signify her meaningless descent into irredeemable degradation. But now that she has the desire, ability, and freedom to take agential control over her own life, what once would have been considered soul-destroying menial labor is now seen as "service to a higher ideal."[23] This epiphany occurs in a chapter titled "The Family Silver." Based on this title it might seem that the family is the Irvines, because these are the people who employ Bella. But at the end of the chapter, Mrs. Irvine has Bella polish a splendid silver tea service. Bella does her job enthusiastically, and when she finishes she notices an inscription on the silver, which reads: "Isabella Casey, it read, Mistress of her Circumstances."[24] This is an intertextual allusion to the education chapter, and it underscores the novel's agency theme. Different between the two time periods, however, is the Rising, both personal and political. Even seemingly servant behavior (charwoman) can have a sense of meaning and magic if it is self- rather than other-generated. The implication: now that the Irish, through the Rising, have begun to shuffle off the mortal coils of British rule, personal and political actions are infused with more value, meaning, magic, and life.

Such a transformation in relation to personal and political agency could set into motion the process of curing the culture of its "incurious solipsism." This explains the end of the novel, when Bella's daughter tells her mother that she will marry a Catholic. The typical family response is to disown the child for such a clear act of religious defiance, but Bella responds by saying that her daughter's choice is "a good man,"[25] and that she will not "deny anyone's good nature."[26] Entering the world of agency has had the salutary effect of enabling Bella to escape her "incurious solipsism."

What I am trying to illustrate through this brief analysis of Morrissy's novel is that using historical-novel criteria, as Morales-Ladrón does, distorts our understanding of biographical novels like *The Rising of Bella Casey*. There is no compelling reason to accept Morrissy's version of Bella's transformation as an accurate representation of what happened to the real Bella, and it is likely that Morrissy had no intention of treating the story as an actual form of biography or history. Consequently, it makes no sense to suggest that Bella symbolically represents a significant cross section of women from the late nineteenth and early twentieth centuries. Therefore, instead of treating the novel as if it were a historical novel, as if Morrissy were trying to do history or to give readers an accurate picture of Bella or the past, it would make more sense to read it as a biographical novel, as a work that fictionalizes a certain part of a life in order to illuminate a crucial trait of the human condition, specifically the part of the human that achieves some level of personal and political meaning through agency.

Joseph O'Connor has authored a moving biographical novel (*Ghost Light*) about Molly Allgood, an actress who was the lover of John Millington Synge, and O'Connor's remarks in what he refers to as the "Acknowledgments and Caveat" are very useful for understanding how biographical novelists make use of their protagonists. There is a note of defiance in O'Connor's tone in this work, as if he has lost patience with certain types of readers, so he seeks to set the aesthetic record straight in his post-textual remarks, clarifying precisely what readers should and should not expect from such a form of fiction. "*Ghost Light* is a work of fiction," O'Connor stipulates, "frequently taking immense liberties with fact." Thus, "the experiences and personalities of the real Molly and Synge differed from those of my characters in uncountable ways." After specifying that "chronologies, geographies and portrayals appearing in this novel are not to be relied upon," O'Connor cheekily notes that "certain biographers will want to beat me with a turf-shovel." This admission leads O'Connor to issue an apology to "Yeatsians" as well as "scholars of Lady Gregory and Synge and Sean O'Casey." O'Connor's references to these writers are important because he adopts their aesthetic approach, at least to some degree:

> These giants often said they had fanned their fictions from the sparks of real life, renaming the people who had inspired their stories. The practice was sometimes a camouflage, sometimes a claim of authenticity. It was an option I considered carefully but decided against in the end, and so I dare to ask the forgiveness of these noble ghosts of world literature for not changing the names of the innocent.[27]

Like these writers, O'Connor acknowledges that he takes his inspiration from "real life," but he differs from them in that he did not change the names. The *roman-a-clef* strategy has the effect of both camouflaging the person on whom the fictional character is based and authenticating the story and its implicit symbolism and content. Biofiction is different from the *roman a clef* because it dispenses with the camouflaging and it enhances the story's authenticity by naming the character after the historical figure. And yet, the claim to authenticity is compromised, because O'Connor acknowledges that he changes biographical facts and that his characters differ from the historical people. It is for this reason that O'Connor emphasizes that his work is fiction.

Based on O'Connor's claims, we could say that names matter, but they matter in radically different ways based on the genre in which they function. In a biography or a history, the name signifies factual accuracy, insofar as such accuracy is possible. But in fiction, factual accuracy is subordinate to a different type of "truth," and this "truth" will differ based on the specific genre. Ebershoff offers a useful way to think about the distinctive kinds of truths authors give and readers get from specific works. As he says in my interview with him: "I think that every book teaches a reader how to read it. It will give clues to the reader of what it is, what it's trying to be, and what it isn't, and what it's not trying to be. There are signals. This is going to be *this* kind of book, and you can expect this format from this book."[28] Authors strategically cue readers as to how a text should be read, and it is my contention that a biographical novel invites readers to approach it in a radically different way than do historical novels. This is not just the case because of the way the author has built the protagonist but also because of the way the character signifies. To illustrate, consider Hannah Kent's *The Good People*, a novel about a nineteenth-century Irishwoman who killed a four-year-old boy because she thought he was a changeling. In an interview, Kent acknowledges that she only "had two newspaper articles" and "no biographical information"[29] about her protagonist. Given the dearth of biographical material, Kent turned to history in order to construct her protagonist, so her main character, named after the actual person, is a logical product and representation of her environment:

> With *The Good People* I again did a lot of research into the outside world or environment. I looked at the lives led by people who resembled these characters or who could be said to. So that, while everything was imagined with *The Good People*, it was nonetheless likely, as likely as possible.[30]

This characterization reveals much about the nature of Kent's aesthetic approach, which sounds more like the method of the historical novelist than a biographical novelist. Instead of referring to her novels as primarily fiction, she calls them "speculative biographies," and as such, they "borrow from or lean on history in that they are research-led and a great amount of research is required."[31] Thus, she concludes that her novels "reinstall historical context as significant and determining."[32] Kent does historical research in order to give her readers a piece of "determining" history, which stands in stark contrast to the biographical novelist, who fictionalizes the life of a figure from the past in order to give readers a new way of thinking about agential life more generally.

Calling a work a historical novel has an immediate impact. It tells the reader that history is of primary importance, that history is a shaping and determining force not just on the protagonist but also on the readers in the present. Calling a work biofiction has a very different connotation. The Greek word βιός means life, and when biofiction first started to come into being in the nineteenth century the word life was defined in opposition to that which is formulaic and mechanical, to that which is seen as devoid of agency. Biofiction is thus a form of literature that pictures and promotes life, agential life, autonomous life, and as such, it stands in axiomatic opposition to the historical novel, which foregrounds rigid processes and inflexible laws that shape and determine the human in a mechanical way.

Not surprisingly, a radical questioning of the definition of words and the control of language takes center stage in the biographical novel, because the agential use of language is one of the defining features of life. The British authorities dubbed homosexuality a criminal perversion, but Wilde transvalued the dominant view about same-sex relations, as seen in biofictions about Wilde; Europeans saw Christ as the source of authoritative Truth, but Moore exposed the New Testament savior as a politically dangerous fanatic, as seen in *The Brook Kerith*; and the Western world considered colonization a system of social, political, and economic uplift, but Casement revealed its brutally exploitative nature, as seen in the biofictions about Casement. Life for Wilde, Moore, and Casement is defined on the basis of the ability to defy the enslaving system in which they were semiotically trapped and construct a new and radically different one. The Australian hero Ned Kelly is in the same tradition as these three, which Sabina Murray clearly articulates in her essay "A Novel Truth about Casement's 'Irish' Identity." As a child growing up in Perth, Australia, Murray, who is "a half-Filipino, half-American child," identified primarily with the children "predominantly of Irish background." In the nineteenth century, the Irishman Ned Kelly was hanged for murdering a policeman. But as Murray says: "Our hero was Ned Kelly." Therefore, when Murray and her playmates reenacted "the life of Ned Kelly," it was difficult "to find actors willing to play for the other side." This was the case because "in Australia our heroes were bushrangers, and we knew in our blood that the criminals who had been sent to our distant shores—whose history we inherited despite our relatively recent arrival, just as all Americans inherit the legacy of slavery—were largely victims of injustice."[33] The legally defined criminals like Kelly were actually heroes, while the politically sanctioned authorities were the actual criminals. To support her claim, Murray quotes Wilde:

> When Oscar Wilde visited America in 1882, a visit historical for its epic remark-making, he observed, "The Americans always take their heroes from the criminal classes." Yes, he was referring to Americans, but it took an Irishman to notice.[34]

In an essay about Casement, Murray cites Wilde in order to illuminate and justify the Irish inversion of the criminal/hero, which is a central feature of the identity of the Irishman Ned Kelly. Within Murray's framework, distinctively Irish is the following proposition: what is taken as a seemingly ontological given is semiotically inverted, thus requiring readers to question what is presented as an established fact of being. This, I contend, is also the central aesthetic axiom on which biofiction is premised.

To conclude this chapter and book, I want to clarify how this idea functions in Peter Carey's *True History of the Kelly Gang*, a global biographical novel about an Irishman in Australia whose Irish conception of agency as inversion is symbolically exported to the United States. It is my contention that this conception of Irishness in relation to agency and inversion mirrors the form of the biographical novel.

Deep into the writing of *The Secret History of the Kelly Gang*, which would eventually be retitled the *True History of the Kelly Gang*, Carey put together a chronology of crucial events. Significantly, he traces the origins of Kelly's story back to Ireland. Here is the first entry: "1846–1851 The Famine in Ireland."[35] That Carey would foreground Ireland and the Irish in a novel about one of Australia's most revered folk heroes is not an inappropriate imposition. Just months before Kelly died, he wrote what is now known as *The Jerilderie Letter*, in which Ned explains what led him to commit his seeming crimes. In that work, the Irish-Australian bushranger blasts the British for their unjust treatment of Ireland and the Irish.

Kelly claims that "there never was such a thing as justice in the English laws."[36] To the contrary, what people like Kelly could expect from the English justice system is "any amount of injustice."[37] To illustrate, Ned tells the story of Constable Alexander Fitzpatrick, who tried to arrest Ned's brother Dan on April 15, 1878, for horse stealing. According to Ned, "Fitzpatrick will be the cause of greater slaughter to the Union Jack than Saint Patrick was to the snakes and toads in Ireland."[38] This is the case because Fitzpatrick nakedly symbolizes the way British colonial "justice" functions. On the surface, Fitzpatrick is a neutral representative of impartial laws in the service of justice for all, so when he comes to arrest Dan he is behaving as an honest and faithful administrator of law. But when the subalterns fight back by questioning and challenging his justification, it soon becomes clear that a will to power and dominance is the motive more than a neutral and objective commitment to blind justice. At first, Fitzpatrick says that he has a warrant for Dan's arrest, but when Dan asks to see the legal document, Fitzpatrick admits that all he has is a telegram from a sergeant Whelan telling him to arrest Dan. Dan's mother says that "without a warrant" Fitzpatrick has "no business on her premises."[39] At this point, the "trooper pulled out his revolver and said he would blow her brains out if she interfered."[40] But Dan tricks Fitzpatrick and then disarms him, after which the "trooper left and invented some scheme to say that he got shot which any man can see is false."[41] Based on concocted evidence, the authorities arrest and then convict the Kelly matriarch shortly after the event.

This story clarifies why Ned believes that Fitzpatrick's behavior will lead to the death of the Union Jack. To the world the British project an image of being the most advanced and civilized nation because it has formulated a system of laws predicated on universal freedom and blind justice. Based on the projected image of the British, the nation is not colonizing foreign countries for personal and national power and wealth. It is doing so for altruistic reasons, which is why it is a noble and righteous political system. But Ned rejects this view. He holds that the neutral and objective pursuit of justice is just a mask strategically concealing a brutal and ruthless will to economic and political power and control, which is the true motive animating the British colonial agenda. By using Fitzpatrick to expose what Britain is actually doing and how the country is unjustly treating its colonized subjects, Ned believes that he has set into motion a process that could result in the "slaughter" of "the Union Jack."

What specifically makes *The Jerilderie Letter* such a stunningly insightful document is Ned's grasp of ontological inversion in relation to epistemological orientation. The first and most basic example of this is seen in the charge of murder lodged against him. According to Fitzpatrick, Ned shot at a police officer, which is why there was a reward for Ned's capture. To force the Kelly family to turn Ned over to the authorities, policemen visit, threaten, and even tyrannize Ned's unarmed siblings. The officers tell the family that they plan to "blow" Ned "into pieces as small as paper."[42] When writing about this event, Ned becomes so enraged that he threatens corresponding violence. After noting how he is characterized in the papers as "the blackest and coldest blooded murderer ever on record," Ned declares: "if I hear any more of it I will not exactly show them what cold blooded murder is but wholesale and retail slaughter, something different to shooting three troopers in self defence and robbing a bank."[43] Ned and his gang killed three policemen who pursued him, but the wronged bushranger insists that what he did was self-defense and not murder. Fitzpatrick's untrustworthy testimony, which the police acknowledge ("the police all knew Fitzpatrick had wronged us");[44] the violation of Ned's family; the excessive amount of weapons the police had in their possession; and the aggressively threatening postures of the police are just a few reasons why Ned claims that what he did qualified as self-defense rather than murder.

But after describing this inversion in naming in relation to his personal life, Ned applies the idea to the political, which makes him an early postcolonial thinker in the tradition of Casement, Du Bois, Césaire, and Fanon. Policemen seemingly serve the general good, but Ned realizes that their true purpose in Australia is to solidify English power and to subjugate the non-English, like the Irish. Thus, Ned says that a "Policeman is a disgrace to his country."[45] At first it might seem that "his country" is Australia. But this is not correct. Ned claims that the Irish policeman in Australia "is a traitor to his country ancestors and religion," who "were all catholics before the Saxons" took control of their land. After which, the Irish "were persecuted massacred thrown into martyrdom and tortured beyond the ideas of the present generation." For Ned, an Irishman who works for the English like a slave "ought to be ashamed of himself."[46] Since the police in Australia are actually working for the English, an Irish policeman can only be considered a deserter of "the shamrock, the emblem of true wit and beauty." Indeed, such a position means serving "under a flag and nation that has destroyed massacred and murdered their forefathers by the greatest of torture."[47] To inspire active dissent and resistance, Ned references Irish heroes ("many a blooming Irishman") who, "rather than subdue to the Saxon yoke, Were flogged to death and bravely died in servile chains but true to the shamrock and a credit to Paddys land."[48]

When discussing the inspiration for and composition of *True History*, Carey emphasizes the importance of *The Jerilderie Letter*, which "is an extraordinary document, the passionate voice of a man who is writing to explain his life, save his life, his reputation." But Kelly's focus is not just on himself. As Carey says, Kelly "wants us to see the injustice suffered by the poor farmers of North-Eastern Victoria." In other words, Kelly's story, as communicated through *The Jerilderie Letter*, is a clarion call on behalf of an oppressed and downtrodden community, and as such, it has a trans-spatial as well as a trans-temporal significance. Carey indicates this when he explains how the story relates to his own upbringing: "What I finally wrote grew not just from *The Jerilderie Letter* but my first 10 years of life which I spent in the very small country town of Bacchus Marsh."[49] What readers get in *True History* is not a provincial story of a single abused Irishman in a small region of nineteenth-century Australia. Rather, Carey fictionalizes the story of Kelly to give readers a vivid and poignant picture of the downtrodden, the poor, and the oppressed in a wide range of places and times.

Carey clearly indicates that that is what he is trying to accomplish by comparing his novel to William Faulkner's *As I Lay Dying*. In an interview with Nathanael O'Reilly, Carey claims that the "notion of creating a sort of poetry from an uneducated voice, like Faulkner does in *As I Lay Dying*, was attractive to me then and still is now."[50] In his interview with Robert McCrum, Carey specifies that giving "rich voices to the poor"[51] is what he has taken from Faulkner. Obscene poverty crushes the wickedly brilliant Addie, the sensitive seer Darl, the pregnant adolescent Dewey Dell, the good-hearted but unimaginative Cash, and others from the Bundren clan. Faulkner's 1930 novel is pure genius, a funny, sensitive, perverted, and poignant picture of life in the irredeemable abyss of soul-debilitating poverty. That Carey considers it a model for his own work certainly makes sense, but noting the differences between the two is of vital importance. Postmodernism flourished between 1930 and 2000, thus mandating the rise of a new way of literary signifying, one that was more anchored in the historical and the empirical. So naming his protagonist after the actual historical figure is important, because it gives more credence to Carey's portrayal of the living conditions of the persecuted, the oppressed, the downtrodden, and the poor. In other words, this story is not the seething product of an overheated imagination, which is something people could say of Faulkner's *As I Lay Dying*. By stark contrast, Carey's story is persuasive and compelling because it is more anchored in actual biographical fact.

In *True History*, Carey foregrounds Ned's Irishness, which consists of the same rebellious energy in pursuit of individual and political agency that animates biofiction—this, in part, explains why the Irish have become so central to the origins, evolution, and rise of biofiction. In the Australian context, the English demonize the Irish in the same way they do in Europe. Described as "Irish thieves,"[52] "Irish rubbish" (TH 25), an "Irish mutt" (TH 74), "Irish devils" (TH 101), and "Irish Madmen" (TH 272), "all micks" are characterized as "a notch beneath cattle" (TH 28). This demonization strategy works, because the Irish are treated as inferiors within the culture. For instance, while in school, Ned is placed in a role of responsibility and authority, but this is the case because the teacher "had no other choice for everybody with an English name had taken a turn" (TH 28). A lack of freedom to locate one's self geographically or politically is a defining feature of being Irish in Australia. As Ned notes, his parents had been "ripped from Ireland like teeth from the mouth of their own history" (TH 92) and the English in Australia intend to "gaol" as many rebellious Irish as possible, including "brothers & uncles & cousins" as well as "mothers & babies too" (TH 143). The assault on Irish dignity and persons is strategic, coordinated, systemic, and comprehensive.

This brutal treatment by the English has devastating consequences. It leads to the death of Ned's father, which is why Ned describes his corpse as "bulging with all the poisons of the Empire" (TH 35). After the Kelly patriarch's death, the

Englishman Bill Frost enters into an intimate relationship with Ned's mother, and given his seemingly ontological superiority he lays claim to the Kelly house ("In any case said Bill Frost its my home" [TH 98]) and casts the Kelly children into the role of servants. As Ned says when he arrives home from a lengthy stint away: "I discovered Bill Frost sitting in my chair with a big plate of mutton stew in front of him and it were bring me this & give me that" (TH 107). A position of authority and privilege over the Irish is his birth right as an Englishman, and he does not hesitate to take what he considers rightfully his.

In response to being treated as the wretched of the earth, the Irish internalize a sense of rage against the colonizing and imprisoning machine. Significantly, even if a person is not Irish, he or she becomes a *de facto* Irish person on the basis of having internalized this rage-filled spirit. Ned indicates this most clearly through his description of Ben Gould, a hawker whose cart got trapped in a bog on the Kelly's land. Here is Ned's portrayal: "Had we looked deep into Ben Gould we would of seen a similar fury at the centre of his soul for though he were not Irish he carried the same sort of fire I mean that flame the government of England lights in a poor man's guts every time they make him wear the convict irons" (TH 163). The unbridled yearning for individual agency is the logical product of England's sometimes subtle, sometimes overt, enslavement of the non-English, the Irish in this case.

Striking is the degree to which this passion for agency leads Ned to reject history. A member of the Kelly gang, Steve Hart is a friend of Ned's brother, and he frequently tells stories about Ireland and Irish history. But Ned is not impressed: "you would think Steve Hart were a Professor to hear him on the state of Ireland blah blah blah rattling off the names of his heroes" (TH 204). For Steve, knowledge of history would enable Ned and his gang to formulate a strategy against the English in Australia. But Ned says that "this queer boy's daydreaming were no defence at all" because "all his Irish martyrs couldnt get us decent land" (TH 204). It is when the Kelly gang is on the run that Ned expresses his objections to history most clearly. While in hiding, "Steve Hart began to sing some mournful song in the old language," but Ned "told him to be quiet," because, as he insists, "we would write our own damned history from here on" (TH 255). History will not dictate who Ned is, how he should behave, or what will happen. Ned will create history as an agential being in his own right. So important is this idea that it explains Ned's motivation for writing his *apologia pro vita sua*, which is written for and to his daughter: "each day I wrote so you wd. read my words and I wrote to get you born" (TH 336). Writing is not simply a record of what happened. It is an instrument that gives birth to life. To be more specific, through writing Ned creates life, agential life, a life of meaning and value in and through and for his daughter.

Given the importance of writing, the control of narrative is of ultimate importance for Ned. When people hear his side of the story, many (even most) sympathize with him and turn against the English-controlled Australian authorities. To get the people's support and to justify himself, Ned authors a letter, which he tries to get published. But those in power refuse to allow Ned's story to get widespread circulation, so they strategically silence him. Frustrated and angered, Ned decides to take his message directly to the people. During a robbery at Faithfull's Creek Station, Ned tells his story to twelve men who were held captive. He invites the captives to ask questions, and Ned explains what really happened, which contradicts the narrative in the papers. This experience has an enormous impact. As he says: "In the hut at Faithfull's Creek I seen proof that if a man could tell his true history to Australians he might be believed" (TH 312). Were Ned's version of the story to be heard, people would start to raise questions about the justness of their current living situations and the way the government strategically controls resources and power.

The reason why Ned's narrative appeals so much to the twelve men at Faithfull's Creek is that his story is also their story. After telling the men how the authorities arrested his mother and took away her newborn child in order to retaliate against Ned, he reflects on the response of his auditors:

> And here is the thing about them men they was Australians they knew full well the terror of the unyielding law the historic memory of UNFAIRNESS were in their blood and a man might be a bank clerk or an overseer he might never have been lagged for nothing but still he knew in his heart what it were to be forced to wear the white hood in prison.
>
> (TH 312)

Telling his story has effected a reversal in judgment. Instead of seeing Ned as a ruthless perpetrator of the horrific crime of murdering policemen, the listeners understand Ned, his plight, and the rationale behind his actions, so they now see the Australian authorities as the true criminals. What, in part, enables the everyday Australian to come to this conclusion is his or her own experience, for "the knowledge of unfairness were deep in his bone and marrow" (TH 312). Ned's and Carey's universalizing strategy has an immense power, and it recalls the conclusion of Ralph Ellison's brilliant novel *Invisible Man*, which ends with the following line: "Who knows but that, on the lower frequencies, I speak for you?"[53] Ellison pictures the journey of a young black male who is systematically divested of dignity and rights in a wide range of groups, places, and institutions in the United States. The story might seem idiosyncratic, but by concluding with a direct address to the reader, Ellison suggests that what is happening to the narrator also happens to many everyday people, like the readers of his novel. What Ellison has done, then, is to give readers frameworks for seeing how systemic forms of marginalization and oppression function. Carey does exactly the same thing, but because his biographical subject is an actual historical person, the effect on the reader is more powerful and intense. Names matter, because what Ned has experienced is not a wildly concocted story of an overwrought fiction-maker. It is a "true history" of an actual person, and while his story may be an extreme case, it functions to illuminate what is happening to so many other people, which can only be heard at a lower frequency.

Insofar as the Irish are concerned, the Ned Kelly story has a significant global and universalizing meaning and value. Carey could have emphasized Ned's Australian upbringing to the exclusion of his Irish heritage. But he did not do that. In fact, Carey goes out of his way to import Irishness into the text, which he does most clearly through the fictional character of Mary Hearn, Ned's lover and the mother of his fictional daughter. From "the village of Templecrone" (TH 201) in Ireland, Mary's father suffers horribly as a consequence of the English colonization of Ireland. The Hearn patriarch is a blacksmith who frequently cares for horses. An Englishman named Lord Hill leaves his horse with Mary's father, but he fails to pick it up at the agreed-upon time, which forces Hearn to bear "the cost of feeding & stabling" (TH 287). Local Irishmen despise Lord Hill, because he has seized Irish land, so to punish him they torture and kill his horse while he is stabled with Mary's father. Eventually, the men are caught and hanged, and Mary's family suffers devastating consequences as well. This story usefully parallels what happens to Ned and his family in Australia, thus suggesting a transnational dimension to English crimes against the Irish, the poor, and the downtrodden.

But Mary's story is not simply one of suffering and abuse. She is Ned's helpmate, and as such, she gives him useful advice for combatting the English-Australian authorities and for devising effective strategies for seizing and advancing individual agency and political autonomy. But she realizes that Ned's fight against the authorities is destined to fail, so she emigrates to the United States. There she gives birth to her daughter, which she communicates in a telegram to Ned: "DAM AND FILLY AT PASTURE IN SAN FRANCISCO FEED IS PLENTIFUL" (TH 336). Ned can barely contain his joy: "My daughter it were you. You was born. You was in a foreign land but safe at your mother's breast I roared like a bull my breath burst forth & froze in that clean Australian air" (TH 336). All along, what Ned really wanted was the freedom to live, work, and love, the kind of freedom that is granted to legitimate citizens of a free and democratic nation. As Ned says: "I wished only to be a citizen I had tried to speak but the mongrels stole my tongue when I asked for justice they give me none" (TH 342). Ned rejoices because he believes that his daughter will have the opportunity for the freedom that was denied to him.

But, symbolically, what the daughter's emigration to the United States suggests is the globalization of the Irish spirit, which is that fight for individual agency and political autonomy. In his interview with McCrum, Carey claims that for Australians Kelly "is like Thomas Jefferson. That is the sort of space Kelly occupies in the national imagination."[54] That all citizens should have a legitimate "right to life, liberty, and the pursuit of happiness" is the founding principle on which the nation is based, and Ned is an Australian hero in the same way that Jefferson is because he best made the case for democratic freedom and universal rights by exposing English abuses and violations. But what Kelly adds to Jefferson's freedom-discourse is his distinctively Irish postcolonial sensibility. In his interview with O'Reilly, Carey locates his work within the postcolonial tradition, but he indicates why that is a problem, especially for contemporary academics: "it seems to me that when academics think of postcolonial literature they tend not to think of Australia, and postcolonial basically seems to me to be a sort of code for a certain sort of black literature."[55] The postcolonial sensibility is at the core of biofiction. Decolonizing the mind in order to make individual agency and political autonomy possible is of crucial importance. This is a specific instance of an ontological reversal in relation to epistemological orientation. But because the postcolonial has so often been defined in relation to non-white political movements, colonized countries like Ireland and Australia oftentimes get overlooked. And yet, when we examine the standard thinking and practices of postcolonial writers, theorists, and practitioners, it becomes clear that someone like Kelly was an insightful contributor who provided a revolutionary template on which postcolonial writers have built.

Scrutinizing the dominant political narrative; questioning who established the authoritative legal frameworks; decolonizing the communal minds; transvaluing the pervasive systems of knowledge; shifting power to the poor, the marginalized, and the dispossessed; inspiring the wretched of the earth to fight for individual agency and political autonomy; and imagining new and alternative possibilities for social thinking and political being—these are just a few of the postcolonial strategies that the Irishman Ned Kelly enacted in Australia and then exported to the United States through his Irish wife and daughter.

The form of fiction that mirrors the personal and political objectives of so many Irish is the biographical novel, and the genre name matters a great deal. Calling works like *The Rising of Bella Casey* and *True History of the Kelly Gang* historical novels would suggest that they emphasize the role of external forces in the shaping and determining of the protagonist's identity, thus distorting what these works do, because the biographical novel came into existence as a rejection of and a counter to the determinism and even fatalism implicit in the historical novel. In a sense, the historical novel, with its emphasis on a representational figure from a specific time and place, takes the colonization of the mind as a necessary condition of human being, which is why Olga Tokarczuk refers to it as an aesthetic form that reinforces conservative schema. The biographical novel, with its emphasis on an anomalous figure that evades determinism and originates a new way of thinking and being, takes the decolonization of the mind as an epistemological starting point for meaningful and agential human living, which is why it can be described as an aspirational aesthetic form. That certain humans have been able to enhance life by creating new ways of thinking and being provides a template for such action but it also inspires readers to think more freely and to live more fully. As such, the biographical novel is more about the present and the future than it is about the past; it is more about the reader than it is about the real-life figure; and it is more about what we can become than what is or has been. Given Ireland's history under British rule, it only makes sense that the Irish have done so much to originate and advance biofiction.

Appendix: Interview with Mario Vargas Llosa

Lackey: You have done many interviews over the years, but this one is unique because we are going to focus exclusively on your biographical novels: *The Feast of the Goat*, *The Way to Paradise*, and *The Dream of the Celt*. As a scholar of the biographical novel, I found your epilogue to *The Dream of the Celt* illuminating and useful; but why did you include an epilogue in the Casement novel, but not in the other two?

Vargas Llosa: I'll tell you why I wrote this novel. I am a great admirer of Joseph Conrad. I think he has had a great influence on my writing. When I was reading a new biography about Conrad, I discovered the first person he met when he went to the Congo was Roger Casement. By this time, Casement had already been in the Congo for eight years. The meeting between the two men was absolutely essential because Conrad, like many people, was convinced that the King of Belgium was a great man who was fighting against slavery and introducing Christianity into the Congo. The Congo belonged to the King of Belgium because fifteen countries convened in Berlin and decided to give the Congo to the King of Belgium as a gift. He received the country, which was eighteen times the size of Belgium, as a gift. He had been strategizing this for years, creating an image of himself as a very generous kind of missionary that was fighting against slavery and introducing the true religion to the natives of the Congo. The image of himself was absolutely different from what he was as a real person. He was never in the Congo. For more than twenty years, it was not Belgium but Leopold who owned the Congo, where he introduced a kind of monstrous system in which the companies that he managed to bring to the Congo had almost total power. It was a criminal system, one of the worst for exploiting natives in any country in the world.

Lackey: Most people couldn't see it as criminal, but Casement eventually did. Is that why you decided to include an epilogue to *The Dream of the Celt*, but not the other two.

Vargas Llosa: Actually, Casement, like many people, went to Africa looking for adventure, and he was fascinated by the British explorers, but when he arrived there he discovered the kind of system that the King of Belgium had imposed in the Congo and he was absolutely terrified and fascinated by this, and so he started to document little by little and with great discretion what was happening there. When Conrad arrived in the Congo, he was already documenting the brutalities, the abuses by the different companies that were committed against the natives. These companies could act with total impunity. The system was terrible, even criminal, and without precedent until then. I was fascinated by this, especially when I discovered that Conrad had a contract as captain of a ship for several years. He was there only six months, but he was terrified. He and Roger Casement were good friends, and Casement informed him little by little about the brutality and exploitation occurring in the region. Conrad, after taking many notes, eventually resigned the contract, and returned to Britain with a very different idea of what was going on in the Congo.

Lackey: Why did you write a biographical novel about Casement instead of Conrad?

Vargas Llosa: Because the life of Conrad is very well known. But few people know about Roger Casement, who is a complicated figure. During World War I, he supported Germany, and he even tried to recruit Irish prisoners of war to work with the Germans in order to overthrow British rule in Ireland. The British discovered this, so they put him in jail. To discredit Casement with the public, the British government fabricated a false biography about Casement, one that documents his sexual adventures with other men. The diaries were arranged in such a way to destroy Casement, and it worked because in Ireland there was great reluctance to recognize him as a patriot.

Lackey: Let me ask a question about Roger Casement's mental awakening. You went to the National Library of Ireland to do research there, and I went there, too, to look at all the documents you looked at. Those unpublished documents in the National Library brilliantly chart Casement's transformation. At first, he supported British colonialism. But after a while, he started to turn against British colonialism and even the British themselves, which is one of the reasons why he started to become a freedom fighter for the Irish. Was Casement's Irishness what enabled him to see the horrors in the Congo? Or were the horrors in the Congo what enabled him to see that Ireland was being colonized in just the same way?

Vargas Llosa: The second one! He was not an independent thinker at all when he went to the Congo. He was very young when he went there and he was fascinated by the great explorers—British and American ones, also. But it was in documenting the crimes that were committed against the Congo people that he discovered that Ireland was a colony. At this time, he secretly became more politically independent. It had to be secret because he was officially appointed consul of Great Britain in the Congo. So he led a double life. He was a British diplomat at that time, but he was independent at heart.

Lackey: But most people who went to the Congo could not see that what they were doing were atrocities against human beings. What enabled Casement to see what so many others could not?

Vargas Llosa: He was not an exploiter. He went to become an explorer and he couldn't become an explorer. Most of the people who went there wanted gold and to enrich themselves. He was an idealist. An adventurer, if you want, but he was also an idealist, and when he discovered the monstrous crimes committed there, this changed him.

Lackey: In your epilogue, you talk about *The Motives of Proteus*. In fact, you use a quote from that book as the epigraph to the novel. Because of your epigraph and epilogue, I read that book, which focuses a lot on the transformation of consciousness.

Vargas Llosa: I think that is what happened with Casement. He became aware of all these problems when he was in the Congo. He didn't go there to discover this at all. On the contrary, he thought, as many young people in the world at that time, that it was the time of the great explorers. He went there looking for adventures, looking for an extraordinary kind of life. And what he discovered is hell. The monstrous exploitation of the natives, the way in which the European exploiters destroyed the communities. My impression is that the Congo has never recovered from this destruction. Never. It is still in such chaos and total disarray because of what happened during the late nineteenth and early twentieth centuries, when the Congo was the personal possession of the King of Belgium.

Lackey: The Spanish novelist Rosa Montero says the following about the biographical novel: "when we read a biographical novel, we're not really going back and trying to understand these actual people." According to Montero, she would say somebody like you wrote the Casement novel in order to help us understand how transformations in consciousness occur. So, while the novel focuses on somebody like Casement, it is really about us and how we can undergo a similar kind of transformation.

Vargas Llosa: I think that is a perfectly acceptable way to read the novel because my impression is that until now, particularly in Belgium, there is this idea that Leopold II was a kind of messiah that wanted to save the Africans from the Arab slave traders; this is a total fabrication. Leopold II was humiliated that Belgium was the only important monarchy in Europe which had no colonies. So he decided to acquire colonies, disguising himself as a kind of great protector of the African people, a hero with nice Christian missions; he sent missionaries to the Congo, and they did his work. So that was the reason why these fifteen countries convened in Berlin. Not one African country participated. Just European and American countries decided to give the Congo as a personal gift.

Lackey: When Virginia Woolf was writing her novel, *Mrs. Dalloway*, she said, "I wanted to criticize the social system and to show it at work, at its most intense." This is a common theme in all your biographical novels. In *The Feast of the Goat*, you show how Trujillo establishes a system of total dominance rooted in a type of masculine patriarchal power. There are two protagonists in *The Way to Paradise*, Flora Tristan and Paul Gauguin, who try to expose the sickness of Western culture, the decadence of that culture. *The Dream of the Celt* pictures colonialism in the Congo, the Amazon, and Ireland. We could look at these novels as history, and some people read them that way. But when I read your novels, I think you are using history to show us how to think about political structures, structures of exploitation, degradation, and violation. There seems to be a real commitment to social justice on your part. Do you think that one of the roles of the novelist is to expose structures of oppression and exploitation?

Vargas Llosa: I was a great follower of John Paul Sartre when I was a student, but I eventually distanced myself from his ideas and political positions, because he had become very radical. I went to France, where I lived for eight years, and I was deeply disappointed by Sartre. When I was a student in Lima, I read Sartre with passion and believed him. I think Sartre's idea that literature was not a purely idealistic kind of vocation, but that literature could play an important role in the historical transformation of societies gave me a kind of assurance that if I became a writer, if I became a novelist, I could at the same time without renouncing my vocation contribute to the revolution that I thought at the time was essential for Latin America. We could put end to the exploitation of the natives and eliminate enormous social and economic inequalities. I moved away from this narcissistic understanding of social matters, but Sartre's main idea I still think is right: that you could be a citizen of a very poor country with brutal inequalities and through writing novels or poems you could make people much more conscious of the brutal differences—

Lackey: Can you clarify what you mean with an example?

Vargas Llosa: Take the case of Roger Casement. He worked very hard for many years informing people and fighting against colonialism. He was fighting against the abusers and the tortures and the crimes that were committed in the colonies. Casement shared what was happening with Edmund Morel. He was also a great fighter against colonialism at that time and he received information from Casement, secret of course, but for many years he also worked hard to expose the crimes that were committed in the Congo and he also became an independent for the same reasons. Flora Tristan was also a great fighter, and an idealist. She was convinced that the most exploited people in society were women and workers. And so, she had this idea to found an international movement in which women and workers would fight to liberate women and workers from this exploitation, discrimination. She was a social fighter moved by moral reasons.

Lackey: But she was not a fan of literature. In the novel, she makes a few unkind remarks about literature and about poets.

Vargas Llosa: She was not an educated woman. At that time, women didn't receive a formal education. She was married to a monster and she was very courageous because she escaped.

Lackey: But she was very smart.

Vargas Llosa: Yes, she was very smart, but she was not an educated person. She did not receive any formal education. She left her husband, and at that time, when a woman abandoned a marriage, she should go to prison. So she disappeared for almost ten years and I think that she was probably a servant in England. Nobody knows why she went to England. There is no clear record of this.

Lackey: So you made up some of this?

Vargas Llosa: I invented it. I invented many things, but not the political realities. She was seduced by the Chartist movement in Britain and she persuaded some to join the Chartist movement. She wrote a book about England. She went to brothels, for example, disguised as a man because that was the only way in which she could explore the sexual exploitation of women.

Lackey: I would like to ask a question about things you made up. In your novel, Flora has a sexual relationship with the Olympia from Manet's painting. Is that true? Is that made up?

Vargas Llosa: No. I invented it.

Lackey: Why did you do that?

Vargas Llosa: Why? I invented many things just because I wanted to fill the puzzle.

Lackey: The Olympia painting is really important to Gauguin, as you highlight in the novel. Is that one of the reasons why you invented that relationship?

Vargas Llosa: Yes, it establishes links between the two characters. Let me explain this. Gauguin was not moved by social or moral matters at all. He had this theory that art in Europe, in the Western world, was in total decline at that time. Why? Because civilization is killing art. The art which is really created is the art that is produced by savages, by primitive people, primitive cultures. He wanted to be a great creator, a great artist. And he tried to become a primitive man, a very primitive man. He hated civilization. He thought civilization was the end of the arts. Flora was deeply committed to social matters and she wanted the liberation of women, of workers, and this was not at all a preoccupation for Gauguin. What he wanted was to return to the primitive world and that is the reason why he went to Panama, Haiti, and then finally to Tahiti. As he discovered that Tahiti was still in the process of civilization, he went to the Marquesas Islands, the most primitive island in the world, because he wanted to become a primitive. But he was not preoccupied by social matters at all, unlike his grandmother. He wanted to get rid of all social, moral, and civilized matters. He became a kind of savage in Tahiti. That is the reason why he was detested by the natives in Tahiti and on Marquesas Island. They considered him an abuser of women and he had already this very serious illness that was contagious with all the women he abused. But, in the world of art, he had this conviction and he tried to be exactly the kind of savage that he thought was indispensable to be a great artist. And in a way, the kind of painting that he did was deeply influenced by his idea of primitive art, which was not only for pleasure, but also a kind of religion, a kind of philosophy, an explanation of the world.

Lackey: What is the difference between history in a history book and history in a novel?

Vargas Llosa: I think an historical novelist can use history, but historians cannot use literature because I think that would distort real history. I think history is kind of a raw material for a novelist and the biography is also a raw material for a novelist. I don't think a novelist can really get rid of history and biography. I think the novelist is using it as a raw material, something that you distort and change, but literature makes possible an understanding of history better than history itself.

Lackey: Why?

Vargas Llosa: I think because you do not have this distance that you usually have with history when history is written by historians. They have to find truth. This is not an obligation for a novelist at all. Take, for example, the Napoleonic Wars in Russia. The historians can explain that *War and Peace* is full of errors, but actually when you read *War and Peace*, you really live the Napoleonic Wars in Russia as if you were a participant in these wars. This vivid experience is much more lasting than the old historical studies and books that explain what was really happening during these wars and I think this is what happened with Conrad, this is what happened with Thomas Mann's *Buddenbrooks*. These works give you a vivid experience of what happened, of what is happening, or what will happen.

Lackey: This idea of "what will happen" is really crucial for many novelists. For instance, in 1957 William Faulkner talked about his Percy Grimm character from *Light in August*, and he said that Grimm was the first Nazi stormtrooper in literature. He published that novel in the early 1930s, before he even knew about the Nazis.

Vargas Llosa: So before. That is fantastic! I think that is the case for many novels. The Orwell nightmare is something that anticipates the kind of technological dictators of the future. In many cases you have novels that open your eyes to things that will happen.

Lackey: That's exactly what happened when I read *The Feast of the Goat*. The novel is about Trujillo, but as I was reading it, I was thinking about Donald Trump, about some of the strategies he is currently using to institute a kind of dictatorship in the United States. Obviously, the United States is not like the Dominican Republic, but some of the things that Donald Trump is doing as a leader resemble what Trujillo did as a dictator.

Vargas Llosa: Some of the things, yes.

Lackey: So this is my question: how does literature enable us to see the way certain structures function in the future?

Vargas Llosa: I think that is the case exactly. I think the novel prepares us for things that will happen. In many cases, things that probably won't happen, And there is a very simple reason for this: when you are living you never have the kind of total experience that you have in a novel, in which you can follow not only the acts, but what precedes them in psychological terms as well as the conduct of the people and the consequences. This kind of total perspective you never have happen in real life. It's only in literature that you can have this total experience in which time is revealed in past, present, and future. This never happens in the real world. You never have the perspective to judge the way in which the conduct is predetermined by certain psychological experiences. I think this is what is probably the most important social role that novels have. Pleasure is essential. Pleasure from the language and characters, but I think in social terms, you are better prepared to face the future and face the present and understand the way in which the mechanism of the social can push you in one direction or another. I think this is the role that great novels have played in history. Of course, there are novels that are just entertaining. But if you think of the great novels, I think they are great for social, political, and philosophical reasons, and not only literary ones.

Lackey: Let me briefly pursue your *War and Peace* reference. We think of *War and Peace* as a historical novel because the main character, let's say Pierre (though there's more than just Pierre as a main character in that novel), is an invented figure, whereas in *The Feast of the Goat*, Trujillo is not an invented figure; he's an actual historical figure.

Vargas Llosa: There are lots of inventions in *The Feast of the Goat*.

Lackey: A lot of scholars would say that *War and Peace* is a historical novel because the protagonist is invented, while *The Feast of the Goat* is a biographical novel because you named the protagonist after the actual historical figure. Why did you do that? Why didn't you create a fictional character? Urania is also a main character in *The Feast of the Goat*, but she is invented. Is that right?

Vargas Llosa: Yes, she is an invented character.

Lackey: And I have to tell you, that novel made me sick. I mean physically sick because I was so horrified. I could sense that you were building up to the ending when she was going to be violated, and it made me sick. As a character, she is symbolic of Trujillo's victims, many of which were women. Is that right?

Vargas Llosa: Absolutely, absolutely. I think particularly during the Trujillo dictatorship women were the major victims. It has something to do with Latin American machismo. Machismo is so brutal, especially in the context of a dictatorship. I remember I was deeply moved when I went to the Dominican Republic to present the book after it was published. I read a letter in one of the important journals in the Dominican Republic. A man wrote a letter to the journal saying, "After reading this book, I had felt the necessity to tell the story of my sister." And what he told was that his family was very devoted to the Trujillo family, and very close to and great admirers of Trujillo himself. His sister was violated by Ramfis, the eldest son of Trujillo, and this was such a catastrophe for the family. The mother was almost crazy after that, the family moved to the United States because they couldn't live in the Dominican Republic after the catastrophe. He said, "When I read this book, I couldn't believe that it was not inspired by the case of my sister. But of course, there is no way in which Mr. Vargas could know about my sister." But these things were happening in the Dominican Republic during the dictatorship. Yes, I had invented it. He had not told me the story of Urania. But, you know, I wrote this novel because I went to the Dominican Republic in 1974 or 1975 to do a documentary for the French Radio Television. It was kind of a touristic document, but it wasn't my first visit to the Dominican Republic. I heard incredible things about the dictatorship, despite the fact that he had been killed eleven years prior. Particularly, there was one thing that impressed me so much that they told: that during the visits that Trujillo did to the country, he received as a gift, from peasants mostly, girls. Girls were given to him because the persons knew that he liked them very much, and I think this is a typical Latin American fantasy. I met an assistant of Trujillo, a former officer, Canila Shea. He was friendly and I asked him, "I have heard this. Is this true? That Trujillo received these girl peasants as a gift?" and he told me, "yes! It was a problem for the chief, you know, because he didn't know what to do with his girls. In some cases, he married them with military officers, with soldiers, but in many cases, he didn't know what to do. He didn't want to be impolite with the peasants." And I said, "you are telling me that this is true? That he received the daughters of the peasants as gifts?" "Yes, of course, many." Well, I think that is really unthinkable because when we think of that happening during the 31 years of dictators, it is really absolutely incredible. And it was probably this that pushed me to write the novel. I started to read about Trujillo, I took notes, and suddenly I discovered that I was already working on a novel about the times of Trujillo.

Lackey: Colum McCann has written some wonderful biographical novels and he argues that the biographical novel enables readers to get a better grasp of the idea of freedom.

Vargas Llosa: I think this is true. But the term biographical novel makes me nervous because when you write a novel, you are not morally obliged to truth, not at all. You are obliged to do a good novel and a good novel is always full of lies, inventions, fantasies, all distortions of real facts. And this is the right of the novelist: to produce these distortions.

Lackey: To what end?

Vargas Llosa: There is one reason: a novel must be a good novel and to be a good novel you are obliged to take liberties with the truth, with historical truth. But if biographical novels mean that you are morally obliged to give your reader truth–

Lackey: No, they are not.

Vargas Llosa: Good, because literature is different. Literature is different than sociology, different than the sciences. It's fiction, it is something that is invented. The characters in a novel are made of words, not flesh and blood. Just words. Words give you a kind of independence with real characters and real persons, and I think it's very important to make this distinction.

Lackey: McCann makes this same point. He wrote a spectacular biographical novel called *Dancer*. It's about the famous Russian ballet dancer, Rudi

Nureyev. I interviewed Colum, and he said: "90% of the novel is made up—."

Vargas Llosa: I think this is true. The percentage, of course, can vary.

Lackey: So I asked him, "why did you write it?" And he said, Look, I wrote it because of the effect that Nureyev had on a friend of mine. That friend saw Nureyev on television, and it changed his life. So the novel was not so much about Nureyev as it was using Nureyev to clarify the importance and power of art, how art changed the life of his friend. In short, he wanted to explore how art could make people more free. So my question for you: can we have freedom? And two, how can the novel bring about freedom?

Vargas Llosa: I think it's essential.

Lackey: Why?

Vargas Llosa: The role of freedom is absolutely essential. Without freedom, you are so limited.

Lackey: What do you mean by freedom?

Vargas Llosa: Freedom is the possibility to do anything you like. You are pushed to do it when you are writing a novel. With this kind of freedom, you have no limits, moral or political, none at all. I think it's extremely important to have this possibility of freedom in the moral, or political, or religious world. It's a moral disposition, you know? If there's a dictatorship, if there is a society that is very controlling, you need a lot of courage to overcome the limitations. You risk a lot, but I think it's the only way in which you can be a real novelist, a real creator. Otherwise—and I would like to add something to this—that is the reason why in any society in which a kind of control is imposed, immediately literature is considered a very dangerous kind of activity. And that is a reason why in all dictatorships in history, control of literature and culture becomes very essential, very important for power. Because they feel that literature poses a potential danger. And I think that they are right. In Latin America, for example, the novel was forbidden. It was not forbidden in Spain, but in the colonies it was forbidden. The political leaders gave religious and moral reasons, but I think there was a perception that if you give literature total freedom, something will happen that will destroy the status quo. And I think this explains why dictatorships want to take control of this operation that is seemingly so innocuous. In a democracy it seems so innocuous, but it's not innocuous, no. This is particularly well perceived by dictatorships.

Lackey: This is my last question. In all three of your biographical novels, you focus a lot on dictatorships, but you also focus on religion. I'm curious, can you just talk about your thinking about the role of religion either in controlling people, contributing to dictatorships, or enabling certain levels of freedom.

Vargas Llosa: I don't think much about religion because, well, my family was very religious, my mother particularly. But I lost my faith when I was very young. Probably when I was 11 or 12 years, I had a very disgusting experience with one of my teachers. I was in a religious school, in the Colegio La Salle, and one day I went to school when no one was there. And my teacher at that time was an old French Brother and he asked me to come with him to the 5th floor, which was the apartments of the Brothers.

Lackey: Christian Brothers?

Vargas Llosa: Yes, Christian Brothers. Normally, we students never went there. It was totally forbidden. But, he told me that I should come with him and I went there and I had a very nasty experience. I noticed that the Brother was very nervous. Something seemed not normal. When we got into a room, the Brother opened a cupboard and to my surprise he gave me pornographic magazines with nude women. I was completely surprised. I didn't know what to do with these magazines and suddenly I felt that he was trying to touch my zipper. I became so nervous that I said, "I want to go!" and he became very nervous, too. Well, it was something very rapid and nothing happened, but this experience had consequences because until then, I was very religious. I went to mass regularly, but little by little I became less and less religious. And then suddenly one day, and I didn't dare say this to anybody, but I was not a believer anymore. I was not. Everything had become purely formal, a formal way in which faith was not present anymore. And it happened like that! I was in the second year of school. And the next year I went to a military school, and since then, religion has not been a preoccupation for me, not at all. My friends had religious crises when they were adolescents, but I never did, because the Brother cured me of this kind of preoccupation for the rest of my life.

Notes

Introduction

1 For a discussion of scholarly works about biofiction, see my introduction in *Biographical Fiction*. Contained in this anthology are numerous works about biofiction from the 1930s until 2017.

2 I spent a week in early June 2019 working at the State Library Victoria in Melbourne on the various draft versions of Carey's novel, and one of the archivists told me this story.

3 Febvre (1973), "History and Psychology," in *A New Kind of History: From the Writings of Febvre*. Ed. Peter Burke, Trans. K. Folca. New York, Evanston, San Francisco: Harper & Row Publishers, 7.

4 Bode (2017), "The Buxom Biographies," in Lackey's *Biographical Fiction*, 269.

5 Kendall (2017), "Excerpt from 'Contemporary Biography' from *The Art of Biography*," in Lackey's *Biographical Fiction*, 282.

6 Boldrini (2012), *Autobiographies of Others: Historical Subjects and Literary Fiction*. New York and London: Routledge, 66.

7 Kohlke (2013), "Neo-Victorian Biofiction and the Special/Spectral Case of Barbara Chase-Riboud's *Hottentot Venus*," *Australasian Journal of Victorian Studies* 18(3): 13.

8 See Schabert's *In Quest of the Other Person: Fiction as Biography*; Dee's "The Reanimators: On the Art of Literary Graverobbing"; Jameson's *The Antinomies of Realism*; Haan's "Personalized History: On Biofiction, Source Criticism and the Critical Value of Biography"; and Novak's "Experiments in Life-Writing: Introduction." Biofiction scholars who have made a clear distinction between the actual person and the fictional correlative include Jay Parini, *Some Necessary Angels: Essays on Writing and Politics*; Monica Latham, *A Poetics of Postmodernism and Neomodernism: Rewriting Mrs. Dalloway*; Joanna Scott, "On Hoaxes, Humbugs, and Fictional Portraiture"; and Bethany Layne, *Henry James in Contemporary Fiction: The Real Thing*.

9 In 2012, Monica Latham published "'Serv[ing] under two masters': Virginia Woolf's Afterlives in Contemporary Biofictions," which is an extremely important contribution because she so clearly responds to all those scholars who use a biography approach to assess and criticize biofiction. Focusing specifically on

Michael Cunningham's novel *The Hours*, Latham notes how "Woolfian critics complained" about some of the liberties Cunningham took. But Latham rightly responds: "Cunningham is not a biographer, but a fiction writer whose method consists in fictionalizing biographical events. He breaks free from biography, distorts it, and fabricates new events that seem authentic as they encroach on real, biographical material" (415). I am working within the same scholarly tradition as Latham.

10 Najmi (2014), *Gertrude*. Trans. Roger Allen. Northampton, Massachusetts: Interlink Books, 161.

11 Ibid., 184.

12 Ibid., 186.

13 Wilde (2017), "The Portrait of Mr W.H," in *The Short Fiction*. Ed. Ian Small, Vol VIII of *The Complete Works of Oscar Wilde*. Oxford: Oxford University Press, 259.

14 Nietzsche (1967), "The Case of Wagner", in *The Birth of Tragedy and the Case of Wagner*. Trans. and Ed. Walter Kaufmann. New York: Vintage Books, 192.

Chapter 1

1 Wilde (2007), "Historical Criticism," in *Criticism: Historical Criticism, Intentions, the Soul of Man*. Ed. Josephine M. Guy, Vol. IV of *The Complete Works of Oscar Wilde*. Oxford: Oxford University Press, 28.

2 For useful studies that explore how the French Revolution led to the construction of history programs, see Hayden White's *Metahistory: The Historical Imagination in Nineteenth-Century Europe* and Robert S. Lehman's *Impossible Modernism: T.S. Eliot, Walter Benjamin, and the Critique of Historical Reason*.

3 I am grateful to Todd Avery, who has helped me understand how the late-nineteenth- and early-twentieth-century debate about history as science impacted modernist writers and contributed to the rise and evolution of biofiction. For Avery's best work on this topic, see " 'The Historian of the Future': Lytton Strachey and Modernist Historiography between the Two Cultures" and "Art and Ethics: Lytton Strachey and the Origins of Biofiction."

4 Lukács (1983), *The Historical Novel*. Trans. Hannah and Stanley Mitchell. Lincoln and London: University of Nebraska Press, 28.

5 Ibid., 34.

6 Ibid., 19.

7 Ibid., 38.

8 Ibid., 34.

9 Ibid., 60.

10 Ibid., 23.
11 Ibid.
12 Ibid., 24.
13 Ibid., 42.
14 Ibid., 24.
15 Ibid., 20.
16 Wilde (2007), 10.
17 Ibid.
18 Ibid., 30.
19 Ibid., 28.
20 Wilde (2007), "The Critic as Artist," 143.
21 Josephine M. Guy, "Introduction," in Wilde (2007), xix.
22 Philip E. Smith II and Michael S. Helfand, "The Text as Context," in *Oscar Wilde's Oxford Notebooks: A Portrait of Mind in the Making*, interpret "The Portrait of Mr. W.H." as a logical extension of Wilde's essay about history (87–96). But as I will demonstrate, Wilde's views are in irreconcilable conflict with the view of history-as-science, which are of central importance in the 1879 essay.
23 Wilde (2017), "The Portrait of Mr W.H.," in *The Short Fiction*, 269, hereafter cited in text and in notes as PWH.
24 Other scholars who treat and assess the biographical novel as a version of the historical novel, thus distorting what biofiction does, include Lucien Febvre, Beverley Southgate, Marc C. Carnes, Hamish Dalley, Jerome De Groot, Fredric Jameson, and Binne de Haan.
25 Lukács (1983), 301.
26 Ibid., 304.
27 Ibid., 306.
28 Ibid., 303–4.
29 Ibid., 321.
30 Without mentioning Lukács, Smith and Helfand (1989) use his approach to interpret "The Portrait." As they say in "The Text as Context": "For the narrator W.H. is important because he inspired Shakespeare to write sonnets which were historically representative of the spirit of the Renaissance" (92).
31 In *The Copywrights: Intellectual Property and the Literary Imagination*, Paul K. Saint-Amour (2003) has authored a wonderfully insightful chapter about "The Portrait," which emphasizes the point that Wilde was working in an intellectual tradition very different from Lukács. The Marxist critic brings science and art together, oftentimes at the expense of art. But according to Saint-Amour: "the point of Wilde's experiment in amphibian genre, ultimately, is not to merge science and art, but to plead their separation" (107).

32 Consistently, scholars have failed to note that there are two separate theories at work in "The Portrait." Rather, they take it as a given that there is only one theory. For instance, David Wayne Thomas (2004) says in *Cultivating Victorians: Liberal Culture and the Aesthetic*: "The literary theory proposes that Mr. W.H.—the mysterious dedicatee of Shakespeare's *Sonnets*—can be identified as Willie Hughes, a boy actor in Shakespeare's theater company" (160). Jerusha McCormack (1997) makes a similar claim in "Wilde's Fiction(s)": "the reader is free to enjoy its speculative thesis: that the Mr W.H. of the Sonnets is in reality a boy-actor, Willie Hughes" (108). Here is how Joseph Bistrow (1997) puts the matter in "'A Complex Multiform Creature': Wilde's Sexual Identities": "the theory—even if it cannot be credited with empirical evidence—becomes an absorbing act of faith. In fact, it develops into something more than that. The theory turns out to be a complete obsession, one that makes Erskine aghast because there is something 'fatal' about it" (206).

33 McCann (2017), "Interview with Robert Birnbaum," in *Conversations with Colum McCann*. Ed. Earl Ingersoll. Jackson: University of Mississippi Press, 71.

34 McCann (2017), "Do What Is Most Difficult," in *Conversations with Colum McCann*, 181.

35 Wilde (2007), "Critic," 143–4.

36 Wilde (2007), "Decay," 99.

37 Wilde (2007), "Critic," 146.

38 Wilde (2007), "Decay," 97.

39 Lukács (1983), 290.

40 Ibid., 35.

41 Wilde (2005), "Epistola: In Carcere et Vinculis," in *De Profundis and* "Epistola: In Carcere et Vinculis". Ed. Ian Small, Vol. 2, *The Complete Works of Oscar Wilde*. Oxford: Oxford University Press, 126.

42 Wilde (2007), "Decay," 79.

43 Ibid., 92.

44 Moore (1942), Letter to John Eglinton, December 18, 1915, in *Letters of George Moore*. Bournemouth, England: Sydenham & Co, 29.

45 Vidal (2005), "The Art of Fiction L: Gore Vidal," in *Conversations with Gore Vidal*. Eds. Richard Peabody and Lucinda Ebersole. Jackson: University Press of Mississippi, 54.

46 Scott (2017), "On Hoaxes, Humbugs, and Fictional Portraiture," in Lackey's *Biographical Fiction*, 32.

47 McLain (2018), *Love and Ruin*. New York: Ballantine Books, 388.

48 Wilde (2017), *The Incomparable and Ingenious History of Mr. W.H.*, in *The Short Fiction*, 264, and PWH, 204.

49 Wilde (2017), *Incomparable*, 248, and PWH, 278.
50 Wilde (2017), *Incomparable*, 232.
51 Ibid.
52 There have been many studies focusing on Wilde's treatment of homosexuality in "The Portrait." See, for instance, Kate Chedgzoy's *Shakespeare's Queer Children: Sexual Politics and Contemporary Culture;* Lawrence Danson's *Wilde's Intentions: The Artist in His Criticism;* Joseph Bistrow's "'A Complex Multiform Creature': Wilde's Sexual Identities," and William A. Cohen's *Sex Scandal: The Private Parts of Victorian Fiction*. My approach is different because I am interested in the formal elements and structure of biofiction, so I read the story's homosexuality as it functions within the framework of the specific genre.
53 Wilde (2017), *Incomparable*, 219.
54 Ibid., 224–5.
55 For useful studies about Wilde's engagement with Platonism, see Danson's *Wilde's Intentions* and Bistrow's "A Complex Multiform Creature' – Wilde's Sexual Identities."
56 Wilde (2007), "Critic," 159.
57 Ibid.
58 Locating a work within a specific genre has significant ramifications in the way a work is read. Saint-Amour makes this point directly about "The Portrait": "ambiguous genres disrupt the reading protocols of literary culture" (97). Reading "The Portrait" as a biofiction significantly alters the way we interpret and experience the work.
59 Chedgzoy never refers to "The Portrait" as biofiction, but she deploys a biofictional approach when interpreting the novel: Wilde "uses Shakespeare's *Sonnets* to celebrate and sustain a self-conscious culture and discourse of male homosexuality in the late nineteenth century" (138–9). I agree with this claim, but I would add the following: Wilde uses Willie, Shakespeare, and the *Sonnets* to legitimize and promote male homosexuality in his present and for the future.
60 Unigwe (2019), "Biographical Fiction and the Creation of Possible Lives," in Lackey's *Conversations with Biographical Novelists: Truthful Fictions across the Globe*. London and New York: Bloomsbury, 255.
61 Ibid.
62 Montero (2019), "Speculative Subjectivities and the Biofictional Surge," in Lackey's *Conversations with Biographical Novelists*, 164.
63 Montero (2019), "Speculative," 167.
64 Ibid.
65 Ibid.
66 Ebershoff (2019), "The Biographical Novel as Life Art," in Lackey's *Conversations with Biographical Novelists*, 99.

67 Atwood (1998), "In search of *Alias Grace*: On Writing Canadian Historical Fiction," in *The American Historical Review*. 103(5) (December): 1516.
68 Ibid.
69 Wilde (2007), "The Soul of Man," in *Criticism*, 262.
70 Ebershoff (2000), "Author's Note," in *The Danish Girl*. New York: Penguin Books, 271.
71 Ebershoff (2000), "A Conversation with David Ebershoff," in *The Danish Girl*, 8.
72 Ebershoff (2019), "The Biographical Novel as Life Art," in Lackey's *Conversations with Biographical Novelists*, 101.
73 Peter Ackroyd (1983), "*The Last Testament of Oscar Wilde*." New York: Harper & Row, Publishers, 135, hereafter cited in text and in notes as LT.
74 I want to thank Dennis Kersten for all his useful suggestions as I wrote this chapter.
75 Plato (1951), *The Symposium*. Trans. Walter Hamilton. London and New York: Penguin Books, 41.
76 Ibid., 86.
77 Ibid., 87.
78 Ibid., 90.
79 Ibid., 94.
80 Ibid., 101.
81 Ibid., 106.
82 Plato (1961), "*Ion*," in *The Collected Dialogues of Plato*. Ed. Edith Hamilton and Huntington Cairns. Princeton: Princeton University Press, 220.
83 Blake (1988), "*Jerusalem*," in *The Complete Poetry & Prose of William Blake*. Ed. David V. Erdman. New York and London: Anchor Books, 153.
84 See Wilde (2005), "Epistola," 129.
85 Quoted in Nicholas Frankel (2017), *Oscar Wilde: The Unrepentant Years*. Cambridge, Massachusetts and London: Harvard University Press, 200.
86 Ibid.
87 Ibid., 201.
88 Using a Foucauldian model about the classificatory function of naming, Gregory Mackie clarifies how Wilde's reputation was so significantly damaged in 1895 through two public acts: (1) "when extracts of Wilde's own writings were submitted as evidence in a sequence of judicial proceedings that led to his imprisonment on charges of gross indecency," and (2) "Wilde's bankruptcy during the trials and the hasty sale of his literary property in their wake further marginalized the Irish writer by dispersing the books, manuscripts, letters, and records (and paintings) contained in his London house" (9). Gregory Mackie (2019), *Beautiful Untrue Things: Forging Oscar Wilde's Extraordinary Afterlife*. Toronto, Buffalo, and London: University of Toronto Press.

89 Plato, *Symposium*, 93.

90 In "Epistola," Wilde (2005) explains this shift from the ontological to the phenomenological: "Things in themselves are of little importance, have indeed—let us for once thank Metaphysics for something that she has taught us—no real existence. The spirit alone is of importance" (125).

91 Wilde (2007), "Soul," 250.

92 Wilde (2007), "Soul," 239.

93 Alexander Pope (1991), "Essay on Man," in *Alexander Pope: Collected Poems*. London: J.M. Dent & Sons Ltd, Epistle I, ln. 294; 189.

94 Tóibín (2004), *The Master: A Novel*. New York: Picador, 11, hereafter cited in text and in notes as M.

95 This document is held at the National Library of Ireland in the Colm Tóibín Papers, Collection List Number 133. Here are the manuscript numbers: MS44,474/2.

96 Tóibín, Colm Tóibín Papers: MS44,474/10.

97 Tóibín, Colm Tóibín Papers: MS44,474/2.

98 Wilde (2005), *De Profundis*, 184.

99 Tóibín (2019), "The Anchored Imagination of the Biographical Novel," in Lackey's *Conversations with Biographical Novelists*, 228.

100 James (1955), "Letter to Sarah Orne Jewett," 5 October 1901, in *The Selected Letters of Henry James*. Ed. Leon Edel. New York: Farrar, Straus and Cudahy, 202–3.

101 Wilde (2007), "Critic," 147.

102 Wilde (2007), "Decay," 91.

103 Ibid.

104 Marx (1977), "Preface," to *A Critique of Political Economy* in *Karl Marx: Selected Writings*. Ed. David McLellan. Oxford: Oxford University Press, 389.

105 McCann (2003), *Dancer*. London: Phoenix, 41.

106 McCann (2019), "Contested Realities in the Biographical Novel," in Lackey's *Conversations with Biographical Novelists*, 133.

107 Ibid., 136.

108 Ibid., 138.

109 McCann (2003), 148.

110 Ibid., 245–6.

Chapter 2

1 Locating a work within a particular genre has a significant impact on the way a work is read and interpreted. For instance, Jennifer Stevens reads *The Brook Kerith*

in relation to the "generic framework" of the "extensive canon of non-fiction prose works about the life of Christ." Consequently, she concludes that *The Brook Kerith* was not "significantly determined by the events unfolding around" Moore. Stevens (2010), *The Historical Jesus and the Literary Imagination: 1860–1920*. Liverpool: Liverpool University Press, 251. As I will demonstrate in this chapter, biographical novels are primarily focused on the present and the future, so instead of trying to accurately represent the historical past or the biographical subject, the author converts the figure from the past into a literary symbol that can be used to illuminate a more universal reality or to bring into existence a new reality in the present or for the future.

2 The novel was considered scandalous because it was "a blasphemous libel of the Holy Scripture and of the Christian religion" and that it suggested that "Jesus Christ was an ignorant, deceitful, violent-tempered person and a vainglorious impostor" (32), as Dennis Kennedy notes of the lawsuit that Lord Alfred Douglas brought against the author and publisher of *The Brook Kerith*. For a brief discussion of the scandal and blasphemy of the novel, see Kennedy (2016), "*The Brook Kerith*: 'George Moore's Blasphemy,'" *History Ireland*. 24(5)(September/October): 32–5.

3 Moore, quoted in Frazier (2000), *George Moore: 1852–1933*. New Haven and London: Yale University Press, 63.

4 As Theodore Reff says: "From the time Manet exhibited his portrait of Zola at the Salon of 1868, his novel treatment of its setting has been recognized as its most striking feature." Reff (1975), "Manet's Portrait of Zola," *The Burlington Magazine*. 117(862) (January): 35.

5 Zola (1964), "The Experimental Novel," in *The Experimental Novel, and Other Essays*. Trans. Belle M. Sherman. New York: Haskell House, 2.

6 Ibid., 17.

7 Ibid., 20.

8 Ibid., 21.

9 Ibid., 24.

10 Ibid., 25.

11 Ibid.

12 Ibid., 54.

13 Pfeiffer (2018), *From Chaos to Catastrophe? Texts and the Transitionality of the Mind*. Berlin: De Gruyter, 113–87.

14 Ibid., 15.

15 Rubin (2010), *Manet*. Paris: Flammarion, 97.

16 Lethbridge (2013), "Introduction," *Looking at Manet: Writings on Manet by Emile Zola*. Trans. Michael Ross. London: Pallas Athene, 10–11.

17 As Reff (1975) notes: "If Zola had looked more closely at the reproduction of *Olympia* in his portrait, he would have observed that her glance is directed toward him, rather than toward us as it is in the original" (41).

18 Zola (2013), "A New Way to Paint: Edouard Manet," *Looking at Manet*, 54.
19 Zola (2013), 55.
20 This painting is usually housed in the Musee D'Orsay, but I viewed it on June 18, 2018, at the Musee de Monet in Giverny.
21 Zola (2013), 43.
22 Brilliant (1991), *Portraiture*. Cambridge: Harvard University Press, 8.
23 Ibid., 15.
24 Ibid., 82.
25 Ibid., 83.
26 Ibid., 15.
27 Zola (1964), 9.
28 Wilde (2007), "Decay," 79.
29 Ibid., 82.
30 Ibid., 97.
31 Moore (1972), *Confessions of a Young Man*. Ed. Susan Dick. Montreal: McGill-Queen's University Press, 44.
32 Frazier (2000), 54–65.
33 Moore (1972), 95.
34 Moore, qtd. in Frazier (2000), 63.
35 Joyce (1986), *Ulysses*. New York: Vintage Books, 28.
36 As Frazier (2000) says: "Nietzsche played a key role as midwife to a new view of life for Moore" (257). I will discuss Nietzsche's influence on Moore in more depth later in this chapter.
37 Nietzsche (1997), "On the Uses and Disadvantages of History for Life," in *Untimely Meditations*. Ed. Daniel Brezeale. Trans. R.J. Hollingdale. Cambridge: Cambridge University Press, 121, hereafter cited in text and in notes as UDH.
38 Lukács (1983), 60.
39 Ibid., 35.
40 Nietzsche (1989), *Ecce Homo*, in *On the Genealogy of Morals* and *Ecce Homo*. Trans. Walter Kaufmann and RJ Hollingdale. New York: Vintage Books, 326.
41 Ibid., 328.
42 Ibid., 259.
43 Nietzsche (1999), *The Anti-Christ*, in *Twilight of the Idols/The Anti-Christ*. Trans. R.J. Hollingdale. London: Penguin Books, 181.
44 Ibid., 199.
45 Ibid., 181.
46 Ibid., 144.
47 Ibid., 143.
48 Ibid., 168.

49 Nietzsche (2006), *Thus Spoke Zarathustra: A Book for All and None*. Trans. Adrian Del Caro. Cambridge: Cambridge University Press, 6, hereafter cited in text and in notes as Z.

50 Nietzsche (1974), *The Gay Science*. Trans. Walter Kaufmann. New York: Vintage Books, 177.

51 Nietzsche claims that Christ "promoted the stupidifying of man" and "retarded the production of the supreme intellect." Nietzsche (1996), *Human, All Too Human*. Trans. R.J. Hollingdale. Cambridge: Cambridge University Press, 112.

52 Nietzsche (1989), 146.

53 See the Gospel of John 10:1-16.

54 Gospel of John 14:6.

55 See Young (2010), *Friedrich Nietzsche: A Philosophical Biography*. Cambridge: Cambridge University Press, 76–8.

56 Ibid., 185–7.

57 Nietzsche (1967), *The Case of Wagner*, in *The Birth of Tragedy* and *The Case of Wagner*. Trans. Walter Kaufmann. New York: Vintage Books, 155.

58 Ibid., 164.

59 Nietzsche (1954), "Nietzsche Contra Wagner," in *The Portable Nietzsche*. Trans. Walter Kaufmann. New York: The Viking Press, 676.

60 Nietzsche, *Ecce*, 321.

61 For an insightful discussion of the Förster/Elisabeth courtship and relationship, see Diethe (2003), *Nietzsche's Sister and the Will to Power: A Biography of Elisabeth Förster-Nietzsche*. Urbana and Chicago: University of Illinois Press, 36–8.

62 Weaver Santaniello notes how Nietzsche opposed Christian anti-Semitism, which was dominant in Richard Wagner's circle. Elisabeth met her future husband in this circle, which served to reinforce her Christian anti-Semitism. Santaniello (1994), *Nietzsche, God, and the Jews: His Critique of Judeo-Christianity in Relation to the Nazi Myth*. Albany: SUNY Press, 139.

63 Förster claims that Germanness and Christianity were wed in what he refers to as the second phase of Christianity's development. Förster (1881), *Das Verhältniss des modernen Judenthums zur deutschen Kunst*. Berlin: Verlag von M. Schulze, 19.

64 Förster (1883), *Parsifal-Nachklänge: Allerhand Gedanken ueber Deutsche Cultur, Wissenschaft, Kunst, Gesellschaft*. Leipzig: Fritsch, 22. My translation. Chamberlain makes this same claim in the *Foundations of the Nineteenth Century*. This is clearly an idea circulating in the Wagner circle.

65 As Richard S. Levy notes, this petition "received over 250,000 signatures and became the subject of a debate in the Prussian Parliament." Levy (1991), *Antisemitism in the Modern World: An Anthology of Texts*. Ed. Richard S. Levy. Lexington, MA and Toronto: D.C. Heath and Company, 122.

66 Förster, "Antisemites' Petition," in Levy (1991), 125.
67 Ibid., 126.
68 Goebbels (1987), *Michael.* Trans. Joachim Neugroschel. New York: Amok Press, 65.
69 Bridgwater (1988), *George Moore and German Pessimism.* Durham: University of Durham, 57.
70 Ibid., 60.
71 Ibid., 63.
72 Ibid., 67.
73 Moore (1942), *Letters of George Moore.* Bournemouth, England: Sydenham & Co., 34.
74 Quinn, qtd. in Bridgewater (1988), 57.
75 Moore, qtd. in Bridgewater (1988), 58.
76 Halevy (1914), *The Life of Friedrich Nietzsche.* Trans. J.M. Hone. London: T. Fischer Unwin, 271.
77 Ibid., 260.
78 Moore (1942), 21.
79 Shirer (1960), *The Rise and Fall of the Third Reich: A History of Nazi Germany.* New York: Simon and Schuster, 158.
80 Ibid., 159.
81 Ibid., 156.
82 Field (1981), *Evangelist of Race: The Germanic Vision of Houston Stewart Chamberlain.* New York: Columbia University Press, 1.
83 Goebbels (1962), *The Early Goebbels Diaries: 1925–1926.* Ed. Helmut Heiber. New York: Frederick A. Praeger, 83.
84 Field (1981), 452.
85 Ibid., 438.
86 Chamberlain (1912), I.221, hereafter cited in text and in notes as FNC.
87 Quoted in Steigmann-Gall (2003), *The Holy Reich: Nazi Conceptions of Christianity, 1919–1945.* Cambridge: Cambridge University Press, 14.
88 Frazier (2000), 265.
89 It is worth noting that there are only two published volumes of Dujardin's correspondence, one of the letters from Moore to Dujardin and one of the letters between Dujardin and Chamberlain.
90 Zuleika Rodgers compellingly argues that Moore incorporated many of Dujardin's ideas into *The Brook Kerith.* See Rodgers (2016), "A Twentieth-Century Irishman's First Century Palestine: George Moore's *The Brook Kerith,*" in *Sibyls, Scriptures, and Scrolls: John Collins at Seventy,* Volume 2. Leiden and Boston: Brill.
91 Rodgers (2016), 1140.
92 Adolf Hitler (1942), "Speech of April 12, 1922," in *The Speeches of Adolf Hitler.* Trans. Norman H. Baynes. London and New York: Oxford University Press, 19–20.

93 Hitler (1971), *Mein Kampf*. Trans. Ralph Manheim. Boston: Houghton Mifflin, 65.

94 Ibid., 687.

95 Eckart (1999), *Bolshevism from Moses to Lenin: A Dialogue between Adolf Hitler and Me*. Hillsboro, WV: National Vanguard Books, 36.

96 Ibid., 33.

97 Ibid., 35.

98 Ibid., 21.

99 Bytwerk (1983), *Julius Streicher*. New York: Dorset Press, 1–2.

100 All references from the Nuremberg Trials are taken from Yale's *The Avalon Project*, an online database with all the documents pertaining to the case. My citations will reference the URL: http://avalon.law.yale.edu/imt/judstrei.asp

101 Tusa (1986), *The Nuremberg Trial*. New York: Atheneum, 334.

102 *The Avalon Project*: http://avalon.law.yale.edu/imt/judstrei.asp

103 For my most focused analysis of Streicher's anti-Semitic Christian nationalism, see Lackey (2013) "Conceptualizing Christianity and Christian Nazis after the Nuremberg Trials," *Cultural Critique* 84(Spring): 101–33.

104 *Der Stürmer*, March 1929, number 13.

105 Goebbels (1987), 65.

106 Ibid., 65–6.

107 Ibid., 120.

108 Ibid., 65.

109 Ibid., 39.

110 Nietzsche (1966), *Beyond Good and Evil: Prelude to a Philosophy of the Future*. Trans. Walter Kaufmann. New York: Vintage, 131.

111 Nietzsche (1999), 55.

112 Moore (1910), "The Apostle," *The English Review* 5(June): 564.

113 There has been much confusion about these various versions, especially the two play versions of *The Apostle*, which are very different from each other. For the sake of clarity, I will specify the year after the title to indicate which version of the play I am discussing.

114 Ibid., 568.

115 Ibid., 569.

116 Ibid., 573.

117 Ibid., 576.

118 Moore (1911), *The Apostle*. Dublin: Maunsel, 20.

119 Ibid., 29.

120 Ibid., 92.

121 Moore (1916), *The Brook Kerith: A Syrian Story*. New York: The Macmillan Company, 447, hereafter cited in text and in notes as BK.

122 Moore (1911), 15.

123 Ibid.

124 Ibid., 17.

125 Moore (1942), 23.

126 Hobson (2018), "George Moore and New Testament Biofiction: *The Brook Kerith*," *Éire Ireland* 53(1 & 2)(Spring/Summer), 182.

127 Woolf (1980), *The Diary of Virginia Woolf*. Ed. Anne Olivier Bell, Vol. 2. New York: Harcourt Brace Jovanovich, 248.

128 Moore (1910), 574.

129 Moore (1911), 61.

130 Moore (1923), *The Apostle*. London: William Heiemann Ltd, 119.

131 Moore (1910), 574.

132 Moore (1923), 69.

133 For works that discuss the role of Christianity in Nazi Germany, see Doris Bergen, *The Twisted Cross: The German Christian Movement in the Third Reich*; James Carroll, *Constantine's Sword: The Church and the Jews*; Richard Steigmann-Gall, *The Holy Reich: Nazi Conceptions of Christianity, 1919–1945*; Robert Michael, *Holy Hatred: Christianity, Antisemitism, and the Holocaust*, and Susannah Heschel, *The Aryan Jesus: Christian Theologians and the Bible in Nazi Germany*.

134 Tóibín (2019), "The Anchored Imagination of the Biographical Novel," in Lackey's *Conversations with Biographical Novelists*, 224.

135 For my extensive analysis of Faulkner's critique of Christianity, see Lackey (2006), "The Ideological Function of the God-Concept in Faulkner's," *Light in August, The Faulkner Journal* 21(1 & 2)(Fall 2005/Spring): 66–90.

136 In an interview with Mario Vargas Llosa (see appendix), who has authored three biographical novels, I told him this story about Faulkner, and he confirmed that novelists provide readers with frameworks for understanding what will happen: "In many cases you have novels that open your eyes to things that will happen." I will examine Vargas Llosa's *The Dream of the Celt*, a biographical novel about Roger Casement, at some length in the next chapter.

137 Faulkner (1959), *Faulkner in the University*. Ed. Frederick L. Gwynn and Joseph L. Blotner. New York: Vintage Books, 41.

138 For my extensive analysis of Woolf's critique of philosophy, see Lackey (2006), "Modernist Anti-Philosophicalism and Virginia Woolf's Critique of Philosophy," *Journal of Modern Literature* 29:4(Summer): 76–98.

139 Woolf (1989), *A Room of One's Own*. San Diego, New York, London: A Harvest Book, 4.

140 Ibid., 25.

141 Ibid., 26.

142 Ibid., 27.
143 Ibid., 30.
144 Ibid., 31.
145 Ibid., 4.
146 Ibid., 31.
147 Ibid., 35.
148 Lyotard (1991), *The Postmodern Condition: A Report of Knowledge*. Trans. Geoff Bennington and Brian Massumi. Minneapolis: University of Minnesota Press, xxiv.
149 Sellers (2019), "Postmodernism and the Biographical Novel," in Lackey's *Conversations with Biographical Novelists*, 207.
150 Binet (2019), "Reflections on Truth, Veracity, Fictionalization, and Falsification," in Lackey's *Conversations with Biographical Novelists*, 36.
151 Lodge (2019), "The Bionovel as a Hybrid Genre," in Lackey's *Conversations with Biographical Novelists*, 128.
152 Tóibín (2019), 231.
153 Using the idea of "in-depth Christianization," an idea that Michel Foucault formulates, I clarify the processes by which prominent Christians were able to enforce submission to Christian Truth. See Lackey (2012), *The Modernist God State: A Literary Study of the Nazis' Christian Reich*. London and New York: Continuum.
154 For a detailed analysis of in-depth Christianization as it functions in Forster's novel, see chapter three ("'In-depth Christianization': E. M. Forster and the Modernist 'religious sense'") in Lackey (2012), 87–132.
155 For my most extensive analysis of Woolf's critical view of God and religions, specifically in relation to *Mrs. Dalloway*, see Lackey (2002), "Virginia Woolf and T.S. Eliot: An Atheist's Commentary on the Epistemology of Belief," *Woolf Studies Annual* 8: 63–87.
156 Larsen (1988), *Quicksand*, in *Quicksand* and *Passing*. New Brunswick, New Jersey and London: Rutgers University Press, 130.
157 For an extensive analysis of Larsen's critique of the role the God-concept plays in the oppression of African Americans, see chapter three ("No Means Yes: The Conversion Narrative as Rape Scene in Nella Larsen's *Quicksand*") in Lackey (2007), *African American Atheists and Political Liberation: A Study of the Sociocultural Dynamics of Faith*. Gainesville: University Press of Florida, 73–95.
158 Moore (1942), 30.
159 Moore (1942), 24.
160 Orel (1991), "A Reassessment of George Moore's Achievement in *The Brook Kerith*," *English Literature in Transition, 1880–1920* 34(2): 169.
161 Moore, *Letters*, 29–30.

162 In the 1923 version of *The Apostle*, Moore continues his shift in focus. In the Scenario and the 1911 play, the most shocking part of the conclusion is Paul's murder of Christ. In *The Brook Kerith*, Paul does not kill Jesus, and the concluding emphasis is on Paul's journey to evangelize the world. The conclusion of *The Apostle* (1923) is even more haunting than *The Brook Kerith*, because, even though multiple followers of Paul have been informed that Jesus survived the crucifixion in that work, they all support Paul's journey to evangelize the world nonetheless. To underscore that Paul's religious campaign is even more important than Jesus, Moore refers in the Epistle Dedicatory of the play to "Paul's departure for Rome" as "the most momentous of all events for the last two thousand years." Given the content of Paul's message as expressed in *The Brook Kerith* and *The Apostle* (1923), it is clear that this momentous event is not going to have a positive outcome. As for the pre-crucifixion Christ, while he is not portrayed nearly as negatively as he is in *The Brook Kerith*, he is still faulted for having posed as the Messiah and God. In 1930, Moore published *The Passing of the Essenes*. This work also focuses more on Paul than Jesus, but what is most significant is that Paul's fallacious teaching about Christ risen is exposed to the Essene monks and many of them abandon the Essene faith and monastery and commit themselves to preaching the risen Christ, even though they know that Paul's story cannot be true. This work indicates how fanatical forms of faith can easily lead people to dismiss empirical evidence, certainly an important idea in relation to the version of Christianity that Hitler and the Nazis adopted and widely disseminated by 1930.

Chapter 3

1 Kiberd (1995), *Inventing Ireland: The Literature of the Modern Nation*. Cambridge, Massachusetts: Harvard University Press, 4.

2 Yeats (1966), "The Ghost of Roger Casement," in *The Variorum Edition of the Poems of W.B. Yeats*. Eds. Peter Allt and Russell K. Alspach. New York: The Macmillan Company, lines 37–40.

3 King Leopold II (2003), "Letter from the King of the Belgians," in *Fictions of Empire*. Ed. John Kucich. Boston and New York: Houghton Mifflin Company, 106.

4 Kipling (1990), "The White Man's Burden," in *Rudyard Kipling: The Complete Verse*. London: Kyle Cathie Limited, lines 15–16.

5 Yeats (1966), line 11.

6 Ibid., lines 16–18.

7 Ibid., line 21.

8 Ibid., lines 24–5.

9 Ibid., lines 31–6.
10 Vargas Llosa (2012), *The Dream of the Celt*. Trans. Edith Grossman. New York: Farrar, Straus and Giroux, 55, hereafter cited in text as DC.
11 Yeats (1966), "Roger Casement," 581.
12 Yeats (1966), "Roger," line 7.
13 Ibid., line 8.
14 Ibid., line 23.
15 Sebald (1998), *The Rings of Saturn*. Trans. Michael Hulse. London: The Harvill Press, 129.
16 Ibid., 134.
17 Duffy (2014), "In the Fog of the Biographical Novel's History," in Lackey's *Truthful Fictions*, 114.
18 Ibid., 113.
19 Ibid., 114.
20 Ibid.
21 Ibid.
22 Lewis (2016), *Dying for Ireland: The Last Days of Roger Casement*. Self-Published, 137.
23 Murray (2019), "Complex Psychologies in the Biographical Novel," in Lackey's *Conversations with Biographical Novelists*, 182.
24 Ibid.
25 Ibid., 182–3.
26 This quotation is taken from the Roger Casement Letters to Alice Green, which are housed in the archives at the National Library of Ireland in Dublin. I will cite the manuscript numbers. MS 36,204/1; p. 3.
27 Ibid., pp. 17–18.
28 Ibid., pp. 1–2.
29 Rodó (1928), *Motives of Proteus*. Trans. Angel Flores. New York: Bentano's Publishers, 2.
30 Ibid.
31 Ibid.
32 Ibid.
33 Ibid., 3.
34 Ibid., 40.
35 Conrad (1999), *Heart of Darkness*. New York: Penguin Books, 8.
36 Ibid., 12.
37 Ibid., 92.
38 Ibid., 88.
39 For an extensive analysis of the redeeming-idea logic that leads to genocide, see Lackey (2012), "Joseph Conrad and Michael Bakunin on the Redemptive Logic of Western Genocide," 185–222.

40 I interviewed Vargas Llosa at his home in Madrid, Spain on July 27, 2019.
41 Murray (2018), "A Novel Truth about Casement's 'Irish' Identity," *Éire-Ireland: An Interdisciplinary Journal of Irish Studies* 53(1&2)(Spring/Summer): 168.
42 Murray (2016), *Valiant Gentlemen*. New York: Grove Press, 19, hereafter cited in text as VG.
43 Ebershoff (2019), "The Biographical Novel as Life Art," in Lackey's *Conversations with Biographical Novelists*, 99.
44 Murray (2018), 171.
45 Ibid., 169.
46 Ibid., 168.
47 Ibid., 173.
48 Ibid., 172.
49 Ibid., 172–3.
50 Ibid., 172.
51 McCann (2013), *TransAtlantic*. New York: Random House, 55, hereafter cited in text as T.
52 Montero (2019), "Speculative Subjectivities and the Biofictional Surge," in Lackey's *Conversations with Biographical Novelists*, 158.

Chapter 4

1 There has been much confusion about the facts of Eliza's life. For instance, all of the novelists think that Eliza was born in 1835, but she was actually born in 1833. Michael Lillis and Ronan Fanning used a newspaper announcement and a baptismal certificate to verify that Eliza was born in 1833. Lillis and Fanning consistently give readers the most well established facts about Lynch's life. Lillis and Fanning (2009), *The Lives of Eliza Lynch: Scandal and Courage*. Dublin: Gill & Macmillan, 6–7.
2 As Pelham Box says in 1930: "Eliza Alicia Lynch was nineteen years old when she came to Paraguay with López early in 1855 to play her part as a pinchbeck Lady Macbeth. The nature of the influence that for sixteen years the 'lorette parisienne' exercised over the mind of Francisco Solano López has not been adequately investigated. That it was considerable admits of no doubt." Box (1967), *The Origins of the Paraguayan War*. New York: Russell & Russell, 181–2.
3 Lillis and Fanning (1967), 132.
4 I have some reservations about calling *The News from Paraguay* a biographical novel. Lukács argues that the protagonist of a historical novel must be an invented, mediocre figure that the author could use to picture representative realities from

the past. Since Tuck names her primary protagonists after actual historical figures, it would disqualify the work as a historical novel. But if we accept my claim that agency is one of the defining features of the biographical novel, then *The News from Paraguay* would not qualify as biofiction, because Tuck gives readers a panoramic view of the Ella-Franco relationship, and she does almost nothing to convert her protagonists into symbols that illuminate or advance agency. I contend that Tuck's novel is a cross between a historical novel and a biographical novel, but it reads primarily like a historical novel.

5 Costello-Sullivan (2018), *Trauma and Recovery in the Twenty-First-Century Novel.* Syracuse: Syracuse University Press, 19.

6 Shelby (1990), *Demand the World.* London: Barrie & Jenkins, 379, hereafter cited in text and notes as DW.

7 Barrett (1938), *Woman on Horseback: The Biography of Francisco Lopez and Eliza Lynch.* New York: Frederick A. Stokes Company, 1.

8 Ibid.

9 I will use the names of the characters as they are found in individual works. For instance, Lillis and Fanning spell Eliza's name with a *z*, while Graham spells it with an *s*. When I am discussing Graham's Elisa, I will use an *s*, but when I am discussing the Lillis and Fanning Lynch, I will use a *z*. The same applies to Francisco Solano López. In Graham's novel, he is mainly called Solano, whereas in Enright's novel, he is most often referred to as López.

10 Henke (1998), *Shattered Subjects: Trauma and Testimony in Women's Life-Writing.* New York: St. Martin's Press, xii.

11 Ibid., xv.

12 Ibid., xvi.

13 Ibid., xix.

14 Claire Bracken notes that the Eliza Lynch of history has often been referred to "as a Lady Macbeth figure." Bracken (2010), "Queer Intersections and Nomadic Routes: Anne Enright's 'The Pleasure of Eliza Lynch,'" *The Canadian Journal of Irish Studies* 36(1)(Spring): 109.

15 Oates (2014), "Enhanced Symbolic Interiors in the Biographical Novel," in Lackey's *Truthful Fictions*, 183.

16 Enright (2003), *The Pleasure of Eliza Lynch.* London: Vintage Books, 107, hereafter cited in text and notes as PEL.

17 Conrad (1999), 130.

18 See Barrett (1938), 23–9.

19 Rees (2003), *The Shadows of Elisa Lynch: How a Nineteenth-Century Irish Courtesan Became the Most Powerful Woman in Paraguay.* London: Review, 92.

20 Ibid., 93.

21 Bracken and Cahill (2011), "An Interview with Anne Enright, August 2009," in *Anne Enright*. Eds. Claire Bracken and Susan Cahill. Dublin and Portland, Oregon: Irish Academic Press, 16.

22 Ibid., 28.

23 Ibid., 29.

24 Schwall (2008), "Muscular Metaphors in Anne Enright: An Interview," *The European English Messenger* 17(1): 18.

25 Bracken and Cahill (2011), 27.

26 Enright and Kelly (2002), "What It's Like to Have the Future Inside You," *Books Ireland* 252(October): 235.

27 Coughlan (2011), " 'Without a blink of her lovely eye': *The Pleasure of Eliza Lynch* and Visionary Skepticism," in *Anne Enright*, 108.

28 Schneider (2018), "Postnationalism, Postfeminism, and Other 'Posts' in Anne Enright's Fiction," *Studies in the Novel* 50(3)(Fall): 409.

29 Bracken and Cahill (2011), 28.

30 Ibid., 29.

31 Lukács (1992), "Realism in the Balance," *in Aesthetics and Politics*. Trans. and Ed. Ronald Taylor. London and New York: Verso, 33.

32 Ibid.

33 Lukács (1983), 166–7.

34 Lukács (1992), 36–7.

35 Oslen (2014), "The Biographical Novel's Practice of Not-Knowing," in Lackey's *Truthful Fictions*, 193.

36 Scott (2014), "The Masking Art of the Biographical Novel," in Lackey's *Truthful Fictions*, 223.

37 Scott (2020), "A Roundtable Forum with Joanna Scott," in *Conversations with Joanna Scott*. Ed. Michael Lackey. Jackson: University Press of Mississippi, 133.

38 Parini (2014), "Reflections on Biofiction," in Lackey's *Truthful Fictions*, 205.

39 Schwall (2008), 22.

40 Ibid., 21–2.

41 Bracken and Cahill (2011), 31.

42 Tokarczuk (2019), "I Believe in the Novel," in Lackey's *Conversations with Biographical Novelists*, 238.

43 Lukács (1983), 290.

44 Muller (2019), "Stitching up the Auto/Biographical Seam," in Lackey's *Conversations with Biographical Novelists*, 175.

45 Ibid., 172.

46 Cercas (2019), "Resisting the 'Dictatorship of the Present' in the Biographical Novel," in Lackey's *Conversations with Biographical Novelists*, 53.

47 Bracken and Cahill (2011), 17.
48 Ibid., 18.
49 Ibid.
50 Ibid., 17.
51 Ibid.
52 Ibid.
53 Ibid.
54 Schwall (2008), 17.
55 Donoghue (2019), "Voicing the Nobodies in the Biographical Novel," in Lackey's *Conversations with Biographical Novelists*, 88.
56 Ibid.
57 Ibid., 89.
58 Ibid.
59 Ibid.
60 Ibid., 90.
61 Banks (2014), "The Truth Contract in the Biographical Novel," in Lackey's *Truthful Fictions*, 50.
62 Ibid., 51.
63 Ibid.
64 Ibid.
65 Ibid.

Chapter 5

1 Nietzsche (1974), 283.
2 Hutcheon (1988), *A Poetics of Postmodernism: History, Fiction, Theory*. New York and London: Routledge, x.
3 Ibid., xi.
4 Ibid., 89.
5 Ibid., 113.
6 Ibid.
7 Ibid.
8 Ibid., 114.
9 Ibid.
10 Ibid., 113.
11 Ibid.
12 Ibid.
13 Ibid., 114.

14 Ibid.
15 Banks (2019), 45.
16 Ibid.
17 Ibid., 50.
18 Ibid.
19 Ibid., 47.
20 Ibid.
21 Ibid., 47–8.
22 Styron (2017), "The Uses of History in Fiction," in Lackey's *Biographical Fiction*, 143. For my extensive analysis of the way the "metaphorical diagram" functions in Styron's novel, see Lackey (2016), "Separatists, Integrationists, and William Styron's *The Confessions of Nat Turner*," *Mississippi Quarterly: The Journal of Southern Cultures* 69(1)(Winter): 65–91.
23 Banville (1993), *Doctor Copernicus*. New York: Vintage International, viii.
24 Ibid., 3.
25 Ibid.
26 Ibid., 4.
27 Ibid., 12.
28 Ibid., 15.
29 Ibid.
30 Ibid., 17.
31 Ibid., 23.
32 Ibid.
33 Ibid., 34.
34 Ibid., 85.
35 Ibid., 83.
36 Ibid., 240.
37 Ibid.
38 Ibid., 241.
39 Ibid.
40 Ibid.
41 Hutcheon (1988), 113.
42 Ibid., 89.
43 Banville (1973), *Birchwood*. New York: W.W. Norton & Company, 176.
44 Michael LeMahieu has authored an important book about Wittgenstein's impact on creative writers. He mentions Banville, and he quotes the passage I cited from *Birchwood*, but he does not discuss *Doctor Copernicus*. But there is a good reason why. In a footnote, LeMahieu quotes Banville, who says the following about Wittgenstein: "As a young man I considered myself a Wittgensteinian, but for

the little that I read of Wittgenstein, I understood even less." LeMahieu (2013), *Fictions of Fact and Value: The Erasure of Logical Positivism in American Literature, 1945–1975*. Oxford: Oxford University Press, fn #11, 199. My view is that Banville has a basic grasp of Wittgenstein's *Tractatus*, and that he was more indebted to Wittgenstein when he published *Birchwood*, but that he became more critical of Wittgenstein when writing *Doctor Copernicus*, and this happened primarily because he started to realize how Nietzsche's view of language was more consistent with his own worldview than Wittgenstein's.

45 Wittgenstein (1988), *Tractatus Logico-Philosophicus*. Trans. C.K. Ogden. London and New York: Routledge & Kegan Paul LTD, 6.341.

46 Ibid.

47 Ibid., 6.342.

48 Ibid.

49 Ibid., 6.41.

50 Ibid., 4.1212.

51 Ibid., 4.126.

52 Banville (1976), 239.

53 Ibid.

54 Ibid., 6.53.

55 Banville (1976), 240.

56 Ibid., 241.

57 Nietzsche (1989), "On the Genealogy of Morals," in *On the Genealogy of Morals* and *Ecce Homo*. Trans. Walter Kaufmann. New York: Vintage Books, 155.

58 Ibid.

59 Ibid., 157.

60 Ibid.

61 Banville (1976), 206.

62 Ibid., 207.

63 Ibid.

64 See Banville (2012), "Survivors of Joyce," in *Possessed of a Past: A John Banville Reader*. Basingstoke and Oxford: Picador, 333, 335–7.

65 Banville (2012), "Thou Shalt Not Kill," 349.

66 Ibid., 350.

67 Banville (1976), 110.

68 Banville and Aurora Piñeiro (2015), "The Evidential Artist: A Conversation with John Banville," *Nordic Irish Studies* 14: 56.

69 Banville (2012), "The Personae of Summer," 344.

70 Banville and Piñeiro (2015), 64.

71 Ibid., 58.

72 Nietzsche (1968), *The Will to Power*. Trans. Walter Kaufmann and R.J. Hollingdale. New York: Vintage Books, 302.
73 Nietzsche (1989), 80.
74 Banville and Piñeiro (2015), 64.
75 Nietzsche (2006), 6.
76 Berensmeyer (2000), *John Banville: Fictions of Order; Authority, Authorship, Authenticity*. Heidelberg: C. Winter, 127.
77 Ibid., 148.
78 Ibid., 147.
79 Ibid., 148.
80 Wittgenstein (1988), 6.53.
81 D'hoker (2004), " 'What Then Would Life Be but Despair?': Skepticism and Romanticism in John Banville's *Doctor Copernicus*," *Contemporary Literature* 45(1) (Spring), 52.
82 Ibid., 59.
83 Ibid., 68.
84 Nietzsche (1974), 182.
85 Nietzsche (1999), 51.
86 Banville and Piñeiro (2015), 58.
87 Nietzsche (1974), 282–3.
88 Nietzsche (1989), 44.
89 Ibid., 39.
90 Banville (1976), 240.
91 Nietzsche (1974), 283.
92 Nietzsche (1989), 39.
93 Nietzsche (2006), 40.
94 Nietzsche (1974), 89.
95 Banville and Piñeiro (2015), 59.
96 Ibid.
97 Ibid., 60.
98 Ibid.
99 Banville (2012), "The Personae of Summer," 345.

Chapter 6

1 Morales-Ladrón (2016), "Mary Morrissy's *The Rising of Bella Casey*, or How Women Have Been Written Out of History," *Nordic Irish Studies* 15(1): 27.
2 Ibid., 28.

3 Ibid., 29.
4 Ibid., 31–2.
5 Ibid., 32.
6 Ibid., 36.
7 Ibid., 33.
8 Morrissy (2013), *The Rising of Bella Casey*. Dublin: Brandon, 110.
9 Ibid., 119.
10 Ibid., 292.
11 Ibid., 139.
12 Ibid., 196.
13 Ibid., 277.
14 Ibid.
15 Ibid., 254.
16 Ibid., 279.
17 Ibid., 272.
18 Ibid., 334.
19 Ibid., 335.
20 Ibid., 339.
21 Ibid.
22 Ibid.
23 Ibid., 341.
24 Ibid., 344.
25 Ibid., 350.
26 Ibid., 351.
27 O'Connor (2010), "Acknowledgements and Caveat," in *Ghost Light*. New York: Farrar, Straus and Giroux, 244.
28 Ebershoff (2019), "The Biographical Novel as Life Art," in Lackey's *Conversations with Biographical Novelists*, 102.
29 Kent (2019), "Fictions of Women," in Lackey's *Conversations with Biographical Novelists*, 108.
30 Ibid.
31 Ibid., 106.
32 Ibid.
33 Murray (2018), 168.
34 Ibid.
35 This manuscript is housed in the State Library Victoria in Melbourne, Australia. Peter Carey: True History of the Kelly Gang (MS 13475: F Box 3989/2-3), 1.
36 Kelly (2001), *The Jerilderie Letter*. Melbourne: The Text Publishing Company, 16, 18.
37 Ibid., 18.
38 Ibid., 28.

39 Ibid., 32.
40 Ibid.
41 Ibid., 34.
42 Ibid., 40.
43 Ibid., 42–3.
44 Ibid., 53.
45 Ibid., 64.
46 Ibid., 65.
47 Ibid., 67.
48 Ibid., 68.
49 Carey and Robert McCrum (2001), "Reawakening Ned: Robert McCrum Talks to Peter Carey about Wrestling with a National Myth," *The Guardian* 6 January. (https://www.theguardian.com/books/2001/jan/07/fiction.petercarey).
50 Carey and Nathanael O'Reilly (2002), "The Voice of the Teller: A Conversation with Peter Carey," *Antipodes* 16(2)(December), 164.
51 Carey and McCrum (2001).
52 Carey (2000), *True History of the Kelly Gang*. New York: Vintage International, 24. Hereafter cited in text as TH.
53 Ellison (1995), *Invisible Man*. New York: Vintage International, 581.
54 Carey and McCrum (2001).
55 Carey and O'Reilly (2002), 165.

Bibliography

Ackroyd, Peter (1983), *The Last Testament of Oscar Wilde*. New York: Harper & Row.

Atwood, Margaret (1996), *Alias Grace*. Toronto: McClelland & Stewart.

Atwood, Margaret (1998), "In Search of *Alias Grace*: On Writing Canadian Historical Fiction," in *The American Historical Review* 103 (5) (December): 1503–16.

Avery, Todd (2010), "'The Historian of the Future': Lytton Strachey and Modernist Historiography between the Two Cultures," in *ELH* 77 (4) (Winter): 841–66.

Avery, Todd (2017), "Art and Ethics: Lytton Strachey and the Origins of Biofiction," in *American Book Review* 39 (1) (November/December): 5.

Banks, Russell (2014), "The Truth Contract in the Biographical Novel," in Lackey's *Truthful Fictions*: 43–56.

Banville, John (1973), *Birchwood*. New York: W.W. Norton & Company.

Banville, John (1976), *Doctor Copernicus*. New York: W.W. Norton & Company.

Banville, John (2012), *Possessed of a Past: A John Banville Reader*. Basingstoke and Oxford: Picador.

Banville and Aurora Piñeiro (2015), "The Evidential Artist: A Conversation with John Banville," *Nordic Irish Studies* 14: 55–69.

Barrett, William E. (1938), *Woman on Horseback: The Biography of Francisco Lopez and Eliza Lynch*. New York: Frederick A. Stokes Company.

Barry, Kevin (2015), *Beatlebone*. New York: Doubleday.

Berensmeyer, Ingo (2000), *John Banville: Fictions of Order; Authority, Authorship, Authenticity*. Heidelberg: C. Winter.

Bergen, Doris (1996), *The Twisted Cross: The German Christian Movement in the Third Reich*. Chapel Hill and London: The University of North Carolina Press.

Binet, Laurent (2019), "Reflections on Truth, Veracity, Fictionalization, and Falsification," in Lackey's *Conversations with Biographical Novelists*. pp. 33–48.

Bistrow, Joseph (1997), "'A Complex Multiform Creature': Wilde's Sexual Identities," in *The Cambridge Companion to Oscar Wilde*. Ed. Peter Raby. Cambridge: Cambridge University Press.

Blake, William (1988), *Jerusalem*, in *The Complete Poetry & Prose of William Blake*. Ed. David V. Erdman. New York and London: Anchor Books.

Bode, Carl (2017), "The Buxom Biographies," in Lackey's *Biographical Fiction*: 269–74.

Boldrini, Lucia (2012), *Autobiographies of Others: Historical Subjects and Literary Fiction*. New York and London: Routledge.

Box, Pelham (1967),*The Origins of the Paraguayan War*. New York: Russell & Russell.

Bracken, Claire (2010), "Queer Intersections and Nomadic Routes: Anne Enright's 'The Pleasure of Eliza Lynch,'" *The Canadian Journal of Irish Studies* 36 (1) (Spring): 109–27.

Bracken, Claire and Susan Cahill (2011), "An Interview with Anne Enright, August 2009," in *Anne Enright*. Eds. Claire Bracken and Susan Cahill, Dublin and Portland, Oregon: Irish Academic Press, pp. 13–32.

Bracken, Claire and Susan Cahill (2011), *Anne Enright*. Eds. Claire Bracken and Susan Cahill. Dublin and Portland, Oregon: Irish Academic Press.

Bridgwater, Patrick (1988), *George Moore and German Pessimism*. Durham: University of Durham.

Brilliant, Richard (1991), *Portraiture*. Cambridge: Harvard University Press.

Bytwerk, Randall L. (1983), *Julius Streicher*. New York: Dorset Press.

Carey, Peter (2000), *True History of the Kelly Gang*. New York: Vintage International.

Carey, Peter, and Robert McCrum (2001), "Reawakening Ned: Robert McCrum Talks to Peter Carey about Wrestling with a National Myth," *The Guardian*. 6 January. Accessed online at https://www.theguardian.com/books/2001/jan/07/fiction.petercarey.

Carey, Peter, and Nathan O'Reilly (2002), "The Voice of the Teller: A Conversation with Peter Carey," *Antipodes* 16 (2) (December): 164–7.

Carnes, Mark C. (2001), *Novel History: Historians and Novelists Confront America's Past (and Each Other)*. New York: Simon & Schuster.

Carroll, James (2001), *Constantine's Sword: The Church and the Jews*. Boston: Houghton Mifflin Company.

Cercas, Javier (2019), "Resisting the 'Dictatorship of the Present' in the Biographical Novel," in Lackey's *Conversations with Biographical Novelists*. pp. 49–67.

Chamberlain (1912), *The Foundations of the Nineteenth Century*. Volumes I and II. New York: John Lane Company.

Chedgzoy, Kate (1995), *Shakespeare's Queer Children: Sexual Politics and Contemporary Culture*. Manchester and New York: Manchester University Press.

Cohen, William A. (1996), *Sex Scandal: The Private Parts of Victorian Fiction*. Durham and London: Duke University Press.

Conrad, Joseph (1999), *Heart of Darkness*. New York: Penguin Books.

Costello-Sullivan, Kathleen (2018), *Trauma and Recovery in the Twenty-First-Century Novel*. Syracuse: Syracuse University Press.

Coughlan, Patricia (2011), "'Without a blink of her lovely eye': *The Pleasure of Eliza Lynch* and Visionary Skepticism," in Bracken's *Anne Enright*: 107–26.

Dalley, Hamish (2014), *The Postcolonial Historical Novel: Realism, Allegory, and the Representation of Contested Pasts*. New York: Palgrave Macmillan.

Danson, Lawrence (1997), *Wilde's Intentions: The Artist in His Criticism*. Oxford: Clarendon Press.

De Groot, Jerome (2010), *The Historical Novel*. London and New York: Routledge.

Dee, Jonathan (1999), "The Reanimators: On the Art of Literary Graverobbing," *Harpers* 298 (1789) (June): 76–84.

D'hoker, Elke (2004), "'What Then Would Life Be but Despair?': Skepticism and Romanticism in John Banville's *Doctor Copernicus*," *Contemporary Literature* 45 (1) (Spring): 49–78.

Diethe, Carol (2003), *Nietzsche's Sister and the Will to Power: A Biography of Elisabeth Förster-Nietzsche*. Urbana and Chicago: University of Illinois Press.

Donoghue, Emma (2019), "Voicing the Nobodies in the Biographical Novel," in Lackey's *Conversations with Biographical Novelists*: 81–92.

Duffy, Bruce (2014), "In the Fog of the Biographical Novel's History," in Lackey's *Truthful Fictions*: 113–28.

Ebershoff, David (2000), *The Danish Girl*. New York: Penguin Books.

Ebershoff, David (2019), "The Biographical Novel as Life Art," in Lackey's *Conversations with Biographical Novelists*: 93–104.

Eckart, Dietrich (1999), *Bolshevism from Moses to Lenin: A Dialogue between Adolf Hitler and Me*. Hillsboro, WV: National Vanguard Books.

Ellison, Ralph (1995), *Invisible Man*. New York: Vintage International.

Enright, Anne (2003), *The Pleasure of Eliza Lynch*. London: Vintage Books.

Enright, Anne and Shirley Kelly (2002), "What It's Like to Have the Future Inside You," *Books Ireland* 252 (Oct): 235–6.

Faulkner, William (1959), *Faulkner in the University*. Ed. Frederick L. Gwynn and Joseph L. Blotner. New York: Vintage Books.

Febvre, Lucien (1973), "History and Psychology," in *A New Kind of History: From the Writings of Febvre*. Ed. Peter Burke. Trans. K. Folca. New York, Evanston, San Francisco: Harper & Row Publishers, pp. 1–11.

Field, Geoffrey G. (1981), *Evangelist of Race: The Germanic Vision of Houston Stewart Chamberlain*. New York: Columbia University Press.

Förster, Bernhard (1881), *Das Verhältniss des modernen Judenthums zur deutschen Kunst*. Berlin: Verlag von M. Schulze.

Förster, Bernhard (1883), *Parsifal-Nachklänge: Allerhand Gedanken ueber Deutsche Cultur, Wissenschaft, Kunst, Gesellschaft*. Leipzig: Fritsch.

Förster, Bernhard (1991), "Antisemites' Petition," in Levy's *Antisemitism in the Modern World*, pp. 125–7.

Frankel, Nicholas (2017), *Oscar Wilde: The Unrepentant Years*. Cambridge, Massachusetts and London: Harvard University Press.

Frazier, Adrian (2000), *George Moore: 1852-1933*. New Haven and London: Yale University Press.

Goebbels (1962), Joseph, *The Early Goebbels Diaries: 1925-1926*. Ed. Helmut Heiber. New York: Frederick A. Praeger.

Goebbels, Joseph (1987), *Michael*. Trans. Joachim Neugroschel. New York: Amok Press.

Haan, Binne de (2017), "Personalized History: On Biofiction, Source Criticism and the Critical Value of Biography," in *The Biographical Turn: Lives in History*. Eds. Hans

Renders, Binne De Haan, and Jonne Harmsma. London and New York: Routledge, pp. 53–67.

Halevy, Daniel (1914), *The Life of Friedrich Nietzsche*. Trans. J.M. Hone. London: T. Fischer Unwin.

Henke, Suzette A. (1998), *Shattered Subjects: Trauma and Testimony in Women's Life-Writing*. New York: St. Martin's Press.

Heschel, Susannah (2008), *The Aryan Jesus: Christian Theologians and the Bible in Nazi Germany*. Princeton: Princeton University Press.

Hitler, Adolf (1942), *The Speeches of Adolf Hitler*. Trans. Norman H. Baynes. London and New York: Oxford University Press.

Hitler, Adolf (1971), *Mein Kampf*. Trans. Ralph Manheim. Boston: Houghton Mifflin.

Hobson, Suzanne (2018), "George Moore and New Testament Biofiction: *The Brook Kerith*," *Éire Ireland* 53 (1 & 2) (Spring/Summer): 175–97.

Hutcheon, Linda (1988), *A Poetics of Postmodernism: History, Theory, Fiction*. New York: Routledge.

James, Henry (1955), *The Selected Letters of Henry James*. Ed. Leon Edel. New York: Farrar, Straus and Cudahy.

Jameson, Frederic (2015), *The Antinomies of Realism*. London and New York: Verso.

Joyce, James (1986), *Ulysses*. New York: Vintage Books.

Kelly, Ned (2001), *The Jerilderie Letter*. Melbourne, Australia: The Text Publishing Company.

Kendall, Paul Murray (2017), "Excerpt from 'Contemporary Biography' from *The Art of Biography*," in Lackey's *Biographical Fiction*: 275–83.

Kennedy, Dennis (2016), "*The Brook Kerith*: 'George Moore's Blasphemy,'" *History Ireland* 24 (5) (September/October): 32–5.

Kent, Hannah (2019), "Fictions of Women," in Lackey's *Conversations with Biographical Novelists*: 105–8.

Kiberd, Declan (1995), *Inventing Ireland: The Literature of the Modern Nation*. Cambridge, Massachusetts: Harvard University Press.

Kipling, Rudyard (1990), *Rudyard Kipling: The Complete Verse*. London: Kyle Cathie Limited.

Kohlke, Marie-Luise (2013), "Neo-Victorian Biofiction and the Special/Spectral Case of Barbara Chase-Riboud's *Hottentot Venus*," *Australasian Journal of Victorian Studies* 18 (3): 4–21.

Lackey, Michael (2007), *African American Atheists and Political Liberation: A Study of the Sociocultural Dynamics of Faith*. Gainesville: University Press of Florida.

Lackey, Michael (2012), *The Modernist God State: A Literary Study of the Nazis' Christian Reich*. London and New York: Continuum.

Lackey, Michael (2014), *Truthful Fictions: Conversations with American Biographical Novelists*. Editor and Interviewer Michael Lackey. New York and London: Bloomsbury.

Lackey, Michael (2016), *The American Biographical Novel*. New York and London: Bloomsbury.

Lackey, Michael (2017), *Biographical Fiction: A Reader*. Ed. Michael Lackey. New York and London: Bloomsbury.

Lackey, Michael (2019), *Conversations with Biographical Novelists: Truthful Fictions across the Globe*. New York and London: Bloomsbury.

Larsen, Nella (1988), *Quicksand* and *Passing*. New Brunswick, New Jersey and London: Rutgers University Press.

Latham, Monica (2012), " 'Serv[ing] under two masters': Virginia Woolf's Afterlives in Contemporary Biofictions," *a/b: Auto/Biography Studies* 27 (2)(Winter): 354–73.

Latham, Monica (2015), *A Poetics of Postmodernism and Neomodernism: Rewriting Mrs. Dalloway*. New York: Palgrave Macmillan.

Layne, Bethany (2020), *Henry James in Contemporary Fiction: The Real Thing*. New York: Palgrave Macmillan.

Lehman, Robert S. (2016), *Impossible Modernism: T.S. Eliot, Walter Benjamin, and the Critique of Historical Reason*. Stanford: Stanford University Press.

LeMahieu, Michael (2013), *Fictions of Fact and Value: The Erasure of Logical Positivism in American Literature, 1945-1975*. Oxford: Oxford University Press.

King Leopold II (2003), "Letter from the King of the Belgians," in *Fictions of Empire*. Ed. John Kucich. Boston and New York: Houghton Mifflin Company, pp. 106–8.

Lethbridge, Robert (2013), "Introduction," in *Looking at Manet: Writings on Manet by Emile Zola*. Trans. Michael Ross. London: Pallas Athene.

Levy, Richard S. (1991), *Antisemitism in the Modern World: An Anthology of Texts*. Ed. Richard S. Levy. Lexington, MA and Toronto: D.C. Heath and Company.

Lewis, Alan (2016), *Dying for Ireland: The Last Days of Roger Casement*. Self-Published.

Lillis, Michael and Ronan Fanning (2009), *The Lives of Eliza Lynch: Scandal and Courage*. Dublin: Gill & Macmillan.

Lodge, David (2006), *The Year of Henry James or, Timing Is All: The Story of a Novel*. London: Harvill Secker.

Lodge, David (2019), "The Bionovel as a Hybrid Genre," in Lackey's *Conversations with Biographical Novelists*: 119–29.

Lukács, Georg (1983), *The Historical Novel*. Lincoln: University of Nebraska Press.

Lukács, Georg (1992), "Realism in the Balance," in *Aesthetics and Politics*. Trans. and Ed. Ronald Taylor. London and New York: Verso, pp. 28–59.

Lyotard, Jean-Francois (1984), *The Postmodern Condition: A Report on Knowledge*. Minneapolis: University of Minnesota Press.

Mackie, Gregory (2019), *Beautiful Untrue Things: Forging Oscar Wilde's Extraordinary Afterlife*. Toronto, Buffalo, and London: University of Toronto Press.

Marx, Karl (1977), "Preface," to *A Critique of Political Economy* in *Karl Marx: Selected Writing*. Ed. David McLellan. Oxford: Oxford University Press, pp. 388–92.

McCann, Colum (2003), *Dancer*. New York: Picador.

McCann, Colum (2013), *TransAtlantic*. New York: Random House.

McCann, Colum (2017), *Conversations with Colum McCann*. Ed. Earl G. Ingersoll and Mary C. Ingersool. Jackson: University of Mississippi Press.

McCormack, Jerusha (1997), "Wilde's Fiction(s)," in *The Cambridge Companion to Oscar Wilde*. Ed. Peter Raby. Cambridge: Cambridge University Press.

McLain, Paula (2018), *Love and Ruin*. New York: Ballantine Books.

Michael, Robert (2006), *Holy Hatred: Christianity, Antisemitism, and the Holocaust*. New York: Palgrave.

Montero, Rosa (2019), "Speculative Subjectivities and the Biofictional Surge," in Lackey's *Conversations with Biographical Novelists*. pp. 157–68.

Moore, George (1910) "The Apostle," *The English Review* 5(June): 564–76.

Moore, George (1911), *The Apostle*. Dublin: Maunsel.

Moore, George (1916), *The Brook Kerith: A Syrian Story*. New York: The Macmillan Company.

Moore, George (1923), *The Apostle*. London: William Heiemann Ltd.

Moore, George (1930), *The Passing of the Essenes*. London: William Heiemann Ltd.

Moore, George (1942), *Letters of George Moore*. Bournemouth, England: Sydenham & Co.

Moore, George (1972), *Confessions of a Young Man*. Ed. Susan Dick. Montreal: McGill-Queen's University Press.

Morales-Ladrón, Marisol (2016), "Mary Morrissy's *The Rising of Bella Casey*, or How Women Have Been Written Out of History," *Nordic Irish Studies* 15 (1): 27–39.

Morrissy, Mary (2013), *The Rising of Bella Casey*. Dublin: Brandon.

Muller, Stephanus (2019), "Stitching Up the Auto/Biographical Seam," in Lackey's *Conversations with Biographical Novelists*: 169–79.

Murray, Sabina (2016), *Valiant Gentlemen*. New York: Grove Press.

Murray, Sabina (2018), "A Novel Truth about Casement's 'Irish' Identity," *Éire-Ireland: An Interdisciplinary Journal of Irish Studies* 53 (1&2) (Spring/Summer): 167–74.

Murray, Sabina (2019), "Complex Psychologies in the Biographical Novel," in Lackey's *Conversations with Biographical Novelists*: 181–93.

Najmi, Hassan (2014), *Gertrude*. Trans. Roger Allen. Northampton, Massachusetts: Interlink Books.

Nietzsche, Friedrich (1954), "Nietzsche Contra Wagner," in *The Portable Nietzsche*. Trans. Walter Kaufmann. New York: The Viking Press.

Nietzsche, Friedrich (1966), *Beyond Good and Evil: Prelude to a Philosophy of the Future*. Trans. Walter Kaufmann. New York: Vintage.

Nietzsche, Friedrich (1967), *The Birth of Tragedy and the Case of Wagner*. Trans. and Ed. Walter Kaufmann. New York: Vintage Books.

Nietzsche, Friedrich (1968), *The Will to Power*. Trans. Walter Kaufmann and R.J. Hollingdale. New York: Vintage Books.

Nietzsche, Friedrich (1974), *The Gay Science*. Trans. Walter Kaufmann. New York: Vintage Books.

Nietzsche, Friedrich (1989), *On the Genealogy of Morals* and *Ecce Homo*. Trans. Walter Kaufmann and R.J. Hollingdale. New York: Vintage Books.

Nietzsche, Friedrich (1996), *Human, All Too Human*. Trans. R.J. Hollingdale. Cambridge: Cambridge University Press.

Nietzsche, Friedrich (1997), "On the Uses and Disadvantages of History for Life," in *Untimely Meditations*. Ed. Daniel Breazeale. Cambridge: Cambridge University Press.

Nietzsche, Friedrich (1999), *Twilight of the Idols/The Anti-Christ*. Trans. R.J. Hollingdale. London: Penguin Books.

Nietzsche, Friedrich (2006), *Thus Spoke Zarathustra: A Book for All and None*. Trans. Adrian Del Caro. Cambridge: Cambridge University Press.

Novak, Julia (2017), "Experiments in Life-Writing: Introduction," in *Experiments in Life-Writing*. Ed. Lucia Boldrini and Julia Novak. Cham, Switzerland: Palgrave Macmillan, pp. 1–35.

Oates, Joyce Carol (2014), "Enhanced Symbolic Interiors in the Biographical Novel," in Lackey's *Truthful Fictions*. pp. 179–92.

O'Connor, Joseph (2010), "Acknowledgements and Caveat," in *Ghost Light*. New York: Farrar, Straus and Giroux, pp. 243–6.

Orel (1991), "A Reassessment of George Moore's Achievement in *The Brook Kerith*," *English Literature in Transition, 1880–1920* 34 (2): 167–80.

Parini, Jay (1997), *Some Necessary Angels: Essays on Writing and Politics*. New York: Columbia University Press.

Parini, Jay (2014), "Reflections on Biofiction," in Lackey's *Truthful Fictions*. pp. 205–15.

Pfeiffer, K. Ludwig (2018), *From Chaos to Catastrophe? Texts and the Transitionality of the Mind*. Berlin: De Gruyter.

Plato (1951), *The Symposium*. Trans. Walter Hamilton. London and New York: Penguin Books.

Plato (1961), "*Ion*," in *The Collected Dialogues of Plato*. Ed. Edith Hamilton and Huntington Cairns. Princeton: Princeton University Press, pp. 215–28.

Pope, Alexander (1991), "Essay on Man," in *Alexander Pope: Collected Poems*. London: J.M. Dent & Sons Ltd, pp. 181–215.

Rees, Siân (2003), *The Shadows of Elisa Lynch: How a Nineteenth-Century Irish Courtesan Became the Most Powerful Woman in Paraguay*. London: Review.

Reff, Theodore (1975), "Manet's Portrait of Zola," *The Burlington Magazine* 117 (862) (January): 33–44.

Rodgers, Zuleika (2016), "A Twentieth-Century Irishman's First Century Palestine: George Moore's *The Brook Kerith*," in *Sibyls, Scriptures, and Scrolls: John Collins at Seventy*, Volume 2. Ed. Joel Baden, Hindy Najman and Eibert J. C. Tigchelaar. Leiden and Boston: Brill, pp. 1128–44.

Rodó, José Enrique (1928), *Motives of Proteus*. Trans. Angel Flores. New York: Bentano's Publishers.

Rubin, James H. (2010), *Manet*. Paris: Flammarion.

Saint-Amour, Paul K. (2003), *The Copywrights: Intellectual Property and the Literary Imagination*. Ithaca and London: Cornell University Press.

Santaniello, Weaver (1994), *Nietzsche, God, and the Jews: His Critique of Judeo-Christianity in Relation to the Nazi Myth*. Albany: SUNY Press.

Schabert, Ina (1990), *In Quest of the Other Person: Fiction as Biography*. Tubingen: Francke Verlag.

Schneider, Ana-Karina (2018), "Postnationalism, Postfeminism, and Other 'Posts' in Anne Enright's Fiction," *Studies in the Novel* 50 (3) (Fall): 400–18.

Schwall, Hedwig (2008), "Muscular Metaphors in Anne Enright: An Interview," *The European English Messenger* 17 (1): 16–22.

Scott, Joanna (2016), "On Hoaxes, Humbugs, and Fictional Portraiture," *a/b: Auto/Biography Studies* 31 (1) (Winter): 27–32.

Scott, Joanna (2020), "A Roundtable Forum with Joanna Scott," in Michael Lackey's *Conversations with Joanna Scott*. Ed. Michael Lackey. Jackson: University Press of Mississippi.

Sebald, W.G. (1998), *The Rings of Saturn*. Trans. Michael Hulse. London: The Harvill Press.

Sellers, Susan (2019), "Postmodernism and the Biographical Novel," in Lackey's *Conversations with Biographical Novelists*. pp: 207–21.

Shelby, Graham (1990), *Demand the World*. London: Barrie & Jenkins.

Shirer, William L. (1960), *The Rise and Fall of the Third Reich: A History of Nazi Germany*. New York: Simon and Schuster.

Smith II, E. Phillip, and Michael S. Helfand (1989), "The Text as Context," in *Oscar Wilde's Oxford Notebooks: A Portrait of Mind in the Making*. New York and Oxford: Oxford University Press.

Southgate, Beverley (2009), *History Meets Fiction*. Harlow: Longman/Pearson Education Limited.

Steigmann-Gall, Richard (2003), *The Holy Reich: Nazi Conceptions of Christianity, 1919-1945*. Cambridge: Cambridge University Press.

Stevens, Jennifer (2010), *The Historical Jesus and the Literary Imagination: 1860-1920*. Liverpool: Liverpool University Press.

Stone, Irving (2017), "The Biographical Novel," in Lackey's *Biographical Fiction*. pp. 115–30.

Styron, William (2017), "The Uses of History in Fiction," in Lackey's *Biographical Fiction*. pp. 131–60.

Thomas, David Wayne (2004), *Cultivating Victorians: Liberal Culture and the Aesthetic*. Philadelphia: University of Pennsylvania Press.

Tóibín, Colm (2004), *The Master*. New York: Scribner.

Tóibín, Colm (2010), "Roaming the Greenwood," in *Love in a Dark Time: Gay Lives from Wilde to Almodóvar*. London: Picdor, pp. 5–34.

Tóibín, Colm (2019), "The Anchored Imagination of the Biographical Novel," in Lackey's *Conversations with Biographical Novelists*. pp. 223–34.

Tokarczuk, Olga (2019), "I Believe in the Novel," in Lackey's *Conversations with Biographical Novelists*. London and New York: Bloomsbury, pp. 235–46.

Tusa, Ann and John (1986), *The Nuremberg Trial*. New York: Atheneum.

Unigwe, Chika (2019), "Biographical Fiction and the Creation of Possible Lives," in Lackey's *Conversations with Biographical Novelists*. London and New York: Bloomsbury, pp. 247–58.

Vargas Llosa, Mario (2012), *The Dream of the Celt*. Trans. Edith Grossman. New York: Farrar, Straus and Giroux.

Vidal, Gore (2005), "The Art of Fiction L: Gore Vidal," in *Conversations with Gore Vidal*. Eds. Richard Peabody and Lucinda Ebersole. Jackson: University Press of Mississippi, pp. 36–59.

White, Hayden (1973), *Metahistory: The Historical Imagination in Nineteenth-Century Europe*. Baltimore: Johns Hopkins University Press.

Wilde, Oscar (2005), *De Profundis and* "Epistola: In Carcere et Vinculis," In *The Complete Works of Oscar Wilde*. Vol. 2. Ed. Ian Small. Oxford: Oxford University Press.

Wilde, Oscar (2007), *Criticism: Historical Criticism, Intentions, The Soul of Man*. Ed. Josephine M. Guy, Vol. IV of *The Complete Works of Oscar Wilde*. Oxford: Oxford University Press, 2007.

Wilde, Oscar (2017), *The Short Fiction*. Ed. Ian Small, Vol VIII of *The Complete Works of Oscar Wilde*. Oxford: Oxford University Press.

Wittgenstein, Ludwig (1988), *Tractatus Logico-Philosophicus*. Trans. C.K. Ogden. London and New York: Routledge & Kegan Paul LTD.

Woolf, Virginia (1980), *The Diary of Virginia Woolf*. Ed. Anne Olivier Bell, Vol. 2. New York: Harcourt Brace Jovanovich.

Woolf, Virginia (1989), *A Room of One's Own*. San Diego, New York, London: A Harvest Book.

Yeats, William Butler (1966), *The Variorum Edition of the Poems of W.B. Yeats*. Eds. Peter Allt and Russell K. Alspach. New York: The Macmillan Company.

Young, Julian (2010), *Friedrich Nietzsche: A Philosophical Biography*. Cambridge: Cambridge University Press.

Zola, Emile (1964), "The Experimental Novel," in *The Experimental Novel, and Other Essays*. Trans. Belle M. Sherman. New York: Haskell House.

Zola, Emile (2013), *Looking at Manet*. London: Pallas Athene.

Index

accuracy
biographical 2–3, 20, 22, 25–6, 52, 70, 95, 119, 133, 156, 183–5, 210
factual 211
historical 17–20, 168–9
of the material world 61–2
in painting 4, 61–2
vs. possibilities 29
Ackroyd, Peter 33–7
aesthetics
authorial self-actualization 22
of the biographical novel 5–6, 10–11, 22–3, 32, 61–2, 70, 133
Copernicus, Nicolaus 193–4
dynamic 46, 49
of the historical novel 16, 22–3, 181
James, Henry 46–50
life-bringing 50–1, 175
Moore, George 71
Nietzsche, Friedrich 63, 94, 193–96
in portraiture 3–5, 59–62
and postmodernism 182–83
renunciation 41–4
representational 19–20, 22
Wilde, Oscar 18, 27–9, 33–7, 46–7, 49–50, 53, 94, 236n31
agency
female 167, 206–7
and history 58, 184, 189
human 8, 31, 94, 125, 131–2, 143, 181, 189, 209
individual 7, 10, 50–1, 142, 148, 217, 220–1
intellectual 188, 208
as inversion 214
narrative 142
overreaction 161
personal 10, 209–10
political 156, 177–8, 209–10, 217
psychological 146–7
psycho-political 8
in the reader 172, 175
recovering 142, 163
restoration of 146
traumatized 8–9, 142, 165, 177–8, 207
Alias Grace 30
Annales School of history 2
anti-Semitic Christian nationalism 68–70, 72–9, 85–8, 95
appropriation 2–3, 184, 190
Archer, Isabel 41
Arrogance 26
art
and authorial self-actualization 22
purpose of 4–5, 24–5, 202–3, 232
and the scientific method 23
subordination to history 18, 20–1, 23
works of 3–4, 122
The Art of Biography 2
"artistic sense" 23–4, 31–2
artists. *See also* creation.
creative vision 25, 30, 58–62, 197
as creators 36, 127, 128–9
cultural diagnosticians 9, 38, 41, 45, 70, 89
cultural role of 44–5, 47, 69–70, 79
and Truth 36
Aryans 69
As I Lay Dying 216–17. *See also* Faulkner, William.
Atwood, Margaret 30–1, 100
authorial present 85
authorial vision of the world 26, 49, 51, 59, 64, 85–8, 92, 94
Autobiographies of Others 2–3
autonomy
art's 23
authorial 51
biographical 24
and determinism 58
divesting of 123

individual 50–1, 67–8, 93, 100, 105, 125, 131–2
lacking 127
national 131–2, 137
political 7, 10, 100, 220–1
reader's 52

Banks, Russell 176–7, 184–5
Bannister, Gertrude (Gee) 109–10
Banville, John 9–10, 182–4, 189–92, 194–8, 202–3, 254n44
Barrett, William E. 143–4
beauty 27, 34–5, 52–3, 101
Beaver, Nick 206–7
Berensmeyer, Ingo 197–8
Bernard, Claude 56–7
Beyreuth 74, 85
the Bible 81
Binet, Laurent 91
Birchwood 189
Blake, William 36
Blonde 156
Bode, Carl 2
Boer War 130
Boldrini, Lucia 2–3, 5
Bolshevism from Moses to Lenin 75
Bonnet, Jenny 176
Book of Daniel 83–4
Brazil 150
Bridgwater, Patrick 70
Brilliant, Richard 59, 61
The Brook Kerith. *See* Moore, George.
Brown, Owen 176–7, 184–5
Bull, John 101–3
Burr 26
Burr, Aaron 26

Canon Wodka 186–7
Carey, Peter 1–2, 213, 216–17, 220
The Case of Wagner 6–7. *See also* Nietzsche, Friedrich.
Casement, Roger 8
and authority 129–30
"Black Diaries" 99, 103
colonialism 100–4, 108–19, 213, 223–6
compassion for suffering 108–12
cultural symbol 104, 123–4
epistemological development 112–16, 131
friendship with Joseph Conrad 224
homosexuality 99, 102–6, 120, 121–4, 133–4, 139–40, 224
intellectual curiosity 130, 132
as an "Irishman" 8, 108–10, 119–20, 134–5
letters to Alice Stopford Green 107–10
liberationist politics 103–4, 108, 120, 224
relationship with Herbert Ward 125–8, 129–30
transformation of 107–8, 113–14, 224–5
transnationalism 123–4, 129–30
Casey, Bella 205–10
censorship 232
Chamberlain, Houston Stewart 72–5, 78–9, 85–6
character. *See* protagonists.
Christ. *See* Jesus Christ.
Christensen, Eivind Adler 121–2
Christian nationalism. *See* anti-Semitic Christian nationalism.
Christianity 65–6, 70, 81
appropriation of 2–3, 184
fanaticism 80–5, 94–5
and Germanness 69, 75–8
and heteronormativity 91
and nationalism 68–70, 72–9, 85–8, 95
in opposition to Judaism 73–8, 85–8
and politics 83, 93–5
psychology 92
skepticism of 83
and violence 76, 78, 82–8
Christmas, Joe 88–9
civilization 228
Cloudsplitter 176–7, 184–5
colonialism 8, 132, 213
in the Amazon 117–19, 123
atrocities 114–16, 133, 223–6
in Australia 215–16
banality of evil 117
in the Belgian Congo 103–4, 108–13, 117, 123, 125–7, 223–6
criminality 130
critique of 101–4
genocide 114–15

in Ireland 103–4, 108, 116–17, 120, 123, 135–7, 144, 149, 166–7, 214–15
justifications for 113, 130–1
master 174–5
narrative 113, 131
in Paraguay 152
as social engineering 135
Spanish 160–1
stages of 118–19
compassion 108–11, 115–16
Conrad, Joseph 103–4, 114–15, 157–8, 223–4
consciousness 48, 52, 143–44, 169, 225
Copernicus, Andreas 188, 190, 194–5, 200, 203–4
Copernicus, Nicolaus
aesthetics 193–4
disobeying authority 186–7
epistemology 186, 188, 192, 195–6, 198
heliocentric model 183, 194, 196, 200
and language 185–8, 190–1, 194–6
love 188, 191–2, 196, 201
physical world 188, 191, 195–6, 200–1
Platonism 187–8, 195–6
Ptolemaic model 183, 194
science 187, 194
transcendence 188, 190–1, 193, 196, 198, 200
two-tiered model of knowledge 191, 195, 198–200
corruption 65, 101–2
Costello-Sullivan, Kathleen 142
Crane, Helga 92
creation
active vs. passive 29, 36, 40, 50
artistic 27, 30, 204
of consciousness 53
of knowledge 9–10
of lives 50–1
of more socially just alternatives 104
of new ways of looking at life 5, 24–5, 28–32, 39, 42, 49, 67–8, 93, 106, 120–1, 175, 212
of realities 36–7, 52–3, 94, 107, 125, 128–9, 183, 203
vs. representation 4–5
of systems 9–10, 38, 125, 193
creative liberties 5
"The Critic as Artist". *See* Wilde, Oscar.
culture 42. *See also* society.
Cunningham, Michael 234n9
Curie, Marie 30

Dancer 52–3, 231–2. *See also* McCann, Colum.
The Danish Girl 30, 31, 128–9. *See also* Ebershoff, David.
de Balzac, Honoré 35, 61
"The Decay of Lying". *See* Wilde, Oscar.
decolonization of the mind 8, 221–2
deconstruction 125, 193, 203. *See also* postmodernism.
Decoud, Carlos 161
Demand the World 143–57
determinism 7, 33, 48, 52–3, 57–8, 63–4, 125, 135, 175–6, 189, 222
D'hoker, Elke 197–8
Doctor Copernicus 181–3, 185–204
Dominican Republic 230–1
Donoghue, Emma 175–6
Douglass, Frederick 136–8
The Dream of the Celt 102, 107–25, 132, 223–4
Duffy, Bruce 104–6
Dujardin, Edouard 73
Dying for Ireland 104–7

Easter Rising 122–3, 208–10. *See also* Irish emancipation.
Ebershoff, David 30, 31, 128–9, 211–12
Eckart, Dietrich 75–6
Elbe, Lili 30, 31, 128–9
Ellison, Ralph 219–20
empirical evidence 21–3, 28–9, 32, 58
epistemology 106, 112, 113–16, 137, 174
and art 4
blind spots 100, 103, 125, 137
Casement, Roger 100, 103–4, 108, 112–16, 131
Copernicus, Nicolaus 186, 188, 192, 195–6, 198
defining humans 123–4
limitations of 44, 117, 126–8, 198–9
naïvety 169
Neoplatonist 188
Nietzsche, Friedrich 199–200
orientation 215, 221
and postmodernism 182

redemptive-principles 114–16
and truth 36–7, 39, 186
"Englishman" 101–2, 108–10, 126, 130, 217–18
Enright, Anne 157–68, 170–3, 177
Erskine 18–19, 21–3, 26, 28–9, 32, 237n32. *See also* Wilde, Oscar.
essence of life 39–40
ethics 1–3, 5, 22, 156–7
"existential map" 50–1, 100, 112, 125, 129, 140
"The Experimental Novel" 57–8. *See also* Zola, Emile.
exploitation 100, 167, 224–7

facts
accuracy 33, 59
altering 2, 22, 155–6, 210–11, 231
vs. fiction 1–2, 91, 119–20, 144–5, 169–70
faith 81
Faulkner, William 88–9, 91–2, 216–17, 229
Febvre, Lucien 2
The Fest of the Goat 226, 229–31. See also Vargas Llosa, Mario.
fictionalize 8–9, 25–6, 31, 49, 64, 71–2, 94–5, 100, 176–7, 184–5, 189, 197, 207, 210, 212, 216
fields of meaning 22
Fitzpatrick, Alexander 214–15
Förster, Bernhard 68–9
Forster, E.M. 91
The Foundations of the Nineteenth Century 73, 85
Francia, Rodriguez 143
Frankel, Nicholas 38
Frazier, Adrian 62, 74
freedom 136–9, 217, 231–3. *See also* slavery and unslaved.
French Revolution 15, 17
friendship 67, 125, 202–3
Frog Music 176
From Chaos to Catastrophe? 57–8

Gaugin, Paul 226, 227–8
Gellhorn, Martha 26
genocide 114–15
George Moore and German Pessimism 70. *See also* Moore, George.
Germany 69, 76–8, 121, 130, 224
Gertrude 3–5
Ghost Light 210–11
"The Ghost of Roger Casement" 101–3. *See also* Yeats, William Butler.
Glave, Edward 127
God 66, 84
Goebbels, Joseph 73, 78
The Good People 212
Gospel of Mark 82
gospels 72, 82–3
Gould, Ben 218
Graham, Cyril 18–19, 21–3, 26, 28–9, 32
Graves, Robert 30
Great Famine 8, 144–5, 158, 168, 170–1, 174
"great novels" 229
Green, Alice Stopford 107–10, 130
Grimm, Percy 88–9, 229

Halévy, Daniel 72
Hall, Desmond 33
Hammond (Henry James manservant) 42–3
Hart, Steve 218
Hawthorne, Nathaniel 49
Hearn, Mary 220–1
Heart of Darkness 103–4, 114–15, 157–8
Henke, Suzette A. 145–7
hero 16, 108, 122–3, 133, 139–40, 153, 216, 221
heteronormativity 91, 103, 105–6
historical novel 23, 29–30
benefit of 17–18
and biographical novel 2, 47–51
causal forces 183, 189
and fatalism 48, 222
predictive capacity 17–18
rejection of 7, 47–8, 105, 124
The Historical Novel 2, 16–21, 168–9. *See also* Lukács, Georg.
historiographic metafiction 9, 182–3, 189, 193–4, 196–7, 203–4
history
authoritative version 171–2, 175–6, 192–3
contributions to life 63
doing vs. using 31, 197, 210, 212, 228–9
historiography 192–3
narrative technique 169–70

as oppressive force 208
and postmodernism 181–2
as raw material 228–9
as science 15–23, 53, 56, 63, 181
subordinate to fiction 181, 184–5, 189
and symbols 122–3
Hitler, Adolf 73, 75–6, 79, 95
Hobson, Suzanne 83
Hochschild, Adam 100
homosexuality 170–1, 213
Casement, Roger 99, 102–6, 120–4, 133–4, 139–40, 224
James, Henry 42–3
Wilde, Oscar 27–9, 33, 38–9, 132–3, 213, 238n52, 237n59
Hone, Joseph 72
Hopkins, Pauline 132
Hughes, Willie 18–19, 20, 26–7, 32, 237n32. *See also* Wilde, Oscar.
human nature 30–1, 84, 111–12, 119–20, 124–5, 134–5
Hutcheon, Linda 9, 181–4, 188–9, 193

I, Claudius 30
I Give You Oscar Wilde 33
idealism 33, 225–6, 227
identity
British 8, 108–10, 119–20, 134
constructed 31, 121, 140
define 135, 139–40
displacement of 3
Irish 108–10, 119–21
and location 133
national 17, 108–10, 113, 125
reinvention 127
self 195
sexual 27–8, 120, 128, 176
theft of 3
imagination 23, 42, 92–3
imperialism 101, 108–9. *See also* colonialism.
The Incomparable and Ingenious History of Mr. W.H. See Wilde, Oscar.
individualism 37, 39–40
Inglis, Brian 99
inspiration 28–9
An Introduction to the Experimental Study of Medicine 56–7
Inventing Ireland 128
Invisible Man 219–20
Ion 36
Irish emancipation 108, 117–18, 121–3, 128, 131–2, 135–7, 207–10

James (the apostle) 87
James, Henry
aesthetics 46–50
The Ambassadors 46–7
Guy Domville 41, 45–6
and the historical novel 47–50
homosexuality 42–3
limitations 44–5
The Portrait of a Lady 41
relationship with Oscar Wilde 40–1, 45–7
renunciation 40–4, 46, 49–50
role as an artist 40–1
transformation 40–1, 46–7, 49–50
James, William 47–9
Jesus Christ
fanatic 25, 66, 71, 82–4, 94–5, 213
as literary symbol 92–3
pre/post-crucifixion 71, 79, 83–5, 88, 92–5, 248n162
son of God/Messiah 83
and violence 82–4
will-to-power 66–8
Jewett, Sarah Orne 48, 51
Joseph of Arimathea 83–4
Joyce, James 128, 185, 194–5
Judaism 69, 73–8, 85–8
justice 37–8, 93, 100, 102, 110, 124–5, 148, 172, 213–15, 226

Kelly, Ned 1–2, 133, 213
colonialism 214–16, 221
criminal justice 214, 216
family 220–1
father's death 217–18
and history 218–19
The Jerilderie Letter 214–16
justice 215, 219–21
narrative control 219–20
ontological inversion 215, 221
and violence 215
Kendall, Paul Murray 2

Kent, Hannah 212
Kiberd, Declan 128
King Leopold II 113, 223, 225–6
Kohlke, Marie-Luise 3, 5

language 138–9, 170–1, 173–4, 183, 185–7, 189–92, 195–6, 212–13
Larsen, Nella 92
The Last Testament of Oscar Wilde 33–7. *See also* Wilde, Oscar.
Latham, Monica 234n9
Layne, Bethany 47
Lewis, Alan 104–7
lies 30, 85, 119, 231
Life Mask 176
The Life of Nietzsche 72. *See also* Moore, George and Nietzsche, Friedrich.
life writing 146–7
Light in August 88–9, 92, 229
limited universal 89
literary forgeries 22
literary symbol
  ahistorical 90–1
  biofictional 91–2
  creation of 8, 49, 51, 88–9, 92
  and history 122–3
  political 103
  representative 10, 16–17, 64
  traditional 90
Lodge, David 91
López, Francisco Solano 141–2, 149–54
Lord Natesby 144, 148–50
love 34–5, 42
Love and Ruin 26
Lukács, Georg 2, 16–25, 29, 64, 105, 168–70, 172, 182–3, 206, 236n31, 250n4
Luke (the apostle) 82–3. *See also* Moore, George.
Lynch, Cavan 144–9, 151, 153, 159, 171
Lynch, Eliza/Elisa 8–9, 250n1
  ability to learn 166, 174
  agency 146–50, 153, 155–6, 158, 160, 163, 165–7
  Asunción 157, 159–60
  child labor 149–50, 154
  children 155–6
  colonialism 144, 149, 160, 161, 166–7, 174–5
  crime 144–5, 147–8, 159–60
  empathy 151
  father's death 144, 159–60
  France 145–6
  Great Famine 144–5, 158, 168, 171, 174
  Mallow (Ireland) 158–9, 162
  murder 161–2, 165–6
  in Paraguay 143, 150–4, 157–68
  Paraguayan War 152–4, 165–6
  poverty 145, 148, 152–3, 226–7
  power 145, 149–53, 161, 165–6
  relationship with Dr. William Stewart 158–9, 164–5
  relationship with Francisco Solano López 141–2, 149–54, 160–6
  self-mastery 145, 146, 151–3, 155–6
  and sex 158, 165–7
  suffering 142, 145, 155
  transformation 149, 152–4, 164
  trauma 145–8, 151, 152–3, 159–60, 168, 177, 207
  wealth 149–50, 153, 162–4, 166
Lyotard, Jean-François 90

machismo 230–1
Magee, W.K. 26, 71, 72, 83, 92, 93
Manet, Edouard 55–6, 58–62, 94
Manyaki, David 138
Marks, Grace 30
Marx, Karl 52
Mary Magdalen 80–2
The Master 40–53. *See also* Wilde, Oscar.
Matisse, Henri 3–5
Maurice 91
McCann, Colum 23, 52–3, 136–9, 231–2
McClain, Paula 26
The Mental, Moral, and Physical Inferiority of the Female Sex 90
metanarratives 90, 193
Meyerfeld, Max 81
Miss Kilman 92
modernists 88–9, 91–2
Montero, Rosa 30, 100, 139, 225
Moore, George 25–6, 55. *See also* Jesus Christ.
  aesthetics 71
  The Apostle (play) 79, 81–3, 85–7, 95, 248n162

"The Apostle"/"Scenario" 79–81, 82–3, 85–7, 95
The Brook Kerith 25–6, 55, 70–1, 81–3, 85–8, 92–5, 213, 240n1, 241n2
and Christianity 70, 79
Confessions of a Young Man 62, 70
and Friedrich Nietzsche 71–2
and Houston Stewart Chamberlain 74, 85
The Passing of the Essenes 79, 248n162
"Prefatory Letter" 81–2
and Richard Wagner 74, 85
moral code 126
Morales-Ladrón, Marisol 205–6
Morel, Edmund 227
"The Moroccan Amido" 3–4
Morrissy, Mary 205–8
Motives of Proteus 108, 225
Mr. Ducie 90
Mrs. Dalloway 92, 226
Muller, Stephanus 172–3
murder 81
Murray, Sabina 106–7, 125–34
The Myth of the Twentieth Century 73

Najmi, Hassan 3–5
naming 10, 183–4, 211–12, 217, 220, 230, 239n88, 250n4
narratives 171, 174–6, 182
narrativizing 131, 142
National Socialism 73
nationalism 68–70, 72–9, 87–9, 94–5, 126–7
Naturalism 58–9
nature of existence 139
Nazis/Nazi Party 73, 85–8
"Nazi Storm Trooper" 89, 229
Neruda, Pablo 30–1
New Testament 75–6, 92–5
Newton, Isaac 190
Nietzsche, Elisabeth 68–9
Nietzsche, Friedrich 6–7, 197–8
aesthetics 63, 94, 193–6
affirmation vs. negation 193–4, 196
The Case of Wagner 68–70
and Christianity 65–6, 74
Ecce Homo 64, 68
epistemology 199–200
"evil enemy" 200–1
friendship 67, 202–3
The Gay Science 202
love 201–3
"Nietzsche Contra Wagner" 68
nihilism 192–3, 199
On the Genealogy of Morals 66–7, 192, 199, 201–2
"On the Uses and Disadvantages of History for Life" 63
"thing-in-itself" 196, 199, 203
Thus Spoke Zarathustra 63–72
transcendence 201–2
transvaluation of values 101–4, 107, 132–4, 140
Twilight of the Idols 198–9
Nostromo 157
"A Novel Truth about Casement's 'Irish' Identity" 133
Nuremberg Trials 76
Nureyev, Rudi 52–3, 231–2

Oates, Joyce Carol 156, 189
O'Brien, Biddy 144, 146, 155
O'Casey, Sean 205, 207, 208–9
O'Connell, Daniel 136
O'Connor, Joseph 210–10
Olsen, Lance 169
Olympia 59–60, 227–8
oppression 100, 104, 111, 120, 124, 131, 138, 144, 174, 220
Orel, Harold 93–4
organized religion 71, 232–3

"paper person" 26, 82
Paraguay 143, 150–4, 157–68
Parini, Jay 169–70
parity 67
past vs. present/future 10, 28–31, 64–5, 70, 94, 100, 207, 222, 229–30
patriarchy 89–90, 167, 226
Paul (the apostle) 79–81, 85–8, 95. *See also* Moore, George.
Pearse, Patrick 131–2
personhood 106–7. *See also* self.
Pfeiffer, K. Ludwig 57–8
Picasso, Pablo 4–5
Plato 28, 33–7, 39–40, 187–8, 195–6, 199, 201

The Pleasure of Eliza Lynch 157–68, 177
Poetics of Postmodernism 9, 181
political systems 8–9, 105, 117, 123, 137, 226, 229–31
Portrait of Emile Zola 55–6, 58–62
"The Portrait of Mr. W.H." *See* Wilde, Oscar.
portraiture aesthetics 3–5, 59–62
postcolonialism 103–4, 136, 138, 172–3, 221–2
post-feminism 173–4
postmodernism 9–10, 90–1, 172–4, 182–4, 205–6, 217
poverty 136–7, 208, 217
procreation 34–5
"Professions for Women" 102. *See also* Woolf, Virginia.
protagonists
  development of 51, 139, 222
  foregrounded 105
  individuality of 16
  invented 16, 250n4
  mediocrity of 19–20, 182–3
  personality 16, 113
  as representative symbol 16–17, 19–20, 31, 124–5, 206–7, 210
  uniqueness of 20, 183, 206–7, 220
  as work of art 128–9

Queen's Jubilee 207–8
Quicksand 92
Quinn, John 71

the reader 53, 100, 172, 175, 177, 184–5, 211–12
reading 128
realism 168–72
"Realism in the Balance" 168–9. *See also* Lukács, Georg.
reality
  absolute 39
  actual 3, 169, 188
  artistic 3, 36–7
  creation of 36–7, 52–3, 94, 107, 125, 128–9, 183, 203
  conceptual 36–7, 132–3
  conventional 36–7
  creation of new 25, 36–7, 94, 175–6
  falsification of 182
  humans' effect on 24
  inviolable 37–8
  and language 186
  objective, social-historical 16–17, 19–20, 63–4, 169
  phenomenological 164–5
  physical 164, 199
  representation of 64, 186
  ultimate 195–6, 203–4
Rees, Siân 161
Reid, B.L. 100
the Resurrection 81
Reverend Leeper 206
The Rings of Saturn 103–4
The Rising of Bella Casey 205–10, 222
Rodó, José Enrique 107–8, 111–12
"Roger Casement" 103. *See also* Yeats, William Butler.
roman a clef 211
A Room of One's Own 89, 90. *See also* Woolf, Virginia.
Rosenberg, Alfred 73
Rossa, O'Donovan 131–2

Sánchez, Camilo 139
Sarita (Herbert Ward's wife) 127
Sartre, Jean-Paul 226
Schiele, Egon 26
Schneider, Ana-Karina 167
scientific method 23, 56–9
scientific sense. *See* artistic sense.
Scott, Joanna 26, 169
Sebald, W.G. 100, 103–4, 121
self 41, 52–3, 106–7, 112
self-consciousness 33, 183
Sellers, Susan 90–1
The Shadows of Elisa Lynch 161
Shakespeare, William 18, 20, 26
Shelby, Graham 143–57
skepticism 83, 169–71, 183
Slammerkin 175–6
slavery 67, 114, 119, 123, 135–39, 167, 207–8, 223–4. *See also* freedom and unslaved.
Smallhorne, Jimmy 52
"smudge" 156, 185, 189, 207
social engineering 135

society 37–8, 85
Socrates 33–6
solipsism 208–10
speculative biography 93–4, 212
Stanley, Henry Morton 113, 114, 126
Stein, Gertrude 4–5
Streicher, Julius 76
Stevens, Jennifer 240n1
Stewart, William 157
Stürmer, Der 76–8
subjectivity 58, 169
suffering 108–11, 136, 142, 145, 155, 220
symbolic understanding 30
Symposium 33–5, 39, 201
systems 7, 9, 57, 124–5, 166, 173, 182, 187–9, 192–4, 205

"Talma Gordon" 132
technology 106–7
Tóibín, Colm 40–53, 91
Tokarczuk, Olga 171–2, 222
Tolstoy, Leo 17
The Tory Lover 48
To the Lighthouse 89
Tractatus Logico-Philosophicus 189–91, 197–8
Transatlantic 136–9
transcendence 64, 189–91, 201–3, 188–91, 193, 196, 198, 200–3
transformation 5, 40, 46–7, 111–12, 210
transvaluation of values 101–4, 107, 132–4, 140
trauma 142, 145–8, 151, 152–3, 156–7
Tristan, Flora 226, 227
True History of the Kelly Gang 1–2, 10, 213–2
Trujillo, Rafael 226, 229–31
truth
  artistic 25, 33, 61–2, 231
  biographical 2
  of Christianity 83
  construction of 39–40, 66, 172, 177
  contracts 184–5
  critique of 39–40, 187
  epistemological 36–7, 39, 186
  fetishization of 66
  fictional 2
  historical 2
  physiological 7
  propositional 190
  surface/submerged 90
  systems of 124–5, 193
  trans-historical 119
  transnational 119, 123–4, 156–7
  transcendental 169
  universal 156
  and women 89–90
Truth 36, 49
  absolute 36–40, 66–8, 182
  ahistorical 90, 182
  Christian 91–2
  Christ's 66–8, 84–5, 93, 94–5
  consequences of 40
  ontological 36–7, 39, 66, 133, 156
  superior to art/artists 36–7

understood notions 106–7
Unigwe, Chika 29–30
United States 220–1
"unslaved" 138–9, 146. *See also* freedom and slavery.

Valiant Gentlemen 106–7, 125–34. *See also* Casement, Roger.
Vargas Llosa, Mario 102, 107–25, 223–33, 246n136
Vidal, Gore 26
violence 76, 78, 82–8, 118, 121–3, 215
virtue/vice 101–2
Völkischer Beobachter 73

Wagner Festival 73
Wagner, Richard 7, 68–70, 72–3
Wallace, David Foster 173
War and Peace 17, 228–30
Ward, Herbert 122, 125–8
The Way to Paradise 226
Wegener, Einar. *See* Elbe, Lili.
White Citizen Councils 89
The Widow of the Van Goghs 139
Wilde, Oscar 5, 61–2, 239n88
  aesthetics 18, 27–9, 33–7, 46–7, 49–50, 53, 94, 236n31
  The Ballad of Reading Gaol 38
  "The Critic as Artist" 24, 28
  "The Decay of Lying" 24, 25

De Profundis 46
"gross indecency" trial 37–8, 46
"Historical Criticism" 18
homosexuality 27–9, 33, 38–9, 132–3, 213, 238n52, 237n59
An Ideal Husband 41
The Incomparable and Ingenious History of Mr. W.H. 26–8
"The Portrait of Mr. W.H." 5, 18–24, 28–9, 32, 33, 132, 237n32, 237n59
prison reform 38
"The Soul of Man" 39–40
women 38–9
will 66–7
will-to-power 66–8
Wittgenstein, Ludwig 183, 189–95, 196–8, 254n44
Woman on Horseback 143–5
women 28, 38–9, 45, 90, 102, 126, 137–8, 141, 146–7, 166–7, 173, 205–6, 227, 230–1
Woolf, Virginia 85, 89–91, 102, 226, 234n9
Woolridge, Charles Thomas 38
Wollson, Constance Fenimore 45

Yeats, William Butler 71, 101–3

Zola, Emile 55–62, 64

www.ingramcontent.com/pod-product-compliance
Lightning Source LLC
Chambersburg PA
CBHW060247100726
47907CB00003B/803